INNOCENT EARTH

DALE E. MCCLENNING

Milton, Ontario
http://www.brain-lag.com/

SF
McClenni

Brain Lag Publishing
Milton, Ontario
http://www.brain-lag.com/

Cover artwork by and © Thomas Budach
Cover design by Catherine Fitzsimmons

ISBN 978-1-928011-21-7

Library and Archives Canada Cataloguing in Publication

McClenning, Dale E., 1962-, author
    Innocent Earth / Dale E. McClenning.

Issued in print and electronic formats.
ISBN 978-1-928011-21-7 (softcover).--ISBN 978-1-928011-22-4 (ebook)

    I. Title.

PS3613.C55I56 2019   813'.6   C2018-905353-4
                                            C2018-905354-2

To my wife, Daphne
For always believing in me

Chapter One
The Event Horizon

Arhus loved looking at the buildings of Jerusalem as he took the elevator to the one hundred and seventh floor. The towers of glass and carbon nano-tube glistened in the rising sun. The glass tube-connected towers formed a ring around the green of the park far below. Leaves turned in the wind, showing dark to light green and back, like a carpet walked over by an invisible man who paced the floor. The sunlight flowing through the glass tubes made rainbows above the treetops. After a rain, the leaves would sparkle in the sun, adding to the effect. It was a few moments of pleasure before the start of work. How such beauty could come from a city that had been erased by nuclear warheads eighty years ago made it more wondrous.

Not until he was almost at his floor did Arhus notice that the others in the elevator were huddled in groups of two or three with their hands to one ear. They spoke in short, hushed tones to each other. Arhus's earpiece was off so it would not intrude on his short morning revelry. As the elevator door opened, Arhus turned his earpiece on with a practised shake of his head. He was immediately onset by a swarm of conversations. Normally, the conversations were calm enough that one could listen to two, three, or even more at once with practice. Today, they were frantic to the point of blurring into each other.

As Arhus walked into the cluster that was his work area, he

spotted Josef Buddo standing in front of a large screen with a crowd of others. Walking up behind Buddo, Arhus tapped him on the shoulder. Josef turned around with a start.

"What's happening?" Arhus asked.

"Haven't you heard?" Josef asked with wide eyes.

"I had my connection off like I do every morning," Arhus replied with a shrug.

"Then you've missed it!"

"Missed what?"

"Titan monitoring station tracked an object coming Earthward at 0.87c!"

"0.87c?"

"Yeah! That means…"

"That our notification of the object got here a short time before the object itself." It was Arhus's eyes' turn to widen. "What goes that fast?"

"Nothing man-made, that's for sure." Josef grabbed Arhus's shoulders. "It's our first contact with other life!"

Josef was all but jumping up and down. Arhus just stood there, staring into space.

"How can you be sure it's another life form?" Arhus asked Josef, trying to get a view of the screen. "Maybe it's just a rock in space."

"Going 0.87c? You have to be kidding!" Josef pleaded for sanity with his hands.

"And it's headed toward Earth?"

"Yes!" After he said it, Josef started to look a little worried.

"Then let's hope it is intelligent or we will not be around to correct each other," Arhus said. A murmur went up from the screen crowd.

"The report is coming in from the moon station!" Ayso said.

"Why can't they just look at it with the telescope?" Miranda asked.

"It's going at almost the speed of light! The image doesn't get there much sooner than the object does. At best, it would look like a smear; at worst, they wouldn't be able to find it in the sky." That was Karlstad.

"Trust a German to know the details, even if he is a diplomat."

"Quiet! What are they saying?" a woman said. Sindie had the

sharpest tongue on the floor when she wanted. Her one hundred pounds of energy could be daunting even for her shorter than average height.

"To repeat," the man on the screen said in an increased volume, "the object has reached the vicinity of the moon and has slowed to one-third the speed of light and appears to continue to slow. We are trying to get an estimate now of where they believe the object is headed on the Earth, given that its trajectory does not change, of course."

"So when will it be here?" Sylva asked.

"At the rate it's going, not long." Karlstad again.

"The object appears to be approximately six hundred metres in diameter and round in nature," the man on the screen continued. "The space authority has just released a picture of the object, which we are going to show you now. Because of the high speed of the object, the picture is a little fuzzy."

The man's face was replaced by a blurred picture of a round object that appeared to be flat on the bottom and domed on the top with a severe angle to the dome from the bottom to the top. It was made of a smooth, shiny material with little variation in colour.

"It's a flying saucer!" Josef called out while pointing at the picture.

"It is!" Sylva answered.

"Who would have guessed?" Arhus said, glib on purpose.

"But where is it headed?" Miranda asked.

Arhus turned from the screen and ran to his work area. Turning on his computer interface en route, he typed in commands solely because it was faster than using the holographic interface. A globe appeared, followed by a moon and vectors representing the moon's path. A small pause while data was retrieved led to a new vector being displayed. A countdown appeared next to the head of the new vector, starting around twelve seconds. Arhus then called up a probabilistic algorithm. Areas on the globe became dark, at first oceans, then mountains, and then a narrowing circle of oscillating dashes that became ever smaller. In a few seconds, the circle was small and a name appeared next to it. Arhus ran back to the screen crowd.

"Here! It's coming here!" he shouted.

"What?!" Josef said, turning from the screen.

"Probabilistic analysis says that Jerusalem is the most likely place the ship is headed." Arhus found himself short of breath.

"Why do I suddenly want to be visiting my parents?" Worry covered Josef's face.

"We are now being told," the man on the screen was saying, "that the most likely destination of the object is Jerusalem."

Exclamations were heard as people headed to the windows or the elevators. Arhus let them pass before making his way to the window, not wanting to be trampled. The scene that greeted him was the sky above eastern Jerusalem, filled with clouds and lightning. Bunching together, the clouds looked like the white foam of a tidal wave marching toward Jerusalem. The wave moved up and curled back instead of toward them as the ocean would. The tidal wave of compressed air flooded the city, obscuring the view of anything but the clouds that marked its progress. Droplets formed on the cooler windows. The clouds were pushed away as a large, metallic object travelled through the middle of the lightning storm straight at the city. It travelled at a speed that seemed impossible to stop before entering downtown. People gasped, some holding onto each other.

"It's going to crash!" a woman yelled in panic.

"Why come all this way to crash?" Josef asked in soft disbelief.

People ran from the window. Arhus stood and watched. If the ship crashed, it would pass through their building. There was no way they could move fast enough to get out of the way.

Against all physics, the ship stopped in mid-air outside of town. The clouds continued to swirl in front of the ship in circles as large as the craft. The air that had been drawn behind the ship kept its momentum and passed along the ship, pulling clouds with it and cleansing the ship of the clouds. No breaths were heard until the clouds dispelled and revealed the ship hovering in place. A common sigh of relief went out as everyone stood and stared at the ship. It felt as if the world stood still.

"LET'S GET OUT THERE!" Josef yelled. The statement was enough to cause half the people to scramble for the elevator. The rest stayed at the windows, staring at the ship. Arhus tried to find any markings, lights, or features on the ship that would give some hint about the beings inside, but there were none. The entire surface was smooth. Even the outer edge had no rim but smoothly transitioned under the ship. He couldn't even tell if the craft was spinning or not.

"Where did it stop?" Miranda asked.

"I believe it is just outside the city proper," Karlstad answered, "above what used to be called the Mount of Olives."

"Shit!" Arhus said. He turned and ran back to his computer.

"What?" It occurred to Arhus that the voice belonged to Eymen. Before he could get to the computer, the media screen caught Arhus's eye. A map of Jerusalem was on the screen with a small, silver circle. Arhus ran over to the screen and stared.

"Damn," Arhus said in what he thought was a soft voice.

Eymen ran up behind Arhus. "What's up?"

"The ship is hovering over the Mount of Olives."

"So?"

"That is where the Bible says Christ ascended into the heavens and would return," Arhus replied.

"You a Neo-Utilitarianism or something?" Eymen asked.

"No, I practice Virtuism," Arhus said as he walked back to the window.

"Then how do you know?" Eymen followed Arhus.

"It helps to understand a language if you understand the cultural background. Christ crosses several cultures, and thus languages, I speak." Arhus made it back to the window. The clouds had settled down and started responding to the winds that normally drove them. The ship hung among them, immobile.

"What are they waiting for?" Eymen asked as they stared at the ship.

"Maybe it takes a while to adjust after stopping so fast." He waited before saying anything else. "Maybe they are waiting to see if we attack."

"Maybe they are waiting for us to say something," Eymen said. "You know, make our greeting first."

"How would we do that?" Arhus asked.

"You're asking me? I'm not a protocol specialist. I just schedule meetings."

"So schedule a meeting with the aliens, will you?" Arhus gave a small laugh with the statement.

"You have their contact information?" Eymen shot back.

"Touché, touché."

As the men watched, their eyes were distracted by the movement of the other buildings' elevators going back and forth to the ground floor. The elevators were packed.

"Where are they going?" Eymen asked.

"Maybe they want to get as close to the ship as they can or be the first to greet our visitors when they come down," Arhus offered.

"I-I think I will let someone else do that job," Eymen said with a stutter, "just in case."

"In case of what?"

"Exactly!"

A light started to appear at the very top of the craft. The light was stark white and as bright as an arc-light. The light grew out of the craft until it was a spherical beacon, a ball of pure, intense light resting at the pinnacle. The sphere was too bright to see inside. Both men held their breaths.

WE... RETURN!

The voice filled Arhus's head. More than just filled, it pushed outward from the inside of his skull. There was pain. He became dizzy and couldn't see because the voice occupied all thought. He felt his knees hit the floor. Covering his ears with his hands did nothing to lessen the intensity of the words that echoed back and forth inside his skull again and again as if they were phantom images. When the intensity subsided, he found himself prone, his forehead touching the floor and his hands on top of his head.

Fighting dizziness, Arhus made the effort to raise his head until he was in a sitting position. Everyone left in the room was on the floor also, some prone and some on their backs. The one exception was Miranda, who had somehow wedged herself between a pillar and the window. She looked uncomfortable, leading Arhus to decide to help her first. Rising to his feet would have been impossible if the windows weren't right there to use as support. Small steps and lots of leaning got him across the floor to Miranda. By the time he got there, he was feeling well enough to stand on his own and lift the woman out of her trap.

"Thank you," Miranda said in a whisper as Arhus helped her

stand.

Trusting she could cope, Arhus turned back to the others. Most were stirring and a few were sitting up. All were holding their heads as if waking from a record-breaking bender. Eymen was attempting to stand and make his way to Akmal, an elderly man who specialized in southern Pacific dialects. Arhus made his way there, too. By the time he arrived, almost falling once, Eymen had turned the man over. Blood seeped from the man's nose. Eymen put his finger to the man's throat and then laid his head on the man's chest. He brought his head up slowly after a few seconds.

"He's dead," Eymen said.

"How?" someone next to them asked. Arhus was still too dazed to recognize the voice.

"His heart couldn't stand the strain, I guess," someone else said.

"Probably more like a brain aneurysm," Eymen said. "That voice was extremely loud."

"If it was a voice," Arhus asked, "why didn't it break the windows?"

"They are pretty sturdy," someone said.

"But the sound would have to come through the windows," Arhus replied.

"It would be a good question for the engineers," Eymen said. Placing Akmal's hand on his chest, he said, "I guess we'll just leave him here until a medic shows up."

"I'll put in a call." Arhus registered the voice as Karlstad after a prolonged second of mental processing.

"All that just to say 'I have come'," Sindie commented.

"That's not what he said," Eymen said, looking at Sindie as he stood. "He said, 'We arrive'."

"I didn't hear either of those," Arhus said, furrowing his brow.

"It's easy enough to settle," Sindie said, turning toward the workstations, smugness in her voice. "We'll just check the building noise monitors."

"If they pick up bird activity on the roof, I'm sure they would have picked up that!" Eymen said, following her.

Arhus did a visual check of everyone else before following. No one else appeared to be suffering more than the rest and all were recovering well. *Whatever it was,* he thought, *it doesn't seem to last long.*

Sindie was busy swiping her finger across the holographic interface. Her face was contorted as if in a struggle. "It has to be here somewhere," she stated.

"What's wrong?" Arhus asked.

"We can't find a record of the words from the alien," Eymen replied.

"That's not possible, we all heard it," Arhus said.

"There's no record. All I am finding is bird noise." Sindie kept moving her finger in the hologram. Bird calls were the only sounds from the speakers.

"Could the aliens have some way of generating sounds only people can hear?" Eymen asked.

"The sensors pick up everything, even stuff we can't hear," Sindie said. "I just don't understand."

Arhus put his elbow in his hand and his hand under his chin. "We're missing something here."

"We're missing a lot!" Eymen said. "We're dealing with a fricking alien! Who knows what we're dealing with!"

Eymen was panting as he spoke. Arhus began to worry he would hyperventilate. Sindie's movements were getting quicker, her breathing was getting faster, and her face was getting red. *We all need to calm down,* Arhus thought.

"What World Council department would handle this?" Arhus asked aloud.

"There's a good question," Eymen replied, straightening up from looking at the display. "I wonder if that's even been decided yet."

"Computer," Sindie said into the display, "who has been put in charge of contacting the alien ship?"

"A commission is being formed," a voice from the speakers said. "Many departments have… volunteered… to be a part of the commission."

"More like they are insisting," Eymen said. "I am sure there are a lot of people who think this will make their careers. I should know, I deal with them every day."

"Computer," Sindie continued, "are the security forces included?"

"Security is asking to be included," the voice replied.

"Of course they are," Arhus said. "Why would we expect any different?"

"Who is the head of the commission?" Sindie asked.

"At the moment, it appears the vice-commissioner Arlan Morresette will be in charge of the commission."

Eymen groaned. "Great, we're doomed."

"Just because you don't like the guy," Arhus said, "doesn't mean he's not competent."

"The man's a pain in the ass," Eymen said, emphasizing the last word.

"Demanding, yes. Particular, yes. Both might be good for what he will be dealing with." Arhus tapped his finger on his chin, not thinking about the commission.

The display changed to a man's face. In fact, all the displays changed to the same face at the same time: Rossarro Cashel, department head of the translator's office in Jerusalem and their supervisor. His face looked like it had been sealed air-tight, but then, that was how it always looked. His eyes scanned back and forth across the screen.

"Where is everyone?" Rossarro asked.

"Some went outside," Sindie replied. "Akmal's dead."

"Dead?"

"Eymen thinks that voice caused a brain aneurysm. We called the medic."

"Shit! The last thing we need is to be losing people right now. I'm calling everyone back. The whole World Council is going nuts. I need some people at the central committee room now and I guess you three are it!" They could see Rossarro's hand in the display, pointing at them.

"I'm not even a translator!" Eymen said, his head pushed back as if by the hand, his eyes wide.

"Doesn't matter! You speak several languages, so you're assigned. Not like any of us speak alien anyway. Now go!"

Rossarro's face disappeared from the screen.

"We better get there right away," Arhus said, resigned. He disconnected his electronic interface from its dock on the workstation and placed it on his wrist on the way to the elevator. Eymen and Sindie already had theirs on. When the lift-car arrived, several medics got off. Sindie pointed the medic toward Akmal as she got on.

When all three were inside, Arhus told the elevator, "Top Floor."

"It's going to be chaos up there," Eymen said.

"It's chaos everywhere, I'm sure," Sindie replied. "They should have sent someone else."

"Thanks a lot," Eymen said.

"Not you, stupid, I meant myself!" Strain covered her face as she fidgeted in place. "I hate dealing with those people. Any people, actually."

"Oh, sorry," Eymen said, more resigned.

"Not that you should be either," Sindie said without looking at him.

Eymen laughed.

"I am sure everyone is going to be on edge," Arhus said in a calm voice, his meeting manner kicking in. "Stay calm, translate the best you can, *but* only when asked, and don't translate anything that sounds like something that the speaker shouldn't be saying."

"Yeah," Sindie said with a small huff, "we don't need another Geneva incident."

"Isn't that the one that doomed computer translations?" Eymen asked.

"Yes. Our biggest job is knowing what *not* to translate," Arhus said.

The lift-car slowed to a halt and the door opened to a short, wide hallway. Six security personnel stood outside a double door, announcing that they were in the right place. Nowhere else warranted that level of security. Arhus led the way to the doors. One of the security guards waved his hand in front of Arhus's face, checked his interface, and opened one of the doors. The manoeuvre was repeated for all three.

Arhus entered a room in less confusion than he had expected. About twenty people were already in the room and more were arriving from other doors. A man in an immaculate, dark green suit walked up to him and raised an eyebrow. The realization that he had not dressed for the occasion flashed into Arhus's mind, but then, most people in the room hadn't, either.

"Translators," he told the man, who nodded once and went back the way he had come. Arhus waited for the others to catch up with him. "Let's take a position over there. When they need us, they will call us over."

Taking a position against a wall that had no doors, Arhus scanned the crowd. The representatives in the room were higher in the organization than he was used to servicing. The thought caused a twitch he had to consciously suppress. The room was filled with commissioners and their aides. Senior Commissioner Mi Kutua stepped to one side of the round table, picked up the gavel, and hit its pad several times. All talking stopped as the commissioners turned toward Kutua.

"I know we are not all here yet," Mi said, "but we need to get started. The others will have to be briefed as they arrive. If everyone would please take a seat."

Mi sat in a chair next to her that an assistant had pulled back. The other commissioners took seats around the table. They seemed to leave as much space between each other as possible. Arhus noted groupings by political interest group, such as the African Confederation and India. The North American ambassador was here but the United Americas representative was not in attendance. That and other absences made Arhus wonder how bad things were outside the building.

"As I am sure you all heard," Mi started, "a commission is being formed to contact our visitors, if that is possible. The make-up of that commission is not our task here," she said in a firm voice. "Our task at the moment is to decide what appropriate actions should be taken due to our visitors' arrival…"

"Should we not first," a man sitting in the African Confederation's group interrupted, "determine what exactly was said?"

The question seemed to cause Mi pause. "We all heard it."

"Yes, we did," the man continued. "But from my discussions with others, we did not all hear the same words."

"I am not sure that matters," Mi countered. "We all heard the same basic message."

"Yes! But why did we all hear it differently?" The man's hand rested on the table with one finger pointing up into the air. "And more importantly, does different people hearing it differently mean that the message was meant to be different to them?"

"We are not here to discuss philosophy," Mi said, her voice becoming more pointed. "We need to set what kind of response will be allowed to this encounter."

"It is not philosophy!" Another member of the African Confederation piped in. Arhus recognized him as Kuwa Tammil. "How can we decide how to respond if this visitor is sending different messages to different cultures? And maybe more important, how is this even possible?"

"It's simple," the North American ambassador said. "It spoke different languages at the same time."

"So loud?" Kuwa asked. "How could they have done so without each of us hearing several languages at once?"

"I don't know what kind of technology the aliens have!"

The discussion, as Arhus had expected, was getting heated. Multiple voices started speaking at once. To Arhus, people looked worried. The representatives were better at hiding it, but several of their aides almost looked sick with worry. Arhus's brain had continued to work on the problem even before Rossarro had contacted them. Three people who worked in the same office, in the same vicinity, had heard different words. How was that possible? Arhus's brain came to a conclusion.

Breaking all protocol, Arhus stepped forward until he was next to the table. Mi was trying to control the conversational chaos, but it was a tough fight. The gavel hit its pad again. On the fourth hit, the conversations stopped.

"Everyone, please!" she shouted. "This is getting us nowhere!"

Ambassador Miguel Montoya from Spain sat across the table from Arhus, looking directly at him. "Did you have something to say, young man?"

Clearing his throat, Arhus said, "We didn't hear our visitors say anything."

"What do you mean?" Mi asked.

"The words were not communicated through our auditory

senses," Arhus replied.

"Then how did we hear them?" Mi asked, suspicion in her voice.

"They were communicated telepathically." The statement brought murmurs from around the table. "That is why different cultures heard different words. Even our little group of translators heard three different phases, most likely because one of us is Turkish, one is Chinese, and I am Dutch. The telepathic communication was interpreted into different phrases by each of our brains. It also explains why it wasn't picked up by the building auditory sensors."

"It wasn't?" the North American ambassador asked. Arhus's brain put a name to the man: Greg Mallard.

"Yes, it was the first thing we checked."

"That is an interesting hypothesis," Mi said. "I am not sure how you would test it."

"You don't have to test it," Mallard replied. "They already did when they checked the auditory sensors. Any microphone in the whole city would have picked up that voice if it was auditory."

"We agree with the hypothesis," the Western Pacific Conglomerate representative Song Bir said. "We have reports from other parts of the world that everyone heard the same thing. There is no way a spoken word could have been heard that far away."

Mi scanned the members seated at the table. The expression on her face gave the appearance that she felt besieged. Arhus stepped back from the table in the least obvious way he could imagine.

"If accepting the hypothesis ends the previous discussion and allows us to proceed to more immediate needs, then I will accept it. Agreed?"

Heads nodded around the table.

"Good. To other business, then."

A central holographic display run by a green-suited functionary kept track of the decisions made in the meeting. Arhus was called on twice for hushed translation advice. The others were not needed. After a couple of hours, the meeting broke up. Mi looked satisfied with the results. The representatives left first, but Ambassador Montoya walked over to Arhus instead.

"Keen observation, young man," Montoya said as he extended his hand. He gave Arhus a firm handshake. "I'm not saying you're right, but it is the best idea we have at the moment."

"Thank you," Arhus replied, trying to keep the nervousness out of his voice. It was the first time an ambassador had shaken his hand. Translators were used to being treated slightly better than furniture.

"Can I have your contact information, please?" Montoya smiled as he asked. Shocked, Arhus raised his hand in an automatic fashion to allow Montoya's interface to scan his. "I have a feeling I will be needing your services in the near future."

Montoya walked away from the stunned Arhus as Eymen walked up behind him. "Big score, that one."

"I am beginning to wonder if any of this day is happening. I am awake, aren't I?"

"It is happening, alright. I wonder how Rossarro is going to react to your direct link to an ambassador." Eymen laughed at this thought.

"Not well, I assume," Arhus said as he exhaled. "Let's get back to the office."

Chapter Two
We, The Humble Few

Everyone else was back in the office when they got back; at least, everyone that had been there before. Rossarro was there also, having arrived not long before Arhus and the others, evidenced by the fact that he was still asking questions about what had happened. When he saw the three exiting the elevator, he strode directly to them.

"What happened up there?!" he shouted.

"Not much," Arhus said. "They asked us to translate twice in private."

Rossarro stared at them for a few seconds as if making up his mind. He huffed and turned back to the general office area. Eymen gave Arhus a short stare, who tilted his head and raised his shoulder as if to say, "what he doesn't know..." Eymen raised his eyebrows, to which Arhus turned away.

"People!" Rossarro was still shouting, but at least at everyone now. "News media has started to show up as close to the ship as security is allowing. We need to get people down there. One, to make sure the security personnel don't get confused, and second, to monitor what is being said by the news agencies."

"You want us to spy on the news agencies?" Miranda asked.

"No! I want you to make sure that no misinformation is communicated and spread farther than we can stop it."

No one spoke, no one dared.

"Now go!"

"Are we really going to do this?" Josef asked Arhus, hoping Rossarro didn't hear.

"Look. There's going to be a lot of people down there. We're going to be needed, if just for our normal job. Let's go out and do that, and the hell with what Rossarro says."

"Right," Josef said, nodding. "Good enough for me. Good thing you don't have a girlfriend anymore to call and cancel a date with."

"Thank you for bringing up such a painful memory," Arhus said as they made their way to the elevator. "What about you?"

"Heck, she gets upset, she can leave. I can always get another."

"Your concern is heartwarming."

"You know me, never get tied down."

"Sometimes I think you take that too seriously." The elevator doors closed and it started to descend.

Arhus and Josef left the path taken by the rest of the crowd and took the 'gerbil tubes', as Josef liked to call them, as far as possible before descending to street level. It proved to be a solid plan, as they could see packed streets below them moving much slower. When they did have to descend, they found a slow-moving press of people, some already carrying hand-written signs saying "Hello" or "Peace." Pushing their way through the crowd was impossible without drawing heated remarks and sneers from those around them. Also, no one seemed to care that they were officials from the World Council.

"This was a bad idea," Josef said for the fourth time as he shook his head.

"In all probability, you are right," Arhus replied. "You know, my apartment is only a few blocks from here and it has a view of the Jordan River. We would have a good view of the ship from there."

"And abandon our assignment?" Josef asked in mock surprise. "I can't believe you're suggesting such a thing." Josef paused for a couple of seconds. "You got any cold beer there?"

"Of course," Arhus said with a chuckle.

"Then I'm all in," Josef said in a more serious tone.

"We need to take a right at the next street." Arhus hopped to make sure of his bearings.

"So, ten minutes from now." Josef sighed.

"We can cut through this coffee shop." Arhus pushed through the people to their right and headed toward the edge of the street. The doors to the shop swung inward, making an easy entry from the crowded street. Most of the people in the shop were standing against the windows, or as close as they could get, so walking through the shop wasn't hard. Josef stopped to get a dark black coffee, no cream or sugar, before continuing out of the shop.

"You don't walk into a shop and not buy something," he said to Arhus's smirk. "That's what my grandfather always said."

"The guy who owned the hat store?" Arhus asked.

"Yeah, him. Why, you think he had an ulterior motive?" Josef gave him a fake shocked look.

"Just don't spill it on me."

The cross street was just as crowded as the ones heading toward the alien craft, but at least they could travel slowly along the building. The main problem was fighting the crowd, which was headed the other way. After ten minutes, they had made it one block to the next intersection, all of fifty feet.

"By the time we get there, it will be lunch," Josef complained. "I hope you have food at your place."

"There's a café on the corner."

"You think anyone will be serving food?" Josef asked in a tone that suggested he thought he already knew the answer. "More important, does it look to you like the people on this street are going the wrong direction?"

Busy trying to find a way across, Arhus had failed to notice that the foot traffic was headed in the opposite direction that it had been earlier. They also didn't appear happy about it. A news crew of three people was still trying to head east against the flow and having little success. News crews consisted of a speaker, or 'voice', someone who many times got a second job as a model, the 'eye', wearing the recording equipment consisting of multiple cameras and an AI strapped to their back to control the view angles that made him look like a robotic bug, and the person who carried the antenna, a long, thin rod with a small, horizontal circle at the top. The antenna carrier also doubled as the eye's escort when they were recording, since the eye's attention could be occupied by up to six displays. It always reminded Arhus of an amusement park character.

"You're right," Arhus said. "Something must be going on."

"I would say," Josef said, leaning against a building, "that if we stay right here, our job might come to us."

The two men stood next to the building and watched people get pushed west along the street. As the cross street was already full, west was the sole direction for them to go. Josef sipped his coffee, almost losing it twice to the flow of traffic. The news crew held its ground in the middle of the street, asking people what was going on but not getting any answers. The crowd didn't look panicked, just disappointed.

The reason for the reversed flow soon became clear. Security personnel were herding the crowd back the way they had come, asking people to return to work or home. For the most part, people didn't fight them and those that did seemed happy with simply voicing their protest before turning back. The people carrying signs showed the most disappointment.

"If they went to all the trouble of making a sign, I guess they wanted to use it," Arhus said loud enough for Josef to hear over the crowd noise, which was ever increasing.

"Wouldn't you?" Josef asked.

The news crew made the biggest protest, for all the good it did them. Standing their ground until Security reached them, the 'voice' went into a lengthy tirade about why they should be let through. Security's response came down to the fact that they believed there were enough news crews closer to the ship already and they weren't letting any more through. Continued protest by the crew brought no change to the security personnel's stance. The crew was escorted west after their emotion had been spent. Not long after, a man in security garb approached Arhus and Josef.

"Move along, please, we need to clear the streets for your own safety," the man said.

Arhus displayed his work identification on his wrist interface.

"Arhus Gint, World Linguistic Anthropology Agency, World Council. We were sent here to provide translation services."

The officer laughed. "Translation? What do you guys think people will be doing down here? Nothing has come out of that ship as far as I've been told and I don't think whoever 'they' are need you to translate, from what we experienced."

"We're here to assist with the news crews," Arhus said.

"With a few exceptions, the news crews are all being sent packing. I don't think we need you to help with them. Now get back down the street." The serious look on the man's face left little chance of misinterpreting his words.

"Let's go, Arhus. I said this was a bad idea." Josef turned to follow the reluctant crowd.

"Thank you for your time, officer," Arhus said before following Josef. As they walked west, he said to Josef, "Rossarro is going to be pissed."

"Let him be," Josef said with a wave of his hand. "Security told us to leave and we left. Let him argue with that."

"You didn't try hard enough," Arhus said in a mock voice, shaking his shoulders back and forth.

"Hey, he can argue with the guys with the stunners if he wants, but I'm not going to," Josef replied.

"Getting stunned once was enough for you?"

"That's for sure! And by the way, weren't you the reason I got stunned in the first place?" Josef's tone lightened.

"I didn't force you to drink all that alcohol at my graduation party," Arhus said, raising his palms in front of him.

"It was your party!"

"And you wouldn't have missed it for the world."

"True, so true." Josef gave Arhus a shoulder bump. "You think Alia is still mad at me?"

"After twelve years?" Arhus asked, looking sideways at his friend. "Yes, I do."

"Just thought I would ask," Josef said with smirk and a shrug.

They didn't hurry back to the office. The crowd would have made it difficult anyway. When they got back to the World Council Centre, they found that several of the displaced news crews had set up near the building in hope of snagging an official who knew something. They didn't appear to be having much luck. From Arhus's experience, most diplomats were more than ready to talk about whatever subject was their pet issue at the moment. He saw more than one eye shut down soon after an official started talking.

After making their way to their building, Arhus and Josef took the elevator back to the one hundred and seventh floor. Most of the office staff had returned. Arhus figured that those that were absent had taken the opportunity for a day off. He couldn't blame them, though he wasn't looking forward to Rossarro's reaction. He considered it lucky when Rossarro wasn't in the office. Arhus didn't care enough to ask if anyone knew where he was and proceeded to a workstation. Several requests awaited his attention. A couple were communal requests so that the Public Relations people could judge the best wording of announcements. Arhus's job was to make sure any nuances in language didn't offend those who read them.

Responding to the requests did not take long. Next, he looked at schedule requests. Several periodic meetings he simply rejected, knowing that recent events made them obsolete. The most surprising was a request from Ambassador Montoya. A gathering was being held tomorrow night and the ambassador requested his personal service as translator. Of course he said yes, though from the request, he could not tell how formal the meeting would be. Hoping that further information would follow, he moved on to other messages. He did not know he had reacted to the request until Josef, sitting next to him, said something.

"What's up?"

"I just got asked to assist Ambassador Montoya at a gathering," Arhus said in hushed tones.

"Holy crap!" Josef said, suppressing the words as best he could. "Directly?"

"Yeah."

"You must have made an impression."

"Or I am in deep shit now." Arhus rolled his eyes, which caused the display to scroll. He had to scroll it back in place.

"Formal?" Josef asked.

"Don't know."

"Shit! Rossarro will have a royal fit if it is a formal occasion. You said 'yes', didn't you?"

"Of course! What else am I supposed to do?"

"Prepare a last will and testimony?" Josef said, looking back to his screen.

Arhus let the comment go without a reply.

"Don't worry, I will scrape up your remains afterwards."

"You're a true friend," Arhus replied, irony dripping from his voice.

The rest of the messages were more normal, though one was personal, rare at work since the computer was supposed to segregate those to his station at home. It was from his ex, which was why the computer let it through. The message made him think that a lot of people everywhere were hearing from relatives who hadn't talked to them in a long time. Arhus selected the message to display and not verbally. He had no hope it was an apology.

It didn't take long looking at the message to see it was Biel Chant fishing to see if he knew anything about the visitor. *What did you expect?* he asked himself. *I guess* boring *guys are only good for information and a place to crash when you need it.* Arhus sent a rejection notice for the message and permanently deleted it, proud that he didn't feel any guilt while doing so.

A small display to the side started to flash, so Arhus changed the channel selected. The display he had been looking at shrank to a few centimetres per side and a news broadcast took centre display. Sound was automatically activated. A quick look showed that everyone's display was on the same channel.

"Citizens of Jerusalem," an official-looking woman said. She was dressed in the official World Council overcoat, something bureaucrats did when addressing the public. Arhus noted that her lips' movements did not precisely match the words, indicating that she was being translated by computer. The thought of such an important announcement being translated by computer made Arhus nervous, but someone higher had made that decision.

"We understand that everyone is interested in our visitors, but we ask that you do not clog the streets trying to view them. Essential services must be able to travel through the city. This includes medical services responding to some less fortunate side effects of our visitor's message. Monitors are being installed at strategic points and views of the ship will be provided for your information on regular news broadcasts.

"We also ask that the multitude news agencies not send news crews to the site. We do not know the effect of so many signals near the craft, but we consider it safer if we limit such activity to as few as possible. All information will be shared equally to all concerned."

"Are they kidding?" Josef said. "Do they think our news teams are going to crash the ship or something?"

"The World Council Executive Committee," the woman continued, "is taking all necessary steps for contact with our visitors. I must emphasize that no contact has been initiated by our visitors other than the one statement already made. We are not speculating at this time as to why, but surmise that the effects that the communication had on humans was not intended and that our visitors are re-evaluating their communication methods."

"Trust a bureaucrat to claim not to be speculating and then do it," Arhus said in a soft voice.

"Information will be provided as it is known. Thank you for your cooperation." With that, the broadcast stopped and Arhus's previous screen was displayed.

"Can you believe that?" Josef asked him, leaving out the 'BS' part that should have been said.

"What else did you expect? For them to invite everyone to a party for the aliens?" Arhus asked.

"That sounds like a great idea!" Miranda put in. Arhus had been so focused, he had not even noticed she was sitting next to him. "We should organize one! You know, a 'bring-your-own party beverage of choice' for the aliens."

"And how do you expect to invite them?" Arhus asked. It was meant as a real question, but Miranda didn't appear to take it that way.

"You don't think they are monitoring every broadcast on the planet?" she asked.

"Let me put that another way," Arhus said, keeping his voice as normal as possible. "You don't think that they haven't received about a thousand invitations already?"

"Oh," Miranda said, crestfallen. "I hadn't thought of that."

"I would bet that the World Council has been sending out invitations since the ship arrived," Josef added.

Miranda sighed. "You're probably right. It was a nice idea, anyway."

Arhus looked at the time. It read two in the afternoon. "Crap, no wonder I'm hungry," he said aloud.

"Your stomach catch up with your head?" Josef asked.

"Why didn't you say something?" Arhus asked.

"I figured you would be too distracted before you figured it out for yourself."

"Aren't you hungry? You're always the one complaining about not going to lunch soon enough."

"Starved!" Josef turned from his display to face Arhus. "Shall we go?"

"Might as well. Feels like everyone is holding their breath until the aliens do something." Arhus looked around the room. "Anyone else want to go to lunch?"

"We went without you," Sindie said without looking. "Those that could eat, that is. Can't expect us to wait for you all the time." The last remark was made with a half-hidden smile.

"Well, carry on, then," Josef said in a fake authoritarian voice. He got several looks, but no replies.

The cafeteria was on the twenty-third floor, just above the tree tops. Well stocked at all hours of the day, today proved to be rather sparse. Maybe it was the day's events, maybe it was because they were so late. Arhus didn't know and decided not to complain. Most of what was presented appeared to be items that took little preparation, which would indicate that much of the staff had not shown up for work. It hadn't looked like this since over a year ago, when about two-thirds of the staff was out at the same time with an unexpected strain of flu. The whole city had smelled like puke for a week. The memory still made Arhus nauseous.

Fixing a salad plate which included a healthy portion of sunflower seeds and protein slivers, Arhus took a seat near a window. The competition for such seats was very low. Josef followed with a plate of barbecue meat and potato wedges.

"That probably contains pork, you know," Arhus said with a smile, knowing that while Josef had Jewish heritage, he never acted like it.

"Yeah, get the good stuff," Josef replied with emphasis.

"What would your grandfather say?"

"'I hope you got a good deal on that!'" Josef replied.

Arhus laughed.

Arhus ate for a while before talking. It was always better to let Josef get about half of his food in his stomach before expecting conversation. "What do you think the aliens meant by their message?"

"The immediate conclusion," Josef said after swallowing, "is that they want to us to believe that they were here before."

"Well, there are a lot of old stories about aliens in saucer-shaped craft," Arhus pointed out with his fork.

"Yes, but maybe the aliens know that and made their craft look that way just to correspond with the stories."

"Entirely true, I guess, though cynical."

"Cynical is my middle name, I thought you knew that by now."

"I keep forgetting." Arhus took another bite of salad, chewed, and swallowed. "What if they have been here before?"

"Which time?"

"Maybe all the times," Arhus said, rolling his eyes and flipping his hands.

Josef laughed. "The so-called sightings in the twentieth century, actually any sighting since about 1800, have been proved false. So you are left with the ancient sightings."

"The Hebrews, Incas, Mayans, Egyptians, etc.," Arhus finished for him.

"Correct. And those records are so old and done by people who were so technologically backwards that they won't have known a spaceship from a balloon!" Josef took a bite of barbecue for emphasis.

"Except they were able to form world-spanning empires without our technology," Arhus responded.

Josef swallowed hard. "I'm not going to get into your old debate about how capable ancient civilizations were because they could do a lot without electricity and internal combustion engines. I'm just saying that if anyone with a hover vehicle today went back in time, it would be easy to convince the local population you were an alien from another planet or a god."

"All of which doesn't prove that aliens didn't show up back then."

"So we have established that we can neither prove nor disprove they were here before, and I am not sure we can take their word for it, either." It was Josef's turn to emphasize his words with his fork by driving it into a potato wedge.

"Why not take their word for it? What would they have to gain by lying?"

"I don't know, and that's what concerns me. Who knows what they want or care about? Not us, that's for sure. If they are *really* alien, it could take us years or even decades to understand how they think or what motivates them. In the meantime, we have to make sure we don't end up on their dinner plate!"

Arhus laughed. "You've been watching too many old movies."

"It was metaphorical," Josef said with a shrug. "Even if they give us what we think is a fair trade, how are we supposed to know if, according to the universe's economy, we didn't just get screwed?"

"Wow," Arhus said, taken aback a little, "you're that cynical?"

"Someone's got to keep a clear head," Josef said between bites.

"Clear and vacant are two different things. If a trade is seen as good by us, that should be good enough. Which, by the way, is not the question I was asking. So you think the aliens at least want us to believe they were here before?"

"What else?"

"Maybe it is a poor translation." Arhus again pointed with his fork. At least it had salad on it this time to be less threatening.

Josef stopped eating and raised his head to look at Arhus. "Don't even go there. If we start thinking that the aliens don't understand what they are saying, we'll spend all our time trying to figure out what they are saying and get caught in a quagmire. I won't jump into that!"

"You're right," Arhus said, eating the salad on the fork. "We have so little information at this time it's frustrating."

"Maybe *that* is the point."

"What does that mean?"

"Maybe the aliens are keeping information from us in order to see what conclusions we draw." Josef gave Arhus a smirk.

"Sounds like a very *human* trait," Arhus replied with his own smirk.

"Some traits would have to be universal."

"Another very human-sounding statement."

"I take it that the conversation topic is over? Are you done yet?"

"No, but if you want to go back to the office, don't let me stop you." Arhus took another bite of his almost eaten salad.

"That's okay, I've been watching you eat long enough I'm used to it." A more genuine smile followed the comment.

"Are you saying I'm slow?"

"Only when it comes to girls."

Arhus was tempted to throw what was left of his salad at his friend, but then, Joseph was right. Girls were Josef's specialty, not Arhus's. His last relationship proved that. It had been over for two months before Arhus threw in the towel. He was sure Biel was through with it before then and just didn't tell him. The fact that she had someone else ready for her to move in was proof of that.

Arhus finished his salad on those unpleasant thoughts, put everything back on the tray, and hauled it to the return dolly. The building could have used robots to clean up, but the administration felt that it made people more responsible to clean up after themselves. *That is what they tell everyone, at least. Of course, I never see any of the top brass eating in the cafeteria.*

When Arhus and Josef made it back to the office, Rossarro was back and yelling at people for being in the office. The two were able to slip in and make it to their stations unnoticed most of the way, but Rossarro turned around right as they got close.

"At least here are two guys who tried!" Rossarro said, gesturing to them. "What have you got for me?"

"Nothing, I'm afraid," Arhus said. "The security officers chased us off."

"And you let them?" Rossarro's mood was turning less friendly.

"We had no choice." Arhus didn't look away or blink from Rossarro's stare.

Rossarro turned away after a few seconds. "You're all a disappointment."

"We had no business being there," Arhus said, still staring at Rossarro. *Enough is enough.*

"I give the orders around here," Rossarro said, turning back around, pointing at Arhus, "and you take them."

"I don't know what you expected to accomplish by this stunt..." Arhus started.

"And you don't need to! You do as I say!"

"Maybe I should file a grievance and we'll see who the administration agrees with."

The statement caused Rossarro to pause and look worried. It might not be the best time to file a grievance, but they were taken seriously. Rossarro looked around the room as if thinking and then turned back toward his office. "Everyone back to work," he said over his shoulder.

Arhus dared to take a breath. His shoulders sagged and he felt like he lost an inch in height.

"Brave," Josef said in his ear, "but you know you'll pay for that."

"Let him try. I'm going to log our orders today so there is a record of what was going on." As Arhus turned toward his station, he caught a worried look from Miranda and a smile from Sindie, the first he could remember receiving. It left him to wonder what it meant.

"I'll file one, too. We can't let this guy get away with this." Josef moved to a station.

Arhus sat at his station, but before he could start the report, he noticed that he had another message. Opening the message showed that it was from Ambassador Montoya's office, informing him of the time, place, and dress code of the gathering. Arhus let out a sigh of relief when he saw that dress was business and not formal. Formal events came with many other protocol rules.

"Maybe no one has time for protocol anymore."

Chapter Three
Hello World

The sun was just coming over the horizon when Arhus rode the elevator to his office. Earlier than normal. He hadn't slept much the night before and decided he might as well go to work. The café at the corner of his block had yesterday's leftovers on display instead of fresh croissants from the oven. He didn't ask if people were out late or just hadn't bothered to show up for work.

Arhus wasn't the first one in the office. Half of the staff was there, and a few looked like they never made it home. At least Rossarro was not in the office. He could have been hiding in his office, but Arhus put those chances at slim. Rossarro was not known as an early bird. One new item was a large holographic display in the centre of the office, displaying the latest news feed on the alien ship. Holographic displays weren't as detailed as screens, but everyone could work and still keep one eye on the news. As tired as Sindie looked, Arhus decided she had installed the display. Where she procured it was anyone's guess.

As Arhus made his way to his preferred workstation, he noticed the windows' automatic tint changing as the sun showed its whole face. How tired he still was showed when he momentarily panicked as he sat down, thinking he had forgotten his interface, but then he realized he had never taken it off yesterday. Shaking his head and setting his coffee on the table, Arhus commanded his computer on and then called up messages. The fact that his message screen was already full didn't surprise him, almost none of a work nature. There was another message from Biel, which he deleted, and then he set her name to hide-display.

The display in the centre of the room changed, drawing the attention of Arhus and everyone else sitting at their station. The fresh and alert 'voice', due to makeup, Arhus decided, was shown with the alien ship in the background.

"We are receiving word that something is happening at the top of the ship where the globe of light appeared yesterday." Arhus could see the man unconsciously cringe with the statement.

"If I was that close, I would be nervous, too," he said to himself.

The camera view distorted to show the voice and the top of the ship at the same time, a view that would have seemed strange if one had not been so concentrated on the ship. Arhus reminded himself to breathe. The top of the ship slid open by splitting down the middle and disappearing to either side. Light came from inside the ship, but not the intense light of before. The voice was talking, but Arhus paid no attention. A transparent globe, solid like glass, rose from the ship. As it rose, inside he could see a large chair. On the chair sat a large, humanoid figure, one that had to be much taller than any person. Next to the seated person stood a smaller humanoid figure whose features did not become clearer even when the camera magnified the view. Inside the globe flowed another shape, wispy with an ever-changing definition, that moved like a flying snake around the other two figures as the sphere moved.

"Oh my..." Arhus said softly as he watched.

"What are they?" someone asked.

Josef said something in Yiddish.

"Yes," Arhus responded. "They fit the descriptions very well."

"Descriptions of what?" Sindie asked from her workstation.

"The holy trinity," Arhus said. "Father, Son, and Holy Spirit or Ghost."

"That's religious, right?" Sindie asked.

"Central to the Jewish and Christian religions," Josef responded.

"You mean that they are the God of the Bible?" Sindie asked.

"No," Arhus said, "we are saying that they appear in the same form as the God of the Bible."

Conversation stopped as they watched the sphere leave the ship and float above it. The seat, or throne as Arhus now thought of it, rested on a platform. Underneath the platform, concentric wheels, iridescent bluish-green in colour, turned within each other. On the edge of each wheel, elliptical white shapes with dark centres rotated. The wheels gyrated within each other on several axles.

The sphere moved toward the camera. It took a few seconds for Arhus to realize that it was moving toward the World Council buildings. He looked east out the windows, but could not see anything and turned back to the display. The camera still followed the sphere, which took no notice of security forces, news crews, or hover drones. All gave way before the sphere. The voice on the display had stopped talking. Arhus watched until he started to see the building on the other side of the green and then stood and sped to the window. Others followed.

The sphere made its way to the centre of the buildings in an unhurried manner. News drones followed at a discreet distance. The sphere lowered to just above the treetops. The sun had cleared the horizon and now shone through the sphere. Arhus could see the seat, which appeared to be made of clear crystal, maybe diamond, with gold edges and swirls throughout. The base was a green colour and could have been made of emerald. The dome on the top of the sphere did not refract the sunlight. It was if it didn't exist. The disembodied being inside the sphere continued to swirl around the others.

The world had gone silent. No sounds reached Arhus's ears, as if they had been cancelled out or silenced. The thought raced across his mind that it might be an effect of telepathic communication, but it felt more like the world was holding its breath, waiting for the being to speak. It didn't wait long.

"We are EO-AY." The communication felt telepathic, but was not the overwhelming force that it had been before. This one felt more conversational, but still commanding. Arhus could not see any mouth on the being or see him move in any way while the words resounded in Arhus's head.

"We have returned to claim our own," the voice continued. "Those that are pure will be chosen. Those that are not pure have no place with us. We shall send forth our messengers to find our own so they may know that we desire them to be with us. If they will, they may join us in our home.

"All others are not welcome in our home. We shall set guardians around our home to keep out those who are not welcome.

"We are EO-AY. We are jealous of ours. If you test us, you shall be subject to our wrath. None shall stand before us. We are EO-AY. Do not test us." Instead of the words beating Arhus's head from the inside, it only sounded like they were shouted at the top of someone's lungs.

The sphere hovered for a while, as if waiting for a response. There was none. Slowly, the sphere rose back to its original height, turned, and proceeded back to the ship. Hover drones followed the sphere.

As the sphere disappeared into the ship, Arhus felt like he breathed for the first time since it appeared. The others around him sounded like they had the same response. The sun was well above the World Council building, causing Arhus to look at his watch. At least two hours had passed. It seemed impossible that that amount of time had passed. Did telepathy distort one's view of time? Or had the alien's presence been that awe-inspiring?

"Look at what time it is!" a female voice said. Arhus ignored it as old information.

"God doesn't exist in normal time." The voice belonged to Sindie, who was standing close by.

"What?" Arhus asked as he turned toward her. Then he shook his head. "I mean, why would you say that?"

Sindie sighed as she looked up to him, her head tilted. "I practise Hutchisonism," she said, as if admitting a fault.

"Dang, I would have never guessed," Josef said.

"So you believe in God?" Arhus asked.

"Sort of," Sindie said. "Hutchisonism, as it is practised today, doesn't believe in the same form of God that traditional religions had, but we do believe in a higher existence."

"So do you believe that is God?" Josef asked, pointing out the window.

"No, not in the sense that Hutchisonism believes or traditional religions mean it," Sindie said, closing her eyes and shaking her head.

"Be easy on her, Josef," Arhus said, putting his hand on his friend's shoulder. "We're all adjusting to a lot here."

"Sorry," Josef said to Sindie. "I keep having this nightmare that I'm going to have to tell my grandmother that she was right."

"Oh, please," Arhus said, humour contorting his face, "don't do that. We'll never be able to live with it."

The statement made Josef laugh and regain some of his composure. He took a deep breath. "Now what do we do?"

"We go back to work. I am sure we are going to be flooded with requests very soon. God spoke and everyone is going to want to know what he said." Arhus tried to give them a genuine smile.

"Oh, please," Josef said with a groan. "Don't make me interpret God. That didn't turn out very well for my ancestors."

"Don't worry, I think they got rid of the death penalty a couple of hundred years ago." Arhus slapped him on his back and then turned toward Sindie. "Are you alright?"

"Yeah, I'll be okay," she said, her voice more steady. "Like you said, a lot to take in."

"Let's not make more of it than it is," Arhus said.

"But that's the question," Sindie replied.

"That's for someone else to decide."

The first thing they did was to have everyone record what they had heard for comparison to each other and the audio records, which existed this time. All of the versions were very close with some minor differences, like 'will' for 'shall'. That fact seemed to comfort people. Before the comparison was done, messages started to come in from other departments.

"Can you believe this?" Josef said to furious strokes on his display. "Some guy wants to know how many different synonyms there are for 'guardian.' Do people really need to be led by the hand on everything?"

"Don't be too hard on him, some higher-up probably told him to ask," Arhus said. "You know what they are after."

"Yeah," Josef said with a sigh. "They want to know if they will be armed."

The number of messages seemed to have increased proportional to the size of the message. Arhus couldn't answer them fast enough, even though most were simple to answer. Lunch came and went without notice or hunger pains. People started to look tired. The new broadcast in the centre of the room became repetitive, as if they were afraid people would forget what had just happened. Speculation was rampant from all sides and the news seemed to glory in it, all restraint or reason removed from what they displayed. Arhus could believe that they thought it didn't matter anymore.

Arhus saw his hand shake a little and took a break long enough to take a few deep breaths and look at the time. It showed ten after three. "Darn," he said, not able to keep a slight quiver out of his voice.

"Sugar getting low?" Josef asked.

"You let me miss lunch," Arhus accused without any bitterness.

"You're a big boy. You know you need to eat regularly." Josef never stopped interacting with the display.

"I have to go get something to eat, and then I have to get ready for tonight, so I won't be back." Arhus waved at his display to close it down.

"And disappoint all the people asking these stupid questions? How dare you!" Josef laughed at his own joke.

"You can console them for me." Arhus waved his hand at Josef. "Tomorrow, man. Don't wait up for me."

"Never do," Josef said, not watching Arhus leave, but then stopped. "Hey! That's my line!"

Arhus took the lift to the cafeteria and picked out some high-sugar food that he started eating before even paying for it. The attendant said nothing. It wasn't the first time this had happened.

Getting past the news crews was harder. The ones that hadn't cornered someone already roamed the plaza, stalking their next victim. "Must be out of volunteers," Arhus said to himself. It took only a few steps for one of the voices to run up to him and try to engage him in a conversation. Arhus held his hand to the man's face, knowing that the man would back down if his face was covered. Conceit was more than common in the job.

Arhus had to fend off two more news crews before getting across the plaza. He felt released from a bond as he walked out of the World Council Centre into a normal city street. It might just have been his sugar coming back up, he admitted to himself, but the other reason sounded better. On the way to his apartment, he picked up some milk, fresh eggs, and a fresh loaf of bread, because it smelled good and he was just happy that the shops were baking again. He had to admit to himself that he was spoiled by the fresh bakeries. Packaged bread just didn't seem appealing anymore.

At home, Arhus put away the food, broke a piece of bread off the loaf and filled his mouth with a bite, and proceeded to the closet to remove his suit from its plastic bag. Careful not to drop any crumbs on the clothes, Arhus removed the plastic and laid the clothes on the chair to examine them. Finding no stains by the time he finished the bread, Arhus decided a shower would be in order first. Plus, he would have to look to see if he had any cologne left, though he didn't remember any.

"I wonder if that has anything to do with Biel leaving?" he asked himself with a quick laugh.

Chapter Four
What We Don't Know

Though in his best suit, Arhus felt under-dressed for the occasion. True, many countries had different ideas of what business dress constituted, but many of the attendees looked much better dressed than him. *Then again,* he reminded himself, *they are here to be heard and I am not. Maybe that is the point.*

Ambassador Montoya came in soon after Arhus arrived. Arhus glided over to stand just behind the man and was surprised when he offered his hand.

"Thank you for coming, young man," Montoya said.

"Ah, of course," Arhus said haltingly.

"Being a translator was a convenient excuse to have you here tonight," Montoya whispered.

"Excuse me?" Arhus did not have to fake his confusion.

"We are living in times that we have never imagined," Montoya started. "We are going to need people who can think along new veins and you proved the other day that you can. You will act as my interpreter, but unless I am speaking, do not feel afraid to tell me what you think about what you hear. It will look natural, so you need not worry."

"So you asked me here as an adviser?" Arhus asked. *This is too strange.*

"Yes, if it helps you think that way. Now, I must meet some others before they take offence." Montoya walked in a stately manner toward the small crowd. Arhus followed at the appropriate distance.

The conversation was composed of diplomat small talk for which translation was not required before the meeting started. Mercifully, it didn't last long, because people were in a hurry to get the meeting started. Another long, oblong table was occupied. Arhus noticed that all the chairs around the table were full and no representative was left standing. He took it as either good planning or purposeful intent.

"Thank you all for coming," Senior Commissioner Mi Kutua started. "We have a lot to discuss and decide. While there are other items I would like to discuss first, I hold no illusions that the message that was delivered today isn't the first item people want to discuss. This naturally includes what it means and what we are going to do about it. For once, I will let everyone else speak first."

The comment brought suppressed laughs from those around the table. Arhus could feel the mood of most attendees lighten and relaxed himself a little, knowing that tension in such meetings could bring its own difficulties. He could see that most were eager to speak, but cautious about speaking first. All but a few.

"If I may," Greg Mallard spoke up. Mi gave him a nod.

"I think it is very clear what this alien intends," Mallard said in a firm voice. "They intend to gather people to take back to wherever they came from. The only question that remains is whether we are going to let them."

"I think you are making an assumption," Arlan Morresette said, pointing at the American. "There was no mention of people in the speech. They said they would take what is theirs without specification. Until these messengers are sent out to identify what they think is theirs, I say we wait and see what they want."

"Really?" Mallard asked, looking genuinely surprised. "You have any doubt what these guys want? They are following the pattern established in the Christian Bible and it is pretty clear what God comes back for. I think the true question is why they want us."

"I believe," the representative from the African Confederation said, "that the statement about taking the pure means that they will be selecting the best, smartest, most capable of us to take as their slaves back on their planet. If this was not so, then they would have asked us to supply representatives."

Without a list of who had been invited, Arhus had no chance to check names before the meeting. It would have been a severe breach of conduct to look during the meeting. Thinking that this would not be the last meeting those here would be having, he went through mental exercises to memorize those present he didn't know.

Arlan Morresette interrupted. "Again, gentlemen, we are assuming. Assumptions in these types of circumstances can lead to unfortunate instances."

"And why not assume the worst?" Mallard asked. "That way, anything else will be a pleasant surprise."

"Such assumptions are dangerous," Arlan countered, leaning with his elbows on the table. "They create certain mindsets that can destroy any positive outputs."

"Like the aliens taking several thousand of our best and brightest with them?" Mallard asked. The accusation was clear in his voice.

Arlan gave the man a dirty look, but then looked away. "Until we have clarity, I am not making any assumptions. If our visitors take action at their current rate, tomorrow will provide answers to at least some of our questions."

"So you intend to just sit there and wait?" Mallard asked.

"I intend," Arlan said in a precise tone, "to see what tomorrow brings, and until something does, I intend to try and continue to form a communication link with our visitors to establish some kind of rapport."

"This is useless discussion at the moment," the African Confederation representative piped in. "The important question is whether we allow people to go with any alien invitation."

"Allow?" The statement clearly hit a sore spot with the American.

"The first question," Ambassador Montoya spoke up for the first time, "is whether we have the legal right to prevent people from going with the visitors."

The statement caused a stir. Representatives turned to their retainers, asking questions in hushed tones in various languages. It lasted a few minutes until Arlan, who had not turned from the table, spoke.

"As an issue of global security and border control, this issue falls squarely into the World Council's sphere of power."

Arhus was sure the American was going to laugh. Avoiding a diplomatic situation, the man held his laughter. Arhus leaned over to Montoya's ear and whispered. Montoya nodded and turned toward the faces at the table.

"You fail to consider one thing, Mr. Morresette. If our visitors decide to take some people with them, do we have the power to prevent them from doing so or do we even dare try? The technology that they have already demonstrated far exceeds ours, there is no question about that. What other technology they might possess, we have no way of knowing. Do we really want to find out the hard way?"

"So we just roll over and give in?" Mallard asked with a wave of his hand.

"There is a great distance between giving in and engaging in armed resistance," Montoya replied.

The statement calmed the room a little. The American in particular appeared to settle in his seat, looking thoughtful. Arlan's face took an expression of self-assurance, as if he had been justified by Montoya. Montoya did nothing to discourage the look, demonstrating his diplomatic skill, in Arhus's estimation.

"Gentlemen," Montoya continued, "this discussion is going nowhere. We must decide what we are going to do now, tonight, or tomorrow morning, even if the visitors do nothing. Everything else can be sent for study."

"I agree," Arlan said quickly. "We need to get representatives in front of the news and stop the wild speculation being aired. Secondly, we need to take a more measured approach to trying to establish contact with the visitors. Third... we need to establish a better perimeter around the ship, including drone flights. Fourth, and more importantly, if any 'messengers' are sent out from the ship, we need a way to track where they go and who they talk to."

"And how are we supposed to know that before we've seen them?" Mallard asked.

"What I am talking about," Arlan said, closing his eyes, "is that we need to have all satellite coverage over Jerusalem possible and it needs to be linked to coverage in other areas so that tracking information can be transferred immediately."

Heads nodded all around. Mallard's head turned down and away from Arlan as the man reasserted his authority in the meeting.

"Legal can handle the question of whether we can restrict access to the visitors or not. Mi, I defer that to you. Hatuar, get the military better organized on this and move the perimeter as far back as possible. I know we can't move it into the city without displacing people, which would be unpopular, but we need to make sure no radical has access. Miguel, we need to find a way to make contact. I would be glad to hear any ideas someone has on how to do this. With the ship hovering several hundred meters in the air, we can't knock on the front door."

"I believe patience is needed on that front," Montoya said. Arhus thought Arlan looked like he wasn't finished speaking. "I don't expect our visitors to make any other contact for a couple of days, but I think we need to have a presence near the ship ready for contact at all times, back far enough to allow it to land, which will also allow it to be seen. I am sure I will have plenty of volunteers, but I would rather keep the military out of the operation to present the least intimidating presence possible."

"That is reasonable," Arlan replied, taking back the conversation. "I will handle the media. We need to have just one information conduit if we are going to have any information control. Have the word passed down that no one is authorized to speak to the news, starting now."

"You can't seriously believe that you can enforce that," Mallard said in disbelief.

"Why not?" Arlan sounded serious.

"Because just saying so will cause more people to think about doing it! Don't you know anything about psychology?" Mallard threw his head back.

"We have to set a policy! That policy must be communicated to everyone immediately. Not that we make a big deal or threaten people, but if someone publicly flaunts the policy, we must take action. My assistant is prepared to send the policy to everyone as soon as we are agreed."

The statement brought surprised looks from everyone. Arhus did not understand. It seemed efficient. A few muffled huffs came from the representatives. Hushed talk between those seated at the table was traded and then quieted down. Several checked their interfaces. Arhus could see a copy of the memo on Montoya's.

"The wording is simple. I felt that it would be better in this first memo to keep it that way. Plus, it will be easier to agree on, of course. Please take a moment to review." Arlan sat back in his chair like a teacher that had just told his class to start their tests.

It didn't take long for the representatives to read the memo. Some shrugged, others looked thoughtful as if trying to decide on changes, always risky from Arhus's experience. No one spoke, which Arlan took as acceptance after a minute.

"If there are no objections," he said, pausing for a couple of seconds before continuing, "I will have the memo sent."

Arlan tapped his interface, a look of satisfaction on his face. Arhus heard several breaths being taken. Arlan smiled as he looked back to the others.

"Good. I feel that this has been a very successful meeting. Hopefully, tomorrow will bring more information for us to work with. Shall we plan to meet again tomorrow at the same time?" No one objected. "If circumstances require us to meet sooner, I will send out a notice. Thank you all for coming."

Arlan stood up, bowed, and walked out of the room. Arhus watched him leave the table and then looked down to Montoya, who didn't seem concerned. Arhus bent down by his ear.

"Does he have somewhere he needs to be?" Arhus asked.

"Maybe it's past his bedtime," Montoya said flippantly. Arhus suppressed a laugh.

"Will you need me for anything else?" Arhus asked.

"I don't think so," Montoya replied. "We didn't tackle the questions I expected tonight and with Arlan gone, I doubt anyone else is going to start anything significant. I will make sure you get the notice for tomorrow's meeting. Now excuse me, there are other issues I must attend to before I leave."

Arhus backed up as Montoya pushed back his chair and stood. Arhus could see that the man would not have to go far to transact his business. Others were already making their way toward him without their translators or assistants. Whatever the 'business' was, they didn't want anyone else knowing it.

Not that I care, Arhus thought. *Ambassadors are always secretive about something, it seems to be a requirement of the job. How many secrets can be left in the world with everyone's lives so connected, their every movement possible to track one way or another, and a computer on their wrist wherever they go? Some people seem to need the appearance of secrecy, if nothing else,* he guessed.

Without ceremony, Arhus left the room, heading for the lifts. Checking the time, he was surprised that the meeting had taken over an hour when so little had happened. Maybe more surprising, he was hungry again. *If I don't want to get my good suit stained, I'll have to go home and change first. It was not a long walk, just more time before I get to eat.*

At ground level, things looked different. They always did. The news crews must have grown tired of trying to find someone who knew anything of value or they had been sent home. A few people still milled around the plaza, looking and pointing up to the tree tops as if something was still there. Other than that, the plaza appeared normal, if you didn't look at people's faces. Arhus knew what they were thinking, because he was, too. *The future has become so unpredictable. Everyday stuff has become inconsequential. If one eats or not, will it matter tomorrow? Does 'god' care? I doubt it.*

If the visitors are the God of the Bible, there are an innumerable number of questions to ask. Did they say all those things that were written down or had men misinterpreted telepathic messages? If they have been misrepresented, what does God really care about? If they aren't the God of the Bible, none of it matters except what they want now. And that's the real question—what do they want? Arhus had the feeling they would find out very soon.

Chapter Five
The Messengers

"This getting in early needs to stop," Arhus said to himself as he rode the elevator to his office. The day before had made him tired enough to go to bed before his normal schedule, but after eight hours, his body had decided it was time to wake up again. He had been through this cycle before and knew it wouldn't end until he either stayed up until his normal bedtime, without the benefit of alcohol, because that tended to put him to sleep, or the weekend came along. For whatever reason, his body knew it could sleep longer in the morning on the weekend and was willing to do so. Of course, that assumed they got a weekend.

At least he got breakfast when it was fresh out of the oven this time of the morning. Arhus knew how much flavour disappeared if you waited an hour or more. It would have been worth getting up if he had something other to do than go into work, but the bakers were the only ones doing anything of note that time of the morning. More was the shame.

When the door opened, Arhus could see that a few people were in the office, the ones who liked to come in so they could leave early if they wanted. Once in a while, someone came in because they needed to be somewhere else in the afternoon, but that was rare. People just left. Sure, they might get yelled at by Rossarro, but the ones who took that seriously were those who made up the time and were never the recipient of his anger, at least for that reason.

Arhus turned on his interface when he got near his table. It starting flashing and beeping at him like an angry hornet, which drew a look from all of the three other people in the room. He managed to turn off the alarms just in time to hear Rossarro's voice.

"Gint! Get in here now!"

"Great," Arhus muttered to himself, "he must have had the proximity sensor on."

Walking into Rossarro's office, Arhus couldn't decide if the man had not gone home the night before or just not bothered to clean up his office the last few days. Not that he cared. Rossarro looked mad enough and hungry enough to bite the head off something. Arhus didn't bother to sit down.

"Why didn't you tell me you were invited to a special council meeting last night?" Rossarro blurted out.

"I figured you knew," Arhus said in a calm voice.

"Knew! How would I have known?"

"Procedures state that all requests are to be channelled through your office before sending notification to the translator." Arhus kept his voice even and calm as if reading from the manual.

"That doesn't mean they did it!"

"How am I supposed to know that?" Arhus touched his chest with his right hand.

"You could have made sure it had been cleared!" Rossarro pounded his fist on the table in front of him.

"That's not part of the procedure." Arhus managed to look a little confused.

"Why didn't you tell me?" Rossarro pounded on the desk again.

"You weren't here," Arhus replied with a small shrug.

"You could have forwarded the message to me! Did you think of that?"

"No, I didn't," Arhus said after looking to think about it for a second. "I don't assume people violate procedure on purpose."

"People do things the wrong way all the time!"

Arhus stared at Rossarro. No words were required, though many came to mind. He watched the realization come across Rossarro's face and then watched it turn to frustration and then anger. Rossarro appeared to be accusing him of something with his eyes. Arhus continued to stare without changing his expression. He knew the next words would decide much.

Rossarro lowered his eyes to the display on his desk. "Get out of my office."

Complying without comment, Arhus walked out, noting to himself that Rossarro had not given him any directions concerning future requests from Montoya.

Outside the office, the work area had not increased in population. As he scanned the room to note who was there, his eyes fell on Sindie. She looked ready to fall over from exhaustion, sitting in front of the central display that had become life-like to the point that Arhus figured they would need military-grade equipment to make it better. Not that he put that past some people's ability to acquire. He walked over to where she was sitting.

"I hate to say it this way," Arhus said in a low voice next to Sindie, "but you look awful. You okay?"

"Can't sleep," she replied, not even looking up, eyes fixed on the scene of the alien ship hovering in the air.

Arhus squatted down so he was level with Sindie's head. "Look, you're not going to make it through the day like this. At least let me take you down to medical and get some Awaken in you before someone comes in and makes a huge fuss."

Turning her head with meaning, Sindie looked at him. He could tell from her eyes that she wanted to argue with him, but he could also tell she didn't have the energy. She took a couple of breaths while Arhus waited, each held for an instant before she let them escape. She lowered her eyes.

"Fine, I'll go." The words sounded as tired as she looked.

"I'll go with you, just to make sure you don't get lost or fall down a shaft," Arhus said with a smile.

"You're all heart," Sindie said. She stood up as if she was covered in concrete. Halfway up, she grabbed Arhus's arm for assistance, but let go as soon as she was standing. Taking a deep breath and holding her head upright, she started for the lift, Arhus standing next to her step for step. Before she made it, she was leaning against his shoulder, though she seemed resolved not to put her head on his shoulder, at least until the lift started to descend and they were out of sight of anyone in the office. She also allowed Arhus to put his arm around her lower back. He could feel some of her weight being shifted to his arm. When the lift stopped, he guided her to the medical centre.

At the door to the centre, Sindie stopped and pushed away. "I'll go in by myself, if you don't mind," she said. "It won't look so bad that way."

"Sure, but I'm going to wait out here for a few to make sure you don't just turn around and come right back out." A large smile accompanied the statement.

"Thanks for the vote of confidence, *mother*," Sindie said as she stepped toward the automatic door.

Arhus didn't stay long. He knew that Sindie prided herself in being able to take care of herself. Just letting him bring her to medical was a huge concession, which also proved how much she needed sleep. Turning back to the lift, he tried to remember if Sindie lived with anyone, but came up with no name. The fact that she rarely talked about that part of her life didn't help him keep current.

The stress caused by the alien's arrival has surfaced in all sorts of ways, Arhus reminded himself. *Did she have a fight with... whoever... and been thrown out, or worse? At least if it is worse, she's in the right place to get taken care of.*

While ascending, Arhus checked his interface. He now had six unanswered calls from his ex-girlfriend. Deciding that they were not going to stop on their own, he spoke at the interface, "Contact Biel." He was not even to his floor when her voice came to his ear.

"Arhus! Where have you been, I've been trying to reach you!"

"I was ignoring you," he replied in a calm voice.

"Why?" she shot back. It seemed a day for not speaking. "Okay, I know why, but things have changed."

"Changed?"

"The alien ship, of course!"

"I'm confused. How does that change us?" Arhus stepped off the lift and walked toward an area of the room with no workstations.

"It changes the whole world! It changes everyone! I would have thought you would have known that!" She sounded a little flustered.

Arhus could feel the anger rising. He had hated when Biel was in one of these moods, unable to see how condescending she was acting, never understanding the precision in language he had to use every day at work. It had been a very gradual grind that had ended up with him not even wanting to talk to her. About all that had been left was the physical and even that became not worth the relationship.

"What I am asking is what does the arrival of the aliens have to do with you contacting me?" he replied.

"Didn't you hear what it said? They are here to take some of us back to their planet. I want to go with them, I *need* to go with them!"

"And that relates to me how?" The conversation was progressing with painful slowness, just like every other conversation he had had with Biel when she wanted something. He sighed, remembering how many times he had told her that he could not read her mind and getting told he should just know what she wanted.

"You work for the government. You need to get me on the list or whatever they are using."

Arhus laughed. It couldn't be helped.

"Why are you laughing at me?" The question was asked with a harsh tone.

"Because you grossly over-estimate my position in the government," he managed to say.

"But you know diplomats and government officials! Surely you could put in a word for me..."

"With whom?" Arhus shot back, anger bubbling in his voice. The suddenness of his words stopped the voice on the other end. "No one is getting near that ship! It's two hundred metres above the ground, for crying out loud. What do you expect me to do, hail a cab for you?"

Silence came from the interface. Arhus thought he could hear Biel breathing, sounding like she had just finished a short run down the hall. Laying odds she was going to cry if he didn't say something else, he decided not to make the situation worse.

"Look, Biel," he said in a soothing tone while rolling his eyes and head backwards, "no one is going near that ship except military and diplomats. If that changes, I am sure the media will announce it faster than I can call and tell you. All I can say is keep your eyes on the news for any changes. Other than that, I don't know anything."

Arhus could hear her breathing change to a less frantic pace. He let his shoulders sag and took a deep breath. *Crisis averted,* he thought to himself. *Something else I didn't need this morning.*

"Look, Arhus, I know I've messed up my life, wasted my time looking for excitement, fun, and the right friends, worried about things I shouldn't and not appreciated the people I should have..."

Arhus closed his eyes and wished it all to go away. But it didn't. Knowing that when Biel starting talking in impossible-length sentences, endless apologies were coming, he started to search his brain for any excuse to break the contact. It had to be one she would believe, which living with her had made that much harder.

"Don't you see, this is my chance to start over, to make my life count, to undo all the waste that I have made of my life and give it real purpose and meaning somewhere with people or beings who don't know what a mess I have made with you and others, not to mention my family and..."

"Biel... Biel... Biel, my boss is giving me a look, I have to go."

"Okay, I know I've taken up your time, just keep me in mind and let me know if there is anything you can do..."

"Yes, I will remember. Bye." Arhus broke contact and leaned against the wall. Air came out of his lungs like a prisoner escaping from a torture pit. He felt beat on and was developing a headache. Walking back to his workstation, he flopped in the chair and looked at the time.

"All that and only seven in the morning," he said to himself.

"Let me guess," Josef's voice came from behind him. "Biel."

"How did you know?" Arhus laced the statement in sarcasm and an eye roll that Josef couldn't see.

"Trust me, I know the symptoms." Josef sat down at the station next to Arhus and held his interface at the desk interface to active the displays. "I've seen that look enough times that I'm tired of it."

"I'll trade you places."

"No, thanks!" Josef recoiled from Arhus. "I like myself too much for that!"

Arhus's brow furrowed. "Did you ever wonder that maybe I just like beating myself up?"

"That would explain the women you pick." Josef's right forefinger pointed upwards with the statement.

"And where is my best friend when I am making these bad decisions?" Arhus asked, turning toward Josef, his face puckered toward the middle.

"Oh, right," Josef said with a laugh, "like you ever listen to me. I tried to introduce you to someone I thought would be perfect for you, but no, you had to make up your own mind."

"Wait!" Arhus's eyes got wide. "You mean the lady boxer with arms thicker than mine?"

"Hey," Josef said with a shrug, "at least you'd never argue."

"Not more than once, that's for sure. Besides, she wasn't that good looking."

"You're thinking of her twin brother." Josef gave his head a small shake.

"You mean there were two of them?"

"I tried to tell you that, but you were just drunk enough not to be able to tell the difference. That really was a missed opportunity. He kind of liked you." Even though his head was not turned toward Arhus, the sly smile was still visible.

"Just shut up," Arhus replied, turning away from his friend in order to suppress the desire to punch him.

Normal work went on for a while, a relief, and the news continued to show a picture of the alien ship as the sun started to come over the horizon and throw rays of light that reflected off the back of the ship. The rays dispersed around the ship, giving a dramatic image from the right angle. Arhus gave the report an occasional glance until a new voice started talking in a more urgent tone. Arhus looked up from his display as the sun made a full appearance.

"Many here are full of expectation," the voice said, "as the visitors have promised to send out their messengers today. As you can see, the military has brought out numerous sighting instruments in hopes of getting a clear view of these messengers before they leave Jerusalem."

"Why do they always say 'as you can see'?" Arhus said, irritation in his voice, his head tilted to the side.

"I think it's tradition," Josef replied. "Besides, if they didn't state the obvious, what would be left to talk about?"

"Some useful information?" Arhus offered half-heartedly.

"I think there's a law against that." Josef continued to type into his display. "Let me know if anything interesting happens."

Ignoring his display and the news voice, Arhus continued to watch the news video. When the sun had risen above the level of the ship, the circle on top of the ship opened, revealing the inner light as before.

"Jos, you may want to look now," Arhus said, not taking his eyes from the display.

When the circle stopped opening, a ring of beings facing inward were raised to the top of the ship. Standing erect as if at attention, the white robed beings' physiques were hard to make out even when the camera zoomed, due to the colour similarity and light from inside the ship. The news voice was talking with hurried words, but they were lost on Arhus. As the platform reached the outer hull, the light from inside the ship disappeared.

"Twenty, I repeat, twenty beings have just exited the ship," the news voice said, almost shouting. "Can these be the messengers that the aliens have promised?"

"Wa!" Arhus replied, as if the man could hear him.

All at the same time, shapes unfolded from their backs, transparent shapes on both sides. No more than a second afterwards, the beings launched into the sky, dispersing equally from each other upwards, like rockets from a launch pad. They left no trail. The blurred view of the extension from their backs were the sole indication that they were flying.

"Holy..." Josef muttered as the beings disappeared from the site. "Do you know what those look like?"

"Angels," Arhus replied. "They look just like angels have been described for ages."

"You don't think they really are... you know what?" Josef's voice trembled with the question.

"Either they are or our visitors have gone to a lot of trouble to make them look like it." Arhus peered at the display as the top of the ship opened again and more messengers were raised. This time, the platform had concentric rings of beings. When the platform stopped, the outside ring flew off first, followed by the next inner ring until all had launched, each taking its own track. The top opened again.

"Crap!" Josef exclaimed, tilting forward with the word. "How many do you think they are sending out?"

"No idea. How many people do you think they could get on that ship?"

The statement shocked Josef's brain out of its stammer, causing him to sit up straight. His head turned one way and then the other as if to measure the spacecraft. "I would say a couple thousand, easy. Of course, it depends on how many beings are already inside and how much space they take up, not counting the ship systems."

"And if you were taking only humans back with you?" Arhus asked.

Josef looked at Arhus, his eyes wide. "I never thought about that. In that case, I would say ten thousand easy, probably more like twenty."

"I heard a report that speculated about it last night. If you weren't worried about giving everyone a comfortable room and gave them some kind of transport tube instead, like in the old sci-fi movies, they estimated that ship could hold twenty-five thousand and leave plenty of space for ship systems." Arhus watched another wave of beings. They appeared to be exiting the ship faster now.

"What the heck would they want with twenty-five thousand people?" Josef asked.

"Colonization," Arhus offered, "experimentation, cultural studies, a food supply on the way home?"

"Don't even kid about that," Josef replied without humour.

"Yes," Eymen said from the other side of Arhus. "That's not even funny."

"Just using the plots from almost every sci-fi movie the first hundred years they were made." The comment was nonchalant even with the emotions from the others.

"Where do you think they are all going?" Miranda asked. As if in reply, the news voice came back on.

"The military is tracking the beings that have already left. They appear to be scattering around the globe at a speed that exceeds what a human could withstand, though they don't appear to be leaving a supersonic wake. How they are doing this is anyone's guess, but it does make them harder to follow. We are trying to get a complete count of the beings, but estimate that two hundred have already left the ship."

All activity in the office had stopped as people watched wave after wave of beings leave the ship on the display, so many that they became a blur until they had separated far enough from each other.

Arhus dragged his eyes from the scene to look at his companions in the office. About half had their mouths open in shock. A few hands twitched. He wasn't sure some of them were breathing. On impulse, he looked out the window to see if any of the beings were hovering outside the window, trying to get in, but saw only the fading glows of those flying overhead. He could hear no noise from outside, something he never thought about until now, when there was none and assumed there should be. Movement in the office was limited to that on the display, to which he returned his attention.

Without any indication of diminishing, the stream of beings leaving the ship stopped. Those at the end flowed up and outward, following the others like a rear guard. Anticlimactically, the platform raised empty and sealed the ship. The camera watched the last of the beings disappear from the site and then had the presence of mind, or just luck, to scan those standing nearby. Soldier and citizen alike stood looking upward, the same expressions on their faces as on those in the office. After a short pause, Arhus could hear people breathing again. At first, they looked at each other without talking, waiting for someone to become brave enough to give voice.

"What does it all mean?" Sylva asked.

"It means there are a lot of people on the invite list," Josef said.

"But no one here?" Karlstad offered.

"Not yet at least," Arhus answered. "Who knows how many people each of those, whatevers, has been sent to contact?"

"Start with those farthest away and work your way back," Karlstad said. "That is what would make sense."

Arhus's interface started to chime, flash, and vibrate at the same time. Someone wanted to talk to him and labelled it urgent. He just hoped it wasn't Biel. Twisting his wrist, he turned the interface and looked at the message. It wasn't Biel.

"Gint," he said after waving his hand over the interface.

"Ambassador Montoya would like you in his office immediately, top priority," a female voice said. She would have been pleasant-looking if she hadn't been so scared.

"I'm on my way," he replied, pushing his seat back.

Josef's head turned his way with an unspoken question.

"Don't know," Arhus said in reply. "I'll let you know when I know something."

"Don't evacuate without me," Josef said in a voice that Arhus could not tell was serious or not.

"Never. Who else would carry my luggage?" That brought a laugh from Josef as Arhus left for the lift. Once inside, he could see others at the windows, scanning the skies. Each floor that he passed revealed more, some more crowded than others. When he reached his destination, the number of gawkers was down to none. The hallways, though, were full of people rushing back and forth, who had to be avoided if a person liked his body parts where they were supposed to be located.

Arhus entered Montoya's reception area to be waved into the open door of his office. With all the people rushing in and out, it appeared the practical solution. The office itself looked like it had been hit by a paper bomb and too many people had volunteered to clean it up, making it worse with their efforts. Assuming he was to report to the ambassador, Arhus looked around until he located Montoya and then made his way through the maze, finishing his trek at the end of Montoya's mahogany desk.

Montoya's head assistant, a man whose name Arhus had failed to learn, saw Arhus first and started directing a few people toward a door on the side wall while diverting most of the others elsewhere. Looking at Arhus, he gave his head a quick jerk toward the door. The handful of people heading through the door looked more important to Arhus than he felt, even the younger man in the well-tailored suit. The group was made up of four men, including Arhus, and two women. All were older than he was, except for a well-dressed man who couldn't have been over twenty-five. Arhus recognized two of the men from the council meetings, but did not know their names, since they had not spoken. He pegged them all Montoya's allies. One of the women was dressed as a rabbi.

Their destination was a private audience room with padded chairs, two couches, end tables, and a refreshment console on one wall. Arhus took a station near the window while several of the others took bottles of drinks from the console and downed them with the speed of the thirsty. No smell of alcohol came across the room to Arhus, which he took as a good sign. Montoya and his assistant came in last, the assistant closing and locking the door from the inside.

"Thank you all for coming," Montoya said, making his way to the middle of the room.

"Is there somewhere else you thought we would be?" the young man asked with a chuckle.

"Given the state of events," Montoya replied in his ambassadorial voice, "I have no idea what anyone will do. But since we are all here, we will begin."

"May I ask," Montoya's assistant interrupted as he pointed at Arhus, "why *he* is here?"

"Don't be so suspicious, Alonzo," Montoya said with a chuckle. "He has proven himself to be very insightful. To the business of the day, then. These beings that left the ship, the, the... whatever we are going to call them."

"Why can't we just call them 'being' or 'winged being' if you want to be more precise?" one of the men said with a Spanish accent.

"Do you really think people will go for that?" the lady not dressed as a rabbi asked. She had on formal business attire common to diplomats with an eastern-Asian flair to it. Her accent was one Arhus could not place, due to the fact it was so slight. He assumed she came from long-time diplomatic corps, maybe even generations long.

"We can't worry about what people will think, we have to do something decisive," the young man said.

"But we have to refer to them somehow," Montoya answered.

"Why don't we just call them what everyone is going to call them?" Arhus put in. "Angels."

"The few remaining religious people in this world," the rabbi said with a firm voice, "and be sure there are getting to be more every day, will not stand for the government to sanction them as angels."

"I didn't say 'sanction' them," Arhus retorted. "Use some kind of conditional wording or something, but people and the media are going to call them angels and we are going to look silly if we stand up and try not to do the same."

No one spoke, looking at each other. As a group, they looked at Montoya. The man answered their looks and then nodded his head.

"You are correct. We will refer to them as 'beings that have the appearance associated with angels' or some such wording and then use implied parentheses when we use the word later. Will that do for everyone?" Montoya looked around at those in the room, each of whom nodded. "Good, that is settled. We can move on to other issues."

"Like what are the religious experts going to say about these beings?" the rabbi asked.

"No, Annalisa," Montoya corrected, "like what are the people going to think? I couldn't care less what the so-called experts are going to say. There are so few of them they will be drowned out by all the other voices. The people are going to have some real questions and we need to be ready for them, even if we don't have the answers."

"You're not worried that this is a matter for the special council?" the young man asked, sarcasm clear in his voice.

"Those bureaucrats, Bahir? I wouldn't trust them to choose a lunch menu. The food would be cold by the time they decided on the first course." Montoya walked to the refreshment console and snatched a bottle of water from a tub of ice.

Arhus found himself relaxing just enough to notice the international flavor of the group. Bahir looked Middle Eastern, now that he thought about it. Annalisa was obviously Jewish. She shared enough facial features with Josef, she had to be. The other woman, he decided, was from Singapore or maybe Malaysia. Of the two other men, one appeared to be eastern European and the other Spanish. The fact that Montoya had managed to create such a diverse political group impressed Arhus. *Maybe,* he thought, *they are representatives from sub-factions. That would be impressive.*

"I think the question Ambassador Montoya is referring to," Annalisa said, "is whether our visitor is God or not."

"You are correct," Montoya said as he came back among the group.

"Preposterous!" the Spanish man said.

"Really, Vicente?" Montoya asked. "Do you think that an alien that came to earth six thousand years ago wouldn't have appeared as a god to the people, particularly if he wanted to?"

"No," Vicente answered, straightening himself. "I meant that it is preposterous that he *is* God."

"And if any of you start saying that God is just a construct of people's minds," Annalisa said as she stared, "I'll punch you. And I don't mean the pleasant type."

The comment drew a few laughs, though no one acted as if she was kidding. Arhus didn't think she looked *that* big, but then again, Josef had told him about some of his people's martial traditions.

"I am not suggesting he is God as we think of Him and make no allusions to the God of the Bible." Montoya spread his hands in supplication. "I am just saying that if people today think of this visitor as God, then what hope did ancient man have back then? None at all, that is for sure."

"Are you asking if the aliens have taken the appearance of the God of the Bible to influence mankind?" Annalisa smiled as if she liked where the conversation was going.

"Entirely possible," Vicente added, "and not a bad stratagem. If nothing else, you confuse people and buy yourself time."

"And why go through the whole deception?" the eastern European gentleman asked. "Clearly they have technology superior to our own. Wouldn't that be good enough? Why go through all the effort to create the right forms? What do they want?"

"They said what they want, their own," Annalisa answered. She looked around the room. "People. They want people."

"As if enough people on the planet wouldn't have gone with them voluntarily?" Bahir asked.

"They don't want just anybody," Arhus answered. "I don't know what they are looking for, but I am sure they want very specific people."

"Who?" Bahir asked. "Who are the pure?"

"I assume," Montoya took a drink before continuing, "we are all about to find out."

They all just stood, not speaking, some with their chins in their hands. Arhus, sure he had said more than enough already, was happy to stand there in silence. Montoya sat in one of the high-backed padded chairs. It seemed to be a signal for the others to sit. Arhus waited until all had settled before taking a spot on one of the couches. Montoya restarted the conversation by looking at his assistant.

"Has there been a count of the messengers, Alonzo?"

"We have received no official count yet," the man answered.

"Have they provided an estimate?" Montoya's voice edged a little.

"No. I think they are afraid to say in case they are wrong. Because the beings are white and move so fast, the system is having a hard time telling one from another. The images tend to blur, also, making it even harder, even at a distance from the ship."

"So much for our much-touted technology," Bahir said with a huff.

"No one has any idea?" Annalisa asked.

"Approximately five thousand."

Everyone looked at Arhus, questions displayed on their faces.

"You have some intelligence that we aren't party to?" Alonzo asked.

"No, I converted the problem into a linguistics one." Arhus looked at the faces, which showed no comprehension. "Some linguists, me included, enjoy getting into the technical aspects. One of these is speech patterns, particularly how fast people speak. When people are unsure of themselves or making public speeches, they will start slow, gradually increasing the number of words per minute they talk. This rate of increase follows well-established patterns.

"Applying this type of analysis to the beings leaving the ship, I made an estimate of how many came out of the ship in the first waves and the rate of the waves at the beginning and end of the event. With the amount of time total, I could then apply one of the known algorithms and establish an estimate for the number of messengers that were sent out. Please remember, it is a rough estimate."

"How confident are you in this estimate?" Vicente leaned forward on the edge of the chair he had chosen.

"Pretty sure. There is always the possibility they were trying to deceive us to their numbers, but I have no reason to think they would do that."

"And the estimates of how many people they could fit on their ship?" Montoya leaned back to look at Alonzo, who was still standing close by the ambassador.

"Twenty thousand, at least. Maybe more." Alonzo's voice was flat and mechanical.

"Then I would say that our friend's estimate is not far off," Montoya said as he nodded his head up and down.

Friend? Arhus thought. *Did he mean that? Translators are thought of as invisible. Have I somehow been invited to some inner circle or something?*

As Arhus considered, the conversation continued without him.

"Do we expect that there are any more of these 'messengers' inside the ship?" the eastern European gentleman asked.

"No way to know," Alonzo answered. "Given the size of the ship and the fact that it is here to transport humans, I find it unlikely that there are many more of our visitors on the ship. I doubt more would be needed to defend themselves, given their advanced technology."

"You're not thinking something desperate, are you, Ionut?" Montoya raised an eyebrow.

"I just want to know all information in case decisions are required later." Ionut flipped his wrist in dismissal and sat back in his chair.

"I agree with that sentiment, but the last thing we want to do is start being stupid. We have no idea what our visitors are capable of and I, for one, don't want to find out the hard way."

Montoya gave each of his guests a look and received a small nod from each. He even looked at Arhus, who gave the most enthusiastic nod. Montoya gave him a small smile in return, one used by parents or teachers. Arhus managed a small one in return, feeling like he was five years old again.

"The special council didn't answer the critical question," Vicente shot into the group, sitting on the edge of the chair's seat. "Are we just going to sit by and let people board that ship?"

"What do you propose we do about it?" Bahir giggled, looking toward the ceiling as his hands spread wide. "Cordon off the ship with troops? Build a fence?"

"What kind of signal do we send if we allow any alien to show up and take twenty thousand humans with them like we are sheep?"

Vicente's fist pounded his knee.

"What kind of signal do we send if we try to prevent them?" Montoya's voice calmed the discussion.

Vicente opened his mouth to speak, but after a few seconds closed it. Staring hard at Montoya, Vicente took a deep breath and let it out. "I know that we don't have the border controls that plagued our history for ages, but this is different. Our borders are open because we know each other and have worked though our differences."

"Most of them, at least," the well-dressed woman said. Now that he had all the names of the others in the room, it bothered him that he did not know hers.

"Yes, yes, there are still minor issues to deal with. If there wasn't, we wouldn't have jobs, now would we? But these visitors, we have no information on their identities or their goals. What is their planet like? What is their society like? How do they intend to treat these people they say they want? Do they even have food on their planet to feed them? Does it have an oxygen atmosphere?"

"These are all good questions," Montoya said in a tone much calmer than Vicente's. "Unfortunately, we have the answer to none. And unless our visitors decide to provide the answers, I doubt we will ever find out. I have no confidence that force would produce the answers either."

"I say let the aliens handle the problem," Annalisa said from behind a glass filled with ice and water. Arhus realized that he hadn't even seen her get up and retrieve it.

"What does that infer?" Vicente asked.

Annalisa tilted her head toward Vicente. "Do you expect that only twenty thousand people are going to try and get on that ship? A million would not surprise me. Do you want to deal with a million people trying to push their way into that ship? Let the aliens deal with it, I say. They created the problem."

"And if they don't deal with it gently?" Vicente asked, emphasizing the last word.

"Then you will get what you want. If the aliens get violent, popular opinion will go against them and we will have the excuse we need to step in. Before that, you will just be a target for people's scorn." Annalisa raised her glass to Vicente.

"There is wisdom in your words, Annalisa, as always," Montoya said with a nod.

Arhus was startled to realize that this was not just another political group, it was a well-designed organism. Each member was like the parts of a highly-crafted sentence, playing their part on purpose or because that was who they were. *Did Montoya create this group or did it come together naturally? What is my part? Should I even think about it?*

Vicente's comment broke Arhus's internal questioning. "You still have not answered the question of what we do now."

"Let us open that question to all here. Suggestions?" Montoya leaned back in his chair, folding his hands together in front of himself.

"It would be easier," Bahir started the conversation, "if we could talk to our visitors face-to-face. They must be intelligent enough to know that they are going to attract many more humans than are invited. The fact that they are being selective implies that they must have some method of rejecting the enthusiasts."

"Good luck doing that." Ionut laughed. "They are keeping their distance, hovering over that hill with no sign of any entry except for the platform on top."

"Maybe that is what they need," Arhus found himself saying, though not looking at anyone. "Maybe they need space. People tend to crowd around as close as possible. Maybe if we moved them back, the ship would come down to the ground."

"Ridiculous!" Vicente said with a shake of his head. "There is plenty of room for the ship to land."

"You're thinking like a human," Arhus replied as he turned to the man. "Our idea of space and their idea of space could be completely different, particularly if they live in space instead of on-planet."

"Very true." Montoya pointed with his drink bottle. "It won't hurt to move the lines back further. And if it brings the ship to land, it will be more than worth it. Are you suggesting that we remove our forces after the ship lands?"

"After it *lands*, yes." Annalisa closed her eyes and smiled. "One way or the other."

"I am sure we are ready to go that far," Montoya said, his face showing he was not amused at the statement. "The World Council is not here to prove or disprove your theological debates."

"We will need more troops if we are going to make the lines longer," Ionut said.

"That can be done," Montoya said, recovering some of his easy nature.

"Will we be able to trust them?" Ionut asked.

"As much or more than anyone. If we start worrying about that, we will be in trouble." Montoya stood up and walked to the refreshment console. He placed his drink on the counter, looking away from the group. "I believe this meeting is over for now. Thank you all for coming."

Startled by the abrupt end, Arhus sat while the others stood and proceeded toward the door they had entered. When the others had passed, Arhus stood and followed. Before making the door, the Asian woman turned and waited for him to catch up.

"That was very clever, counting the messengers that way," she said as he drew close.

"Thank you, Ms…"

"Smith."

Arhus did a double take.

"My grandfather was British and the family kept the name. I think they liked the shock factor. I am a special envoy from the Western Pacific Conglomerate."

"Meaning?"

The woman laughed. "Don't worry, I'm not an assassin or a spy. Well, not any more than any of us are spies here, I suppose. Officially, I represent one of the larger business conglomerates, but in reality, I am here to help push Conglomerate policy."

"Wait," Arhus said, shaking his head. "There are conglomerates inside the Conglomerate?"

"About a dozen, yes. They are organized around function and size, such as business, banking, mining, and policy, though they all dabble in policy, of course." The woman talked as they walked out of the room. The outer office was almost vacant without Montoya there to hold people. Those still in the office looked like staff.

"If I can ask, what is the function of this little group I have been invited to? To advise Montoya?"

"Yes, but more than that. It should be clear to anyone who works here that one person cannot shape events in any significant way. Individually, we were all powerless, even with the positions we held in our respective governments. Montoya brought us together, showed us how to be influential, almost like a tradition for him to pass down information."

By this time, they had reached the reception area and headed toward the hallway. Ms. Smith did not seem concerned that someone would overhear the conversation. With all the activity around them, Arhus figured she was right to assume people were too busy to listen in to conversations, a well-practised art form for assistants.

"Our governments know we are part of this group," she continued, "and, typical of them, expect to use it to their advantage, as they do all relationships. In a way, they are correct. It's not like we are traitors to our country, but we do have the greater concerns of mankind in general in mind also."

"I am still unclear why I was invited to the group or what is expected of me."

"Montoya likes to choose people of intelligence and insight. He thinks you are one. He also chooses a very diverse group, if you could not tell. Bahir is considered a spoiled rich kid by most, Ionut is a general, Vicente is a bureaucrat, Annalisa a priest, and Alonzo is a bodyguard, of course."

"Yes, a very diverse group with different points of view."

They had reached the lifts. Ms. Smith stepped into one and turned so that she still occupied the entry just inside the doorway. "Just be yourself and I am sure you will be a valuable asset. If not, you will not be asked to attend anymore. Good day, Mr. Gint. Ninety-four."

With that statement, the doorway closed and the lift descended. Arhus watched until it was out of sight.

"I guess I go back to work then," he said to himself and waited for the next lift.

Chapter Six
Fallout

In the lift, Arhus checked the time. Deciding to attend his blood sugar needs, he rode down to the cafeteria to eat an early lunch. It also gave him the opportunity to look in on Sindie. The nurse said that he had just missed her. The nurse sounded pleased that she had slept several hours after taking the drug, though she voiced the opinion that Sindie could stand with a good night's sleep. Arhus provided no guarantees.

Arhus walked back into an office area full of busy people. Rossarro was nowhere to be seen. Josef looked about to pull his hair out. As Arhus sat down next to his friend, Josef disconnected his conversation and placed his head on the table.

"You okay?" Arhus asked.

"The whole human race has gone mad at the same time," Josef said between his arms without looking up.

"The messengers?" Arhus guessed.

"Yes! The messengers!"

Arhus turned toward his own console and pulled up an interface. Messages filled his screen, all marked high priority urgent. Not able to imagine what people would want to know, Arhus paused before opening any of them, looking for any other subject to address. He sighed when he realized no other subject but the messengers existed at the moment. The temptation to erase all the messages ran high.

"What could all these people possibly want?" Arhus said out loud, not expecting an answer.

"Mostly they want to know what language the messengers speak," Josef replied, his head still down.

"How the hell are we supposed to know that?"

"I guess we're supposed to know whatever people want us to know." Josef's voice sounded as weary as his actions.

"Do we have any recordings of their voices?"

"No."

"Then how are we supposed to know what they are speaking?" Arhus searched the messages for attached recordings but found none.

"And thus my frustration," Josef replied.

"To hell with them," Arhus said under his breath.

"My sentiments exactly," Josef replied in a similar manner.

Shaking his head, Arhus moved all of the messages to storage and looked at the central display. The news showed pictures of the messengers talking to people, but provided no audio records of the interactions. Arhus assumed telepathy was in use. The people looked too shocked to respond. Turning back to his personal display, Arhus had the computer display the known locations of messenger interactions. Dots populated the globe across eastern Asia, southern Africa, the western Americas, and Scandinavia.

"Just as I would have done it," Arhus said out loud.

"What?" Josef asked, looking up from his display from the corner of his eye.

"The messengers started at the farthest points on the globe from the ship."

"Hmm, makes sense."

"Are we tracking who they are talking to?"

Josef's head turned away from the display. "I never thought to find out."

"Computer," Arhus said, "do we have a list of who the messengers have been talking to?"

"The list is being compiled," a voice responded. "Would you like to see the compilation so far?"

"Yes," Arhus said, but then added, "and I will need as much information on these people as we can get."

"What are you looking for?" Josef asked.

"Anything that is common, or not common, for that matter." Arhus's eyes scanned the list and information as it came in. The list was already thousands long. On a smaller part of the screen, the globe continued to add white points, growing ever closer to Jerusalem.

"Computer, start running comparison analysis on the people listed: ethnic backgrounds, family history, jobs, religious associations, anything they might have in common or complete dissimilarities."

"The analysis will take a few moments," the voice replied. "Should I include new names to the analysis as they arrive?"

"Yes. Report any finding to me."

"Certainly." The voice sounded too cheerful to Arhus, considering why he was asking.

"You're trying to find out why those people were selected?" Josef asked.

"It would be the first step in understanding why our visitors are here."

"How would they know any of this?" Eymen was sitting on the other side of Arhus, staring at the analysis being displayed on his screen.

"Besides the same way we will?" Arhus asked back.

"So you think they have tapped into our computer databases since arriving?" Eymen's voice sounded shocked in the way of someone who comes home to find out they had been robbed.

"Plus the fact that those messengers could have their own sensors to find the correct people," Josef added.

"I am more concerned with the who than the how at the moment, though. 'How' we can always look into later," Arhus said with a wave of his hand.

Arhus waited and watched the computer analysis. A correlation factor was shown at the bottom of the display, but the number did not change much. Additional names made it smaller. Men and women were, for all purposes, evenly represented. All major ethnic groups in the countries visited made the list. Even education categories showed no significant correlation.

"Do you think it could be random?" Josef asked.

"Would you come all this way and then choose random people?" Arhus asked back.

"They seem to be avoiding the very young and the very old," Eymen commented.

"Which makes sense. They would have it worst if space travel is stressful. Better to pick those who are more likely to survive."

"But they are not choosing many children, and then only older ones." Eymen pointed at the screen.

"Maybe they understand our protective nature when it comes to children," Josef suggested.

"Computer," Arhus said, "of the teenagers who are selected, how many are orphans?"

"All of them."

"What about the others? How many have families, namely their own minor children, or are in a religiously-united marriage?"

"None."

"That confirms it," Josef said, a smug smile showing up on his face. "They appear to prefer people without attachments that would make them want to stay, like kids and a spouse." Josef's face changed. "Hey! How come I didn't get an invite?"

"Computer," Arhus said at the display, ignoring Josef, "can you compare medical records of those chosen?"

"I am sorry," the voice said, "that information is private."

"What were you looking for?" Eymen asked.

"I just thought that there might be a common physical feature that the visitors were looking for."

The news coverage continued with views of all kinds of people facing a messenger. When the news voices asked them what was said, the information boiled down to an invitation to join the aliens, or EO-AY, to be precise. Some people looked excited, but many looked confused or shocked. When asked if they would go, most did not know, with a few excited acceptances and firm negatives. After watching a while, Arhus's brow furrowed.

"You notice something about who they are asking?" Arhus said aloud.

"Want to be more specific?" Josef asked.

"Most people don't think about it much, but there are a few areas of the world that are still 'primitive' to preserve a specific culture. I don't see any of those people being visited by our messengers."

"Would you?" Josef shot back. "I mean, if they are primitive, how would we know?"

"They'll not all *that* primitive," Arhus replied. "And even the most primitive have some kind of monitoring to make sure no one messes with them."

"Yes," Eymen piped in. "There are a couple of villages near my parents' home that keep the old traditions, but they still have modern communication and news services."

"But even those I don't see displayed. I would think the fact that a messenger visited such a place would draw a lot of attention." Arhus looked back at his display, but the correlation factors were not getting any better. "Damn, I wish I could see those medical records."

"Maybe you should ask your ambassador friend," Josef said in a sing-song voice.

"I'll have to remember that next time I see him," Arhus said in a serious voice. Synchronous side looks between the friends brought them eye-to-eye for an instant.

A quick look at the globe in the corner showed that the points of lights were converging. Arhus swept his fingers to bring the image to the centre of the display. The closer the points came to Jerusalem, the faster they appeared. The area to be covered was smaller, but they were becoming more rapid and closer than his eyes could distinguish.

"Guys," Arhus said, pointing at the globe, "guys, I think..."

His words were interrupted by a flash of light, followed by a constant glow from behind. All three men turned to find a messenger standing behind them. It was the height of a tall human. Its wings were either translucent or some kind of energy field. The messenger had a vaguely human face and human arms showing from the sides of a long robe with vertical folds that reached to the ground.

The intruder alert sounded in the room, a klaxon designed to eliminate the possibility of being ignored. Red lights flashed along the wall and a voice advised those present to leave the area if possible. No one moved, just stared at the messenger, fixated at the sight. Arhus looked behind the being and noted that the windows to the building were still intact and no glass lay on the floor. This made his eyes go wider when he looked back at the messenger, who, except for his wings, looked solid.

The messenger's head turned from side to side and then turned to Eymen and stared. Eymen's head jerked back and his mouth came open, but his eyes remained fixed on the messenger. Arhus watched both of them. He thought he could feel power pulsating from the being, but could not hear any conversation in his head or out loud.

Is this how they are choosing people, by the fact that they are able to communicate individually with them? How do they know?

As quickly as it had appeared, the messenger turned, spread its wings, and flew out of the building without shattering the windows. Arhus couldn't decide if it was his imagination or if the windows had changed while the messenger had flown through them, as if it had changed their physical properties. When it was gone, the windows appeared as they always had.

As if on cue, security guards appeared in the lifts and ran into the room, weapons drawn. Four faces scanned the room to find stunned faces all looking their direction. One touched his belt and the intruder alert ceased, leaving a sound hole in the room more noticeable than the alarm had been. The man stepped forward.

"What happened here?" he demanded.

"Messenger," someone managed to say, pointing out the window it had left.

"Only one?" the man asked.

"Yes."

The man turned and spoke into a mouth-piece, signalling his men back to the lift with his hand. The men gave one last look around the room as if to verify the situation and then turned to follow. Once they were inside, the lift descended.

The security people vanishing was like a signal for people to move. Eymen became the centre of attention, questions coming fast with many repeats before he could answer.

"What did he say?" was the first immediate question from most people.

"He said I was invited to join the EO-AY on his journey back to his home. He said I didn't need to bring anything with me, all would be provided."

"Did he threaten you?"

"No, in fact, he was quite polite."

"Why you?"

"I have no idea."

"Eymen," Arhus said, verbally pushing his way into the conversation, "this is the perfect opportunity to find out why certain people are being invited. Do you have any physical abnormalities that you know of?"

"No," Eymen replied, a little shocked. "My tests have always come back normal."

"So no deficiencies, either?"

"No."

"So what makes you different from everyone else in this room?" The question was asked with some indignation from someone out of direct eyesight.

"I have no idea." Eymen looked around at the faces. "I am sorry, but I had no idea this was going to happen. I have never been religious or as excited by the aliens' arrival than many. As far as I know, there is no reason they should have chosen me."

"Random," Josef muttered. "It has to be random."

"I'm not so sure, but we aren't going to prove otherwise here." Arhus got up from the workstation and went the window. Everyone else was gathered around Eymen as if they expected him to disappear or turn into a frog. The only person that joined him at the window was Sindie.

"You feeling better?" he asked, giving her a quick look.

"Yeah, still tired, though." Her eyes were more of the regular tired than the exhausted tired.

"You want to talk about why you're not sleeping?" Arhus looked out the window, knowing that staring would pressure her.

"Not really, but I guess you deserve to know." Sindie took a deep breath and let it out slowly. "These aliens, they scare the stuffing out of me."

"Why?"

"Not sure I know. I'm not worried they are God, but maybe I'm worried they're not, which begs the question if they are as benevolent as we would like them to be. Maybe it's not knowing that scares me, particularly when I'm alone. It's like that ship is staring at us."

Arhus turned his head toward her. "Aren't you with…"

"Not anymore. Been, I don't know, five weeks maybe. Said I worked too much. Imagine that."

"Weren't you staying at his place?"

"Yeah, had to move out. My uncle's third cousin's letting me stay at his place, but the room is small and it's not real comfortable. If fact, when it's nice out, I'd rather sleep outside, if that tells you how bad it is. Plus with all that's going on, I really don't want to be alone."

"You don't have a friend to stay with, something better?"

"Not anyone I would want to. Never thought about it before we broke up, but most of my friends are guys and that didn't seem like a good idea. You know, show up at some guy's door and say, 'Hey, my boyfriend kicked me out, can I stay here?' Can you imagine what they would think?"

Arhus couldn't help but laugh. "Yes, I can."

"Then, just when I started to think about finding my own place, this happens." She waved at the ship in the distance.

Arhus stood for a few moments, both of them in silence, taking in Sindie's words, before he spoke. "Can I make an offer without you taking it, well, the way those offers are normally taken?"

Sindie looked at him, eyebrows raised. "Now you have to say it so I don't die of curiosity."

"My place has one of those sleeper-chairs, which is more comfortable than my bed, to tell the truth, plus the bedroom has a door. Come over to my place. At least you won't be alone somewhere. One of us could take the couch and the other the chair if you don't want to be in a room by yourself. Trust me, I've slept on both before, so it was good I had the foresight to make sure I picked a model that's good for sleeping."

Sindie just stared at him for a few seconds. "Why would you go out of your way for me?"

"Because you're my friend." Arhus turned back to look out the window. "And not that I would tell anyone, but if Biel did hear about it, maybe she would stop calling me."

Sindie huffed a laugh. "Oh, I see how you are. You just want to use me, just not in the normal way guys use girls. Wait, come to think of it, it's not *that* unusual."

"Well?" Arhus said after a dramatic pause.

"Thanks. I mean, sure, thanks. If I can just get a good night's sleep, I'm sure I'll feel a lot better." She stared out the window at the ship, and then said, "Just don't tell Josef. I don't want the whole world to know."

"Half the world. His relatives would take care of the other half."

"Exactly."

Their conversation was interrupted by a shout from behind them. The voice could only belong to one person, based on the volume as well as the distinctive tone.

"What the hell is going on out here?" Rossarro's voice echoed throughout the room. Faces turned his direction.

"Eymen was visited by a messenger," someone on the other side of the group managed to say.

"Eymen! My office!"

Eymen pushed sideways through the crowd around him and, head tilted down and shoulders slumped, walked to the office. Furtive looks followed him and were directed around the group after he disappeared.

Arhus took the opportunity to check the time on his interface. "What?"

"What?" Sindie asked.

"It's after three already." Arhus double-checked the central display. It agreed.

"What?" Sindie said, creating a sense of déjà vu. "How is that possible?"

"Were we that absorbed in the news reports that we didn't notice how much time passed?"

"Or can the messengers somehow affect time?"

The comment caught Arhus off guard, causing him to look at her with a blank expression. It didn't help that any reply fled from his head.

"Some kind of time dilation. It would allow them to travel around the world faster, wouldn't it?"

"Those are two different time effects, you know," Arhus said when he was able to speak.

"Why couldn't it work both ways?"

Arhus shrugged. "Not sure how you would prove it. Sounds a lot better than we just lost track of time and wasted the day, though."

The comment made Sindie laugh, followed by a long, deep yawn. Sindie looked embarrassed by the yawn, hiding her face until it was over.

"You okay?" Arhus asked. "The Awaken wearing off?"

"The nurse didn't give me Awaken, she gave me a sleep-inducer, said I was too tired for the Awaken, it would stress my system too much." She half-suppressed another yawn, but it refused to be defeated.

"Maybe you should call it a day before you lose the battle?" Arhus looked around. "I doubt anything else is going to happen here today. Why don't we leave now while everyone is preoccupied?"

"Not a bad idea. I need to stop and get some fresh clothes, for tomorrow." They both turned toward the lifts and tried to walk without looking tired. Sindie fussed with her hands as if she wished she had something in them to add to the deception. When they turned around in the lift, no one was watching. Sindie let out a sigh of relief when the floor disappeared from sight.

"Biel left a few clothes at my place, some of the Knockers she bought for some unknown reason and then pronounced as hideous." Arhus turned to watch the trees come up to meet them.

"The one-piece ones?" Sindie asked.

"Yeah, even got one with the added skirt and button front. I guess it's supposed to be dressy. Kind of ruins the effect if you know what it is. If you ask me." The leaves waved in greeting as the lift passed the top of the trees.

"I always liked those. Does the self-adjusting size really work?"

"No idea. Didn't try them on. You're welcome to, though."

Sindie laughed. "Guess I just might." Another yawn followed. "I don't know if I can make it through a restaurant wait and stay awake. Maybe we should pick up supper on the way."

"I've got food in the apartment unless you have special diet needs or are afraid to try my cooking," Arhus said, looking at Sindie after the statement.

"You cook? That I have to see."

"It's hard to imagine that I cook?" Arhus asked with a smile.

"It's hard to imagine that anyone in our office has time to cook," she replied with a roll of her eyes.

"Takes as much time as sitting and waiting at a restaurant for your food." Arhus shrugged.

"I wouldn't know. The women do all the cooking in my family, the ones who stay home and don't work, that is. Add to that the fact they make enough for three times the number of people at the table and it's not hard to imagine why I never had to cook."

"Must be nice." The way he said it made Sindie look at him.

"I grew up with it so I never thought much about it. You an only child?"

"Yeah. Mom and Dad both worked so I was home by myself after school. And then on Saturday mornings they would 'sleep in,' or so they said. Growing boys have to eat, you know. I made a lot of bad pancakes before I learned how to do it right." Arhus looked back when he was done talking and tried to give a reassuring smile that said that it had been no big deal, but was not sure she bought it. "Besides, when I reached junior high, I started hanging out with Josef and there was always food at his house."

Sindie looked like she was going to say something sensitive and touching, but then her face changed as if she had decided they didn't know each other well enough. The door of the lift opened and she faced forward to exit. The front door was close, so the conversation stopped until they were under the trees in the plaza.

"I hope you learned to make something besides pancakes," she said with a smirk.

"Sure," he said and paused for a couple of steps. "Crepes."

The comment earned him an elbow to the arm.

Arhus looked out his all-glass porch doors and windows. The alien ship took up a large part of the view, but the mountain with its trees was also visible and some of the valley in the distance. The ship still had no lights or other features common to human ships, but just hung in the air like an ornament, defying gravity.

Arhus laughed to himself, thinking that Sindie had either been truly hungry or impressed with his cooking, betting on the former. He could see her fading as she ate, not wanting to stop, but the need for sleep caught up with her as the blood rushed to her stomach to deal with the food. When she surrendered and realized that she had brought nothing to change into, she asked if he had anything she could use. Since one of his 'tourist' shirts reached her knees, it was not hard to find her something. She went into the bathroom to change and had been in there long enough that he was beginning to wonder if she had fallen asleep when he heard the door open.

Sindie walked into the room and sat down on the couch next to him, laying her head on his shoulder. The way her body slumped, he wondered if she could raise it again if she wanted.

"You can take the bed," he said. "I'm not going to sleep yet."

"Do you mind if I just sit here for a few?" she asked. "I don't feel like being alone."

"Sure," Arhus said with a small smile. He stared at the ship and wondered what it would bring next. He wanted to turn on the viewer and see what was happening, if all the messengers had returned, but he didn't want to disturb Sindie and thought the news might make her edgy. Besides, some birds were chirping outside the window, having built a nest on top of the building in some of the decorative structure. *How often do I just sit and listen to them?* he asked himself.

"That thing scares the shit out of me," Sindie said after a while.

"Why?"

"I don't know. Maybe that's why. Someone that advanced could do whatever they wanted, couldn't they? So why are they here? Will they come back and want more of us? Are we just some kind of harvest to them?" Arhus felt her shift almost as if she was trying to hide behind him.

"It would seem logical that if that's all we were, they wouldn't be so nice." Arhus tried to sound reassuring, but didn't try too hard. Translators were taught how to calm someone with their voice and he didn't want to seem like he was working her. "If we were just some kind of harvest, then they could just send troops and take what they wanted, right?"

"Unless they were afraid we would damage ourselves in the process and that would make us less valuable. Maybe psychological damage is the worst kind for what they need."

"I am sure we could think up a sinister scenario for any action they took. We have to deal with what they are doing at face value or we'll paralyze ourselves."

"I guess," Sindie said with a sigh. "It still makes me nervous. People are such sheep. I'm sure there are thousands that would blissfully walk onto that ship no matter what anyone told them, not having any idea what is waiting for them."

"Millions, I am sure." Arhus laughed. "Maybe we are better off without them."

"Are they the kind of people you want representing humankind in the universe?" Sindie asked.

"Well, I sure don't want to send a bunch of politicians, *that's* for sure."

"Stop trying to depress me," Sindie said as Arhus had a little chuckle.

The conversation came to an end. Arhus sat and listened as Sindie's breathing slowed to the level of sleep. A soft snoring sound started and her arms went limp. After half an hour, he moved, gently placing her head on the pillow at the arm of the couch. Her feet were already curled up on the couch, so he placed a comforter-sheet over her. Looking at the kitchen, he decided that the dishes could wait until tomorrow. Pulling the pillow from the other end of the couch, he found another comforter-sheet under the couch and sat in the chair.

"Recline position one," he said. The chair began a slow transformation into a sleeping position with the head slightly elevated. Arhus put the pillow behind his head and the sheet over himself. He was within arm's reach of Sindie if needed.

"Windows opaque," he said out loud. The porch windows and doors became a smoky black colour that blocked any outside view.

Chapter Seven
Resistance

While Arhus's alarm was set with plenty of time for him to be ready for work, no consideration had been made for two people to prepare. The fact that he, being an early riser that rose before the alarm went off, had always used it as a last resort in case he overslept, only made matters worse. Breakfast would have to wait, but showering, shaving, and other preparations were required. For about the thousandth time, he told himself he was going to get the whisker removal process done so he could be done with shaving.

When Sindie came out of the bathroom for the second time, she was wearing the Knocker with the extra skirt and false blouse so that it looked like a complete outfit. It still maintained the full-length legging that were the hallmark of the Knockers. When Arhus saw her, his eyes went wider.

"I must say," he said to Sindie, "that you look better in that than Biel ever did." As soon as he said it, he hoped that Sindie would not read into the statement and could feel his cheeks wanting to blush.

"It helps if you have something to fill it out with," Sindie said, gesturing down her body, causing Arhus's cheeks to threaten harder. "You always seemed to like the skinny ones."

"So you're saying that it fits better if you have a fat ass?" Arhus said as much to cover his reaction as to tease Sindie. The comment earned him a pillow thrown to the face.

"Come on, if we're late, people will ask questions." Sindie walked to the front door, putting her interface on as she went.

They fast-walked to work, bypassing the bakery and breakfast shops by mutual consent. When they reached their building and stepped into the lift, Arhus asked for the twenty-third floor.

"I've got to eat or my blood sugar will get too low," he said as if to no one in particular.

"Oh, that's right. Could you pick me up a croissant while you're there? Chocolate?" Sindie asked.

"Sure, and I'll get something for Josef," he said as he gave her a look.

"He'll appreciate that," she replied in a nonchalant voice.

"It will keep him from complaining that I didn't think of him."

The comment made Sindie laugh. "Yes, let's avoid that at all costs," she said.

Arhus got off the lift when it stopped at twenty-three. In the cafeteria, he picked out Sindie's croissant, a bagel for Josef, and a doughnut and breakfast sandwich for himself. The sandwich was half gone before he left the cafeteria. He had it gone before the lift reached the office.

Arhus dropped off the croissant to Sindie as he walked to the workstation next to Josef. He managed to place the bagel on the table in front of his friend without a snicker before sitting down. Josef took a quick glance at the table and then at his friend.

"The doughnut isn't for me? No breakfast sandwich?" Josef asked as if hurt.

"Nope," Arhus said, taking a bite with a grin beneath.

"So because I'm Jewish, I get the bagel," Josef said in a slight sing-song.

"No, because I know you like them. If I wanted to be cliché, I would have brought you some lox, too."

"Please, no!" Josef recoiled. "No raw fish for breakfast!"

"See, you should be thanking me," Arhus said, sitting down and taking another bite of doughnut.

"What would be the fun in that?" Josef picked up the bagel and took a bite. Through a mouth of bagel, he said, "At least you got blueberry."

"Friends are supposed to know what each other likes, right?" Arhus shot back.

"Is that why Sindie is wearing Biel's outfit?" Josef asked without looking at Arhus.

"Who says it's Biel's?" Arhus did not look at Josef.

"Nice. Don't just deny the question, because I can tell when you're lying a mile away. But you failed to answer the question." Josef let the statement stand for a minute before continuing. "Is there something I should know, before I find out some other way, that is?"

"No, there is nothing to tell," Arhus said firmly. "She's been having trouble sleeping, so I invited her over to my place. Just to sleep, that's all, by herself. This morning she needed something to wear and, as you know, Biel left what she didn't want." Arhus turned his head and aimed his serious face at his friend. "That's it. You don't need to be talking about it."

"Fine, fine." Josef raised his hands in a defensive gesture. "Just thought it might be a good idea for me to know before the whispers started. By the way, Sindie does look better today, not as tired. So I guess that rules out a night of passion."

"So what's happened since yesterday?" Arhus said, steering the conversation away from his private life.

"Not much, at least that anyone is saying. It looks like all the messengers have returned." Josef moved his display, throwing away old messages. "I guess we wait for whatever they do next."

"Maybe not," Arhus said one word at a time. When Josef turned his way, he found Arhus staring at the central display. His gaze quickly followed. A scene of a soldier pointing a weapon at one of the messengers caused him to switch sound to the central display.

"This was the scene yesterday," the news voice was saying, "in Indonesia as soldiers tried to prevent the messengers from talking to citizens of that country..."

"Yesterday?" Josef exclaimed.

"You know how the government is there, controlling all information going out of the country. I'm surprised we heard about this so fast." Arhus's voice held no tension, but his face was a different matter, tightening around the jaw.

"Even though the messenger had already talked to an individual, we are told," the voice continued, "the soldier here is threatening the messenger if it tries to talk to anyone else in the country. The messenger doesn't look phased by the presence of the gun or what the man is saying. In fact, we are not sure why it stayed around to listen."

The scene showed a soldier, Indonesia being one of the few countries to still maintain its own army, holding a rifle at waist height, aimed at the messenger, while he screamed in Indo-Chinese. The messenger made no response to the man, standing with his wings folded. It made no apparent attempt to fly away. This caused the man to shout louder and then raise the gun to his shoulder. Arhus heard a gasp go through the room. The soldier continued to shout as he pointed the weapon at the messenger's head. People in the background started to pull away from both individuals, but faster from behind the messenger. People started to voice alarm.

The news eye must have had a directional mic pointed at the scene, because the noise of the crowd did not drown out the soft *psst* of the gun being fired. The gun jerked back in recoil a few centimetres. Without smoke, a firing rifle was not much to watch, so eyes were fixed on the messenger. But nothing happened. A scream in the background drew the camera eye to the crowd behind the messenger, where a person lay on the ground with another kneeling over them, screaming. The news eye turned back to the soldier and messenger, who had not moved. The soldier lowered his gun and stared. The messenger, without facial features to read, appeared not to react.

Without warning, the messenger's wings unfurled and the messenger shot into the air, straight up. The soldier stared upwards, oblivious of the person who charged him, tackled him to the ground, and beat him with his fist. All he could do was cover his face. Other soldiers moved in and the scene disappeared.

"Shit!" Josef said, still looking ahead. The sentiment was echoed around the room by others.

"And there was no reaction from the ship since?" Arhus asked, turning back to his display and starting frantic searches.

"None that I have heard of," Josef said, his mouth still open and his body hitting the back of the chair.

"Well, the aliens do like to take their time," Arhus said in an offhand manner.

"Must have to decide by committee," Josef said flippantly.

Arhus stopped. His head slowly turned toward his friend, who looked back, dumbfounded.

"What?"

"Josef, I think you may be more right than you know. We saw three beings in the orb. What if they have some kind of governance that requires that they come to a consensus before acting?"

"You mean like a collective mind?" Josef was still dazed.

"No, a collective mind would come to a consensus quickly, or at least I hope it would, for its own sake. I mean more like a committee that might include a lot more beings than we saw in the orb."

Arhus's display started to flash in one spot and an alert sounded in his ear. "Crap! I gotta go."

"Where you going?" Josef asked as he watched Arhus stand.

"The ambassador awaits," Arhus answered and took hurried steps to the lift. "Not hard to tell what he wants to talk about."

As the lift rose, Arhus looked out toward the alien ship in the distance. As quiet as ever, it gave no hint as to what was going on inside. When he reached his destination, he noticed that it appeared that the picket line had been moved back toward town. There also appeared to be fewer people at the lines. Knowing how easy it was for people to be bored, it didn't surprise him, but he also wondered how many more would show up, given the latest events.

Ambassador Montoya's office was as busy as the first time he had visited. The lady behind the desk looked at him as he entered and nodded to a side door with her head. A well-muscled man stood next to the door and opened it just in time to let him in without slowing down. Everyone but Bahir was already present, looking nervous.

Montoya gave Arhus a quick look when he entered, but waited until the door was closed before he spoke. "We're not going to wait for Bahir, so let's begin. We need to talk about Indonesia."

"Seems to me they got what they deserved," Ionut said in a voice that was low but loud enough to be hear.

"Agreed." Annalisa nodded her head as she spoke.

"I'm not going to argue in their favour," Montoya said as he waved the comments off. "I am more interested in what we are going to do or not do because of it."

"Nothing," Vicente stated in a flat voice. He swept his hand across his body in a dismissive manner. "They want to be isolated, so they can handle their own problems."

"You might not think that if you lived closer to their country," Ms. Smith said. Her look and voice were both stern, leaving Arhus to wonder where she was from. He knew conglomerates could pull from all over the globe. Maybe the imprecise nature of her accent was intentional.

"Indonesia is not in the Western Pacific Conglomerate," Vicente said, turning and walking toward the woman, his back straight as if he was on parade. "Why would you care what happens to them?" His right eyebrow rose as if in defiance.

"True, but they are not far, in global terms, from some of our interests, and anything too drastic might affect us also. Plus the fact that we don't want to deal with millions of refugees, either." Smith looked Vicente straight in the eye, unflinching, unblinking, her jaw set like a stone statue.

Vicente stared back for a few seconds, broke the stare, and laughed. "Damn, woman, I do wish you were a duellist. It would be such fun!"

"Enough of games," Montoya said in a voice that left no room for division. "The incident in Indonesia was something I was hoping we could avoid, but I suppose now I was being too optimistic. The Security Council is going to be looking for recommendations for action, so we need to have the one that will be acted on."

"I don't think we need to say anything, at least as far as the aliens go," Vicente continued. "It's not like they are listening to us anyway. How many messages has the government sent and there is no reply? I am sure they will make some statement to the people that the behaviour in Indonesia should not be imitated, but that is standard stuff."

"I am not sure what you are asking of us," Ionut said. "Are you asking for action against the Indonesian government?"

"That is always a possibility," Montoya said, leaning into his high-backed chair, letting the cushioning swallow what small part of him it could. "It would be one way to show the aliens we do not support their actions."

"So now we care what they think?" Vicente asked.

"Not like action against Indonesia has ever done any good," Annalisa said with a huff. "The people, most of them at least, have shown no interest in removing their government. It's almost as if they like having an incompetent dictator to blame."

"It is very convenient," Ionut said with a chuckle. He walked to the refreshment console, moved a panel that had no handle or other similar feature, and removed a bottle that Arhus identified as holding beer. The door closed itself as Ionut turned back toward his seat.

"A little early for that, is it not?" Montoya asked.

"Not in Indonesia," Ionut said as he popped the top off with his thumb, letting it spin to the floor. He drank half the bottle in his first pull. "If the world is going to act like this, I need a drink."

Montoya huffed, but turned back to the group. "Ideas, we need ideas."

"Morresette is such a fan of doing nothing, I say we do that," Annalisa answered.

"You just want to see the wrath of God in action." Vicente pointed at the woman with a shake of his finger.

"Who doesn't?" she answered in a calm voice. "And it would give us some idea of their offensive capability if they did."

"So true!" Ionut piped in from behind a chair, bottle still in hand. "Let's just see what these messengers are capable of!"

"I'm not even sure they are actually there," Arhus said quietly. All eyes turned to him. Swallowing first, he continued. "We had one show up in our office. I watched it fly through the glass windows of our building without any effects. How could they have done that if they were solid in any sense?"

"So you are suggesting they are made of energy?" Montoya asked.

"No," Arhus pushed down one eyebrow without looking at any of the others. "We know the aliens speak telepathically. I am beginning to wonder if these messengers were mental illusions."

"That stretched across the world?" Vicente asked, his eyes wide. "Do you know the kind of power that would take?"

"Maybe they have something on their ship that generates it," Ionut said before a swig that finished the bottle. After he swallowed, he headed back toward the refreshment console.

"It's a possibility we cannot dismiss," Montoya said, nodding his head. "The possibilities such a device would imply are significant."

"More reason for us to do nothing," Vicente said, his right hand making a flat, sweeping gesture in front of him. "If these messengers are not even there, then there was never any danger. Us acting would only show us to be ignorant!"

"Sometimes it can be an advantage for your enemy to think you are ignorant when you are not." Montoya's hands were fingertip to fingertip across his body as his elbows rested on the arms of the chair.

"Or afraid," Annalisa added.

"Correct also," Montoya agreed with a slow nod.

"I am so glad you all agree with me," Vicente said, a smile implying triumph.

Alonzo bent down and whispered into Montoya's ear. It was a short message. Montoya stood up and started toward the door.

"We are going to have to suspend this meeting," Montoya said. "The alien's orb has exited the ship again and is headed this way. I think the purpose of our meeting has been superseded." His fingers waved at Arhus to follow. Arhus fell into step at the appropriate distance.

The hallway was full of people walking the same direction, the general assembly room. No one was giving way to anyone that Arhus saw, but at least they were moving at a fast pace. The room had a display large enough for all five hundred seats. Now the room held at least twice as many people, standing in every spot available that was not a main aisle. Montoya headed straight to his seat near the front. Arhus, conscious of how far forward they were, squatted down against the low dividing wall behind Montoya's seat.

On the display, the orb was just entering the circle of World Council buildings, moving at a faster pace than before. It appeared to hold the same passengers. Arhus thought the shorter being had better defined facial features, but it could have been his imagination or a trick of the interior light. With the third being swirling around at what he interpreted as an agitated pace, it was hard to tell. The scene made him wonder if the 'spirit' was an emotional projection of the other beings' feelings, which sounded strange, but he reminded himself anything was possible.

The orb came to rest at the same spot it had stopped before. The central display made him feel like it was sitting in a front-row seat of an auditorium. He also knew that everyone had the exact same view, something he figured was a political necessity. The short being inside the orb took a step forward, standing in front of the seat inside the orb.

"You were told," a voice different than the previous voice said inside his head. The voice was not as loud and more human sounding, almost like it came out of a human throat. Arhus could not see a mouth move, if one existed. He had to remind himself to breathe. "One of you has not heeded our warning. They will now be punished."

The being stepped backwards to his place beside the seat. At least Arhus could see legs moving this time. Could the beings change their appearance or were these beings artificial constructs? Maybe they were mental images also.

The orb returned to the ship at its increased rate. The hole at the top of the ship did not close after it entered. Within a few seconds of the orb disappearing, beings could be seen rising from the ship. They were twelve in total. Their appearance brought gasps from the observers.

The creatures were tall, taller than the messengers had been, maybe three metres. They had six wings each, two at the top of the shoulders, two mid-body, and two just below the knees. The pair mid-body was much larger than the other pairs. The head had four faces, each pointing a different direction. One was the face of a man, one was the face of a lion, one like a face of a cow, and one like the face of an eagle. They were dressed in the robes that the aliens seemed to prefer, with a belt around the waist. When the platform reached the outer edge of the ship, the beings' wings started to beat rapidly. All twelve creatures shot from the ship at the same time, travelling in the same direction. The satellite viewers followed the group and a number at the bottom of the view displayed their velocity, counting up rapidly. *They don't travel as fast as the messengers, at least initially, and they continue to accelerate,* Arhus thought, *so these creatures must have mass. Either that or the aliens are getting better at their illusions.*

A small globe in the centre of the display showed the creatures' route, straight for Indonesia. The magnification of the view gave Arhus the feeling he was flying next to them. The large centre wings were a blur, extending well above and below the creature. The smaller wings remained more level. The velocity reached Mach 3 and kept increasing. *They can't be real wings.* He could see no sign of a weapon on the creatures.

The speed kept increasing. Arhus's interface vibrated on his wrist. Looking down, he saw a message from Montoya. "*At this rate it will not take long.*" Arhus nodded without looking at the man. With his free hand, he typed in a message while looking at the room display.

"*I think these are real,*" he sent.

"*Will find out,*" came back. "*Weapons?*"

"*Will find out.*"

He couldn't help but smile.

Watching the creatures fly was mesmerizing, like watching magical creatures from a fairy tale. They swayed back and forth as they flew. At times, they changed position with each other, reminding Arhus of migrating geese. The ethereality of the wings gave them a glittering appearance. The smaller wings appeared more solid, at times moving in the same direction and sometimes opposite. He could not tell any difference between the creatures. *Wouldn't individuals have differences? Or is that a human idea?*

The velocity indicator at the bottom started to decrease, bringing Arhus out of his revelry. A second display in the lower right corner showed fighters taking off from an airstrip. Twelve planes took formation in the air, thrusters glowing red, wings pulled back in attack formation. Voices came over the sound system.

"Fighter squad, do you have the targets?" The accent was all wrong for Indonesia. Arhus thought he recognized the voice doing the translation.

"Negative," the same voice said. "There is nothing on our sensors."

"Satellites indicate they should be in range."

"I repeat, Control, there is nothing on our scopes."

Arhus watched the creatures reach into their belts and pull out a metallic cylinder. The arms had free movement in between the top and middle wings. The creatures held the cylinders to one side and forward, just under the front wings. The distance between the creatures and the planes disappeared rapidly. As the two views merged, red lengths of flame emerged from the cylinders. Frantic calls from the planes and their control could be heard in the background.

It happened so fast the scene was a blur of red, followed by sparks and smoke. The creatures continued, leaving behind plane halves to fall from each other. The twelve creatures had each taken one plane, destroying all twelve at the same time and then flying back into formation as if nothing had happened. The planes had not even fired.

Whispers started in the hall. More planes were launched, but by now the creatures had reached the coast, flying just above tree-top level. They were moving so fast that landmarks were indistinguishable. Arhus overheard someone say that the creatures were so low that sensors would not be able to find them. *As if they had been any use before,* he thought.

As the planes flew ineffective search patterns, the creatures flew straight to Jakarta. It made Arhus wonder how they knew where to go. *Do they have internal guidance or do they receive telepathic signals? Maybe they use magnetic lines like birds? I doubt we'll ever know.*

A large city came into view. The speed indicator started moving at an unreadable speed. The creatures flew between buildings, weaving from one street to another. The distance between the creatures grew until it was clear they were forming a full circle. The display split into two, one following the creatures from a more elevated view and one on the Central Government Building that held the administrative offices. Armed guards lined the arches of the upper level and the doorways of the ground floor. Heavier weapons stood at the front door, two automatic pulsators with their own tracking sensor. The sensor spun in wild circles, unable to find a target.

As they neared the government buildings, the creatures took a near-vertical upward turn. They came down on the guards in the top arches from straight overhead. One instant the guards were standing at their station, the next, severed body parts adorned the building or were falling toward the ground. There was no blood spatter to be seen. The body parts were still falling when the creatures blurred past the pulsators, which exploded into red waves of energy. Two of the creatures continued around the building. Four flew back to the top of the building and took positions on the dome. The rest landed in front of the building and then walked inside.

At first the display remained the picture of the exterior of the building. It did not take long for those in the room to react.

"Splice into the interior cameras!" someone shouted. "We need to see what's going on inside!" Murmured conversations came from all directions, along with the sounds of people shuffling in their seats. Arhus looked around. People were bent toward each other or waving at the display, strong demands on their lips.

Silence came in a few seconds when the display scene changed to the inside of the building, making Arhus wonder how the visual was obtained. The view looked to be from the corner of the room, implying a security camera. Six creatures walked across the central hall under the dome, wings wrapped around their bodies like armour, but no flame-swords visible. At the other end was a line of security guards, weapons raised. Arhus could see the tips of the weapons shake. The guards were shouting at the creatures, who appeared unconcerned with the men. The leader creature had a lion face toward the guards, complete with lion-like snarl. The creatures made it to the centre of the room before a weapon was discharged, evidenced by the distinct sound made by the energy discharge. The invisible shot caused the lead creature to pivot slightly as if hit on the right shoulder by the impact, accompanied by a slight flare on its wing, but there was no other visible effect or slowing of its pace. The guards started to lose their shooting stances, some even lowering their weapons from their chins.

A guard with more decorations than the others stepped forward and raised a pistol. A sharp crack startled Arhus as much as the realization that the man was using an outdated slug-throwing weapon. The slug had even less effect on the creature than the previous weapon.

"I didn't know they still used those," Arhus said, more out of surprise than in conversation.

"Pulling out all the stops," Montoya said over his shoulder.

The creatures reacted. Swords were drawn and a blur of flame-coloured curves made quick work of the men standing in front of them. The faces of the creatures showed no emotion except for the continued snarl of the lion face on the lead creature. Without pause, the creatures pushed open a double door and continued their march. The camera switched to a new room, an assembly hall in the standard amphitheatre layout. The room was empty of any people. The creatures walked across the room to a door in the back wall of the stage area. The front creature opened the door and entered, followed by the others.

"My mind keeps telling me this is just a movie, but it's real," Arhus said as he stared as blankly as the others. "It just doesn't seem possible."

"I'm sure it will hit us later." Montoya's voice seemed so far away.

"Not looking forward to that. Guess I'll save the throwing up till later."

Again the camera changed. This time, the room had occupants, but the shaken guards threw down their weapons and ran out two side doors. The one person left stood behind a large, polished wood desk. Arhus recognized Prime Minister Angga Sargsyan. *In control of Indonesia for the last twelve years and showing no inclination to let anyone else take over,* Arhus thought. Sargsyan was shouting at the creatures, shaking a pointing finger at them while he talked. A translation appeared at the bottom of the screen, standard stuff about how Indonesia was a sovereign country and they had no right to force their will on his people.

If the creatures understood the speech, they gave no indication. The lead creature strode to the other side of the desk, drew his sword, and beheaded the man as he spoke. Arhus considered it a mercy that the flame weapon prevented blood from spraying from the wound. Still, he found himself holding down fluid in his throat at the sight as he watched the head fall to the ground and the body follow. The creature showed no such reaction, but returned its sword to its holder at the waist, turned, and walked back the way it had come. When the beings reached the assembly hall, they spread their wings and flew through the room, through the central hall, and out the building. Outside, they were joined by the other creatures and headed west on the same track they had arrived, this time gaining a high altitude instead of hiding along the buildings.

The display changed from the creatures to one of the city. People came out of buildings and looked to the skies and pointed. It was clear to Arhus that if they could see the creatures, the view was soon lost. The people turned to each other, talking and throwing their hands about.

"What will happen there now?" Arhus asked in a low voice. "From what I have heard, Sargsyan killed or kicked out anyone that looked like a rival or a successor."

"Chaos," Montoya replied. "Months of it, if not years. There may even be a popular revolt, if you believe some of the reports."

"That would be interesting. There hasn't been an uprising in almost two hundred years."

"With good reason. Modern weapons are very efficient. Any uprising would need support from the military to succeed. If different factions in the military pick different sides, things could get bloody fast."

"Any idea if that will happen?" Arhus watched the track of the creatures on the global display. A single light was used for the entire group with no close-up view.

"No. So little information has come out of the country, there is no real way to tell."

"Will the World Council get involved if people start dying?" Arhus asked with a hint of pleading in his voice.

"We have no authority. Indonesia is not a member."

"Still…"

"Intervening would cause some serious questions about the authority of the Council and there are members looking for an excuse to accuse the Council of over-reaching." Montoya sighed as he talked.

The central display changed to the alien spaceship. A lone figure was raised on the top platform. As the camera zoomed in, Arhus saw it was the shorter of the two main beings. The close-up allowed him to see that the facial features were indeed more distinct and human-like than they had been before. It had a mouth, nose, and ears. The eyes were still closed-over or closed. No hair could be seen anywhere. The figure wore the same white robe.

"Our punishment has been executed." The being's mouth moved and the same voice they had heard before spoke. "Our wrath is satiated. Similar actions on your part will result in similar responses.

"There is no need for fear. We have only come to retrieve our own, to take them to our home. Accept us and our mission and all will be well with you. Our blessings will be upon all those who follow our will. Punishment will be to those who do not."

With those statements, the platform lowered again into the ship, remaining open after the figure had disappeared. Small, quiet conversations started around the room. The central display became small and lights brightened in the room. Arhus reminded himself to breathe again and found himself sitting on the floor.

"I would suppose the world is sure of that now," Montoya's voice said with a touch of mirth, a touch more than Arhus felt the situation warranted. No one watched the creatures fly back to the ship. Arhus found that odd. He had known what was going to happen from the beginning and yet it had held everyone's attention as if they were not sure.

"Will you be needing me anymore, Ambassador?" Arhus managed to ask, his voice soft and strained.

"No, thank you." Montoya's head turned toward him slightly as it spoke, but turned right back to his colleagues when finished.

Forms must be maintained, I guess, Arhus thought as he stood. His legs had some shakes in them at first, but they disappeared as he walked. When considering why, he realized that, while having seen people supposedly die in movies, he had never seen what his mind couldn't dismiss as pretend. It scared him how much impact the sight had on him. *But it should, right?* he asked himself. *Shouldn't watching another human being die affect you deeply?*

Others were leaving the room also. Some appeared affected by events, others talked to each other with no external emotional response. Reminding himself that he had no idea what these other people had experienced in their life, he tried not to judge, but it was hard. A few he wanted to grab and demand if they realized they had just watched a person being executed, but he held his peace.

My training as a translator has served me soooo well, he thought as he walked. *Hold your tongue unless asked, that is our way.*

It became easier to ignore everyone and only look up when required to make his way back to the office. Even in the lift, he did not make eye contact. Enough people must have been acting that way, because he was left alone. He did hear a few soft inquires that caused him to think they had been made by others familiar with the people they asked. Believing that there were a few genuinely concerned individuals made him feel better.

When the lift reached his floor, though, Arhus raised his head, put on a brave face, and walked normally into the room. It was not hard to tell that everyone had been watching events and a significant number looked disturbed by them. Sylva, an older lady, was sitting in a chair with her eyes closed and her head in her hands. Darmay was trying to reassure her. Worse, though, was Ayso, who was having trouble breathing and looked like he might bolt for the door. Arhus made a quick inquiry to his interface to make sure medical had been called, but the wait time was not encouraging.

"Where have you been?" asked Josef in a hurried voice. At the same time, Arhus caught Sindie's eye and she appeared to relax a little.

"Working," Arhus said with more calm than Josef. "I assume you didn't miss anything."

"If you mean we watched a man get his head cut off, yes, we saw that. As you can tell, it upset people." Josef looked around and took a breath with a slight shake of his head. "Any pearls of wisdom from on high?"

"No. I think people are still processing."

"Our visitors clearly have a much higher level of permitted violence than people are used to." Josef turned back to his friend. "What do you think it means?"

"I think it means," Arhus said, his voice becoming firm, "that we better cooperate, at least until we know a whole lot more about our visitors than we do now. Clearly they have no fear of our weapons, which I am sure they know all about."

"How?" Strain from the events peppered Josef's voice, alongside uncertainty.

"If they are telepathic enough to send messages to our mind, they might be able to read them also."

Josef just stared at Arhus for a moment before saying anything. "I hadn't thought of that."

"I don't think we can take any chances and better assume the worst." Arhus searched the room. "Where's Rossarro? Shouldn't he be overseeing this chaos?"

"Haven't seen him since the broadcast stopped. He wasn't around afterwards."

"Why do I get the feeling he is playing some angle in all this?"

"Because he always is? Personally, I hope he chokes on whatever it is and get fired for it." Hatred for the man, normally well hidden, had made a full appearance.

What have we got to lose? Arhus thought. *Who knows what the world will be after these visitors get done with it?* "Hold down the fort, I need to check on some people." Arhus patted Josef's shoulder as he walked farther into the room.

"Me!" Josef protested. "Why me?"

Arhus did not answer. Walking through the room, he looked at those he could see clearly. Most appeared to be coping, but also looked as though they would need time. At least no one was panicking. Arhus walked to Rossarro's office just to say he looked, but it was empty. Examining the man's desk gave no clue to where he might have gone. Neither did Arhus's interface. Arhus sighed and walked back toward the door. Before he reached it, Sindie walked into the room. Concerned that she brought more bad news, Arhus stopped short, but she only walked up to him and leaned on him.

"I'm so glad you are here," she said in a soft voice.

"Are you okay?" Arhus was not sure if he should put his arms around her or not.

"As fine as I can be after watching *that*," she replied.

Arhus finally decided to lightly put his hands on her shoulders. Sindie made no protest, leaning in more if anything. "I don't suppose Rossarro left any instructions?"

"Of course not. Oh, and by the way, I reported him absent from his post."

Arhus pushed Sindie back far enough to look her in the eye. "You did what?!"

"People are a mess out there! And they're his people! Where is he?

Who knows!" Sindie reburied her head into Arhus's chest.

"I didn't say he doesn't deserve it," Arhus said softly as he patted her on her back. "I'm more worried about you."

"Hell with that," Sindie said into his chest.

I bet a lot of people are feeling that way, Arhus thought. *With all the stress people are going through, it's not surprising. I would just hate for Sindie to suffer for it.*

"Let's get back out there with everyone else."

She shot him a questioning glance.

"At least they won't be able to say we abandoned them." He smiled cheerfully at her.

"Throw my words back in my face, thanks," she said, but added a small smile afterwards.

Arhus let Sindie get a few steps ahead before following. He didn't make it back to the crowd before his interface beeped at him. Stopping to look at the display, a short message played into view.

"What is it?" Sindie asked from the other side of the display.

"I'm being summoned again," he answered, not looking up.

"Well, aren't you becoming Mr. Important?" Sindie said playfully. She waved at him as he looked up with in protest. "Go! We'll handle things here. Besides, you're terrible with people."

"Thanks for making me feel better," Arhus said in a staccato sentence. Sindie giggled and pushed him toward the lifts. "I'm going, I'm going!"

Arhus walked to the lift, but before announcing a floor, thought and asked for the twenty-third instead. As the lift moved down, he checked the time and confirmed his decision. The day was rapidly moving along and he made a mental note to make sure he took care of his blood sugar. He didn't have much time, either. When the door opened, he moved with a quick pace to the cafeteria, picked up three of the nutrition bars in the rack, and proceeded to checkout.

"Must be busy if you are eating those," the checkout lady said as she watched him scan his interface to pay for the bars.

"I'm surprised you have any left," Arhus replied with a smile as he picked the bars up.

"We had a big backlog," the lady said with a laugh of her own. Arhus nodded as he left for the lifts again.

Arhus had the wrapper open and took the first bite of the nutrition bar by the time he stepped on the lift. It took two tries for the lift to understand what floor he wanted. If he didn't think too hard about the taste, the bar was an acceptable substitute for a meal. The three bars were supposed to give him enough nutrition for a whole day, but he hoped he didn't have to use them all the same day. He had enough stress to deal with as it was.

The bar was swallowed and the wrapper in his pocket by the time he reached the one-hundred and twentieth floor. The stops along the way helped. The hungry looks from other passengers surprised him at first, but were not enough to tempt him to share his stash.

Making barely a pause to receive a nod from the receptionist, Arhus walked into the conference room. Being the last to arrive did not surprise him, figuring the others had come directly from the assembly hall. The whole group was there, milling about and talking between themselves. Except for Montoya, who sat in his chair like a king on his throne. For a reason he couldn't place, it bothered Arhus. Since he was thirsty from the nutrition bar, Arhus walked over to the refreshment centre. Sandwiches and fruit adorned the top of the counter.

"Of course," Arhus said to himself as he took a plate and put two sandwiches and an apple on it. He also took two bottles of cold mineral water and walked to an out-of-the-way chair and sat down.

"Let's begin," Montoya said as Arhus took his first bite of sandwich. The others took seats or stood behind chairs. None looked happy, not even Annalisa, but they did not look as upset as Arhus felt.

Who knows what they've seen in their life, Arhus thought as he chewed, *but it does make them feel a bit cold.*

"I know the day's events have been hard on people and much of the population will be upset," Montoya began. "A Security Council meeting has been called for an hour from now. Frankly, I am surprised they are waiting that long, but I assume Arlan needs to collect his thoughts. I thought we could take the available time to consider... issues... before the meeting. This may be the last time you get to air your feelings."

Montoya looked around at the group. Arhus avoided his eyes by looking down at his plate and concentrating on eating. The sandwich was tuna, very fresh, reminding him of the food back home. The question of whether it was real tuna was quickly put from his mind. At the moment, it didn't seem to matter and it tasted a lot better than the nutrition bar. He began to wonder how much food he could smuggle out when the meeting ended.

"Anyone?" Montoya said.

"That was quite a display our visitors put on," Bahir said. "A display of power. I am sure every government is analyzing the recording to discern the creatures' capabilities."

"Visual images will never tell us enough," Ionut said.

"I doubt there is a way to learn about the creatures without having one to study," Vicente said. "Their propulsion system alone is incredible. Do they use those wings or is it all for show? There is no way to tell without examining one."

"I am most disturbed by their form," Annalisa said. The confidence Arhus had heard before was no longer present. "Our visitors are taking this God imitation too far."

"So you do not believe they are God?" Bahir asked, playfulness in his voice.

"Of course not!" Annalisa's head snapped in Bahir's direction and she stared at him hard. "Don't even speak such blasphemy!"

"Behave, Bahir," Montoya said firmly. "We need to work together, not have fun at each other's expense."

"It's a question the whole world is asking!" Bahir shot back. "If you don't know that, you haven't been listening!"

"Of course it's not God," Annalisa responded with equal volume. "This is a display of technology, not miracles."

"Which would look like miracles to more primitive people." Bahir slapped one hand into the other palm as he spoke.

"We are not primitives!" Annalisa drew her head and shoulders back as if insulted.

"We aren't, but five thousand years ago, they were! What do you think they made of a floating chair or angels that could not be attacked?" Bahir's eyebrow rose with the question.

"I think these 'primitive' people you speak of were much smarter than you give them credit," Ionut said without looking up.

"That doesn't matter. They had no thought of technology such as ours, much less these aliens. Most of them were amazed at simple machines that rolled across a stage or made music by themselves!" Bahir's arm waved at Ionut.

"Being amazed and knowing who God is are different!" Annalisa's fists were clenched and she sat on the edge of her chair, feet pulled back as if ready to spring.

"Enough!" Montoya shouted. "This is getting us nowhere!" He stared at the others as if daring them to continue. His breath was short and quick, the effect visible in his moustache. Seconds went by unused. Montoya's breathing calmed.

"I think it is obvious," Vicente spoke up, "that the Security Council will now see our visitors as more of a threat than before, but will have no ideas on what to do about it."

"That should be seen by the dumbest of those fools," said Ionut.

"What do we say?" Montoya asked.

"Nothing," replied Vicente. "There is no answer to give. Anyone who shows resistance is risking the same response."

"So we just roll over?" Ionut asked with a shake of his head and a tone that led Arhus to think it was not a question.

"We do better than that," Vicente said, taking a step toward the large man, arms waving in emphasis. "We help them. You heard them. Those who obey will be blessed. Who knows what technology they will give us. And for what? A few thousand people who want to go anyway? Why is this even an argument?"

Vicente turned back and returned to where he had been. Straightening his suit jacket, he turned toward Montoya and took in a deep breath, his chest expanding as if in preparation for a response. The others, who had been watching the short parade, turned toward Montoya also and waited. After a moment, the older man spoke.

"Is that our recommendation? Cooperation?" Montoya asked.

"What else is there at this time?" Bahir asked back.

"I say inaction," Annalisa ventured. "The committee is good at it and slow to take decisive action anyway. They appointed that snail-plodding sycophant Morresette to their special committee, didn't they? If that wasn't a clear message, I don't know what is." Annalisa huffed with her statement. There was a few moments of silence before anyone else spoke.

"I have no opinion at this time," Ionut said.

"The Eastern Pacific Conglomerate will advise waiting, of that I am sure," Ms. Smith said and then smiled. "That assumes they aren't already trying to show the visitors how cooperative they can be, which wouldn't surprise me in the least, for the same reason Vicente stated. They love new toys."

Montoya sat and appeared to think for a while, his gaze passing from one to the other. Arhus finished the first sandwich and was trying to decide between the second one and the apple. Both had their good points, but the apple would be noisy if no one was speaking. Given the fact that he was the only one eating, he didn't want to draw attention to it. He was just about to throw all caution to the wind and take a bite from the apple when Montoya spoke.

"I want to hear what our new friend has to say. Mr. Gint, would you care to give us your opinion on what our next move should be?" Montoya raised an eyebrow with the question.

Arhus's hand stopped and he looked at the man. Disappointment at having to put the apple back down ran high. *People don't appreciate fruit enough.* Resigned, he took a breath, lowered his hand, and looked straight at Montoya.

"We need to stop reacting," Arhus started. "Everyone in the whole world is worried about what the visitors will do next and what do we do about it. The simple truth is we don't know and there is no way to know. They are *aliens* and don't think like humans. Hell, we can't predict the actions of humans half the time.

"I say we forget about this 'gathering of our own' and work on establishing face-to-face contact with the aliens. They must be anticipating such contact because one of them is taking on a human appearance. If they weren't planning on personal contact, why would they bother?"

"Maybe it is for the people they will take with them," Vicente interjected.

"With just one of them making the transformation? I don't think so. Besides, if you are going with 'God' to his home, I doubt you worry about if he looks human. In the Bible, God didn't take on a 'the form of man' until he planned on spending more than a few minutes with people." Arhus's hand rolled the apple as he spoke.

"You think they mean to leave the shorter one here when the ship leaves?" Montoya asked.

"I hadn't thought of that, but it's a possibility. And if he/she/it does, there is going to be tension about where he stays, that is for sure. A first good relationship could go a long way to securing his presence and any benefits that entails, particularly if he maintains the parallels to the scriptural Christ." Arhus took a bite of apple. As he was more than ready to eat something, he figured it was a good way to demonstrate he was done talking.

Montoya leaned back in his chair. "The boy has a point. While everyone else is focused on reacting to the past, we focus on developing the future."

"My point exactly," Vicente said with a tilt of his head and a flip of a hand.

Bahir let out a single muffled laugh before speaking. "Makes sense to me."

"And if we can develop a dialogue, maybe we can clear up this 'God' thing once and for all," Annalisa added.

"Then it is settled," Montoya said as he slapped his palms to his legs. "We tell the council to do nothing and pursue our own agenda, made easier by the fact that I have managed to have myself appointed to the task of getting the visitors to talk to us."

Montoya looked at the antique clock on the wall. "Now I must go. I will keep in touch with assignments."

Arhus ate his apple as the others rose and made their way to the door. The small conversations that had happened at the end of other meetings was not present, each seeming lost in their own thoughts as much as he was in his apple. By the time Arhus was done, the last of the others were just leaving. He rose from his chair to throw the apple core away, but before he turned to leave, Montoya spoke.

"A word, young man. Walk with me." Montoya had also risen and gathered some papers into a folder.

Arhus chuckled. *Montoya must be one of the few people in the modern world that still uses paper.*

Montoya turned toward the door without waiting for Arhus, who wiped his face and hands on a refresher towel and hurried to follow.

As he did, he regretted not snatching more food for others at the office. *True, they could go down to the cafeteria, but I bet many haven't thought about it. Maybe I should shepherd people down there when I return.*

"You continue to contribute good advice," Montoya said as he also walked and signed electronic forms handed to him by staff. "I wonder how you became so knowledgeable about our situation."

"I've watched a lot of old science-fiction movies," Arhus replied. The comment made Montoya laugh and look up from his forms.

"Now we are relying on Hollywood to set policy?" Montoya asked through the laughter.

"It would seem that Hollywood put a lot of thought into alien encounters from the number of movies they made."

"Our own self-paid think-tank. How convenient. I want to make you our point of contact with the visitors. Since you are a translator, you will be a natural choice. If I can get our policy enacted, it should not be hard to get you assigned. Any problem with taking the assignment?"

"My boss will have a *fit*, I am sure," Arhus said as he rolled his eyes.

"Cashel? He is no longer in the picture, as they say." Montoya laughed at his own quip.

"What happened?" Arhus asked, only noticing the quip afterwards.

"Backed the wrong horse. Much too quick to pick sides, if you ask me. His champion falling out of favour has led to his disgrace and re-assignment back to his own country."

"All in a few days?"

"It can happen fast. There will always be those who try to use a situation for their own advancement, which can be very tricky in the best of times, and these are not the best of times."

"Can't say I'm surprised or sad. The guy always was a prick. What's my department supposed to do?"

"It will get a new head as soon as possible, but that might be a while with everything else going on. Until then, you might show some initiative. Does wonders for getting a new job." Montoya's head turned long enough to give Arhus a meaningful glance. Arhus looked back, his eyes going wide.

"You kidding?"

"No, I am not."

"What were you just saying about power grabs?"

"That you have to be smart about it," Montoya said with so much calm that Arhus began to wonder if he was imagining the conversation. "I will let you know when you are assigned to the visitors."

Montoya turned to an aide, who was handing him a display and engaged in a quick conversation. Arhus stopped walking, knowing when he was dismissed from the many times it had happened.

"Invisible again," Arhus said to himself. As he turned, a thought occurred to him. *Is following Montoya the best path for me? Look what happened to Rossarro. Am I setting myself up for the same consequences? It doesn't appear that I have risked much, but if I am assigned as the liaison to the visitors, maybe I should rethink my position. Once in the position and accepted by the visitors, I doubt they would remove me without some drastic measures. Until then, though, I have people to take care of.*

Chapter Eight
Regrouping

Medical arrived before Arhus made it back to his office area. One team was attending to Ayso and another Sylva. Several more people were being interviewed by people from counselling services. The rest were standing or sitting in groups, talking to each other. Arhus thought it looked like what should be happening. *Is it the new position that makes the difference? I would like not to think that I care more just because I'm their boss now.* But then, he didn't have long to think about it when Sindie ran up to him.

"Well?" she asked.

"Just more bureaucrats trying to make up their minds what to do," he answered.

"Great, just what we need: indecisive bureaucrats." Sindie gave a small giggle with the statement, but it did not feel as if it came from mirth.

"Is everyone doing well here?" Arhus asked.

"Yeah, if you don't expect any work to get done." The laugh that went with that statement was genuine.

"Heard through the grapevine that Rossarro got canned, so I guess it depends on what our new boss thinks," Josef said, coming up from behind Sindie.

"He thinks everything is just fine, what everyone needs," Arhus replied.

"And just how do you know what he would think?" Josef said, hands on his hips.

"Oh my gosh, they didn't!" Sindie exclaimed.

"Didn't what?" Josef asked.

"They promoted Arhus!" Sindie jumped up and hugged Arhus.

"Wait! You mean that the bureaucracy did something reasonable for a change? The world must really be coming to an end." For all his bluster, Josef still managed a stunned smile.

"Now you *have* to do what I tell you," Arhus said to him with a smile.

"And the monster emerges." Josef rolled his eyes.

"And dooon't you forget it," Arhus said in his best Quick Draw McGraw voice. Josef couldn't help but laugh. "Who's in charge from medical?"

Josef pointed to a woman on the other side of the room. Arhus made his way to the woman and held out his hand. It took the woman a second to process the gesture.

"Arhus Gint, newly approved supervisor here. Thank you for coming." Arhus gave the hand two good shakes before disengaging.

"Winlow Corsent, Psychological Technician," the woman replied. "Glad to be of help, at least what help we can." The woman leaned closer. "I think my own people are still dealing with what we all saw, but I think it helps them to help others."

"Is there anything the rest of us can do?" Arhus asked. The woman looked worn around the eyes, like she had been crying. *Well,* he thought, *they are people, too.*

"Has anyone eaten since the incident?" Corsent asked.

Arhus looked around, not noticing food containers or wrappers. "Probably not. I'll get that organized." Arhus turned, but then turned back. "Any suggestions?"

"Comfort food, whatever shape that is."

"So meat for the men, chocolate for the women." Arhus gave the woman a smile. She gave him a nod of appreciation.

Arhus made his way back across the room. He grabbed Josef by the shoulder as he went and then walked over to a group containing Karlstad and Eymen. He walked Josef into the group.

"Gentlemen, I need you to go down to the cafeteria and bring up food for everyone. I'm not sure what the selection should be, but get what you can and charge it to the department. Take Kat and Mus to make sure you get some female food, too. More is better than not enough."

"Can't people just go down to the cafeteria themselves?" asked Karlstad.

"I'm not sure they would and I don't know how busy it is. If it's pretty empty, let me know and I will drag everyone down there, but I would guess they are busy, at least the tables are occupied, that is. Not sure how much people feel like eating, but they need to. Thanks, guys."

"Giving orders already, I see," Josef said.

"Delegating authority," Arhus replied.

"Just don't throw it this way," Josef said with a wave as he walked away.

"Just makes me want to do it even more," Arhus said with a laugh.

"I might need a transfer!" Josef yelled back.

"Not on my watch," Arhus yelled back.

"What's that all about?" Sindie asked from behind.

"I sent them for food for everyone."

"Good idea. I'm starving."

"You want to go with them?"

"Too much to be done here. Follow me."

Arhus was bounced from one task to the next that seemed to require a supervisor's attention. He hoped that all the activity had not been what made Rossarro act the way he had. His next thought was that maybe he had to do all this because Rossarro hadn't, which erased any growing sympathy for the man. The cafeteria called to verify that his department was going to pay for the food, which he agreed to without asking for the total. It didn't matter in the long run and he didn't want to react in a way that would cause problems.

Once people were fed and the counsellors had worked them, Arhus could see that they were looking less stressed. Arhus started to send people home as they recovered. A few requests blinked on the interfaces, but he figured they would wait until tomorrow. Most people were gone by the time he noticed that Sindie was still in the office. Once he thought about it, it made sense. He waited until they could talk without being overheard.

"I still need a place to stay," Sindie said first in hushed tones.

"You don't feel different about it now that I'm your boss?"

"About you?" she asked with some surprise. "No. We've known each other too long for that. But I think we better not spread it around. People might not think as... platonic... as we do."

"Not that I was advertising before," Arhus said with a small chuckle, "but you are right. Co-workers being together are one thing, but this is another. Not that it's not done, but people have enough to worry about as is."

"Agreed. We'll leave separate. Where you want to meet?"

"Feel like a drink?" Arhus scanned the room while he talked. The last person was entering the lift as they spoke. It made them leaving separately seem strange, but he figured it would be a good habit to start.

"Do I ever! You like Irish pubs?"

The question startled Arhus enough to make him pause before answering. "Do you? I never imagined you as an Irish pub sort of gal."

"Hey, if you're going to drink something, it might as well be worth remembering." She gave him a shake of her head while she said it.

"Let me guess, you're one of those liquid bread types."

"Some nights that's called supper."

"The stuff they serve, I can understand it." He was still trying to imagine Sindie downing a black stout. It just seemed strange.

"How about the pub about three blocks north of your apartment?" Sindie offered.

"Sure. Meet you there in about twenty minutes. I guess with all the food that got brought up, we don't have to worry about supper." Arhus looked at the tables that the food had been placed on. Some had been taken home, but some still remained. "Not sure what to do with what's left."

"Unless you want it, just leave it. The janitorial staff will either take it or throw it out. My money on the 'take' option. You ever notice how rarely they bring their meals?" Sindie raised an eyebrow.

"No, can't say I have." Arhus scratched his head just because it seemed the right response.

"Trust me, with all the lunches and dinners they have in the building, they don't need to bring anything unless they're picky about what they eat."

Arhus shrugged. "Fine. Twenty minutes?"

"See you there."

Arhus stared out the window at the alien spaceship hovering in the air. Sindie sat next to him on the couch, slumped down enough so that her head rested against the back of the couch. Both had their feet on the coffee table, per bachelor pad etiquette, though it had to be positioned at an angle to the couch so they both could reach.

"It doesn't scare you anymore?" Arhus asked.

"Naw," said Sindie, her speech somewhat slurred. "I guess that now that I know that they can hurt people, I'm not as afraid. One of those 'fear of the unknown' kind of things."

"It would have nothing to do with being slightly drunk, would it?" Arhus gave her a look over his shoulder.

"Who, me, drunk? No way!" She flapped her arm to the side in a way that made Arhus wonder where it had been intended to go.

"You're the one who had three pints, not me."

"I've done worse." Her head tilted over to look at Arhus, stopped by the couch cushion from going farther.

"And walked home afterwards?"

"I never said that." A finger waved in the air. "By the way, why did your girlfriend leave you?"

"I wasn't exciting enough for her," Arhus said with a shrug, looking back at the spaceship.

"In bed?" A small whiff of dark ale went with the question.

"She wasn't that specific."

Sindie rolled over to her side, putting her head on Arhus's shoulder so that she looked at him from a few inches away. "Maybe I should find out for myself?"

"Maybe you should sleep it off." Arhus gave her a frowning stare.

"A girl likes company. You should know that. Tell you what, I'll go to bed and you can follow when you're ready."

Sindie made her way to her feet, steadied by Arhus to prevent falling down. She kept one hand on any available furniture or wall as she made her way to the other room. Arhus listened to make sure she didn't fall or run into something breakable, finally hearing her land on the bed. Five minutes later, he could hear her snoring softly. He turned back to the sight of the ship.

"So what do you have in store for us tomorrow?" he asked the ship.

Chapter Nine
Welcome Mat

The next morning, Sindie said nothing about the night before, to the point that Arhus wondered if she even remembered what she had said. He decided there was no way he was going to bring up the subject. Not wanting to wear Biel's clothes more than she had to, Sindie decided to stop by her parents' on the way to work. Arhus didn't ask what all she intended to pick up. Just going to work was stressful enough.

Without a way to avoid it, Arhus walked into the supervisor's office and connected his interface. A slew of messages appeared, most of them routed by the computer to specific personnel based on their current assignments. He sent these to be stored. The second-largest batch was those that would have been assigned to Akmal, but had not been re-assigned to anyone else. *Trust Rossarro to ignore these,* he thought as he picked two appropriate people and had the computer split the incoming requests between them. *No reasons to overload someone.*

With most work assigned, Arhus turned his attention to the blinking request that had arrived five minutes before his arrival. The message was from Montoya's office:

Arhus Gint
Department Head

Jerusalem Translation Office

Sir,
Please bring all equipment and personnel you deem necessary to establish face-to-face communications with the alien visitors to the central security station located west of the alien ship. You shall establish all protocols and procedures required to prepare for and participate in communication with the visitors until a format for more formal interactions can be agreed upon between both parties. These efforts supersede all other previous assignments.

Ambassador Miguel Montoya
Central Council Office
World Council

"That's pretty clear," Arhus said to himself, sending an acknowledgement reply to the message. Looking around, he picked up a leather bag about six inches deep and placed it on the table. "At least Rossarro left everything here," he said with a chuckle. "Computer, disconnect main interface module and power supply for transportation. Shut down the display and store for transport."

"Acknowledged," a voice replied. The central display went off and the thin antennae that created the display folded into its base. Arhus heard clamps and cords disengaging, and then lifted each component and placed them in the leather case. On a whim, he opened the desk drawers until he found some pads of paper and pens and placed them in the case also. Pressing the sides together to seal the case, he extracted the strap and placed it over his shoulder as he stood.

In the office area, most people had made it to work, though Sindie had still not arrived. He was glad, because he knew she would volunteer if present. Walking out between the tables, he cleared his throat and waited for people to turn his way.

"I have a new assignment that will take a while. In my absence, Josef will be taking over." He pointed a finger at his friend. "And no argument from you. I need someone here I can count on. I am going to establish a diplomatic station near the alien ship. I need a voice processing specialist, a theorist, and a government liaison.

Volunteers?"

Arhus looked at those present. None looked eager to join, though several raised their hands or stepped forward. Josef looked wistful, as if hurt he had been chosen to stay behind. Arhus chose Eymen, Miranda, and Darmay and told them he was going to the security station and they could follow when they had gathered their required equipment. Sindie arrived on the lift that arrived to take him to ground level.

"What's going on?" she asked.

"I've been assigned to set up a liaison station near the spaceship in case we can entice them to come out and talk to us."

"I'll come along," she offered without thought.

"I already have my team," Arhus replied in an even voice. She gave him a strained look. "One, I need people here I can count on. Two, I put Josef in charge, which means someone has to watch him."

"Thanks," she said, clearly not meaning it.

"And three, with the… other arrangements… I thought it would be easier this way. If you find something else, I can always change my team members." He gave her a look that parents give kids when they are expected to agree. Sindie didn't answer for a few seconds.

"Just because I understand doesn't mean I like your reasons," she said with a small huff.

"The burden of leadership and all that," Arhus replied in a British accent.

"What about my burden of making sure Josef doesn't do anything stupid?"

"*Too* stupid. I sure he will do something stupid, just as long as it has no lasting effect."

Sindie rolled her eyes. "Oh, that makes it so much easier."

"Besides, you can be the unknown consultant." He gave her a smile.

"You better keep me informed, mister, or you'll never hear the end of it!" She poked him in the chest for emphasis.

"Won't expect anything else," he said as he stepped onto the lift. "Ground."

A smile was Sindie's parting gift. When she had disappeared, he turned to look outside. The item that had come to dominate his life hovered on the horizon, filling a good portion of the view. *How much is its arrival affecting people not living in its shadow, on the other side of the world, for instance? Are they still watching the continuous reports or have they gone on with their lives? Are those who have been chosen making their way here or are they waiting for some kind of ride? What if they don't have the means to travel to Jerusalem? Did the aliens already think of that? Most importantly, why haven't they landed? What are they waiting for? For more of the 'chosen' to show up?*

Used to having a lot of questions running around in his head, Arhus felt that they all seemed pathetic now. *What is a disagreement between nations when an alien spaceship capable of projecting images into everyone's heads hovers outside of town? Do they monitor events on the planet and laugh at us? Or do they judge us primitive and thus ripe for the plundering?*

But then, all those questions pale against the real question. Is what the aliens said right? Do they 'own' the planet, seed humanity on it, and thus have the 'right' to harvest for their work? The thought scared him, not one he wished to think about for long. *If this is humanity's initiation into true galactic law, it is a mind-numbing blow to humanity's ego. If there is any left after the aliens leave.*

On the ground floor, Arhus did not hurry to the ship site. Instead, he looked at people as he walked. Many looked over their shoulder, even though there appeared to be no reason to do so. Most walked in groups, but some appeared to want to be alone. There was little chatter between people as they moved about, and what conversation that existed was done in hushed tones.

The city, at least this part of the city, had taken on a different character. It made Arhus wonder what the city would be like when the ship left. *Will people sigh in relief or become paranoid? What if some other alien shows up and makes the same claim? Probably extreme, but it might not matter. Humanity is behind the curve. Will our visitors help us catch up?*

Arhus encountered a small crowd when he reached the security station. Around twenty people stood next to the security agents, a couple arguing with them. Arhus got close enough to listen in on the conversation.

"You're not listening!" a woman all but shouted. "We were INVITED!"

"Ma'am, I don't care if you were invited," said the security agent dressed in the formal green outfit of the World Council Security Units, "I have no way to get you to the ship!"

"Just let me through and let me stand under the ship! I am sure they will send someone down for us!"

"Someone already tried that and nothing happened!" the agent shouted back. "So until something changes, you will have to stay outside the perimeter!"

"I will not!" The woman made the mistake of grabbing the agent. The agent placed his right palm on her shoulder. Arhus knew what coming. The woman started to shake for about five seconds. When the agent removed his hand, the woman fell limp to the ground.

"Get her out of here and move the others back one hundred yards!" the man commanded the other agents around him. One bent down to pick up the woman and throw her over his shoulder while the others formed a walking wall, causing the crowd to back away. Arhus stepped aside to let them pass before making his way to the agent.

"I said no one is getting in!" the man said just short of a shout when Arhus got close.

Arhus held up his interface. "Display ID," he said aloud. "Arhus Gint, Head of Jerusalem Region Translation Department for the World Council." He waited while the man verified the information with his own interface.

"Can't say I see much need for you to be here," the man said with a laugh as he looked at his interface.

"I have been sent to set up a diplomatic liaison point in hope that it will be used by our visitors to arrange formal representation and interaction."

The man punched at his interface to verify the statement.

"So that's what that's for," the man said, using his thumb to indicate a small, mobile office behind him. "Arrived this morning with no instructions, of course."

"Are you in charge of this station?" Arhus asked.

"Lieutenant Benjamin Amster at your service, at least from zero-eight-hundred to sixteen-hundred during the day." The man didn't salute, but then, there was no need. "Where do you want the building?"

"Along the edge of the barrier, this side, with the door facing parallel with the barrier toward the gateway here," Arhus said as he waved toward the gate.

"Not in front of the gate?" Amster asked.

"No. And we'll need an awning, three metres wide would be good, put just this side of the gateway and attached to the building. Can we widen the gateway to match the awning and remove the gate?" Arhus turned back to the lieutenant.

"We can do whatever you want. I'm just confused why the building isn't in front of the gateway if we are removing the gate." Amster started to look concerned.

"We want the meeting point to look inviting and not restricting. Of course, we can't prevent the aliens from going where they want, but this is a physical acknowledgement of their freedom to move about as they will. We'll also need a table and some chairs. Some cooling units in the awning would be good, we might need to be outside a lot and we don't want people overheating in the sun." Arhus turned about, examining the rest of the surroundings.

"We need to move the security units away from the station," Arhus continued. "I guess that might mean you need to move your men to control the crowd farther away. I'll leave it up to you, but I don't think we need another barrier farther out."

"How am I supposed to control the crowd if I don't have a barrier?" Amster asked.

Military thinking, Arhus thought. "Give them an alternative. We're going to need a processing centre for these 'chosen,' if nothing else than to know who is showing up. That's not my assignment, but just a suggestion. It doesn't matter if the aliens have anything to do with it or not, as long as the people think they are being helped to their goal."

"I'm not authorized to do that."

"Then get authorized. If you can't, I'll pass it to the Central Council and have it authorized." Arhus tried not to let his voice increase in volume, but not with total success. *Too much needs to be done for delays.*

"I'll get it authorized," Amster said. Turning to his men, he started to give instructions.

And save yourself the embarrassment of someone else getting it done, Arhus thought to himself as he took up a position out of the way. *Watch it, don't get too cynical.*

The rest of his group arrived by the time the building had been moved into place. Power and communications were turned on in short order and a water tank appeared. Arhus was glad that he had chosen just three others. More would have been crowded inside the building, though Arhus figured that he could have requested a larger building. Once the interfaces were working, Arhus went to Eymen.

"Did we ever get any correlation factor for the people chosen by the messengers?" Arhus asked.

"No. In fact, it seemed to be random on purpose as far as region, ethnic group, or other social factor. Do you think it was random?"

"Not in the least. Did we ever get permission to examine the medical records?"

"No, and I am not sure who we would even ask." Eymen shrugged.

"I do." Arhus made a quick call and turned back to Eymen within a couple of minutes. "Try now."

Eymen's fingers moved on the interface. "Wow! I don't know who you talked to, but we now have access to everything!"

"Look for common physical features, particularly gene sequences." Arhus watched the interface as Eymen worked.

"I don't see any common anomalies in the records," Eymen announced.

"How about what's not there?" Arhus asked.

"You mean like recessive genes?" Eymen looked up.

"We have learned to suppress or hide most medical problems. That doesn't mean the tendencies don't still exist for heart disease, diabetes, even cerebral palsy. Check for any commonality."

Eymen went back to the interface. At first, his motions were intermittent, but then became quicker and more insistent. "This is interesting. As far as I can tell, none of the people have any tendencies toward any abnormal medical conditions. They're all..."

"Perfect," Arhus said.

"Well, medically speaking, yes, I guess you could say that. Guess I never thought about it before. I had relatives that had problems, but I never thought about myself." Eymen looked at the names on the screen.

"So now we know who they are looking for." Arhus put his hand to his chin and stared at nothing in particular.

"It makes sense, I guess," Darmay said. "They would have the best chance of surviving the move to another planet. Even if a person suppresses a medical condition, you have to have medicine periodically."

"I think it is more than that," Arhus said, not turning toward her. "I think they want perfect specimens. Eymen, check the list for genetic proximity."

Eymen went back to the interface for a quick request. "You're right," he said after watching the interface. "No one is a close enough relation that they risk any genetic problems."

"So they intend to breed humans from their genetically perfect specimens?" Miranda asked.

"We can't discount that possibility, and it would go along with our other observations." Arhus's posture didn't change.

"Do you think these aliens go around creating planets with human inhabitants?" Miranda asked. "Why would they do that?"

"You're assuming they just move them and let them repopulate." Arhus pointed a finger her way when he said it.

"What else could they do with them?" Miranda asked.

"Use them as a commodity," Eymen offered. "I'm not sure what they would do with that commodity, but people have used all manner of objects throughout history. Maybe pure races are a commodity in the universe."

"That has to be about the weirdest idea I have ever heard," Darmay said.

"That's because you are human, living in a society that values human life," Arhus said. "Not all societies in the past have valued human life. In fact, in some, a human life was almost worthless because they were so common. Most people don't remember those times in history."

"You mean slavery?" Eymen asked.

"For one example, but there were others where if you weren't part of the elite, you meant less than a decent horse or someone's dog. We have a hard time understanding that, but it did exist."

"And, by extension, we may be worth even less to an advanced alien race," Miranda said, a haunted sound in her voice.

"It's a possibility. Look at the Old Testament Jehovah God that these aliens seem to be imitating. You could make an argument that non-Jewish races were worth very little to Him when compared to his chosen people." Arhus came out of his contemplative stance and started walking around.

"A tradition carried on by others in much of our history," Eymen said, shaking his head.

"Regrettably, yes," Arhus agreed.

"How does this all help us?" Miranda asked.

"Knowing why they are here and what they are after is the first step in understanding the situation. Now, if they decide to talk with us, that knowledge might change the whole tenor of the discussion. Everything up and running?" Arhus asked, using his tongue to activate the microphone switch between his teeth, a small motion that could be kept hidden from an observer. The feel of the switch in his mouth sitting just outside of his right rear teeth had become one that was unnoticed.

All three heads nodded, indicating reception in their ear-pieces.

"Good. Now we just have to wait until the security agents get the rest set up. At the speed which the aliens seem to react, nothing will happen until tomorrow anyway." Arhus looked at the small group. "Lunch? On the department?"

"You don't have to ask me twice," Miranda said, pushing her chair back.

Standing under the awning, Arhus stared at the spaceship. *Do they even know or care what is going on down here? All I can do now is wait, but how long will we have to wait?* He looked back at the new tent that was being set up west of their building: the new processing centre. The lieutenant had wasted no time getting it set up. Arhus wondered what they would do with the people once they were 'processed,' but then, that wasn't his concern unless they wandered into his area. He turned back to stare at the ship. Footsteps drew his attention as Eymen walked up to stand next to him.

"I'm surprised you selected me for this assignment," the man said.

"Why? You're a good theorist." Arhus turned back to the ship.

"Because I had a messenger. I thought you might be worried I would get on the ship as soon as it was possible." Eymen stared at the ship alongside him.

"Truth be told," Arhus replied, "I thought it might give us an advantage in getting their attention." Arhus paused from talking for a few moments. "Besides, if you were going to run off to some alien spaceship, I would rather know about it right away instead of finding out as I watch you walk into the ship. Plus it would give Josef less to complain about to me."

"Well," Eymen said with a laugh, "when you put it that way, it makes sense. I'd hate to stress Josef out."

"I would like to see him stressed out for once. All the years I have known him, I have never seen him stress over anything. Kind of eerie, if you ask me."

Both men stood and stared at the ship, which never moved, not even a little in the wind. No lights showed. The ship presented a round plane of silver-coloured metal. Without apparent means of support, it became unreal if stared at long enough.

"So, you thinking of taking the aliens' offer?" Arhus asked.

"I don't know," Eymen replied. "The thought of going to another planet is intriguing, but leaving everything you know is scary. And it's not like I can just hop the next transport home if I don't like it there."

Eymen continued to look at the ship, or maybe beyond it. "I'm just not sure. I'm thirty-one. Do I want to start my life over? Sure, I have plenty of time, but I just don't know. If I had more information about where we were going and what we could expect there, it would be easier to decide."

"Hopefully, if we can get the aliens to talk to us, we will find out more details. I'm sure you and a lot more people want to know."

"When do you think something will happen?"

"Not before tomorrow morning. They seem to like the morning."

"I wonder why."

"Work me up a full psychological evaluation and I will be able to tell you." Arhus smiled to himself.

"Sure, I'll have that on your desk first thing in the morning," Eymen replied flippantly.

"Appreciated. Will make my job a lot easier." It was times like this that Arhus understood people's old habits like smoking. It gave them something to do when they had nothing to do but wait.

"If anyone wants to go home early today, they might as well," Arhus said. "It might be the last day they get to."

"You sure?"

"Yeah, too much activity already around here at the moment anyway. But be here early tomorrow, just in case."

"So are we going to have any other assignments while we are here or just wait around for the aliens to stop by?"

"Waiting for them to stop by is our sole assignment for now."

"Maybe I should bring some cards to spend the waiting hours."

"I can't officially endorse it, but that doesn't mean I need to say something, either."

Eymen laughed. "See you tomorrow, boss."

"'Arhus' will do. None of this 'boss' stuff. I'm saving that for Josef." The comment made Eymen laugh even harder as he turned to go.

Arhus stayed for a while and stared at the spaceship. Somehow he felt it made a difference, though he couldn't say why. A feeling that something would happen tomorrow wouldn't leave him. *Just hopeful thinking,* he told himself, but didn't believe himself in the least.

Chapter Ten
Hello, My Name Is...

B efore the sun came up the next day, Arhus was standing under the awning, looking at the ship. The rest of the crew showed up a short while afterwards, about the time the coffee had finished brewing. The new processing centre was finished, a quick job in Arhus's judgment, and it looked like they had brought several sleeping units to the area. *They will need a lot more,* Arhus figured. It was too bad there were no hotels on this side of town or they could have commandeered one. He was sure the World Council would have paid the place a good rate, plus the fact that they would be charged for all the rooms from the start. It almost made him wish he was in the hotel business.

The night before, Sindie had been full of questions, most of which he didn't have answers for. She still didn't mention the night before and Arhus figured that she had either forgotten it or was too embarrassed to mention it. With all that was going on, he didn't need a scene to complicate his life, so he let it go. This close to the ship, the thought of it was enough to fill one's mind.

Footsteps behind him interrupted Arhus's thoughts. He turned to see Lieutenant Amster next to him. The lieutenant's uniform looked as if it had come fresh from the dry cleaners and showed none of the dust that tended to accumulate on everything.

"Good morning, Lieutenant," Arhus said. "The processing centre went up fast, I see."

"Yes, we can move quickly when we want to," Amster replied. "I'm told to expect even more people today. They are starting to arrive from out of country by just about every mode of transportation. If our visitors don't start taking them soon, we could be overrun." He paused, shifted his feet, and then spoke again. "Do you think they will respond?"

"I have no idea. I hope so. I don't want to spend the next month sitting out here waiting for nothing."

"I'll trade you jobs," Amster said in a low voice.

Arhus went to answer, stopped for a second, then said, "I was going to say no, but give me a week and I might agree."

That caused Amster to laugh as he walked away. By the time he cleared the awning, though, he was back to his military command voice, directing the placement of new equipment. Arhus continued to stare at the ship, at the moment a shadow against the sky. Eymen came out of the building and walked up with two mugs of coffee.

"You need coffee?" Eymen asked, holding out a mug.

"Need? No, but I'll take it." Arhus took the mug handle and tasted the coffee. "Turkish?"

"Of course. If you're going to drink coffee, you might as well drink the best." Eymen took a sip of his own mug.

"In your unbiased opinion, of course," Arhus said.

"Of course. Just because I am Turkish doesn't mean we don't make the best coffee." If he hadn't said it so straightforward, Arhus would have thought he was teasing.

"Thank you. I am sure this will keep me awake, that's for sure." Arhus took a full swallow. "Have you thought about what to serve our visitors if they do come around?"

"I'd start with water before we know if they even drink liquids. Water is pretty universal across the galaxy, so they would have to be very different not to consume it."

"How different?"

"If they are that different, we will not be able to enter their part of the ship. Of course, it would explain that chair they run around on also, holding a small micro-environment for them, so maybe they are that different. Of course, the creatures they sent out did fine."

"If they are even alive and not machines," Arhus responded, indicating with his mug with the comment.

"True. Our lack of knowledge about our visitors leaves everything in doubt." Eymen took a drink of his own coffee while looking far off.

"We do what we can. Here, take this back with you," Arhus said, holding out the cup. "I don't want to drink too much and have to run inside all the time, but thanks, I appreciate it."

"Sure, no problem. Anything we should be doing?" Eymen took the cup in his empty hand.

"Keeping alert. Are the communication buds working?"

"All set up. You want everything recorded, I assume?"

"Yes. Now we just wait." Arhus gave Eymen a pat on the shoulder and smiled. "And try not to fall asleep. We don't want to embarrass ourselves."

"That won't be a problem. The tension around here should keep everyone awake." Eymen turned back toward the building, leaving Arhus alone to stare up.

Soon after Eymen left, sunshine started to appear over the horizon, announcing the approach of the sun. The sunlight caught on the underside of the ship, appearing first at the closest edge to the horizon and then creeping across the bottom face. Arhus had not noticed before the stark flatness of the bottom of the ship. It was featureless, leaving Arhus to wonder, if it did rotate, would he be able to tell? The bottom did not appear to have accumulated any dirt or wear, shining in the sun like it had just been cleaned.

"If nothing else, they could share how they keep it so clean with us. That could be really useful," Arhus said to himself.

As the sun rose over the horizon, the spaceship was blanketed in full illumination. Though he was not standing underneath the ship, he still felt that if it fell, it would land on top him. He dismissed the silly thought. *Maybe it is just the size of the ship that makes me think that way, or maybe it is a metaphor,* he thought. *Not a pleasant one at that.*

The reflected sun made it hard to continue to stare at the ship. Arhus shaded his eyes with his hand, trying to block out the reflection while still looking at the ship. It was only a matter of time before the sun would be high enough to end the reflection off the bottom of the ship, but the rays were quite intense, almost as if the ship was magnifying them.

"Darmay, get the camera feeds of the ship to the physicist. I think the sunlight may be indicating some sort of field on the bottom of the ship. Maybe they can determine something."

"Sure thing, boss, but don't you think they would have seen that before?" Darmay's voice asked in his ear.

"One, don't call me boss. Two, they haven't been standing here before. It appears that the sunlight reflecting off the bottom of the ship is more intense than that coming from the sun. I have no idea what I am talking about, but I thought it was worth a shot."

"Right away, patching the feed in now."

Maybe today won't be a total loss, Arhus thought.

"Hey, boss," Miranda's voice came over the comm. "They say the ship is descending."

Arhus looked urgently at the ship. With the sun in his eyes, he couldn't tell if the ship was moving, but he trusted the message. With all the instrumentation that had to be aimed at the ship, any slight motion would have been detected. He looked for what seemed to be a minute, but couldn't tell a difference.

"How fast is it moving?" he asked.

"Really slow, about a metre every second. Guess they are in no hurry," Miranda's voice said.

"Guess not," Arhus replied.

The change in the refection of the sun was the sole indication Arhus had of the ship's movement, that and the sounds coming from behind him, indicating a lot of activity and interest by the surrounding crowd. Hating to take his eyes off the ship, Arhus turned his head to look behind him. Security was filling ranks as those who claimed to be called tried to get as close as allowed. Arhus was sure that some of them would run under the ship and get crushed when it landed if they were allowed.

Why do people act so stupid? he thought. *Are they that desperate?*

Turning back to the ship, Arhus did a quick calculation in his head. It would take about ten minutes for the ship to land. He was glad he hadn't drunk more coffee, not wanting to leave.

Ten minutes passed, the slowest ten minutes Arhus thought he had ever experienced. While the ship was descending, he noticed several things. The first was that there was no wind caused by the descent of the ship. There was so little air movement that the dust on the ground did not move. The second was that while the bottom of the ship was flat, the ground was not. As the ship neared the ground, extensions came out and compensated at differing lengths to the ground. The ship settled on the ground with no sound. No sound of machinery shutting down came from the ship. No lights showed while descending or once on the ground.

The settling of the ship brought a hush from the surrounding crowd. Even after it settled, it was as if they were waiting, expecting something to happen right away. Arhus didn't. The pace of the visitors was becoming very clear. Still, he was determined to wait as long as he could. *Hopefully, the fact that the ship landed the day after we set up is not a coincidence, but then, no one can be certain,* he thought to himself.

After a while, the crowd grew restless. Arhus could hear them rustling and talking even from a distance. Every so often, he could hear someone ask in a loud voice to be allowed to go to the ship. *Ridiculous,* Arhus thought. *What do they expect to do once they get to the ship, walk through the side of the ship?*

What are they waiting for? Arhus thought. Not trained in diplomacy, he tried to think back to what he had heard or, to be more accurate, overheard during his career. The first that came to mind was, *Diplomacy is like chess, move and counter-move. We made the first move by setting up the meeting station. Did that lead to the counter-move by the visitors of landing the ship? If so, are they now expecting another move by me, and what is it?* His choices didn't take long to consider.

"I'm going to walk halfway to the ship," Arhus said after activating his microphone with his tongue. He thought he heard the activation of a microphone, but no voice came over the network.

The edge of the ship was thirty metres from the awning. With no indication of where to expect a door, Arhus walked straight toward the ship, assuming the aliens would have positioned a door in front of him. Without any deliberate speed, he covered half the distance to the ship and stopped, standing with his arms to his side and his weight evenly split between his feet, spaced just inside his shoulders. He had worn formal dress today, possibly too optimistic, but just in case. At least he was in the shadow of the ship, so the sun was not beating down on him. While he stood, he realized that he had not brought an umbrella and was thankful it was not raining.

Time ticked by, minute by minute. *Humans would be ready for immediate departure,* Arhus thought, *but then, these aren't humans. Then again, could they be human's ancestors, the gene pool corrupted over time? That would be interesting and explain some of their statements. And some of our myths.*

Without a sound, two lines appeared in front of him along the curve of the ship, maybe three metres apart. All sound behind him stopped. A section of the outside of the ship rotated outward, the upper lip meeting the ground when level, creating the end of a ramp. Arhus looked inside the ship, which was lit by a light coming out of the ship, illuminating the ramp. He tried to look farther into the ship, but the view was a white haze.

"They're using some kind of obscuring light field to prevent me from seeing into the ship," he said. *Or are they using their telepathy to prevent me from seeing anything?* he thought. *If they can make us imagine messengers, convincing my brain that nothing is there would be easy.*

Arhus was wondering if it was his turn to make another move when two figures started to come through the haze near the edges of the ramp. They were over two metres tall, about seven feet in imperial units. They were humanoid and each carried a sword in front of them pointed upwards, the hilt held in the middle of their chests. The swords appeared to be made of a silvery metal which appeared firm, though the metal in the middle of the sword appeared to flow like mercury if he looked at it long enough.

Could the sword be a field that holds the metal to an exterior shape? Arhus wondered. *What would be the advantage? The field would keep the edge sharp, avoiding wear. Mercury? It would provide weight for the blade, that's for sure. The user would have to be pretty strong to use it effectively, though.*

The two beings walked down the ramp, turned, and took up

positions on either side of the end of the ramp, facing away from the ship. When they turned, Arhus could see that they were two of the creatures that had been sent to punish Indonesia, their human faces in the forward position. Once settled, they turned their swords and planted the points into the ground in front of them, hands on the pommels.

Quite a statement. Can they turn their heads? Or do the different forward faces indicate rank or duties? Every time we encounter our visitors, it creates more questions.

Two more figures appeared in the haze. These were shorter and, like the creatures, they were dressed in long, white robes that reached their ankles. Instead of carrying weapons, their hands were placed inside the opposite sleeve so that the arms were crossed in front of them. None of the four figures displayed wings, but Arhus thought that the robes were large enough that they could be hidden inside. The newest two figures had no hair on their heads, not even eyebrows. They walked past the creatures several metres and stopped, standing two metres apart.

Arhus waited, sure someone else would exit the ship. Miranda's voice in his ear-comm confirmed his own thoughts.

"Stay there. If they had wanted you to enter the ship, one of the two in front would have walked forward to invite you in."

"My thought exactly," he replied. Arhus did not change his position, wanting to keep his hands in the creatures' sight at all times.

His wait was not long. A lone figure appeared in the centre of the ramp. It walked in at a slower, stately pace. As it came out of the haze, Arhus had a strong impulse to kneel, one that grew stronger as the figure neared. Fighting off the impulse, he could see that the figure was a humanoid being in a white, ankle-length robe. It appeared to be just under two metres tall, average shoulder width, and had hair on its head.

"I assume the Council is getting this?" Arhus said to his mic.

"They are hurrying to transports," Miranda's voice said.

As the figure neared, Arhus could see that its skin was a light olive colour. All the facial features—nose, ears, mouth, even eyebrows—were of an average size, none particularly large or small. The eyes were brown. Even his hands and feet looked to be average in size. It looked male by human standards. The figure stopped at the perfect distance to shake hands with Arhus but did not extend his.

"Welcome to Jerusalem," Arhus said in a clear, even voice. "I am Arhus Gint, representative of the World Council..."

"We know of you, Arhus Gint," the figure said in a smooth, pleasant voice, one that Arhus could imagine would capture anyone's attention. "We have been interested in talking to you."

Me? Or the World Council? raced through Arhus's mind. *Darn, they could probably hear that.*

"How may I address you?" Arhus asked, trying to concentrate on the conversation.

"We are EO-AY," came the reply.

"I thought maybe you would have a name to indicate just yourself," Arhus said in a delicate fashion. The figure appeared to think for a moment.

"I am the Subordinate." It looked at Arhus as if reading his thoughts. "No, I am more than an assistant. We are equal, but I am not the Dominant by choice."

Arhus started to say something, then paused, then reconsidered. *What harm can it do?* he thought. "You are the Son?"

"That term could be used, though not entirely accurate in the physical sense," the Subordinate replied.

Arhus made a small bow. "We have set up a shelter with chairs and refreshments. If you would like, we can talk there."

"That will be accepted," the Subordinate replied, waiting for Arhus to lead.

Arhus turned and walked to the awning. He saw Eymen bring out a pitcher of iced water and two glasses and set them on the table, retreating to stand near the door. It was also the first chance Arhus had to look at the surrounding crowd. Many were kneeling, some with their heads lowered and their hands together. Some looked excited, others looked scared. Most of the security unit was facing the crowd, but the few that were looking his way had the same shocked/scared expression on their faces.

I just have to get through long enough for the experts to get here, Arhus thought to himself.

Walking as composed as possible, Arhus made his way to the table and chairs without turning around the entire trip. When he did, at the chair, he noted that the two 'messengers' had followed them. He pulled out one chair and then proceeded to the other side of the table to the other chair. The messengers did not approach the table but took up positions three metres from the awning opposite the building. The Subordinate walked to the chair that Arhus had pulled out and sat down without pulling up to the table. Once seated, Arhus picked up his own glass and took a drink. After he had set it down, the Subordinate picked up his glass and took a small sip, then placed it back on the table.

"As I am sure you are aware," Arhus started, "we have many questions."

"Humans have always had many questions," the Subordinate said. "What are your questions, Arhus Gint?"

The way the question was asked caused Arhus to pause. "Do you mean my personal questions?"

"Of course," was the reply.

Arhus stared for a moment, unable to do anything else. "Why would you worry about my questions?"

"As we said, we are interested in you." There was no change in expression, making the face hard to read.

"Why me?"

"Your demeanour has drawn our interest. Since our arrival, you have handled yourself well, as noticed by your superiors."

"Did you somehow ensure that I would be stationed here?"

The Subordinate seemed to consider for a moment. "Events move as we desire them."

That's a non-answer, Arhus thought. He decided to not worry about that line of questioning. "You said you are here to collect your own. And do what with them?"

"Take them to our home."

Arhus took another sip of water just to see if the Subordinate would follow suit. He didn't. *Probably doesn't need to,* Arhus thought. "Where is your home?"

"Far enough away that it will not matter to you for ages."

"What will they do there?"

"They will do our will."

"I am sorry, that is not very specific."

The Subordinate looked at him with no apparent effort to answer. There was no sign of compassion, no sign of anything from his face. *Is this the face of God?* Arhus wondered. *Why not ask?*

"Do you claim to be the God of the Old Testament and the Christ of the New Testament?"

The Subordinate's expression still did not change. "We are EO-AY."

"Are you Yahweh also?"

"That is a name created by the humans. There are many things that we have told them on previous visits that they did not understand, that their minds were not capable of understanding."

"So you have been here before?"

"Of course. We made this world and placed the humans here."

"So you terraform worlds and seed them with humans? To what end?"

"It is our will."

"To what end?"

"Our ways cannot be understood by humans."

This could go on forever without finding out anything, Arhus thought.

"Do not worry, Arhus Gint," the Subordinate said, as if reading his thoughts. "We mean you no harm."

Arhus heard the whine of transport vehicles overhead. *The cavalry has arrived.* The Subordinate and the messengers took no notice. With no clear area to land between the crowd and the barrier, the vehicles landed behind the crowd.

"My superiors have arrived. They will want to talk to you." Arhus felt relief flooding his body.

"We do not wish to talk to them," the Subordinate said. "We came to talk to you."

The flood stopped and was replaced with panic. He stumbled through the next statement. "They will have many questions. You wish me to bring them to you?"

"We have no interest in their questions. We have interest in our purpose."

"Am I part of your purpose?" Arhus's voice quaked when he

asked.

"If you wish to be."

Arhus experienced a small amount of relief at the statement. His mind swam with the Subordinate's statements. *A lot of people are not going to be happy. I'm not sure Montoya is going to believe me. At least we have the recordings to back up my report. Some people will be mad that I was the one chosen. Montoya placed me in this position, I didn't ask for it. They have nothing to complain about. Of course, that never stopped anyone before.*

There was a commotion at the entrance where security was restraining people. The crowd had started to get restless when the dignitaries started to push their way through. The Subordinate made no motion but the messengers moved from their positions to ones between the awning and the entrance.

This isn't going to last much longer, Arhus thought. *I better get to an urgent point.*

"Are you... is your ship ready to take those you summoned?"

"They may come at any time. Only the chosen may enter."

"We cannot check if they are chosen."

"Our guards will know."

The Subordinate stood up. Arhus followed. A small group of people led by Montoya broke through the crowd at the entrance. The messengers closed together, forming a two-person wall. Noticing that their visitor looked to be leaving, Montoya quickened his pace, waving at the messengers to get out of his way. The Subordinate glanced back at the oncoming crowd. They stopped in their tracks.

"Walk with us," the Subordinate said to Arhus.

Of course, he followed.

"We know your leaders will want to sit with us, but there is no requirement for such a discussion."

Arhus didn't say anything for several steps. "How do I reach you if I have questions? Do I wait here at this station or do you send for me?"

"If you wish to speak, come to the ship."

That's it? Arhus thought. *How did I rank this?*

"Thank you for coming to talk to me, Subordinate. I am sure I will be coming to talk to you soon."

"We look forward to it."

Arhus stopped a few metres from the end of the ramp. The messengers had followed behind them. The creatures did not move or even blink, from what Arhus could see. The Subordinate paused and turned his way.

"Until we meet again, Arhus Gint."

"Until next time." Arhus made a small bow, fighting back the urge to do more. He watched as the Subordinate and the messengers entered the ship. The view inside the ship was still obscured. When they had disappeared, the creatures moved to positions in front of the ramp. Arhus estimated that their swords would allow them to reach from either edge of the ramp to the middle.

"Tell me we recorded all of that," Arhus said as he turned around.

"We got nothing right after you sat down," Miranda's voice said over the ear-comm.

"What?!" Arhus started a fast pace back to the station.

"Yeah. They must have turned on some kind of jammer."

"Damn it! Now Montoya is only going to have my word on what was said."

"Is that a problem?" Eymen asked.

"He's not going to like what was said, is all."

Arhus and Montoya's party reached the awning about the same time. Montoya looked mad, but also confused. Whatever the Subordinate had done to them, it had delayed them until he had entered the ship. When Montoya looked at Arhus, the anger was still there and appeared to be directed his way. His group included Alonzo and Annalisa, but also some others that Arhus had not met, two men and one woman.

"Why didn't you stop him?!" Montoya demanded.

"And how was I supposed to do that?" Arhus said with less force than he would have wanted.

"Tell him we wanted to talk to him." Montoya was waving his arms with every statement.

"I did." Arhus could feel the heat rise in his face and tried to control it with proper breathing.

"And how did he reply?"

"He said they had no desire to talk to my superiors."

"What?! How can that be? Doesn't he know who we are?" Montoya was turning as he waved his arms. "Who does he think he is, showing up on our planet and taking people as he pleases?"

Saying nothing bought Arhus a little time before Montoya looked at him and said, "Well?"

"He claims that the human race belongs to them because they made the planet and seeded it with humans. It would appear that they believe they can do whatever they want with us." Arhus knew the statement would not go over well and it didn't, leading to more fuming from Montoya and company.

"I want to listen to the recording!" Montoya bellowed.

"There aren't any," Eymen said. Applauding his bravery and loyalty, Arhus hoped that speaking up didn't cost Eymen his job.

"How can there not be any?"

"As soon as the visitor walked under the awning, our signals were jammed. All we recorded was static." Eymen stood firm, not cowering. Arhus reminded himself to give the man a raise, if he didn't leave with the visitors.

"Unacceptable. Entirely unacceptable. This is a failure, an utter failure!" Montoya walked up close to Arhus and lowered his voice for the first time. "If this is some kind of power grab, you will regret it."

"You are the one who gave me this assignment," Arhus replied in the same low voice. "I didn't ask for it. So anytime you want to replace me, go ahead. From what he said, there is no reason for us to be at this station anymore."

It was clear from Montoya's eyes that he used his bluster to intimidate people quite often. While frustrated, Arhus knew he had also given Montoya an immediate way out of the situation. A small bit of recognition showed in Montoya's face.

"You have learned very well working here," Montoya said, and then turned back to everyone else in a calmer voice. "There is no further need for this station. You may go back to your normal assignments. I want a detailed report."

"Did he say anything else useful?" Annalisa asked, stepping in front of the rest of the followers.

"He said his name was the Subordinate." Arhus watched the group's faces. Only Annalisa showed any reaction to the statement, a tilted head and a piercing look. *She understands the implications of that,* Arhus thought. "He also said the ship was ready to accept those that were invited."

"Do we let them?" one of the men in the group asked. He was dressed in a suit and tie, something done almost exclusively by lawyers.

"We have no choice," Montoya replied, somewhat deflated. "The World Council won't give us the authority to stop them."

"But we can't verify that they had a visit from one of the messengers. How are we supposed to screen them?" the same man asked.

"The Subordinate said that the guards at the ship would know who to let on and deal with any that had not been invited." Arhus watched the reactions that came with the information. Wide eyes and some concerned looks were seen, except for Alonzo, who grew a knowing smile.

"Is that wise?" the same man asked in a shaky voice.

"I am sure that it will take a couple of examples for people to get the message," Montoya said in a detached voice that sounded older by the second. "Let's go."

"I will inform the lieutenant," Arhus volunteered as he watched the group turn and leave. "Might as well, as my last act."

He followed a small distance behind the group. After they were allowed to pass through the crowd, Arhus found Lieutenant Amster. He was talking on his comm. Arhus could guess what about. Walking around to get Amster's eye, he was rewarded by Amster disengaging from his conversation to engage Arhus.

"Give me some good news," Amster said.

"You can let people through when you are ready. The ship will accept them."

"About time. These people are going crazy here. I won't be sorry to see them go." Amster spoke into his comm. "Sergeant, start letting those that have been processed through. Get the rest processed and then let them pass." Amster's sigh was huge after he turned off the comm.

Arhus continued, "We will not be needing our station anymore. Our job here is over."

"Already?" Arhus could see the lieutenant's head swim.

"Seems our guests weren't interested in talking to our politicians."

That brought a laugh from the lieutenant. "Can't say I blame them. Maybe they are smarter than we are. Excuse me." The lieutenant walked past Arhus toward the other security guards.

Waiting for some of the crowd to clear made sense to Arhus. Those allowed through had the dreamy look of little children approaching a giant holiday tree filled with presents. Most of them, at least. A few had a different look, one of desperation. Arhus worried about those, worried what might happen when they reached the ship. He was not sure he wanted to watch, but he also wasn't sure he could not watch.

With the logjam broken, access to the station was easy. Eymen, Miranda, and Darmay were standing under the awning, watching one person after another walk by. They all looked at him when he approached, questions on all their faces.

"Pack up here, we're done," Arhus said.

"Already?" Darmay asked.

"Yes. It was a short vacation, hope you enjoyed it while it lasted." Arhus gave them a small smile. "Take the rest of the day off if you want."

"I think I'm getting to like working for you," Miranda said with a chuckle.

"Don't get used to it, we're back to normal in the office tomorrow." Arhus made the comment without emotion.

"So much for better working conditions," Darmay said while rolling her eyes.

"Let me on, I say!" came from the direction of the ship.

"Here we go," Arhus said, turning toward the scene.

A man was standing in front of one of the creatures. The creature had his sword level, barring the man's way. The creature's face did not wear a pleasant expression. The man's wore one of desperation.

"Please, please, let me on. I know I am supposed to be on that ship, even if I didn't get an invitation. I *have* to go, don't you see? It's where I belong!"

The creature reached out with one hand, grabbed the man by his shirt, and threw him four metres to the side through the air with a rough landing. The man rolled another two metres. The creature returned to its position with the sword point in the ground. After a few seconds, the other people continued to board the ship.

"No, no, no, no!" the man yelled as he stood up. With a groan of a yell, the man charged toward the ship's ramp. The woman who had been nearing the ramp jumped aside. The creature that had thrown the man did not move until the man had almost made the ramp. With the sword moving fast enough to appear as a blur, the creature swung the sword tip over his head and across the path of the man. The man's body, due to its own momentum, fell in two pieces onto the ramp. The creature went back to his stance. From the haze of the ship came a messenger carrying a staff. Stopping at the body, he touched each half with the staff. The body ignited in flame. The flame and the body disappeared together, leaving the ramp as it was before. Without comment, the messenger turned back and walked into the ship.

The woman that had jumped aside stared for a few moments and then approached the ramp with caution. When no challenge came, she hurried up the ramp into the ship. The others, all who had stopped to watch the confrontation, continued toward the ship, except for two, who turned and ran back to the entrance.

"I doubt they will have to make that demonstration too often," Arhus said, heading into the building.

"I can't believe they did that," Miranda said, still staring at the ship.

"I can't believe we're going to let them get away with it," Darmay replied.

"What do you expect the World Council to do about it?" Arhus said through the open door. "What do you think they *can* do about it?"

"We should talk to the visitors, offer to do something with those who aren't chosen, something humane," Darmay said.

"They don't wish to talk to our leaders." Arhus put his computer and associated equipment in the travelling case. "I'm going to the office to write up a report on my encounter."

"Then we have to do a better job of screening them," Miranda protested. "Eymen was working with a list of those who were given an invitation before."

"But we don't know if we have a record of all who were invited," Eymen answered. "In fact, there is no way for us to know. We could only track the messengers by sight and they travelled very fast, plus there were a lot of them. There is no way we know that we tracked all of them to all their destinations."

"So we just let those... aliens... kill people?" Miranda continued.

"The real truth is," Arhus said, coming out of the building, "the Council would rather have the visitors deal with them than the Council deal with them. This way, they can throw up their hands and claim not to be able to do anything. 'The visitors are too powerful, what can we do?' Avoids a lot of protest and accusations."

"Is the Council that cold?" Miranda asked.

"Don't kid yourself," Darmay piped in. "They're all politicians out to save their own skin. If a few people kamikaze themselves on the visitors, what do they care?"

"We can't do anything about that now. We can only hope that people see that incident on the news and take it to heart," Eymen answered. "Some won't, for sure, but most will. After *that* happens several times, people will get the message. Maybe security will get better at finding those who are lying."

"They were probably assuming no one was lying," Arhus said. "Now they will install detectors at the entrance to screen better. See you tomorrow, people."

With that said, Arhus walked back toward the entrance of the office. Almost no one noted him leaving. He did catch the eye of Lieutenant Amster, receiving back a look that told him the lieutenant had already figured out about the lie detectors and was not looking forward to using them. *There are going to be a lot of unhappy people soon, even with all the ones who will be happy being allowed on the ship. They will be gone, the unhappy ones will be staying, making life miserable for everyone else.*

How selfish of the aliens, Arhus thought, *leaving us with all the problems. Isn't that just like people in charge?*

Chapter Eleven
The Unlucky Many

Not being a real drinker didn't mean that Arhus never drank hard, it just meant he needed a good reason. Today seemed like a really good reason. He had just swallowed his third tumbler of whisky when Sindie entered the apartment to find him standing at the window, staring at the grounded spaceship. The ice cubes clunked in the glass as he lowered it from his lips, the sole sound in the otherwise quiet room.

"Tough day?" Sindie asked as she set down the items she was carrying in a chair.

"Historically significant would be more like it," Arhus replied without turning around.

Picking up the bottle on the coffee table, Sindie brought it up to eye level. "You going to save any of this for me?"

"Not if you're slow." Arhus turned, walked back to the table, gently took the bottle from Sindie's hand, and refilled his glass, setting the bottle back on its spot on the table.

"You want to talk about it?" Sindie offered.

"You're just trying to slow down my drinking," Arhus said, pointing with the glass before taking another sip.

"Darn, you figured out my plan. Don't drink it all before I can get a glass." Sindie walked into the kitchen just far enough to grab the first glass in reach and then walked back. Sitting on the couch, she picked up the bottle, filled the glass, and set it back. "Better get it while I can."

"That might apply to everything in the world, as far as we know." Arhus stayed standing while taking another sip.

Sindie patted the couch next to her. "Sit." She waited until Arhus made a movement to do so before resuming talking. "I saw you on the news today. I assume this attitude has to do with what our visitor said?"

"They don't care about us." A little of his drink splashed from his glass when he sat down, but Arhus paid no attention. "At least, they care about those who are the chosen. Everyone else is on their own, as long as they stay out of the way, that is. Get in the way and poof, you're gone."

"I saw the guy get cut in half and incinerated. Quite a statement." Sindie took a small sip of her own drink, small enough to make it last a long time.

"They don't even want to talk to our leaders. Haven't they seen any of the old sci-fi movies? That's the first thing they are supposed to ask."

"These aliens don't care about our so-called rules, that's clear. They also don't care about our political institutions either."

Arhus took a large drink. "I'm scared, Sindie, terribly scared. I'm not sure what is going to be left of the human race when they're done. Are they just going to leave us alone after they take their cut or are they going to purge the planet and start again? After how many thousands or millions of years to get twenty thousand acceptable specimens, are they just going to wait longer for more or are they going to reseed the planet with better stock?"

"What are you talking about?" Sindie looked at him, confusion rampant on her face that Arhus didn't notice.

"The Subordinate, the one who came out and talked to me, said that they seeded humanity on this planet. It seems obvious that they did so to generate their near-perfect specimens. So once they have them, what about the rest of us?"

Sindie set her glass down. "But we have conquered most of the diseases known to man and cured most of the inherent conditions. Now we are even getting to where we can fix the genetic codes. Hell, they eradicated sickle cell already. If the aliens started over, we would have to conquer all those diseases again."

"Unless they started with superior stock on a world where those diseases were already gone. Then they could create even better stock, couldn't they?" Arhus drained his glass and went to pick up the bottle.

"Slow down there, hero," Sindie said as she moved the bottle away. "I don't think genetics work that way. If I remember right, regressive traits, those you don't want, tend to propagate even if you start with good stock. Twenty thousand near-perfect specimens is about all you could get with everyone on Earth now. If you started over, those recessive genes would get into the pool that much faster."

"So what are you saying?" Arhus's expression showed more confusion than normal.

"I'm saying your idea that the aliens are going to 'clear the field' and start over here is wrong." On a whim, Sindie pushed her glass farther away also. "It wouldn't get a purer strain of humans, you restart the same problems. They would be better off to let us continue to fix our own genetic problems and create a purer race that way."

"So why come now? Why not later, when the sample size could be bigger?" Arhus's head waved a little and he blinked a little too much. "Why'd you move the bottle?"

"So I could make sure you had some chance of understanding what I said. Who knows why they came now? Maybe twenty thousand is all they need or all they can fit on a ship. Maybe they are running on some kind of schedule. You want the answer to that question, go ask them."

Arhus's head came up. "I just might."

Sindie's eyes narrowed and her head tilted forward. "You know something no one else knows, like some secret password?"

Arhus laughed, a laugh that was more driven by alcohol than anything else. "I'm sure the news reports didn't tell you everything."

After listening to him laugh, Sindie asked, "You care to share?"

When he had controlled himself enough, Arhus said, "They like me, the aliens. They think I'm interesting. Said I could come talk to them anytime."

"Really?"

"Yeah, lucky me." Arhus reached for the bottle, but Sindie brushed his hand away.

"How do you rate so high?"

"Don't know. Not sure I want to. Haven't decided if it's a good thing or not." Arhus gave Sindie a look questioning her loyalty.

"This means you could take questions to them for the Council. Do you know what power this gives you? Did you tell Montoya this?"

"No. He didn't ask and I didn't say, like that old government policy, you know. Why you withholding my whisky?" The word 'whisky' was horribly slurred.

"Because I want to hear this. Get unconscious later, on your own time." Sindie stared back.

"I am on my own time," Arhus protested.

"Right now, you are on my time. You going to tell Montoya?"

"Wrote the report already. Sent it before I left. Scheduled it for tomorrow morning."

"That should create a stir."

Before she could say any more, Arhus's interface on the table rang. He made no move toward it so Sindie activated it. A woman's voice came from the speaker.

"Arhus? Arhus? Are you there? It's Biel."

"Shit," Arhus said under his breath.

"I saw you on the news," Biel continued. "You haven't called. Arhus, I need to get on that ship! I told you that already and you promised to get me on that ship!" There was a short pause. "Arhus, are you listening?"

Arhus leaned forward. "Did you get visited by a messenger?"

"Are you drunk? You're never drunk. No, a messenger did not invite me, but I need to get on that ship!" The voice sounded desperate.

"If you didn't get invited, don't show up. Didn't you see the guy get chopped in half?"

"But you can straighten things out for me, right?"

"YOU'RE NOT LISTENING, WOMAN! You never listened, just wanted what you wanted. Well, this time you don't get it! If you're not invited, then you're not good enough for them! You get it?"

Sindie sat by and just listened, not trying to calm Arhus in the least. When he looked at her, she had a small smile on her face as if she was enjoying the exchange. Biel started crying.

"Arhus, how can you be so cruel to me?" she said through the sobs.

"It ain't me, baby, it's the aliens. You don't like it, go complain to them."

More sobs came through the interface. "I'll call you back when you're not drunk."

The interface signalled that the connection had been closed. Arhus leaned over the device. "Interface, deny all future calls from Biel."

"Done," the interface said.

Arhus turned back to Sindie. "What?"

"Nothing," Sindie said between giggles. "Just watching the show."

"You don't approve of the way I handled it?" Arhus reached again for the bottle. Sindie didn't stop him.

"I'm surprised you didn't tell that bitch off months ago. Serves her right." Sindie picked up her own glass and took a sip.

"You never liked her." Arhus waved at her with one hand while the other lifted the bottle to his lips. He swallowed twice.

"I never liked the way she treated you," Sindie corrected him. "She always treated you worse than you treated her."

"Josef seemed to have the same opinion." He took another swallow and fell back into the couch while doing it.

"Because we're your friends, you idiot!" Sindie slapped his shoulder, not that Arhus seemed to feel it.

"Friends. Right." Arhus took another swig.

"And that's enough of that for you," Sindie said, reaching up and taking the bottle out of Arhus's hand. Resistance was minimal. He looked her way, tilted his head forward as if to sit up, stopped, and then leaned back into the couch.

"We'll discuss that later," Arhus said as he waved a finger in the air in a random pattern.

"Sure we will. You just stay right there." Sindie went into the kitchen area, found the bottle cap, placed it on the bottle, and stored it in the refrigerator. Her own glass went on the table. Walking back to the couch, she found Arhus passed out on the couch, mouth open, arms drooped over the side and back of the couch.

"Well, tit for tat, I suppose," she said. His legs were moved on the couch and the arms to his side. She took his shoes off, but decided that was all that was required as far as clothing went. Pulling him by his feet was the only way to get his head onto the pillow next to the arm of the couch, though it could have been done more gently. She found a thin blanket and threw it over Arhus's prone figure.

"Nice to see that you are human, too," Sindie said to the reclining figure. "Not that I wanted you drunk, but it's always nice to see that the golden boy has some tarnished edges. Makes the rest of us feel better."

Sindie returned to the kitchen, picked up her glass, walked out onto the small porch, and sat in one of the chairs stored there. She raised her glass toward the alien ship and then took a sip.

"I don't know what your interest is in Arhus, but we aren't going to let you destroy him, that's for sure, whoever you are."

The next morning, Arhus was sure he had two heads and they were at war with each other. A hangover pill was the solution, but making it to the bathroom and finding the pill container was more of a challenge than he remembered. Hoping it wasn't a sign of old age, Arhus swallowed a pill and then made his way to the kitchen for something to drink. Water was recommended by doctors, so that's what he had. In a few minutes, the pill took effect and his two heads came together and stopped fighting. Eyes closed, he heard footsteps enter the room and hoped it was Sindie.

"What time is it?" Arhus asked.

"You're not late yet, but you're working on it. But then, you're the boss, too, so I guess it doesn't matter."

"Matters more," he said as he opened his eyes. "I've never seen that outfit before."

"Maybe you never looked," Sindie replied. "I'm off. Try not to be too late."

"Wait," Arhus said with a wave. He took a breath. "Did I do anything to embarrass myself last night?"

"Besides getting drunk? No, don't worry, your honour is still intact. Later." Sindie waved as she turned toward the door.

"Be right there." Arhus watched her go. It wasn't until then that he saw he was still wearing the same clothes from the day before. "That answers at least one question. Better start with a shower."

The shower and shave made him feel better, the clean clothes even better. The hangover pill also helped him feel rested. Not hungry yet, he decided to pick some breakfast up on the way into work. Looking around, it was clear that Sindie had straightened up before she left. He would have to mention that to her. If she kept this up, it would be obvious that there was more than a bachelor in the apartment.

Shrugging, Arhus headed for the door. Once outside, he headed for the bagel shop. If he was going to be late, he might as well appear to have an excuse. He ordered three dozen bagels and a breakfast sandwich, the latter which he ate on the way. There was a steady stream of people headed the opposite direction, many with hopeful expressions on their faces. It was not hard to guess where they were going. Arhus marvelled at the eagerness of the people.

"If you're that eager to leave Earth, then good riddance to you," he said to the crowd. *Then again,* he thought, *maybe I am being too hard on people. Society relishes the new, the different, the exotic, and this is as exotic as you can get. It would have been nice if humanity could have chosen at least some of those that went, but then, would we be better at choosing than the aliens? Well, at least a few that would be considered to be the best of us. Then again, who knows what they would be like outside of the limelight? Who knows what anyone is truly like?*

"If anyone, the aliens do, since they can read our minds," he said to himself. A thought went through his head. "I wonder if they were reading my mind while I was drunk. If so, I wonder what they found?" The thought was amusing.

In the office, people seemed to be more interested in the bagels than Arhus, which suited him fine. One person, Josef, was more interested in seeing Arhus.

"I hand the reins back to you," Josef said as he patted his arm, "and not a moment too soon."

"Something happen?" Arhus asked.

"Responsibility. I avoid it at all costs, as you well know." He wasn't laughing, but then he smiled. "And now I have to make a choice. Do you always have to make my life more complicated?"

"I live to make your life complicated, you know that," Arhus replied. "Does anyone have a count of how many people have entered the ship?"

"Everyone does," Josef replied through a mouth of bagel. "The news is keeping a running tally. Check the central display."

Arhus turned toward the centre of the tables. The central display held a view of the ramp to the alien ship. A steady stream of people, spaced about three metres apart, was walking into the ship between the creatures. A number in the lower right corner increased by one every time a person walked onto the ship.

"Anyone else try to sneak onto the ship?" Arhus asked, his voice trembling a little at the end of the question.

"Yeah, a woman did," Josef answered. When he saw Arhus's panicked look, he added, "No one we knew."

Arhus let out a deep sigh. "At least there's that." He took a moment to compose himself. "How much work did you leave me?"

"All the stuff I wasn't qualified to handle, or in other words everything that is handled by the supervisor." Josef took another large bite of his bagel.

"Thanks a lot. Remind me to give you all the 'choice' assignments."

"Figured you were already doing that." Josef waved his bagel and walked to his table.

There was enough work waiting for him once he re-initialized his interface that Arhus figured he would be busy all day. It was not to be. Before he could start into the first request, an emergency request buzzed in.

"Arhus Gint," he said after activating the request.

"Mr. Gint, this is the office of Ambassador Montoya. He would like you to come to his office at your earliest convenience." The voice sounded like it belonged to his receptionist.

"I'll be right there," Arhus said before ending the connection. "I have to go," he said to Josef.

"You just got back!" Josef protested.

"It's just a meeting, I'll be back. Try to keep yourself together." Arhus patted Josef on the shoulder.

"As long as you get back today," Josef said with a pointing finger.

Heading to the lift, Arhus asked for the one hundred and twentieth floor. "Get it over with fast, I hope," he said aloud.

"Get what over?"

Turning, Arhus found someone he didn't know standing in the lift behind him. Surprised he could have missed the person standing there, he said, "A meeting."

"I hate meetings," the man said. "Half the time they don't get anything done."

"Have to agree with you there," Arhus said with a smile.

The lift came to a halt. "My floor," the man said. He raised an eyebrow. Arhus took the hint and moved out of the way.

"Sorry," Arhus said as he moved. "Head in the clouds, I guess."

"No problem. Have a nice meeting."

"Thanks," Arhus replied. As the lift started moving again, he said, "But not likely."

Riding alone to his destination, Arhus looked over the city. He could still see the ship, though it was on the ground. For a while, he tried to decide if he was mad at the arrival of the aliens or not. The emotion would not surface. *Some good has happened. Rossarro is gone, that is good. I have been promoted, which is supposed to be good. Plus, I hope, Biel is gone for good. Not sure I would have said that before, but now I am.*

The lift stopped. The walk to Montoya's office was short for being familiar. Ushered into the meeting room, Arhus found the full group plus two of the people that had come to the ship, one man and one woman. Arhus wondered why he was last, but then remembered that he had just turned on his interface.

"Good," Montoya said, walking his way and holding out his hand, "we're all here. First, I want to apologize to you for yesterday, young man. I was extremely disappointed that our visitor wouldn't see me. You understand, I am sure."

"Of course," Arhus replied as he let Montoya pump his hand.

"Please, join us. We all have questions." Montoya waved a hand toward the seating area.

Arhus walked into the area, but kept standing. Montoya followed and took his normal seat. The tension rippled across his skin, leaving

Arhus wondering who would speak first. Once Montoya was seated, his wait was over.

"Your report says that the alien never overtly claimed to be God," Annalisa said, the words bursting out like caged animals. "Are you sure about that? From what you report, they never said one way or another in a definite manner."

"Yes," Arhus replied. "The Subordinate stated that they had made the world, terraformed I assume, placed humans here, and implied they had been here before, but they didn't claim to be a god as we understand the term."

"That leaves us in an interesting theological situation," Annalisa said. She looked at the others in the room. "Which none of you are interested in, I am sure, so I'll drop the subject."

"The theological aspects, yes," Montoya answered, "but I am sure there are other consequences which we will need to discuss. For now, we'll go on to other issues."

Preventing himself from rolling his eyes, Arhus took a steadying breath. *I hope I don't have to answer the same questions over and over.*

"Now," Montoya continued, "as you can imagine, people are very concerned about what is going to happen to those who go with the aliens. Not me, personally, but there are quite a few who want to know. Is there any way, in your mind, that we can find out? Maybe if we form the question correctly?"

"We can always try a trick question," Bahir put in.

"That won't work," Arhus responded. "They use telepathy, remember? The Subordinate spoke out loud to make me feel more comfortable, I am sure. You can't use a trick question if you know, and thus they know, you are trying to trick them."

"Good point," Ionut said with a laugh.

"The Subordinate showed no inclination to answer the question," Arhus continued. "I don't think asking the question again will make any difference. They aren't human, remember, and none of the normal tricks are going to work. For example, because they are telepathic, they show no need to continue talking when the other person is silent."

"Fine, we'll accept that for now," Montoya said with a wave of his hand, as if throwing the question over his shoulder. "But you do feel like you can take other questions to them?"

"Yes, but I don't think I should walk in there with a laundry list of questions. I think the Subordinate is trying to appear and act human. Maybe he likes interacting with humans or maybe it is just his job. Either way, his demeanour was calm, casual, not diplomatic at all. It was more like a conversation between friends than a negotiation."

Fingering his interface, Montoya looked down for a second and then back up to everyone. "I have sent all of you the list of questions we generated. Mr. Gint, I want you to look at this list and tell us which you think are the most likely to get answers, if you can."

Arhus brought up his own interface and pulled up the list, studying it for a moment. "We already have the answer to the first one. They are looking for genetically perfect people."

"No one is genetically perfect," the man from the previous day said. "Everyone's code has at least minor imperfections. True, there are people who do not have major imperfections."

"I forgot to introduce you. Mr. Gint, Dr. Worgung, geneticist. And this is Ms. Reffert, psychologist." The lady's name was pronounced in a French fashion. Arhus nodded to both, noting Ms. Reffert's intentional dropping of any title.

A rebel, Arhus thought, *but what's her cause?*

"As perfect as it gets, then, if that is the way you want to say it. Either way, it is clear they are taking the 'best' specimens they can get."

"The question is why?" Ms. Smith said.

"Why not?" asked Bahir. "They have ten billion people to choose from, why not take the best? Education and skills can all be trained."

"But what about talent?" Ms. Smith shot back. "Not everyone has true talent, such as music or physical ability."

"We still don't even know what decides talent," Bahir shot back. "Maybe they do. Maybe they can train talent like we can train education."

"Speculation will get us nowhere," Montoya interjected. "Until we know for sure why, talking about it does no good."

Do I mention it? Arhus thought. *Hell, why not.* "Maybe we are a commodity, anyone think of that?"

The room turned silent with shock. Annalisa stared at Arhus, then Montoya, and then back to Arhus. Ionut looked at Vicente and then Bahir, who gave him a lifted eyebrow. Ms. Smith continued to looked at Arhus, but settled back into her chair as if something revealing had been said. Dr. Worgung looked to consider the idea in his head.

"That's... disturbing," Ms. Reffert said out loud, though not at someone.

"Because you are human." Arhus scanned the room while he talked. "We raise animals for food and hides, we raise some animals for the chemicals they make in their bodies that are not practical to create any other way. We even still use stomach juices from cows to make cheese. These aliens are nothing like humans, for all the Subordinate now looks like us. Why should we expect them to see us in a different light?"

"You don't think they want to eat us, do you?" Bahir asked, laughing at the idea.

"No, I am not even sure they eat and drink as we know it. I am just saying that humans are pretty capable, adaptable creatures. Such characteristics, I would think, would make a good commodity."

"But why wait until now?" Montoya asked.

"Who knows? Maybe it took this long to get back to us. Maybe we are now advanced enough. Does the reason really matter?"

"No, it doesn't." Redness covered Annalisa's face. "If that is their real reason, well, they better not tell us, is all I have to say."

"If it is, they are not going to tell us," Montoya said in a sure voice. "Continue with the list, young man."

Turning back to his interface, Arhus again studied the list and started throwing away some questions. Sometimes when he did, he would make a comment like "vague" or "stupid," not caring who had suggested it. He didn't worry about how many he was throwing out. The list was longer than he expected and after halfway through, it started to get repetitive. Deciding that Montoya had just compiled the list without having to tell anyone no, Arhus cut with no thought of consequences. No one objected as he did, which told him that either Montoya had told them not to or they weren't surprised when it happened. *Maybe the questions didn't come from them at all.*

When he was finished, the list still had twenty questions. Still feeling like there were too many, Arhus went through the list again, taking out five more questions. There he stopped, waiting for the aftermath.

Montoya studied the reduced list for a while. Everyone else appeared to be waiting, so Arhus waited, too. Head bobbing up and down while he read, Montoya took his time before raising his eyes to Arhus.

"Do you think you can ask this many at a time?" Montoya asked.

This many? Arhus thought. *I was expecting him to complain about how many I took out.* Arhus thought for a minute before answering. "I doubt it. I don't know how many he will take before balking. If the New Testament is any indication, maybe the only one we have, I doubt I can ask more than three or four at a time."

"Three or four? That will take forever!" Vicente's head jerked up.

Shrugging, Arhus just sat and looked at Montoya. The realization that he didn't care anymore freed him from worry. *The aliens aren't here to negotiate; they aren't here to trade or win our approval. They are here to do what they want to do and we can't stop them, no matter how hard we try.*

Is that the definition of God? Arhus wondered.

"It is imperative that we learn as much as we can as fast as we can," Montoya continued. "I am sure as soon as all the invited guests are aboard, the ship will leave. I believe that the most important question is what our visitors are going to leave behind."

"You mean what they are going to pay us for all these people?" Bahir asked.

"I wouldn't put it that way. If our visitors are the same ones recorded in history, they always left something, if only knowledge. There is much they could teach us, that is obvious; their space drive engines, if nothing else." Montoya said it as if it was a reasonable expectation.

"Do you think they are going to give us that?" Bahir said in a manner that did not expect an answer.

"It's just an example. What else are the most important questions?"

Montoya asked the question, but Arhus was pretty sure by the man's expression that he had already decided what the answer should be. *Since he's a career diplomat, does the man consciously learn to talk that way or is it a part of his nature? Are we are what we are or are we what we become? Maybe the visitors know.*

"What do they expect us to do when they leave?" Annalisa said. "If our records are accurate, they have always left instructions for mankind when they leave. True, we were a lot more primitive then, but I would like to know their expectations, even if I don't plan to keep them." A smile that wasn't a smile crossed her face.

"Fair question," Montoya replied. "What else?"

"When can we expect them back?" Ionut offered.

"They've never answered that before, if that was them," Arhus pointed out. "Not sure they will answer it now."

"But our ideas of time are more advanced now," Montoya countered. "It is a good question, even if they don't answer it. One more."

I can see how this is going, Arhus thought. *To hell with religion, get to the nitty-gritty.*

"Are there others out there and can we expect a visit from them?" Vicente offered.

"Yes, very important, very important indeed." Montoya nodded his head while he spoke. "I am not sure they will tell us, but that is a question of utmost importance."

"Do you mean other EO-AY or other races?" Arhus asked.

The question seemed to take Montoya by surprise. His brow furrowed and his finger went up and down several times.

"Both!" Ionut said.

"Be careful asking about others," Ms. Smith piped in while lounging in her chair. "Their enemies might be called 'the devil' and nothing more."

"Even that would tell us something," Ionut responded, "like they have enemies."

"True, but you will have to ask the question carefully and try to ask a follow-up question, depending on the answer." Montoya continued his musing. "A lot of information could be implied by the answer they give."

"With our visitors," Arhus cautioned, "I am not sure that 'implied' means anything. They are ambiguous to begin with and appear more than willing for us to misunderstand what they mean."

"We will have to be very careful," Montoya agreed, shaking a finger in the air. "And we need to keep the answers away from the press. They will draw endless conclusions from any statement, most of them wrong, I fear."

"That you can count on," Vicente said.

"So, young man," Montoya asked with renewed vigour, "when can you talk to our visitors?"

"Tomorrow morning, I would propose," Arhus answered.

"Tomorrow? Why not today?" Montoya's voice rose in volume a little.

"They appear to like to act in the morning, for whatever reason. Maybe it fits their normal day cycle."

"I would prefer this afternoon," Montoya said with some force.

"All their actions so far have been finished before noon. If you want answers, I would suggest not pushing them." *And I would suggest not pushing me. I have other work I need to do, you know,* Arhus thought to himself. *I wonder if the visitors heard that?*

"Fine," Montoya agreed with a wave of his hand. "First thing tomorrow morning. How can we be sure they will know you are there to talk to them?"

"That I am not worried about," Arhus said with a small huff. "Now, if you will excuse me, I have other duties between now and then to attend to. Good day, gentlemen and ladies."

Without waiting to be dismissed, Arhus stood and left the room. The action made him feel powerful. *Why not?* he thought. *I am the designated ambassador, I should have some power now. If they don't like it, they can try to get someone else. Fat chance of that.*

The lift took a few minutes to arrive, making Arhus stand and wait. When it arrived and he walked on, Ms. Smith followed him onto the lift, but did not ask for a floor. Arhus asked for his floor but said nothing to the lady, letting her start the conversation. The lift started to move.

"That was brave," Smith said with a small smile.

"Leaving the meeting?" It was not a real question.

"Yes, what else?" When Arhus made no immediate answer, she added, "Feeling powerful can be dangerous. It can have dangerous consequences."

"What is he going to do, replace me?" Arhus responded.

"He might try," Smith answered.

"I doubt our visitors would take kindly to that." Arhus said nothing for a few seconds, then added, "And if they did, all for the better."

"Am I detecting an attitude about our visitors?" Smith's smile grew.

The lift stopped at the one hundred and seventh floor. Not waiting for Smith to move, Arhus walked off. He was followed by Ms. Smith. Seeing he had company, Arhus walked to his office, waving off anyone who approached. Stopping inside his office, he waited for Smith to enter the room and then waved the door closed before walking around the desk and sitting in the chair. Smith slid into a chair on the other side of the desk.

"I'm worried about when our visitors leave and what it will mean," Arhus said after taking a breath.

"How?" Smith swivelled in her chair.

"Chaos. The visitors totally change our perspective of the universe, and possibly ourselves. We pride ourselves in our independence, our science, our control of our destiny. That has all changed or will change. It might take a while, but it will happen. People will begin to doubt, which will make them insecure, and insecure people are stupid. If our visitors don't leave us with some direction, I am afraid the human race might destroy itself, or at least its soul through doubt and worry." Arhus closed his eyes as he talked, either to block the vision or to see it, he wasn't sure.

"You don't think the world will just sigh in relief at not being destroyed and go on from there?"

"At first, yes, but it won't last. As far as we knew, we were the most advanced life form in the universe. We have been proven wrong in a big way."

"Maybe we will be inspired to be better?" One side of Smith's brows went up and down.

"When faced with an impossible standard, most people despair."

"Impossible?"

"How many people do you know that have developed telepathy?"

It was Arhus's turn to raise an eyebrow.

"It may only be the effect of a machine."

"Made by whose company on Earth?"

The question caused Smith to take a deep breath and let it out slowly, frowning while she did so. She kept so tight a rein on her expressions, Arhus did not know if he saw frustration or not. *Maybe she just feels she was losing the argument, or maybe she agrees.* He decided to take a different tactic.

"What is your opinion?"

Smith stared at him for a minute. Arhus let her. When she had stared enough, she said, "Why do you think the visitors always communicate in the morning?"

"Maybe they watched too many old movies. You know, always attack at dawn."

Smith huffed. "I doubt that."

"Maybe it fits with their normal cycle, or maybe it is their tradition."

"I have been considering it in my mind, but I have not come up with a good reason."

"Maybe they need the sunlight to power their ship?"

"What? There wouldn't be enough power in the sunlight that hits their ship to power it."

"Maybe they only need to power the telepathy."

Smith laughed and leaned forward in her chair. "Power it enough to send messages all over the world? Do you have any idea how much power that would take?"

"No, I don't." Arhus's expression got thoughtful. Tilting his head one way and then the other, Arhus's lips scrunched from side to side. "Hmmm."

Smith narrowed her eyes. "What are you thinking?"

"Just a wild idea that may have no basis in factual science at all," Arhus said as his fingers started to drum the desk.

"Care to share these ideas?"

"Not until I find out if they are even possible or I am just stupid." The finger drumming stopped. "Will there be anything else?"

"If your idea does have merit, I would like to hear about it. Other than that, I will leave you to your duties." Standing, Smith made a small bow. "Good day."

The woman had left the office for over a minute before Arhus got up from his chair and exited the office. People must have been watching the door because several got up and came toward him as soon as he was clear. His expression did not seem to encourage them to say anything. Lucky for them, Sindie was one of them and had no such caution.

"Look," she said, "you seem to be dedicated to ignoring us today, but there is work that needs to be addressed."

"Can't Josef take care of it? I haven't revoked his temporary status yet," Arhus asked.

Sindie paused, then inhaled. "Most of it, yes," she said as she sagged a little.

"I need to run down to Communications to ask them about something. I hope to not be long. Whatever Josef can't address, I'll look at when I get back." He started to walk off, but saw Sindie wasn't done with her questions.

"Care to tell anyone what that meeting was about?" she asked.

"My status in Montoya's special group."

"You getting kicked out?" Sindie's eyebrow rose as she asked.

"If I'm lucky. Excuse me." With that, Arhus walked past the small gathering toward the lift. Not turning around once inside, Arhus asked for the thirty-second floor and watched the trees get closer as he descended. He didn't even look at who entered the lift at the two stops it made before his destination.

Why are the people responsible for ensuring open communications for all the World Council stationed so low in the building? he wondered as he walked onto the floor. *Yes, the equipment doesn't have to be on the top floor, but it just seems odd.*

Sending his identification ahead of him, Arhus walked past the front desk, but was still intercepted by a young man standing inside the communications department area. Arhus tried not to sigh.

"Can I help you?" the young man asked.

"No," Arhus replied, continuing to walk, "I'm here to see Johann."

"Is he expecting you?" The man looked put off by Arhus's answer.

"We're old friends, he won't mind." Arhus waved a dismissal to the young man, who still followed anyway. *Probably his job,* Arhus thought, *but I don't have time to be polite.*

The front of the communications office was dedicated to service personnel and technical support provided through the interfaces. From the size of the room, this support appeared to be over half of their business. The back of the office held equipment and the true technical experts, in software and hardware. Arhus assumed that Johann had not moved desks and knew where to find him. Johann wasn't the type to change habits on a whim and wanted to be close to the hardware anyway.

A slight detour was needed, as it turned out. It didn't surprise Arhus that Johann had managed to get his own office, of course still filled with communications hardware along the back wall. Smiling, Arhus walked to the office and opened the door enough to poke his head in.

"I'm looking for a socially inept engineer, you got any around here?" Arhus asked.

"Arse!" Johann shouted as he swivelled his chair around and stood up. "Come here, stranger!"

Walking into the room resulted in a bear hug from Johann, lifting Arhus off the floor. Since Johann was head-and-shoulders taller and twenty kilos heavier, it was not hard to do. The young man stuck his head in the door.

"Thanks, Den," Johann said, looking at the young man once he let Arhus go. "You can go back to your duties."

Den gave a quick nod and exited the room, letting the door shut. Johann slapped Arhus on the shoulder a couple of times, shaking his head as he did.

"Where you been? I haven't seen you in, what, a year? Fine way to treat your old university pal," Johann said with a laugh as he went back to his chair. "Sit down, sit down. This a social call?"

Johann's face lit up a little with the last comment, leading Arhus to believe that his friend had not changed his habit of keeping a bottle of vodka and several glasses in his desk. Johann called it being social, but Arhus had spent his university years with the man and knew his fondness for vodka.

"Actually, no," Arhus said, sitting in one of the chairs. There was no desk or table between the chairs. All surfaces had been moved to the side and occupied with hardware or test equipment. "I have a technical question."

"Translation software? I hope not. You know I do hardware." Johann sat in a large chair in front of Arhus.

"No. This is a strange question that comes from some work I've been doing for Ambassador Montoya, though I am not here in connection with his office." Arhus's hand made a flat sweep in front of him.

"Yeah, I heard you were scooped up by the big boys. Even talked to an alien! What was that like?" Johann leaned on one elbow as he bent forward.

"Not as interesting as you would imagine. The one I talked to is trying very hard to look and sound human."

"Boring! I'd rather talk to a real alien myself."

Arhus started to say something, but then stopped, his brow coming down to his eyes. "Did you get a visit from a messenger?"

"Naw. What would those aliens need with an engineer who knows less than they do? Doesn't mean I wouldn't relish the chance to talk to them, though."

"You and a lot of other people." Arhus rolled his eyes. "Anyway, I've been thinking a lot about how the aliens seem to come out and make announcements in the morning when the sun comes up. Maybe that's their culture, but maybe not. What you might not know is that they use telepathy to communicate."

"Telepathy?" Johann interrupted. "How can you tell?"

"There are ways, but that's not important to what I have to ask." Arhus put his hand up in front of him, palms toward each other. "Given these two facts, though, it made me wonder if they are connected. I know this will sound strange, but I was wondering if somehow they are using the sunlight as a carrier wave or booster wave to send out their telepathic signal." Arhus brought his hands together and then extended them.

"Booster?" Johann looked skeptical. "Sunlight, individual rays so to speak, isn't that energetic to begin with, compared to most communication forms we use, so I don't see how it would help."

"I don't mean a power boost, I mean a speed boost." Getting more animated, Arhus continued. "What if they can put telepathic signals on the sunlight and absorb its speed? That would allow a weak signal like telepathy to travel huge distances fast."

"True," Johann said with a laugh, "assuming you could do it in the first place. But then how would you get it around the world?"

"It doesn't have to stay with the sunlight. Once it has speed, maybe it bounces off the ionosphere or is relayed through satellites. Maybe they positioned reflectors or relays before they made their first announcement. Who knows? First we need to find out if they are using the sunlight or not."

"But why use sunlight?" Johann said. "Why not just use communications channels like we do?"

"Secrecy?" Arhus offered. "To make it more impressive? To a primitive race, it would seem like magic. Think about it. They landed close to the World Council headquarters. Maybe that distance is how far their telepathy works all by itself. If so, they can read the minds of people in, say, Jerusalem, but not around the world. Of course, with all the instant communications that goes on, they wouldn't need to read everyone's mind."

"That's for sure," Johann said, leaning back in his chair. "People have no filter these days. Plus, with all our information in the info-space, they can access anything they want to know."

"Everything but what our leaders are thinking. Then, if they can implant thoughts into our leaders' heads, they can even affect policy and actions even more!"

"Whoa." Johann's eyes got wide. "That's a heavy thought, one I'm not sure I want to consider."

"We need to consider everything. But I came to you to find out if there is a way we can tell if they are using sunlight as a booster signal. What do you think?"

Watching as Johann's face contorted, Arhus gave his friend time to think, knowing it wouldn't be a fast process, but a thorough one. Once the seed was planted, he knew he might have to come back later for any kind of answer, the length of time depending on the difficulty of the question. After a few moments, he checked his interface, sure that Johann was too deep in thought to care. He took care of a red-blinking request before Johann made any kind of sound.

"You really like asking the hard questions, don't you?" Johann asked while shaking his head.

"Can you look into it?" Arhus asked, leaning toward his friend.

"I can try, but don't expect any miracles. And don't expect anything fast either."

"I understand. I appreciate it." Arhus gave him a small smile.

"Hey, by the way, how's that girl of yours? What was her name?"

"Biel, and we separated a couple of months ago."

"What happened? She was a real looker."

"I wasn't exciting enough," Arhus said with a shrug.

"I bet you're exciting now!" Johann's eyes twinkled as he fisted Arhus's shoulder.

"And not interested in her anymore. What about you and Karie, still together?"

"Of course," Johann said, spreading his arms wide. "Where is she going to get a hunk of man like this anywhere else?"

"Any corner apothecary?" Arhus offered.

Johann laughed. "Not likely, not likely. Don't be a stranger, now you are mister high and mighty, you hear?"

"You could come upstairs, you know." Arhus stood up, wagging a finger at Johann.

"And leave my babies? You sure ask a lot!" Both men laughed. "I'll see what I can find for you."

"Thanks, pal. Appreciate it." He turned to go, but then stopped. "And don't risk yourself with anything, you hear?"

"Risk?"

"Just covering my bases, is all."

"Sure. I'll let you take all the risk. Leaving so soon?"

"You were always so generous. I wish I had time to catch up, but time is a luxury at the moment. Maybe after the visitors leave." With a dismissive wave, Arhus turned and left the room. *Maybe after the visitors leave there will be time, but that feels like a lifetime away.*

The trip back to the office was so automatic Arhus didn't remember it. Desperate thoughts of what else he was missing filled his mind. *There has to be something I'm missing. Translators are taught to listen and watch the speaker and his surroundings. So much is non-verbal, assumed, or cultural and all of it has to be added to the words to know what the person means. But the visitors are harder because I don't know the culture and they tend not to give visual clues. Maybe as the Subordinate becomes more human, he will develop them.*

As the lift was ascending, a thought hit him. *Why is the Subordinate becoming human? It shouldn't take that long for all those invited to reach the ship, a couple of months at the most, no matter how far away they are. Does it mean he intends to stay? Do they know that not all the invitees will accept and that they will need to convince them? Why go through all the trouble?*

Then again, maybe he is the one who is going to interact with the humans during the trip. If they are awake, they would want to interact with their hosts. Is the explanation that simple?

The topic had to be abandoned as soon as Arhus entered the office, because he became the centre of attention. The looks in people's eyes told him they were just nervous and needed to feel like they had a real leader more than that they needed to be told what to do.

One more burden to bear, Arhus thought. *At least it is one that I am appreciated for.*

The thought gave him some comfort, making interacting with *his* people almost reassuring. The questions were easy ones and didn't take much time, leaving plenty to attend to the other items on his interface. It was three in the afternoon before he realized that he had forgotten to eat lunch, the effects starting to grow inside of him. As he chastised himself, Josef walked into the office.

"Hey, you look pale, and I mean paler than normal for a guy who is Dutch and doesn't go outside much." There was concern in Josef's voice.

"I forgot to eat lunch," Arhus said, closing down his interface.

"You should do something about that." For once, there was no sarcasm in Josef's voice.

"Was just about to." Arhus stood up slowly on purpose, thanking his luck that his head didn't spin when he did it. "Want to come along?"

"I, being the smarter of the two of us, ate lunch at the proper time, but thanks. Take Sindie with you. I didn't see her eat anything. She's been monitoring the ship every chance she gets, almost like she is watching for someone she knows."

Arhus stared at his friend. "There wouldn't be some other reason you're suggesting this?" He started walking to the door.

"Who, me? Would I do something like that?" Josef put up his hands and leaned away from Arhus.

"Yes, and you know you would," Arhus said with a small guffaw.

"Darn, caught again!" The fake resignation was well practised.

Arhus shook his head as he walked out of the office. It proved not to be advisable, causing him to swerve a little as he walked. Then Josef was standing next to him without visibly supporting him. People took a look as he walked past the tables, but did not appear to give him a second thought, everyone except Sindie, whose face filled with sudden concern and decided to join the men.

"You forget to eat again?" she asked in a hushed tone.

"When did you become so familiar with my medical conditions?" Arhus asked.

"I have a large family, remember? Name something and we have someone who's had it."

"Malaria," Arhus said with defiance.

"My second uncle," Sindie responded.

"Can you make sure he gets to the cafeteria and eats something?" Josef asked her.

"Sure, no problem. Started babysitting when I was eleven," Sindie said with a shake of her head.

"Wait, hasn't malaria been wiped out?" Arhus asked as they made it to the lift.

"Unless you work for the World Health Organization." Sindie took Arhus's arm while they waited.

"Oh, research?"

"Yeah, so they say. I just hope it wasn't too much vodka."

Once the lift left their floor behind, Arhus leaned on Sindie instead of her hanging onto him. He wasn't that weak yet, but it didn't hurt to be prepared. When they reached the twenty-third floor, he managed to walk, for the most part, on his own from the lift into the cafeteria.

"You mind if I just sit and you get me some food?" he asked.

"Sounds like a plan." Sindie made sure he was in the nearest seat before leaving for the serving line. She came back with a full tray of assorted high calorie food, protein, and two sets of silverware.

"That's right," Arhus said as he picked up a fork, "Josef said you missed lunch."

"I had a power-shake," Sindie replied, taking up a fork of her own, "but if you're buying, why not?"

"I'm buying?" Arhus said through a mouth full of potatoes.

"They have your ID on file. Didn't you know that?" She took a piece of beef from the tray.

"Then why do I always have to scan my interface?"

"Procedure." She gave a shrug.

"And they took your word for all this?"

"Why not, you're sitting right here and you have a reputation for forgetting to eat." She gave him a wink.

"Guess that's not the worst reputation to have," Arhus said as he continued eating.

"Plus, I can count it as our first date," Sindie said, looking down at the food, but then raised her eyes to look at Arhus.

"Schemer," Arhus said with a huff. "Besides, I didn't think I was your type. At least, that is what you've said over the last few years."

"It turns out," Sindie said, pointing her fork at him before taking another bite, "that 'my type' are real dick-heads, so I figured I needed a new type. Not sure what that is, yet, but for sure not what I was after before."

"So fat, dumb, lazy, non-athletic, poor, and ugly."

"About sums it up," Sindie said with a shake of her head. "Know any?"

"I'll give them your number if I run across any." Arhus smiled at her.

They ate in silence for the rest of the meal. Discovering she had forgotten drinks, Sindie got up about halfway through the meal and brought back two large glasses of fruit juice, grape. Arhus chuckled, not realizing how well Sindie knew his taste, though it made him wonder how long she had been watching.

Or maybe she just noticed the container in the fridge, he thought.

"You know," Arhus said when they were all but finished, "we're ruining our supper."

"We don't have to eat supper at six," Sindie said with a flip of her head. "Some people don't eat supper until nine or ten at night, like Spain."

"I wait that long and all I'll want is ice cream." Arhus took his last bite and set the fork down on the plate.

"Nothing wrong with that either," Sindie said through a full mouth.

Laughing, Arhus countered, "Don't let your dietary program hear you say that."

A full fork stopped before entering Sindie's mouth. "Don't have one, turned it off. I have plenty of people in my life telling me what to eat. I don't need a program doing it, too."

"And yet you manage to stay so thin," Arhus replied in a mock female voice.

"That comes from not eating." Sindie took one more bite and threw the fork on the plates. "You good?"

"Yep, for at least four hours. After that, no guarantees."

"Guess I'll take what I can get." A look at her interface took Sindie's eyes down and back up. "It's three-thirty. You going back to the office?"

It was Arhus's turn to look at his interface, causing him to frown. "A couple of requests to take care of, won't take long. I should make an appearance, anyway."

"Fine, let's go." Sindie stood up but didn't push in the chair.

"You don't have to come," Arhus said as he stood up slower and pushed in his chair. His mother would be proud of him.

"We left together, might as well go back together," she said with a shrug.

"Still worrying about appearances?"

"No, in fact. The way I figure it, most of the rules are going out the window very soon, so why worry about it now?" Once she saw that Arhus was steady on his feet, Sindie relaxed as she walked to the lift.

"Can't say I can tell you that you're wrong," Arhus said. The lift showed up just as they reached it. They waited as two women exited and then stepped on. "One-zero-seven."

They stood in silence at first, Arhus watching the floors go by. "Did you ever think of all the people who work on all these floors?" he asked without looking at Sindie.

"No," she replied.

"Do you wonder how many got invitations?"

"No," Sindie said flatly. "I didn't and it's not my concern if they did."

"What if one of them was a relative?"

Sindie huffed. "I have plenty of relatives. The visitors can have a few, as far as I am concerned."

"What if it was one you cared about?"

"They would still make up their own mind. I doubt any of my relatives would go, except for cousin Lou, and the visitors would do us all a favour by taking him. He's a real pain in the ass."

"Somehow I doubt they would want him, but who knows. Have any of your family said if they got invites?"

"They wouldn't. The whole family would be trying to talk them out of it." She paused for a second, then added, "Except for cousin Lou, that is."

The lift stopped. As they entered the general area, Arhus could see that about half of the crew was getting ready to leave. That wasn't unusual. Splitting, Sindie went to her station and Arhus walked toward his desk, getting stopped for a question once on the way. He did see Josef's eyes on him at one point, making sure he was fine. Arhus gave him a quick nod.

The biggest surprise was that he had no messages or requests from Montoya's office. *Did my performance have that big of an effect? Or is my assignment for tomorrow morning enough to satisfy Montoya?* Finding himself not caring, Arhus pushed it from his mind and addressed the two items on his interface. Both were administrative tasks, like most of the items that had come through the last couple of days. None of it seemed important now, but he didn't want it hanging over his head, either. *Plus, after the visitors leave, there might not be time.*

Finished, Arhus closed down his interface and left the office. Even fewer people were present and most of those were leaving. Josef and Sindie were two exceptions, their attention on Arhus as he left the office. Both turned off their stations and joined him.

"So," Josef said in a cheery voice, "anyone up for drinks?"

"Count me in," Sindie said in the same cheery voice. "You have a female you want to invite along?"

Josef's eyes got wide. "It's going to be that kind of night?"

"I thought you always had a girl around somewhere. Plus, I would hate to cramp your style."

"Finding a girl is never a problem," Josef said with a wide grin. "There are always plenty to go around."

"Fine, you go fishing while we drink," Sindie said with a shrug. "We can rate your catch."

"Oh, you'd like that, wouldn't you?" Josef gave her a suspicious eye.

"Come on, you two. We can settle this in a more appropriate location." Arhus herded the two toward the elevator.

With his feet up on the coffee table, Arhus lounged on the couch. With the ship on the ground, they had been able to move the patio furniture so that they blocked the view of the ship, leaving a view of the stars and the mountains. The beauty of the sight reminded Arhus of what he had been missing since the ship's arrival.

Sindie plopped herself down on the couch next to him. Not drunk this time. She was just starting on inebriation, enough to relax but not enough that she had an excuse for anything she did. Arhus marvelled at her restraint, but had not said anything. True, it had been entertaining to watch Josef 'work his magic' in the tavern, failing several times before succeeding. But Arhus had called foul because he recognized the woman as someone he had seen Josef with before. The objection had been raised when the woman had gone to freshen up. Josef had tried to argue that the fact made the feat harder, not easier. Sindie had jumped on the statement immediately and it had not been long before Josef had said goodnight to his uncontrollably laughing friends. The laughter had lasted for almost an hour after Josef had left, both vowing to never let him live the statement down.

"I like this view a lot better," Sindie said as she leaned her head on Arhus's shoulder.

"Me, too. Maybe we had to lose it to appreciate it."

"Not me, I never had this view until right now."

"You know what I meant."

"Will the rest of the human race have the same opinion? Appreciate what we have more than we did?"

"For a while, then people will get back to normal."

Sindie's head came around to look Arhus in the face. "Thank you, negative Naggy. You don't think people can learn something?"

Tilting his head Sindie's way, he replied, "They have to want to learn something. If you're lucky, it will last for the current generation, but when the next one comes around, the effect will start to fade like they were never here."

"You'll never make head cheerleader thinking like that!"

Arhus shrugged at her.

"Well, I will tell you that I, for one, have learned to appreciate things right in front of me more and I mean to keep it that way."

"Such as?" Arhus asked.

Sindie leaned in and planted a kiss on his lips. It was a very purposeful kiss, one full of intent and meaning. For a second, Arhus couldn't decide if he was surprised or not, then his thoughts went to whether he wanted to decide. Sindie was nothing like Biel, nothing like any of the other girls he had any kind of romantic interest in before, which at the moment sounded like a positive. None of those relationships had ended better than neutral. *Maybe I should just get out of my own way.*

The kiss ended, Sindie pulling back a few inches so they could look at each other. "Still making up your mind?"

"No," Arhus said, sliding his hands up her shoulders.

Chapter Twelve
Good Neighbours

As nervous as he was standing in front of the alien ship, Arhus was more glad that he didn't have to encounter Josef this morning. Somehow Josef would know; he always did, and then either teasing or asking for details would follow. If there was one subject Arhus didn't feel like talking about, it was last night. It still felt strange in some ways, though overall it had been more of a revelation than Arhus had thought possible, a revelation in what he didn't know about himself and the old stereotypes that he believed.

With the sun still not showing above the horizon, Arhus stood about three paces from the guards at the alien ship. He had not tried to enter the ship and the guards had not tried to chase him away. As far as anyone could tell, the same creatures that had taken up their original position at the entrance still stood there. At night the ship gave no illumination from inside, so it could be possible that the guards changed while it was dark, but no one had seen anything to indicate that they had. From what Arhus overheard, it had been considered that lights could be focused on the entrance, but no one had wanted to risk upsetting the visitors. It was just more proof to Arhus that the visitors were telepathic, accepting the called without being able to see them and the called not tripping while entering.

Sure that those inside knew he was there, Arhus assumed the calm demeanour that he had developed waiting on diplomats over the years. It did raise the question of why they left him waiting. *Are they sleeping until sun-up? Is it their custom not to engage anyone until the sun rises? That seems silly for space travellers, but humans still hold to some silly customs, so why not our visitors? While curious, it is one of the least important questions.*

The first curve of the sun sent light into Arhus's eyes as he considered the questions, causing him to flinch a little and squint. When his eyes adjusted, he noticed a figure walking down the ramp. Arhus straightened, bearing the hard sunlight in his eyes as the Subordinate approached.

"I am pleased to see you again, Arhus Gint." The Subordinate made an abbreviated bow as he stopped at the bottom of the ramp.

Arhus made a deeper bow, bringing a broad smile to the Subordinate's face.

"You honour me."

"As is proper, Subordinate."

"You come with questions?" It was asked as if the Subordinate did not know the answer. His expressions were getting better, more human. Arhus was impressed.

"Yes, if I may occupy some of your time."

"It would give me great pleasure to do so. Would you like to walk inside the ship as we talk?" The Subordinate's face noted Arhus's slight hesitation. "Do not worry, we would not force anyone to remain on our ship and there are a fair number of the invited to arrive yet."

"It is a very generous offer," Arhus responded, recovering himself, "thank you. I would be honoured to walk through your ship."

"Then please." The Subordinate waved his arm to indicate that Arhus should enter.

Not worried about the creatures guarding the entrance, Arhus couldn't help but glance at them as he took his first steps. As he expected, they made no movement in response to his approach. At least the Subordinate didn't laugh at Arhus's action. As he came close to the Subordinate, the alien turned and walked with Arhus, matching the easy pace that Arhus had set. The bright light coming out of the ship blocked any view of the inside.

"You're not worried I am going to give away any secrets?" Arhus said.

"We did not come to keep such secrets from you," the Subordinate said in his ever calm voice. "Anything you are not told is beyond your comprehension."

The bright light stopped as if it had been a wall that Arhus walked through. Beyond was a corridor of at least one hundred yards with an open area to be seen at the end. Humans and non-humans could be seen walking past the corridor at irregular intervals and plants could be seen. Though the floor and walls he walked through looked like metal, Arhus's footfalls made no sound and their conversation did not echo. As he walked, Arhus noted that the corridor walls had lines in places that could indicate doorways but no means of opening them were shown. The source of the light in the corridor was not apparent either, just seeming to be there as needed. No one else walked the corridor at the moment.

"Impressive," Arhus said, looking around. "Natural noise dampening material, I assume. Do you care to tell me where the light is coming from, just to settle my curiosity?"

"It just is," the Subordinate said.

Arhus was going to ask a follow-up question and then paused. "I would ask how that works, but somehow I know I wouldn't understand the explanation."

The Subordinate smiled in reply, then indicated in front of them. "Ahead is our open area. Here people can meet, talk, eat, and exercise as they please. As you can see, we have placed plants from your planet here to make the area more pleasant."

"Very considerate of you. Is this where people will spend their time when travelling back to your home?"

"No, this area will be removed before we leave." As they neared the end of the corridor, Arhus could see a waterfall, tables, and chairs placed around the area. "Our guests will have to be in their sleeping chambers as we return home, for their protection and health."

"Because the human body can't take travelling at the speeds the ship can achieve," Arhus finished.

"It will be much safer for them, and the journey will pass in a very short time."

"Journey to where?"

"Our home." The manner in which the Subordinate turned indicated a finality to the answer.

"Then will you come back for more?"

"If we deem it necessary."

They walked into the open area. Soft, grass-like plants grew beside the walkways. Bird sounds could be heard, though Arhus did not take the time to locate any actual birds. On the far left side stood a stone table with food covering the top, mostly raw vegetables and fruit. Next to it stood a fountain with clear water running down in multiple thin streams to a basin below. Several hundred people walked, sat, or lounged on the grass in various states of talking, debating, admiring, or sleeping. No one looked stressed or worried.

"This is not everyone who has come aboard. Are there other areas?" Arhus asked.

"Many have chosen to enter the sleep chambers already. They are on the other side of this room." The Subordinate held up his hand to indicate the passageway at the far side and took a step forward. Arhus followed. "There are a few other smaller, quiet areas where guests can read, contemplate, or watch your information announcements, but they do not hold many."

As they walked, Arhus was struck by the fact that no one approached them. The arrival of the Subordinate was either a common event or he was diverting their attention. Arhus did not want to ask since the Subordinate had chosen to give Arhus this time. Plus, he did not know how the aliens would react if he started questioning their methods. Quick glances did not locate any birds, though the songbird sounds continued.

"And what happens if all those invited don't accept your invitation?" Arhus asked as they walked.

"We are sure enough will accept our invitation," the Subordinate said, no hint of worry in his voice.

Arhus let the topic drop and took another track. "You have changed your appearance to look more human. Does that mean you will be staying on Earth when your ship leaves?"

"Would you like for us to stay?" The question was asked as if the Subordinate was not surprised that Arhus's question had been asked.

"I know there are many on Earth that would be eager to accept your company and seek whatever knowledge you are willing to share with us." Arhus almost ran into a woman walking through the room who acted like she was not aware that he was there, having stopped to wave at someone before continuing. Like everyone else, she wore a happy expression on her face.

"But do *you* wish us to stay?"

Stopping, Arhus turned to look face-to-face with the Subordinate. He could read no emotion or anticipation on the face, all information remaining hidden deeper than any diplomat Arhus had ever encountered. Even with that lack of knowledge of the question's intent, Arhus did not feel nervous to give an answer, which was a relief, since he had no idea what answer he wanted to give.

"If you stayed it would… could be quite interesting, if you were willing to share information about yourself and your home world. We have never encountered another intelligent being before now. You are so different that even your philosophy, your way of looking at the world and events, could prove very instructive."

The Subordinate continued to look at Arhus even after he stopped talking, making no effort to say anything. The feeling of being interrogated started in the back of Arhus's head, but he dismissed it as paranoid. *Maybe he is just waiting for me to answer the question, which he knows I have not done,* Arhus thought.

"As for me personally, I don't know if I want you to stay or not. I know that when this ship leaves, there will be tremendous changes, though I cannot predict what they will be. If you stayed, it might help or it might make the changes more sudden and more wide-spread. Would that be good? I don't know."

Smiling at the statement, the Subordinate's face took on a softer tone. "You speak the truth. Change will come, driven by those in power and those not in power now. Some places will not change at all, but some will never be the same. That is the way it always comes to pass. Our presence would affect the speed of the change, not the coming of it."

"But could you help us through it?" Arhus asked with a slight note of desperation.

"If what we say was accepted, then yes. If it was not, it would be worse."

"You can't just tell us what would happen?"

"Please," the Subordinate said as he turned back the way they had been walking and held out his arm, "let us continue to the sleeping chambers so you can see for yourself how our guests will travel."

It was worth a shot, Arhus thought as he turned to continue their journey. The passageway led to another corridor which looked much the same as the first but lined with two levels of small rounded-corner rectangular indents in the walls. The first of these they walked past, but then the Subordinate stopped when they were well into the corridor and touched one of the indents.

With a small sound of air moving, the wall section extended from the wall. Behind it came a gel-filled cushion designed as a bed. The cushion looked deep enough to come well over a person's side, even enclosing his legs and arms. The part closest to the 'door' was shaped to accept a human head and also was raised enough that it would provide ample support. Arhus touched the bed, finding it soft, but firm if pressed far enough. A look inside the chamber revealed tubes and machinery made of a clear material.

"The necessary attachments are made after the person is asleep and removed before they are awake as to not disturb their minds," the Subordinate said.

"Acceleration beds," Arhus said, receiving a nod in reply. "The chambers are filled with gas at the correct humidity and temperature to preserve their skin." Another nod. "Air?"

"One of the attachments delivers fresh, moist air to the person."

"You seem to know what to do," Arhus said absentmindedly.

"Of course. You are ours and we care for our own."

Arhus remembered about not reacting too late. His head jerked up and he stared at the Subordinate, his face filling with more blood than normal. "Then where have you been? Terrible events have happened here. Where were you when Jerusalem was wiped from the face of the Earth? Where were you when hundreds of thousands were slaughtered in Asia? Where were you when one man convinced millions to kill millions more?"

His breaths coming short and fast, Arhus forced himself to stop talking and try to calm himself. *Answer* that *if you will, you arrogant bastards,* he said in his mind.

Nonplussed, the Subordinate replied, "You needed time to grow. Growth can be painful."

"Painful? You consider mass death painful?" A thought ran though Arhus's head, but he suppressed it, not wanting to take the chance that the Subordinate could read his mind. Looking away, Arhus composed himself, making his breathing slow and deliberate. When he felt composed, he opened his eyes and turned to the Subordinate.

"May I see the ship's engine room, the device that propels the ship through space?" he asked.

"It would serve no purpose," the Subordinate replied as he applied a slight push to the door of the sleeping chamber. The chamber retracted with less sound than it had opened. "You would not understand what you see."

"What about your own chambers? Or those of the ones that serve you?"

"You could not abide in our chambers and our servants will spend the time travelling in the centre of the ship." Turning back the way they had come, the Subordinate started walking. Arhus stepped into position next to him.

"You have been very generous and I appreciate all the time you have given to me this morning. As you can imagine, there are many questions that I have been given to ask if possible, many of which I will not even attempt because I find them offensive or ridiculous. One feeling that many have, though, is that since you are asking so many of us to go with you, there should be some kind of exchange on your part, a gift to our world."

Arhus held his breath and then, discovering he was, let it creep out of his lungs. The thought that maybe he should have waited until he was closer to the outside door to ask the question ran through his head, but was dismissed.

"Are not those who join us free to do so?" the Subordinate asked.

"Yes, they are."

"Are they not free to make up their own minds to join us or not?"

"We believe so." The statement caused the smallest pause in the next question.

"Are you not allowed to go wherever you wish on this world?"

"With a few exceptions, yes."

"Then how is their joining us any different?" The Subordinate turned his head to look at Arhus.

"I am not saying I agree with the sentiment, I am just communicating how some of the people feel." Arhus gave the alien a quick look, but did not trust himself to continue very long. The Subordinate looked away.

"And what would they want in exchange?"

"Scientific knowledge, such as knowledge of the universe and what or who might be out there. An indication if we might be visited, other visitors and what they would be like, friendly or not."

The answer did not come for several paces. "You have all the knowledge you need here on Earth. You have conquered almost all diseases and birth defects, you are for the most part at peace, and even those parts of humanity that have not obtained the advancement that you have here are not far behind, far from the primitives that you were at our last visit. We do not see much that you need from us."

"What about other visitors?"

"You are protected by us, you need not worry."

They were halfway across the centre room when the Subordinate stopped. "Would you like something to eat? There is plenty."

"Thank you," Arhus said with a short head bow, "but I made sure I ate this morning before I came and it's a bit soon for the mid-day meal."

"Because your blood is weak." It was a statement and not a question.

How the heck... Arhus hid his feelings. "Yes, I must make sure I eat at regular times."

As their walk resumed, Arhus decided to dare to ask a question. "It was because of my blood condition that I was surprised you took an interest in me. All the other guests that we know of have no bodily weaknesses at all."

"Your condition could be healed. It was because of your keen mind that we thought to invite you."

Healed! "This healing would be one technology we would be very interested in having."

Another pause as they continued until they were in the corridor.

"We will consider this."

"Thank you for taking so much time to talk to me," Arhus said as they walked the corridor.

"We enjoy talking to you. You are more settled than many and yet are keen of mind, an interesting conversation at all times."

"That is very kind of you to say so." Arhus could feel the weight of the genuine compliment as he replied. *If I report that statement to Montoya, he would want to use it for one of his own purposes.*

"There is a woman I know who holds a very high office. She would very much like to talk to you about religious matters, if you were willing. She has questions that I am sure are on many people's minds." Trying to stay calm and even, Arhus made a conscious effort to continue to match the walking pace of the Subordinate, not conveying any anxiety over the question.

"We are not interested in religious constructs created by people or their forms of worship. While in the past it has been useful to bring order and instruction to human society, we feel that they are no longer needed for its development. If some wish to continue with the forms, so be it, but they do not make us more favourable to them than others."

"Some people are very comforted by those forms and structures."

"Then we are happy they have them. All instruction was given to mould people into what they have become. We know that many feel reassured in the familiar. We are glad they have the comfort."

They were now near the entrance. The bright light engulfed them, though it was not as harsh as when seen from the other side. The time to get through the light barrier also seemed faster, but Arhus figured that was because it was directional. As they walked down the ramp, a man was walking up, ignoring the Subordinate and Arhus as he did so. Arhus looked into his eyes, which seemed to be focused on something far away inside the ship. When they had passed the guards, the Subordinate stopped. Arhus turned and bowed.

"Thank you again for your time," Arhus said.

"You are welcome back at any time," the Subordinate said, making a smaller bow.

Arhus turned and walked out of the compound, passing several more invitees on the way. They all had the same far-off look in their eyes after they passed the security gate. *I am sure they made their decision to leave Earth, but what if the decision to change their minds at the last instant has been taken from them? Without being able to prove it one way or the other, the question is moot and no one is going to risk trying to stop someone with the creatures nearby.*

While walking, Arhus pulled up his interface and scrolled through the questions Montoya had given him. "Didn't answer many of these, did he? Not sure there's going to be a point of having the list. Doesn't seem like they want to volunteer any information." Arhus looked up, tilted his head and turned it several times. "The heck with it. Montoya will have to be happy with what he got."

The other side of the gates brought a question to Arhus's mind, causing him to stop and look at those watching the procession. None tried to call out to the people, but waved or stood and cried. Arhus walked over to one of the people crying and tapped her gently on the shoulder.

"Yes?" the woman asked through her tears.

"Do you know someone who went on board?" Arhus asked. "Is that why you are crying?"

"No." The woman shook her head. "I wasn't invited and wish I could go, too."

"Does anyone here know someone who went aboard the ship?" Arhus asked aloud.

"I do," a man said, raising his hand. Arhus walked over to him.

"Did you try to stop them while they were walking to the ship? Did you call to them or anything?" Arhus asked.

"No," the man said, sounding dejected. "We talked about it before she came here. She was determined to go. I just miss her so much and wish she wasn't leaving or I could go with her, but then, she was always better than me."

No one else responded. Looking around with a questioning look on his face, Arhus stared at the crowd. *How can the whole world take the loss of loved ones so easily? Or do the aliens just know who to pick? Did it take ten billion humans to be able to walk off with twenty-five thousand without a fight?*

Disgusted with people, Arhus decided to go straight to Montoya's office and give a verbal report. *The office is far enough that maybe I will calm down by the time I reach it.* Checking his interface, he noted that his time with the Subordinate had not taken that long, maybe half an hour, though it had felt much longer. The crowds were starting to move about town now, the majority coming toward the ship as he went the opposite way. Gawkers or invited, it didn't matter. He was amazed that the presence of the ship still drew so many onlookers.

Maybe it is becoming a tourist attraction, he thought. *A limited time offer, come see the alien ship for yourself! Why bother? The news views show it continually. But then, people do attribute some extra significance to seeing something with their own eyes. At least their eyes aren't vacant like those entering the ship.*

The walk did give him time to clear his head, thinking about what he did and didn't want. He was pretty sure he didn't want to leave Earth with the aliens. He was equally sure he wanted Sindie to stay. Also, he was sure that he wanted nothing further to do with Montoya's little group. They would not be able to understand the coming change, much less get on board with it. Arhus doubted anyone in power in the World Council, the most bureaucratic organization that existed, would be able to adapt and flow with the coming changes. Plus, there was the fact that they might be the targets of the change.

That led him to the question of where he wanted to be when the changes came. It was a complicated question, one that would take much thought. *How long will the transition last? How disrupted will systems like food delivery be?* Arhus wanted to believe the changes would be more about government regulation and how people lived. *How can the world stay so divided knowing that we have been planted here as someone's crop? How can we stay so arrogant knowing that other races are out there with technology that dwarfs ours? How can we not band together knowing others are out there so different from us? Maybe people can not worry if they delude themselves enough, tell themselves they are protected and have nothing to fear. And maybe they will need someone to tell them different.*

The shade of the trees in the park provided a cooling effect on Arhus's mood. The wind rustled the leaves enough to compete with the sound of the people walking below as if demanding to be remembered. Looking at them, Arhus couldn't help but think again that there was much that had been ignored the last few days. It wasn't a pleasant thought and he tried not to dwell on it. He thought about checking the news feeds, but then decided he didn't want to know.

Once in the lift, Arhus was struck by the thought that he had never ridden directly to the one hundred and twentieth floor. Knowing that he should give Montoya a warning that he was coming did not provide any incentive for the action, but the thought of the receptionist catching trouble because he didn't call ahead did. He sent her a quick message that he was coming up and then took his time getting there.

A man was just exiting Montoya's office when Arhus entered. The anxious look on the man's face was countered by the stern look from Montoya insisting that he leave. No words were spoken until the door closed.

"I had the group called, they should be here shortly," Montoya said, moving toward a door that Arhus was sure led to their meeting room.

"I'll report to you and you can decide what to tell them," Arhus replied.

The comment caught Montoya off-guard. He stopped, looked at Arhus, and then sat back down in his chair. Placing his arms on the armrest and bringing his hands up so that his fingertips touched, he looked at Arhus across the top of his fingers. "Fine, as you wish."

"Unless it's not clear, I'm done with your little group. I'm done with politics and people trying to get an advantage over each other." Arhus's voice grew louder as he talked. "Those visitors don't care about us and they don't care about your power struggles. They're not going to show preference to any group and I doubt they will leave us with anything. *We are a farm to them!* Do you hear me? We're wheat to be harvested when ready. In my opinion, you'd be better off figuring out what to do after they leave and everyone starts rioting! Just leave me out of it!"

The man made no attempt to stop Arhus as he turned and stomped out of the room. The thought of taking one of the food or drink baskets ran through Arhus's mind, but it left a bitter taste in his mouth and he dismissed it. Nothing was all he wanted from anything in this room.

If he passed any of the others in Montoya's group on the way to his office, Arhus didn't notice and they didn't say anything to him. *That at least shows they have some sense in them.* It wasn't until he was descending in the lift that his temper and mind cooled. He laughed to himself.

Now I know what they mean about that weight being lifted from your shoulders. After that, I'm pretty sure I won't be invited back or to any other group for that matter. Good riddance to them all.

Looking forward to writing a short, factual report and sending it on its bureaucratic way, he was caught off guard when he walked into a room where everyone was huddled around the large, central viewing screen. The screen showed the docks at Tel-Aviv. A large passenger ship occupied the background and the news eyes were pointed at a man who looked American.

"What's going on?" Arhus asked to the backs of the people he first reached.

"Ship full of American religious fanatics pulled into the harbour under the excuse they were having problems. False, of course." Ayso never took his eyes from the screen.

"What do they want?" Arhus asked, more out of habit than conscious thought.

"What do you think? They want to see God." Ayso scoffed as he spoke.

The view of the man became larger as the camera zoomed. He looked to be fifty, his hair just starting to turn grey. As he spoke, his right hand shot into the air with the unconscious ease of a preacher. His voice was deep and resounding and he wore a two-piece suit that looked last-century. Arhus was sure the look was on purpose, because the suit was neat and pressed and looked new.

"We of the Holy Church of the Messiah have come to behold the return of our Lord and Saviour and beseech Him to take us upon his vessel," the man said, leaning unnecessarily into the camera as one would a mic stand. He was of average height, balding on top, and accumulating the weight that came with age. His voice was clear, though, as a practised orator. "We are not here to create undue trouble, but will exercise our right to assembly where we see fit in an orderly and calm manner, to pray and sing to our God that He might grant us an audience. Our church is the last of the true believers and the whole congregation has sacrificed to allow three thousand of us to be here before our Lord. But we will not forget them either! We will be praying for ourselves and those who had to remain behind, that we might be granted passage onto the vessel here to take the chosen to Paradise."

"Oh my God!" came out of Arhus's mouth unbidden.

"Don't tell me you're one of them," Josef said with a mischievous grin on his face, appearing from among the crowd. "I'm shocked!"

"Be serious," Arhus replied, unable to keep all the disdain from his voice. "This is going to be a nightmare!"

"You think the religious fanatics will take over?" Ayso asked, all seriousness.

"Some might try. I'm sure the Council will try to stop them, but if these are only the first, there won't be anything the Council can do. Even if they don't mess with the guards, just rushing the ship could result in hundreds dead in full global view."

"Would serve them right," came a comment from somewhere.

"It's not whether they deserve it or not. Everything could go to chaos in no time out there. Assuming our visitors don't step in and take control, that is. They seem determined to gather those they want and I doubt they would pause to remove any obstacles, if required."

"You mean like alien martial law?" Josef asked, his voice absent of any of the normal snipe or snark.

"Yes. Then, if the World Council felt compelled to respond..." Arhus let the words drift off. He wasn't alone shivering for a few seconds.

"So what do we do?" Josef asked.

"Do?" Arhus's voice pitched up with the word. He looked at the crowd, all facing him now with the vacant looks of people seeking to be led. *How the hell should I know,* he wanted to yell. *This isn't in my job description! We're translators, not policy makers or law enforcement! What do you expect me to do?*

Staring at the faces, though, he knew he had to say something. The thought of the whole world looking at the news views with the same expression came to Arhus's mind. *No one* knows *what to do. No one has been here before, at least not since ancient Egypt, when godlings ruled people who bent to their every words. But that was so long ago, no one remembers or would be willing to act as a mindless slave. At least not yet, though who knows if it will come to that.*

Arhus cleared his thought and straightened. "For now, we do our jobs. We give no opinions on these fanatics and we stay out of their and security's way. Far away. Hopefully, everything will stay calm. If not, then we change our plans."

People seemed to take comfort in the words. Many nodded their heads and mumbled assent, starting to turn away.

"*And,*" Arhus added, "we keep track of each other! Everyone, have someone else that you stay in contact with at all times and if anyone goes missing, inform me at once! No one slips through the cracks, you hear?"

The statement brought a more vigorous positive response. Arhus was sure that everyone in the office already had someone they kept in contact with, but reinforcing the idea appeared to create unity and security for the group.

"Who made you so smart?" Josef asked, back to his old self as people started to go back to their stations.

"You did," Arhus answered, placing his hand on Josef's shoulder and squeezing.

"Whoa, don't go blaming me for this." Josef smiled as he said it.

At the same time, Sindie walked up to them, her eyes giving Arhus a look that, though it lasted not longer than a blink, sent Josef's head into acting as if he just watched the world's fastest tennis match. A sound like a stifled hiccup came from his lips. Arhus ignored it.

"You two, my office, now. I want to know everything about this church, just in case." As he turned and walked to his office, he listened for anything from Josef, sure a comment was coming. All he could hear was Sindie accessing her interface while she walked, something he wasn't as good at doing. By the time they reached the office, she had the look of someone well informed.

"The Holy Church of the Messiah," she started once in the room, "is based in Kentucky, Owensboro to be exact. Church has some ten thousand members. A little community of their own. The Reverend

Charles Lester Owens, self-proclaimed descendant of the original founders of the town, is the one we saw on the news feed. They call themselves the last true believers in the world."

"Believers in what?" Arhus interrupted.

"The Bible, the Word of God. Old-fashioned stuff, hymns and all," Sindie replied.

"Wow," Josef interjected. "I didn't know they still existed."

"Everything still exists," Arhus said with disdain. "You just don't hear about it anymore because it is so small and the world doesn't care. So they are here because they think the aliens are God."

"It would seem so," Sindie responded. "Reverend Owens has been saying that they fulfill all the prophecies about God but still has some questions that have to be answered, though he doesn't seem to be discouraging anyone from spreading the word either."

"I wonder what High Priestess Annalisa Gideon will say about that," Arhus said in a manner that didn't ask for an answer.

"Nothing good, I expect," Josef said anyway. "In order to get here now, they had to leave pretty soon after our visitors arrived."

"The feeds say that the church took up a special collection to fund those that came, which, by the way, includes children and old people," Sindie said.

"Great," Arhus sighed. "Let's add some helpless victims into the mix, why don't we? All ready-made for a media sensation if anything happens."

"Exactly!" The scorn in Sindie's voice was not hidden. "Manipulators!"

Josef's right eyebrow rose. "You make it sound personal."

"I hate people who use family to manipulate situations. Cowards, all of them."

Arhus was tempted to ask if the feeling came from experience, but stopped and stored it for another time, one with fewer people around. "Where is the city going to put three thousand people on top of all the others that have been arriving?"

"Part of the equipment that the church members brought is tents," Sindie replied. "Plus security is building barracks as fast as possible to hold all the gawkers."

"Well, at least they came prepared. Wonder if there is a tent left to buy in Kentucky." Arhus laughed to himself. His eyes were caught by Josef's expression. "What?"

"About time, I'd say," Josef replied with a small laugh.

"That we got religious fanatics in town?" Arhus asked.

"No!" A smile occupied Josef's face. "You two!"

Exchanging a quick glance, they both looked back at Josef. "What?"

"Oh, please, don't think you can hide it from me." Josef held up his hands. "Don't get me wrong, I have been wondering how long it would take you two to figure it out. And don't act like you don't know what I'm talking about, no way you're hiding it from me."

The last comment caught Arhus with his mouth open before he could say anything. Instead, he took a breath and let it out. Sindie rolled her eyes in a defeated manner.

"I'd appreciate it if you didn't say anything about it to anyone, and I mean *anyone*," Arhus said in a calm voice.

"Hey, far be it from me to get into your personal business," Josef replied, bringing his hands close to his body.

"Since when?" Sindie asked.

"This is different," Josef explained. "Look, I'm happy for you guys. I wondered why this didn't happen a year ago, but it can take time. Of course, it would have been a little less complicated then, but with everything that's happening now, I say go for it."

"I was dating Biel a year ago," Arhus said in minor protest.

"If that's what you call what you were doing," Josef said with a brush of his hand.

Sindie looked at both of them and shrugged. "Anything else you need from me?"

"No, thanks." Arhus's interface beeped at him. Looking down, he found two requests from translation services. He approved and assigned people to the tasks in about ten seconds. Josef was still standing in the office when he finished.

"I would appreciate no jokes or innuendos about Sindie and me, not just in the office," Arhus said to his friend.

"I only kid people when they don't do what I think they should," Josef replied.

"Is that so?" Arhus's head turned downward and his brow

furrowed.

"Hadn't you noticed over all the years?" Josef asked with a smile.

"No, it wasn't obvious at all." Arhus stared at him.

"Fine, fine, no jokes." Josef's head went downward in defeat. "Anything else you need, oh great one?"

"Not that I know, but I'm sure it won't take long. Keep an eye on these Americans for me, will you?"

"Sure thing."

Josef exited the room and Arhus sat down to scan the news feeds about the Holy Church of the Messiah. He found recent sermons by Reverend Owens about the visitors, proclaiming them the most significant event since the death of Christ. On that point, Arhus agreed with him, though he wasn't sure about Owens's version of history. The man liked to hear himself talk, taking twenty minutes to say anything of value. Reading the body language was of more interest. The man strutted, used hand gestures that drew attention to himself, and spoke with personal pronouns.

"One doesn't have to wonder what that guy is all about," Arhus said to himself.

Switching to the current news feeds, Arhus was shown scenes of the Americans disembarking from the ship. Arguments could be seen at different places on the docks, from personal ones to ones with cargo handlers and transport providers.

"What do you expect, showing up unannounced?" he asked the image. Shaking his head, he added, "Nothing good will come of all this."

The camera showing Owens and a small group heading toward Jerusalem in the public transport system seemed significant. Arhus chuckled, assuming that Owens thought himself too important to take care of the details.

"Okay, he could have delegated."

The scene switched to the face of Director Arlan Morresette. *He looks unaffected by the day's events, but then, he is good at that.*

"Sir, what does the arrival of the Americans signify?" a speaker off camera asked.

"Not much," Arlan said, showing no worry. "It's not unexpected that all kinds of religious people would make their way here because of our visitors. The forms that the visitors have taken increased this likelihood. It may be possible that the visitors chose these forms to create such chaos and take our attention off of them and what they are doing here."

A sharp intake of breath was Arhus's response to the statement. "I can't believe he said that! What is he up to?"

Ignoring the news broadcast, Arhus put his elbows on the table and his chin on his fingers. *Montoya's attempt at contact can't be the only one. Surely Arlan has also tried. And my service hasn't been conducive to their advancement either. That must mean he is frustrated and threatened because of his lack of progress. Neither is good, but I can't see how saying so helps his position.*

Arhus's head came up and his eyes went wide. *Unless he is looking for someone to blame for his lack of success!*

The thought wasn't a pleasant one. *The search for the guilty could end up with some strange victims, the least likely being those at the top level who were really to blame.* While unpleasant, Arhus was not worried about himself. *Being a translator has its advantages at times, the chief of those being that you are a conduit, not the action's source. Blaming a translator is risky, requiring the cooperation of other translators, and thus hard to prove. Plus, there is no political advantage to blaming a translator.*

That leaves the target unspecified, at least at the moment. Montoya is the obvious target, but that assumes Morresette knows what I know. Big assumption. But then, I don't know the playing field enough to speculate further.

Which leaves me with one option to follow, Arhus thought, pushing himself away from the table. *Don't worry about it! To hell with the politicians, they can have each other's throats for all I care. I have something else to check on with Johann.*

Chapter Thirteen
Spy Versus Spy

Arhus gave Josef the 'back in a minute' sign as he walked through the office to the lift. Josef rolled his eyes. As he descended, Arhus looked at the road that led to the alien ship, though he knew the Americans would take at least an hour before they got this far, slowed by crowds, news teams, and bureaucrats. He acknowledged the greetings of those who came and went on the lift without registering who they were, an automatic process in the building on a normal day. At the thirty-second floor, he got off and headed straight to Johann's office.

"Anything yet?" he asked as he opened the door.

"What, you expect miracles now?" was the reply from behind the display.

"Yes," Arhus said with a small laugh. "God's in town, we expect no less."

"Then go see him, because I've never promised any."

Arhus walked around the table to stand beside the sitting man. "Do you have any ideas yet?"

"Ideas? Sure," Johann said almost flippantly. "Anything looking like proof? You must be kidding!"

"Right now I'll take ideas." Arhus pulled over a chair and sat down.

"Your idea about sunlight was a good one, but not plausible, though close."

Arhus's head came back a little. "What does that mean?"

Taking his hands away from the display and turning, Johann looked at his friend. "What if they are not using sunlight as a carrier wave, what if they are using it to mask the signal?"

"Mask the signal? So telepathy is similar to sunlight?"

"What if it is close enough that it can get lost in the sunlight, at least near the source? What we need is to search for it on the other side of the world." Johann waved his hands in a half-circle.

"How does that help?"

Chuckling, Johann responded, "There's no sunlight on the other side of the Earth and everyone hears their words at the same time, though there is a very slight time delay, if you look for it."

"Oh, yeah, forgot about that." Arhus thought for a second. "But won't the signal be strong enough for us to notice, then?"

"Sunlight is a relatively 'weak' signal, as communications go. But if it's dark enough, you don't need half a million joules to see it from one horizon to another."

"True. Then why bother hiding it?"

"Because they would expect us to look for it! What advanced-technology culture wouldn't? Thus they need a way to hide it for as long as possible. At least until some clever guy figures out what they are doing." Johann beamed.

"Then it's good I know a clever guy," Arhus said with an exhaling breath.

"I was talking about you, dummy." Johann punched Arhus in the shoulder.

"Me?"

"Yeah, you. Without your initial idea, I wouldn't have even thought to look. Sometimes the concept is the hardest part. After that, it's just engineering."

"Which I will admit knowing nothing about. Guess I should leave you to it. Unless you want lunch, that is?" Arhus stood up from the chair.

"Food? Do you remember anything from college?"

Arhus laughed. "Yes, I do. Just didn't know if you still ate like a horse or not."

Johann stood up. "I didn't shrink, did I?"

The two friends made their way to the cafeteria. True to his word, Johann's appetite had not slacked since college, though Arhus's had. Letting his friend eat, Arhus let work conversations lie until dessert.

"So," Arhus said in what he hoped was a light tone, "how long do you think it will take to check this brainstorm of an idea of yours?"

"How should I know?" Johann replied, moving his shoulders down to emphasize the statement. "We're in new territory here."

"Let me put it another way," Arhus said, cocking his shoulders to one side. "How many more lunches at my expense is it going to take?"

Snorting so hard he almost snorted food, Johann forced himself to swallow before answering. "Let's just say the more you buy me, the greater the chance of getting an answer you like at one of them."

Arhus stared for a moment before saying, "Really?"

"Yes," Johann said, "it's a mathematical certainty." After a pause by both men, he added, "I didn't say buying me lunch would help, just increase the chance of you hearing good news. It does make a nice time to talk about it."

"No holding out on me," Arhus said, pointing a finger. "As soon as you think you know something, I want to hear."

Johann looked up in surprise. "You think I would be able to keep it to myself?"

"Just be careful who you share it with." Arhus withdrew his hand. "I'm not sure everyone would like others hearing about it."

"Politics?"

"Or worse." Arhus went back to his dessert.

"That bad?" The thought caused Johann to put down his fork.

"Could be. I don't think people are going to get what they want from our visitors. Tapping into conversations could be a very big advantage if no one else can."

"You think it will make a difference?" Johann looked confused.

"No, but others might not think that way," Arhus said into his plate.

"Oh, got ya. I never made a point of following politics. Don't you think it could get dangerous around here with all the in-fighting?"

"It's not the in-fighting I'm worried about, it's the out-fighting."

"Out-fighting?"

"Riots, power-grabs through use of force, and so on."

"You think it could get that bad?"

"Yes," Arhus said, staring into Johann's eyes, "in a heart-beat."

"Then we geek-moles will keep our heads down, way down."

"Not a bad idea, even after our visitors leave. Especially after they leave."

Johann went back to his dessert, but without the previous gusto. "Where's all that optimism you had in college?"

"Beat down by the real world, I hate to say. I am a pragmatist now."

"It's because you didn't have a good woman," Johann tossed the comment over his shoulder.

"Thank you for bringing up old sores," Arhus groaned.

"It's true. One of the most important things a woman does for a guy is to keep him from being a grouch."

"I'll work on it when I get time," Arhus said, standing up and grabbing his plate. "Gotta go, a department to run."

"Right! I heard! Congrats!" Johann gave him a big smile.

"Let's hope so," Arhus said as he lifted the tray. "Let's hope we all have jobs a few months from now. Later."

After depositing the tray, Arhus went back to his office. Once again his interface, which he had turned off for lunch, held several requests for him to process. Once done, he turned on the news feed. Not to be disappointed, an image of Reverend Owens filled the screen, but instead of talking to the camera, he was talking to a security officer.

"We are a peaceful group who wish to stand on your perimeter," said as 'pee-rim-a-tor,' "and beseech those inside that there ship to address our requests. We only ask for a small space to do that from."

"Sir, all allocated spaces are occupied," the guard responded.

"As I look around this ship, I see plenty of space not occupied by people." Owens waved his hand as he spoke.

"Sir, not all the space around the ship has been allocated for spectators."

"We are the *only*, and I repeat *only*, American delegation in this country!" Arhus noted a particular cadence that separated syllables in words as if they were different words, like 're-peat,' and wondered if it came from being a preacher. "We have just as much right to stand in front of this ship as anyone else. And if we don't get to do just that, our American diplomats will hear about it. And let me tell you this, they will not be happy about fellow Americans being excluded from this auspicious event!"

The security guard looked flustered. *I'm sure this is not the first time this same conversation has occurred, but Owens is brash enough to make good on his threat. Plus, he has a point. No one country or small group of countries could be allowed 'access' to the ship without brewing trouble, and America is an influential part of the world to exclude. If Owens makes a fuss, it would fan a fire of political activity that security would like to avoid.*

"Let me see what I can do, sir," the guard said and then turned to speak into his interface. Owens held a smug expression on his face, shaking his head up and down and turning back and forth as he did. Appearing to say a cheerful word to the small group of people who had come with him, he looked like a man who was sure he would get his way.

"You have no idea what you might have just started," Arhus said out loud.

As he finished the statement, Sindie walked through the door to the office. "You're watching what's happening, right?"

"Just turned it on a few minutes ago, but I caught the important part, I think," Arhus responded.

"Does that jackass know what he is starting?" Sindie's voice went higher than normal.

"No, I'm sure he doesn't and won't care, if he could even contemplate it." Arhus shook his head.

"Every country will start a mad rush to get their slice of 'alien-front' property. The discussions will last weeks, if the ship is around that long. Even then, half of them will sell it off to the highest bidder after they get it." Sindie's arms flapped up and down as she paced.

"None of which is our concern," Arhus said in a even voice as he turned off the news feed.

Sindie stopped and let her head and arms droop. "I know, I just hate to see this town turn into a market of hucksters. Next thing you know, we'll have souvenir salesmen on the street selling little space ships and statues of God."

"I doubt it," Arhus said, dismissing the comment. "They could never afford the permits. Also, by the time the paperwork got approved, our visitors will be gone."

That brought a laugh from Sindie. She shook her head. "Always a bright side to bureaucracy."

"It has its uses." Arhus smiled as Sindie looked at him. "Something else on your mind?"

A wry smile passed across Sindie's face before disappearing. "You're still disappearing quite a bit. Anything you want to tell?"

"Only if a crazy idea shows any sign of being true." Arhus crossed his arms on his chest.

"Such as?"

"Such as I'll tell you if it doesn't look crazy anymore."

"You're no fun," Sindie huffed.

"I will not be responsible for starting unfounded rumours." Arhus let the statement stand for a few seconds, then added, "That's Josef's job."

"Does he get paid extra for that?" Sindie flipped her finger around while asking.

"No, he does it for free. Now go, I have a report to write." Arhus made waving motions with his fingers.

"Yes, *boss*." Sindie scowled as she turned and left.

The report was accurate and succinct without opinion or conclusions. It was the most basic report that Arhus had written since his first year. While it met the requirements for the report, he knew that those who read it would wish for far more. Once done, the report was sent to the official channels, which did not include Montoya's office. That meant a delay, but again, not something an official could complain about. He had done it according to procedure with no preferential treatment.

Sending the report felt like closing a book or finishing a part of his life. Arhus felt like blowing a horn or throwing a party after it was sent. *It's too much to hope that it will signal an end to my involvement with the politicians, but from this point on, my involvement will be by established processes, which means slow. Slow don't bother me at all.*

His interface beeped at him again. Sighing, he thought that he was discovering that the life of a supervisor filled his mind in an unpleasant way. It wasn't the difficulty, it was the constant interruption. He made a mental note to leave work on time and to turn off the interface when he did.

"No way this thing is going to run my life," he told himself.

Standing, Arhus walked out of the office. He crossed the common room, waving to those who acknowledged him and speaking a few words with some. The central display still showed the Americans near the ship site. Reverend Owens looked to be laying out plans for the place, waving his arms and talking to his people. In the background, Arhus could see that the construction of housing units was proceeding at a fast rate. There was even a large tent with the people exiting holding food.

"Not a bad idea, though I doubt the restaurants are happy about it," he said out loud.

"About what?" Eymen asked.

"The food tent," Arhus replied, pointing.

"Better than people starving," was Eymen's reply.

"Very true." Arhus nodded.

"You off somewhere?" Eymen asked. "Meeting or something?"

"No, just wanted some fresh air. Too much happens for one day anymore."

"Tell me about it. And with these Americans, work will get busier." Eymen shook his head while he talked.

"Job security," Arhus chuckled.

"Pain in the you-know-where if you ask me," Eymen countered.

"True. Be back in a few." Arhus started toward the lift. "Don't let the world fall apart while I'm gone."

"That's not my responsibility!" Eymen protested.

"Just handed you the assignment. If you get in over your head, talk to Josef."

"Oh, thanks, I feel soooo much better already."

*   *   *

Sitting on a bench under a tree, Arhus found that he could do his work just as effectively as in his office. *That might explain why Rossarro was never around,* he thought. The fact that he didn't want to drag himself away from the park also helped make the decision, resulting in his abandonment of the office that afternoon.

As the building shadows got longer, people came outside in greater and greater numbers, walking to other parts of town. No one seemed to be in a hurry and most talked to each other in groups of two or three. Arhus guessed he knew what about, even though he hadn't checked the news feeds since sitting on the bench. When traffic started to get heavy, he noted Sindie exiting their building. She looked around, spotted him, and walked his direction in a casual manner. Reaching the bench, she sat down next to him, but not too close.

"Disappearing again, I see," she said without looking at him.

"World looks a lot better out here," he replied.

"Getting tired of us already?" she asked in a mocking tone.

"No, just the world in general."

"Well," Sindie said with an exhale, "it is the end of the day. You could go out, get something to eat, get a little drunk, and then go home and enjoy the evening."

Arhus chuckled. "Is that what you would recommend?"

"You look like you need it." She still hadn't looked at him.

"Think I should call someone, ask them if they want to go along?"

Sindie turned to look at him. With a slight furrow to her brow, she said, "No. Not unless you are planning on doing it all by yourself."

Chapter Fourteen
And Then the Real Fun Started

The next day, Arhus saw the change even when walking to work. Groups of people made their way toward the visitors' ship. People talked in hushed and not so hushed tones. News crews roamed the streets and walkways. Entering the office area did not rid him of the presence of chaos, just reduced the level. The news report on the large central screen was divided into four sections, showing multiple interviews of different groups. One person had a hat made to look like the alien ship, which brought a disgusted laugh from Arhus.

"The crazies are out today," he said out loud.

"Them and everyone else," Josef said as he walked up from the side.

"You're here earlier than normal," Arhus commented to his friend. The office was half full at best.

"Didn't want to miss the circus come to town." Josef smiled with the comment.

"You never were one to miss a show." Arhus turned back to the screen.

"All the delegates are in session upstairs, too. And," Josef said with emphasis, "we were not invited."

"Too important for even translators."

"Yeah, we might have an opinion, I guess."

Arhus felt the stare from Josef with the comment. He tried not to turn to face his friend but lost the battle. "You implying something?"

"It was your comment that got you involved in the politics of the situation in the first place," Josef said with a shrug.

"I thought I was doing my job."

"And now you have a new one. Like they say, no good deed goes unpunished." Josef continued smiling.

"You think the promotion was a punishment?"

"Aren't they always? You do a good job and they give you more responsibility. Sounds like a punishment to me." Josef tuned back to the screen.

"I'll remember that next time I want to punish you." The comment hung for a while before getting a response.

"And here I thought I was just talking to my friend."

"Just taking your advice," Arhus said with a smile of his own.

"Now you start?"

On the screen, most of the interviewees appeared angry. Loud voices, pointing figures, and waving hands were commonplace. Signs could be seen in the background, the programmable holographic kind. Arhus took comfort in the fact that they were too fragile to use as a weapon. Most had slogans like 'Give Us Our Space' or 'We Deserve Access Too!' He wondered what the signs had read yesterday.

"Any violence yet?" Arhus asked Josef.

"Not that I've seen or heard, but it's only a matter of time. That's if people remember how to be violent," Josef said with a laugh.

"What does that mean?" Arhus asked with a tilted head.

"When was the last time we had a real riot in any except the closed countries? How about an angry protest or even a sit-in, whatever those were?"

"Hmmm," Arhus said as he thought. Josef gave him a few seconds.

"I'll take your silence as a failure to think of one," Josef said. "Sure, there's been a few bar scuffles, but society hasn't seen real violence since the last so-called war and most of that was edited for viewing so people didn't get ideas. Where's the 'We Shall Overcome' or 'Freedom or Death' signs? People would never think of expressing such ideas. I can see why the aliens waited until now to show up. People don't have the stomach for real fighting anymore. Look how they walk into that ship like sheep."

Arhus turned. "You study all this in college or something?"

"You think they have classes on forming protests?" Josef asked incredulously. "Heck no, I did my own research. Don't you remember 'The Rebels' group I formed in school?"

"I thought that was a band."

"See," Josef said with a huff, "my point exactly."

"So all this doesn't worry you?" Arhus asked, waving at the display.

"Worry me? You bet it does!"

Lost for words, Arhus stared at his friend. His brain would not process that. He managed to say, "What?"

Josef turned his direction. "People don't know how to be violent anymore. If they try, who knows what they might do? Intentional destruction is one thing, but random destruction can have terrible consequences."

"I see your point." Arhus nodded his head. "So, should we teach people how to be violent? I think there's not much competition in that market."

"I'm sure the World Council would take a dim view of me starting that business."

"They could be your first target," Arhus encouraged.

"Sounds like a short career to me."

Interface beeping, Arhus looked at his wrist. "Guess I have some kind of staff meeting in a few. Think they'd miss me if I didn't go?"

"I don't want to take the chance," Josef said.

"You take the chance?"

"Yeah, if you screw up, then who knows who we'll get as a supervisor?" Josef gave him a cheesy smile.

"Your concern for me is touching," Arhus said back, deadpan. "I'll be back."

Arhus walked to the lift and waited. Sindie came up with the lift. "Where you off to now, Houdini?" she asked.

"Staff meeting," he replied with a small sigh.

"Don't enjoy it too much, you might turn into a real manager," she said as she stepped off the lift and walked into the room.

Turning back toward the room after he entered, he replied, "Don't think you have much to worry about there."

As the lift doors closed, Arhus said, "Seventy-five." Instead of going down, the lift went up a few floors and stopped. A man and a woman entered the lift after the doors opened and asked for the same floor. This time the lift went down.

"You weren't going up, were you?" the woman asked, slight confusion showing on her face.

"No, wasn't watching the direction when I got on," Arhus responded.

"Gets there eventually," the man added.

The woman looked at the display. "You going to seventy-five also? That's a coincidence."

"Staff meeting," Arhus said without emotion.

"I haven't seen you before, which department do you supervise?" the woman asked, turning his direction.

"Translation."

"Oh! You're the new guy! Took over for what's-his-face." The woman got more animated as she talked.

"Rossarro," Arhus offered.

"Yeah, him. Never saw him much. Not sure what he was about doing all the time. I'm Quita Sholls." She stuck out her hand.

"Arhus Gint." Arhus shook her hand. Her handshake was just long enough and just firm enough to signal meeting a equal.

"Where were you before they saddled you with the translators?" Quita asked.

"Translation," Arhus replied, keeping his voice neutral.

"Oh." The woman looked embarrassed, but hid it well. "So they moved you up? That's unusual."

"Guess we're too much of a problem to saddle anyone else with." Arhus gave the woman a small smile with the comment. Her shoulders eased.

"Anyone can be a pain in the butt," the man interjected, "just a different pain."

"Wait," the woman said, pointing. The lift came to a halt. "I recognize your face from somewhere."

"I hope not," Arhus replied. That brought a laugh from the man as he exited the lift. Arhus let the woman go first before following.

"No, I'm sure I've seen your face before, I know it," the woman insisted.

"The ten most wanted?" the man offered.

"Darn," Arhus said in an even voice, "you figured it out."

The comment brought another laugh from the man. The woman gave him a stare like she would have liked to hit him. "I'll figure it out," she said.

The conference room was a short distance away. The room was almost full by the time they arrived and the last attendees were not far behind, except for one that was ten minutes late. Arhus recognized the woman in front, Fran Diepner, an administration bureaucrat he had done some work for about a year ago. He remembered her being unimaginative and by-the-book, perfect for conducting boring meetings.

"Thank you all for coming," Ms. Diepner started, though she didn't sound like she meant it. "I see our newest addition is attending. At least he is not following in the footsteps of his predecessor. Arhus Gint, please stand and give everyone a wave."

Arhus complied.

"I'll let you make your own introductions. Straight to the agenda."

The meeting that followed was not too different from some where he had provided live translation in the past. At least he was practised at not falling asleep. In his estimation, ninety percent of the material could have been sent to his interface. The last ten percent needed a lot more discussion than was allowed during the meeting, leaving Arhus to wonder how it got done or if the administrative types even wanted them discussing it. No word was made of the on-going negotiations about access to the ship and he was sure Ms. Diepner would be the wrong person to ask.

The meeting was closed an hour and a half after it started. Arhus was impressed by Ms. Diepner's precision in the matter. Not anxious to be recognized and asked questions, Arhus remained in his seat at the edge of the room while others stood and exited, some slow and some with purpose. While they did, he took inventory of who he knew, all of which ended up being first or second level supervision. *A trickle-down meeting,* he thought. *No wonder Rossarro hated it.*

Most of the people were closer to the doors than him when Quita showed up again.

"Now I remember you," she said. "I saw you on the news reports, out by the alien ship, right?"

"Yes, but please don't make a big deal about it," he replied.

"Oh my gosh! What happened? You had a chance! You do something wrong?" The words came faster and louder than Arhus would have liked. He sighed and hoped people didn't notice.

"Turns out they don't want to talk to us," he replied.

"That's a shame. You could have used that to ride up to the top, in the organization and the media." The woman nodded her head while she talked.

"If the opportunity shows up again, I'll give them your name." Arhus stood and looked for the fastest exit from the room.

"You can't mean that! People here would kill for the opportunity!" The woman's eyes went wide.

"That's one of the problems. Excuse me." Arhus slid past the woman and walked with intent to an open doorway. No one else tried to stop him or talk to him but he was sure word would get around. *It doesn't matter,* he told himself. *It will happen sooner or later. Better to get it over with, I guess.*

The lift had a waiting line so Arhus tried to stand unnoticed in the back. It was in vain. A man walked up to him and held out his hand.

"Mr. Gint, glad to see you again," the man said.

Arhus turned, but recognition took a few seconds. "Don, right?"

"Yes. I am surprised you remember me with all the people you meet. I see you've moved up." Don pumped his hand several times before letting go.

Arhus went over the information in his mind. Don was in the HR department, Human Resources, which used translation services extensively. That did not surprise him. Several months ago Arhus had 'graduated' out of HR work, so he hadn't seen Don for a while.

"Thanks. Still trying to figure out if that's good or not." Both men chuckled at the statement. "How you been?"

"Working, just like always. Well, at least until you know what," he said with a shake of his head toward the outside of the building.

"Yeah, I'm sure everyone is that way. Has your department been affected?"

"It sure has." Don rolled his eyes. "Everyone wants to come for an interview from around the world but no one seems to want a job, if you understand what I mean."

Arhus shook his head. "They see you as a free ride to see the aliens."

"Makes doing the job hard." Don looked at the lifts, but the number of people was thinning.

"I can imagine. We've been getting all sorts of strange requests. People asking questions to which they should already know the answer." The front of one of the lifts emptied and Arhus gestured with his hand toward it. Both men walked that direction.

"Everyone has similar problems," Don said as he walked. "By the way, I think I saw you on the news reels. What's happening with the aliens?"

"Nothing." The men entered the lift and asked for their floors. "Turns out the aliens aren't interested in talking, so there's not much to translate."

"But still, you must know something. What do they want with us?"

A small amount of desperation showed in Don's voice. *A lot of people, if not most, must be feeling the same. The unknown breeds fear,* Arhus thought, *and fear fuels the imagination. And the imagination can be very imaginative.*

"They want some of us, about twenty-five thousand at last estimate."

"They want people? Why?"

How to explain this? Let me count the ways. Paranoid, comforting, non-committal? Spreading fear might get me targeted by those in charge and possibly cause panic. Better to give something without the scare factor.

"I think they waited until we were ready for visits from off-world aliens and space travel."

"People have been talking about that for, well, forever, it seems."

"Yes, but was the world ready for it?"

The statement caused Don to pause, long enough that the lift was reaching Arhus's floor. "This is my stop," Arhus said.

"Well, take care. And stay safe out there." Don shook his hand one more time.

"You too. See you next meeting."

"If I can stay awake," Don joked, laughing at his own statement. Arhus chuckled politely in response before getting off.

The common room buzzed with its normal activity. His scheduled meeting past, Arhus's interface started beeping again. Taking a deep breath, he stood still while he addressed each item. Several were from administrators that must be in the high-level meeting about alien access, making him wonder how many support people they had taken with them. Processing the requests, he walked over to where Sindie was seated. He waited until she was finished with the request on her interface display before speaking.

"Can I see you in my office, please?" he whispered just loud enough for her to hear before walking to his office without looking to see if she followed.

Arhus had enough time to sit behind his desk and pull up his display before Sindie walked in. "Shut the door," Arhus said without looking up.

"What's up?" Sindie asked.

"We're getting quite a few requests from people who should be too busy doing something else," he started.

"You mean the secret meeting to allocate alien ship access space?" Sindie asked.

Arhus looked up, but then huffed. "Yes, that meeting."

"So what's the issue?" Sindie sat down in one of the chairs on the other side of the desk.

"I want to find out where the meeting is, based on an estimate of the number of people and the security needs."

A smile spread over Sindie's face. "I'm not sure if this is just curiosity, but I like this side of you. And you want me to set up a program to find the meeting room?"

"Yes, but don't tell anyone you're doing it."

"Oh, sure, my lips are sealed." Sindie passed her pinched fingers across her mouth. "Just curious, why are we doing this?"

"Let's just say I have a bad feeling about the whole thing and I don't like being surprised."

"Works for me," Sindie said, sitting up straighter. "How many people you figure we're talking about?"

"I'm still calculating." Arhus thought for a minute. "Maybe sixty."

"Right. One secret room for sixty coming up. Anything else?"

"Start on the top floors and work your way down, unless you know of any secret rooms somewhere else?"

"For two, yes, but not for sixty," Sindie said with a smile as she stood. "But those can wait. Get back with you as soon as I have something."

"Thanks." Arhus's interface beeped again. Instead of smashing it, which was his first impulse, he pulled up the item.

When he was finished, a thought came to him. Talking to the interface, he asked, "Can I set up automatic assignments that I don't have to approve every time?"

"Of course," the device said back.

"Great! Let's do that." He spent the next ten minutes making automatic allocations with primary, secondary, and in some cases tertiary assignments. The interface would not allow him to allocate everything automatically, but he estimated that his work load should decrease significantly.

As he leaned back in the chair, Arhus felt comfortable in his job for the first time. *What other effort-saving tips has no one told me about?* He asked the interface if there was a time-saving guide for supervisors. Even though he asked the question several ways, it provided nothing. The last resort was to pull up the official description of his job duties and try to figure out something from there. Many of his job title's tasks ended with the wording 'when requested,' which he took to mean whenever his boss wanted to dump work onto him. *I bet those can't be delegated.*

With his life simplified as much as he could arrange, Arhus pushed away from the desk and went into the common area. A buzz of conversation circulated in the room and most people were talking to each other. Arhus walked over to Josef.

"What's going on?"

"The great debate is starting soon," Josef replied.

"What great debate?" Arhus noted a bag of snacks and a drink on the table in front of Josef.

"If our visitors are God or not."

"I didn't know that was a debate." Looking around the room,

Arhus noticed that others seemed be settling in as for a show.

"I'm sure our American travellers prompted the issue. Mr. Owens's declaration that the visitor is God has caused quite a stir. I think he is just playing a political angle. But, I could be wrong." Josef gave Arhus a cheesy smile. "Pull up a chair, this should be good."

Arhus pulled over a chair. "Who's in the debate?"

"Well, Reverend Owens wasn't invited, which I am sure he'll have something to say about. There's High Priest Annalisa Gideon, Sans Marell from the Neo-Utilitarians, Qui Boi for the Buddhist, and some joker named A Then. No idea who he is."

Annalisa was dressed in her formal robes. Sans Marell was an Asian with deep, sun-browned skin and Persian features. He wore a contemporary business suit, tan in colour. Qui Boi was dressed in the traditional Buddhist white robe. Short with a rounded, bald head, Mr. Boi looked the picture of his religion. A Then, in contrast, was dressed in a relaxed, almost party style with a collarless shirt, creased but not pressed pants, and causal shoes. Then looked to be about thirty and had barely-controlled blond hair, blue eyes, and one of those infectious smiles that caused instant trust in people.

"A Then? The fanatic?" Arhus's voice cracked as he sat down.

"You know him?" Josef perked up.

"Yeah, met him once. His real name is Nick Sanders. He was a low level con man before he started this religion stuff. Probably still is. You know the type; dedicate yourself enough to God and he will fulfill all your dreams."

"Which involves lots of money, right?" Josef said with an eye roll.

"Funny how it always works that way, isn't it? I thought he was working the American circuit, trying to branch out. I'm surprised they let him in the debate."

"I bet he headed here as soon as the ship arrived. Maybe the broadcasters just want a lively debate. Ratings, you know."

"They'd get ratings no matter who they put on." The central display changed to the view of a large room. A woman stood in the centre of the view, talking about the event to come.

"I'm disappointed there's no representative from Virtuism," Arhus commented.

"It's not a real religion, more of a club," Josef said. "Moral code without a higher power telling you what to do is not a religion."

"Belief is considered a virtue."

"Yes, but their belief is generalized and they don't believe in God. Not much point having them in the debate then."

"Neo-Utilitarianism doesn't profess a belief in God," Arhus countered.

"A formal belief, no. Some of their members believe in God and they allow it. In fact, their members pretty much believe whatever they want. It's what you get with one of those be-true-to-your-own-self idea systems. Thus some believe in God and some don't. Virtuism only pushes the practice of positive virtues, ergo more of a club."

"Still seems like discrimination to me."

"So says the Virtuist."

"Damn right. Looks like they are going to start."

"Bring in the clowns," Josef cheered.

The scene of the news mouth-piece was replaced with five individuals seated in a semi-circle. Behind them was a glass wall with mountains in the background that Arhus was sure were fake. All participants were sitting, even A Then, to Arhus's surprise. A man at one end of the seats held a small interface screen in both hands. He was the first one to talk.

"Good evening. I am Saul Toch. I will be moderating this evening's discussion, entitled 'Our Visitors and God.' Tonight we have the following with us." Saul made introductions, which included about a minute of titles or background for each individual. Arhus wondered if he had done his own research or the spiels had been provided by each guest. A Then's was the shortest, but Saul did a good job of keeping the same tone as he did when introducing the others.

"The format for tonight's discussion will be as follows. I will ask a question. Each of our guests will be given thirty seconds to answer. They must answer the question given to them. If they do not or go over their times, their microphone will be turned off. Anyone who interrupts another individual will be given one warning. The second time, they will be escorted off the stage. Anyone who participates in argument will be escorted off the stage. This is meant to be a civil discussion. All participants have agreed to these conditions."

"Under threat of the World Council, I am sure," Josef added under his breath. "So much for heated debate."

"Let us begin." Saul shifted in his chair toward the others. "The first question is the one that I am sure is burning in everyone's mind. Do you consider our visitors to be what mankind has traditionally defined as God? Mr. Marell."

"What, no definition of God first?" Arhus's voice dripped with sarcasm.

"You did want to hear them answer *this* question *today*, didn't you?" Josef countered.

Mr. Marell cleared his thought and talked at a calm pace. "The question if the entity that has appeared in its floating chair is God can only be answered by each person themselves. If this entity is God to you, then it is God, at least in your experience. Over human history, objects of much lower statue have been considered gods by humans. What each person has to determine is what they have dedicated their life to and if this entity fulfills that purpose in their life. If it does not, then it is not God to them. If it does, then they can call it 'God' or 'their god' as they please. The individual's search is what is important, the journey and not the end goal. How we conduct that search and what we dedicate our lives to during that search will define us as a person and lead each of us to our afterwards."

"Thank you, Mr. Marell." Saul took a breath. "Ms. Gideon."

"Of course it is not God!" Annalisa dove into the conversation like an eager boxer in the first round. "Just because they pretend to take the forms that are familiar to our scriptures does not make them God, it makes them con artists. Obviously they are more advanced in science than we are, but science is not godhood or spiritual power. These entities people are calling 'angels' may not even have a physical form, but are merely projections or images. We should not let ourselves be deceived! On top of that, at no times have these aliens claimed to be God! If God appeared, don't you think He would claim to be Himself? The whole discussion is preposterous."

The moderator looked as if he had not expected such a vigorous response, his eyebrows flaring up for a moment. He waited a few more seconds after Annalisa was finished than he had after Marell. He looked like he expected a storm to break open. When nothing else happened, he spoke again.

"Mr. Boi."

Boi gave a wide grin. He talked in a slow, modest voice. "If this individual has obtained perfection, then he is to be congratulated. He could serve as another example of what we all may obtain to become one day. I have not had the pleasure of talking with our visitor, so I cannot evaluate his personal perspective on the universe. I would welcome such an opportunity. It would be most interesting to see how the four truths and path of liberation translate into his culture. We may be able to learn much from each other and our own perspectives. There does seem to be a tone of violence in his demeanour, which casts some doubts on the attainment of perfection. But then, I am looking from a human perspective."

"Thank you," Saul said. "Mr. Then."

"Since the World Council has not deigned to share any information about the visitors with us, and since our visitors have also declined to share any information of an evaluative nature, I have to state at this moment that there is no proof that they are God: the visitors or the World Council." The comment brought laughs from those in the room. "There are some very curious traits that our visitors show, such as communicating with the whole world simultaneously, but none of these can't be explained through advanced technology. The real deciding factor will be when they come down to Earth and teach us what they stand for and who they believe *we* are. Of course, it will also be instructive who they choose to be their representatives here on Earth. Will they be common people, like Christ chose, or will they be the established religions with their existing political interests? I await the announcement."

"Talk about non-answers," Arhus commented, leaning toward Josef.

"You don't want to commit too soon," Josef answered. "You might leave an opening for the other guys."

"Thank you all," Saul said. "Now for some more specific questions. Mr. Marell, your... organization... doesn't believe in a God. What would it take for you to believe that our visitors *are* God?"

"I speak only for myself," Marell started, "but the traditional view of God is that He is able to do miracles. I am speaking of true miracles."

"Such as?" Saul interjected.

"One example, which is a significant one for me, is that if these visitors were truly God, why would they need a spaceship?"

"Bravo!" Annalisa said with a shout. The moderator gave her a look, but when she said no more, he ignored the interruption.

"It is true that the document called by some the Scriptures does not state how He would return to gather his people, but I see no mention of a spaceship and cannot imagine why He would need one. Won't God be able to come to Earth by Himself and transport His people to His home, heaven I assume, without one?"

Arhus could see A Then fidgeting in his seat, as if struggling to contain himself. The moderator must have noticed it also.

"Thank you. Mr. Then, you are known to disagree with these arguments. Do you wish to comment?"

"Thank you," Then responded without hesitation. "First, we must not conform God to our way of thinking. Maybe he brought a ship to make us more comfortable with the idea of going somewhere other than Earth. People no longer believe in mysticism, and others just disappearing into thin air could be very disturbing to them. Their loved ones getting on a spaceship and leaving the Earth would cause much less worry about their survival through space. Arguments such as these by Mr. Marell are presented by people who already have made up their minds not to believe."

"So are you saying this is God, contrary to your initial statement?" Saul pressed.

"I am not saying that. I am just saying that we must not require God to conform to our logic. We must leave our minds open to understanding ideas other than to which we are accustomed. But that doesn't really address the real issue. If you believe the New Testament, which many spiritual people say they do, then God was on Earth doing miracles before and people still rejected Him. The demonstration of miracles is not what is required for belief."

Arhus's attention was drawn to Annalisa. Her face was tense and her fists were balled tightly together. The stare she gave A Then reminded Arhus of a cocked pistol. He was sure that if she had the power, she would have thrown fire from heaven at that moment. Saul Toch showed his expertise at handling discussion groups by his next question.

"High Priest Annalisa, you represent the most traditional organization here. Would you care to comment?"

"I certainly would," the woman said, turning back to the camera. "The Word of God has been studied by the most capable scholars for thousands of years. These individuals are experts in religion, language, and context. Would God be so vague as to leave us uninformed after such effort? No, He would not! God wants us to know Him. Would He then be so mysterious that we could not recognize Him when He appeared? The notion is absurd. God is our Father and when a father comes home, he announces himself to his children and they recognize him. These visitors, as they are called, have not announced themselves and are not recognized by anyone."

"I think Jesus was pretty clear when he was here," A Then retorted.

"If you believe he *was* the Messiah, which we *don't*. The New Testament even admits there were charlatans!"

"And his miracles?"

"Exaggerations."

"Of course you would say that. And people would again. Does it surprise anyone that if the visitors are the same God mentioned in the Bible that they don't bother to do miracles? We are becoming a faithless Earth. All the religious groups represented here account for maybe ten percent of the world's population."

Arhus waited for the moderator to shut him down, but it didn't happen.

"We are much larger than that," Qui Boi calmly injected.

"I mean *active* followers, not just in name only." Mr. Then's speech was picking up speed like a revving engine. "The children have deserted the house and their father generations ago. How are we supposed to recognize someone we have never met or even thought existed?"

"Not all of us have deserted our Father!" Annalisa stated. "And that's not Him!"

"Mr. Boi," the moderator said, looking away from A Then, "did you wish to comment on this issue?"

"No." Boi's face never changed and his demeanour showed his dedication to the answer.

"Then let's go to our next question," Saul continued without delay. "Mr. Boi, what do you think should be people's response to our visitors at this time?"

"We must wait," Boi said in his slow, deliberate speech. "We do not have enough information to say for sure who or what our visitor is. Such decisions come from interaction, from conversations, from communing with each other. Until such time, all is speculation without meaning. I am sure once our visitors are comfortable with us, they will engage in such conversations."

"Comfortable?" Saul asked.

"Yes. We must not forget that they are not from Earth. Surely we must seem as strange to them as they seem to us. I can only hope that those who have entered the ship are having such conversations that will lead to our visitors engaging as such with those of us who were not invited aboard."

"High Priest Gideon," Saul continued, "you are very connected to the heads of the World Council. What do they say about our visitors?"

Annalisa didn't even blink. "The World Council does not comment on religion."

"Yes," Saul pressed, "but they have to know more than we do."

"I have not been given any information to distribute to the general public, nor am I any part of the decision-making councils. When the World Council has reliable information, I am sure they will pass it along." The woman gave a short nod of her head with the statement.

"A very good non-lie," Arhus responded out loud.

"She's a bureaucrat," Josef added. "What do you expect?"

"See, evasion," A Then piped in. "The World Council is not sharing their information with the public. I have proof that a representative of the Council visited the ship and returned, and yet they provide no information at all about what is going on! Why are they restricting access to the ship? Why won't they let us talk to our visitors?"

"I don't think our visitors want to talk to you!" Annalisa's voice was sharp as she once again gave the man a hard stare.

"Do you know something you are not sharing with us?" Saul asked, emphasizing important words.

Annalisa turned back to the moderator and spoke with an even voice. "I know this. If our visitors wanted to do something, I doubt we could stop them. That, they have demonstrated to the world. If they are not talking to Mr. Then over there, I can only assume they don't have any interest in talking to a charlatan."

The comment brought the first emotional response to the discussion in the room. Some were in support while others were more in anticipation that the discussion would soon become more interesting in the less-polite way.

"Charlatan?" A Then responded in the loudest voice yet of the discussion.

"People! Please!" Saul interrupted in a equally loud voice. "We agreed to keep this discussion civil and avoid name-calling of any type."

"You expect me to let that comment go unanswered?" Then insisted.

"Yes. It is not worthy of comment," Saul affirmed.

Then sat back in a huff, but uttered the word "relic" loud enough to be heard. The word sent emotion across Annalisa's face, but she held her tongue and settled back into her seat.

"We will not discuss your proof," Saul continued. "We are here to discuss the issue of whether our visitors are God or not, and we will stay on that issue. Next question is for all of you, for which I will give each time to respond. If our visitor does prove to be God, what ramifications does that hold for Earth? Mr. Marell?"

"He's going to waste time with such questions?" Arhus said to Josef, ignoring the discussion.

"You think the effect of our visitors being God is insignificant?" Josef asked back.

"I think the ramifications he is looking for are obvious."

"Such as every religion in the world is wrong?" Josef asked the question with a laugh, but Arhus did not follow suit.

"A better question would be, 'How much do our visitors have to disagree with your religion before you say they are not God?'"

"Do you think these guys can even answer that question?"

It was Arhus's turn to laugh. "You miss the point. If our visitors were God, then the answer would be that religions could disagree with all of it and they would still be God. But we are not just fighting religion here, just like Mr. Then said."

"Of course," Josef said with a wave of his hands. "Being designated as the official religion would cement their place in the world, but are they willing to take the chance that they lose out? Be serious! Can you imagine the Hasidic Jews or Buddhists admitting that they had been wrong all this time?"

"No, I can't."

"Me neither."

They both listened to the panellists talk, though they didn't say anything of note. The sound level in the room rose a notch and people were no longer spellbound by the display. The talk in the room stopped when the moderator took over again.

"Thank you all. We are going to take a short break and then return to our questions."

A communal 'aw' went through the room, except for those who laughed. The display changed to a commercial that people ignored.

"A commercial break?" Josef said.

"Hey, these representatives are under a lot of stress," Arhus said in mock seriousness. "They need a break to catch their breath before the next question."

"You mean before they tear out each other's throats?"

"That too."

The program continued for another hour. So did the vague answers and evasions. All agreed that there was not enough information to make a conclusion, leading many in the room to ask why the program was shown in the first place. At the end of the program, Arhus stood up.

"Well, that's an hour and a half of my life I'll never get back," Arhus said as he stretched.

"You're not leaving now?" Josef protested.

"It's over, isn't it?"

"Yes, but you know that our friend Mr. Owens will be on next."

"They announced that?"

"No, but I'd bet my next paycheck we won't have long to wait." A smug smile took over Josef's face.

Arhus stood while the same woman who had started the program talked, not listening to her comments. "I'll never understand why they feel the need to comment on someone else's comments."

"Because we aren't smart enough to figure out what they said," Josef said.

"So we are bad listeners or are they bad communicators?"

"Yes."

As predicted, the scene changed and Reverend Owens appeared. He was standing with the visitors' ship behind him. People were milling about, waving their signs. Arhus could not catch a glimpse of any security forces.

"Reverend Owens," an off-camera voice asked, "how do you feel about not being included in today's discussion about the visitors?"

Owens took a deep breath and raised his right hand. "The people of the Holy Church of the Messiah are *the* true believers of God. We are the only ones who hold to the scriptures as given by our Lord and Saviour. We are the beacon on the hill, the shining light. Our exclusion from this discussion, as they call it, shows their discrimination against Americans and their persecution of the Word of God. But we are not deterred! We will shine forth! We will stand firm in the truth of God. And we will demand our rights as God has given to all human beings. The Council does not matter! Their man-made religions do not matter! All that matters is God's truth and our dedication to it! God will win and we are on his side."

"So are you saying that our visitors are God?"

"The Bible has given us many signs to look for in our search for truth. Our visitors display those signs. Who are we to say that they are not God? Our human unwillingness to accept God's authority prevents us from accepting the truth that God has come to gather us to Himself as He has promised."

A gasp was heard from Josef. "Did he just declare war on the World Council and every other religion in the world?"

"I'm sure it's not the first time," Arhus replied.

"Talk about two big brass ones!"

"I'm sure he expects to get what he wants, so he might as well act like he is in control of the situation, right?"

"Still, that takes guts to mouth off like that." Josef paused for a second. "What if the World Council decides not to give him access based on a criteria, say, they will allow only official government representatives?"

"Then he will either get himself designated as an official representative or he will cry about how the big, bad World Council is oppressing the common man, from every street corner in town."

Josef laughed once. "He would, wouldn't he?"

"People start wars they think they can win. I'm pretty sure Mr. Owens is here for the long haul." Arhus rubbed his hands on his pants. "I, on the other hand, need to eat something."

"Go ahead," Josef replied, appearing to deflate. "I'm not hungry at the moment. Politics upset my stomach."

"Since when?" When no answer came, Arhus said, "Okay. Hold down the fort while I'm gone."

Turning and walking to the lifts, Arhus noted that most people were discussing among themselves instead of attending to their interfaces. *It's to be expected,* he thought. *The discussions will be* the *topic for the rest of the day, if not longer.*

After entering a lift and asking for the twenty-third floor, Sindie popped in before the doors closed. "Where you off to now?" she asked.

"Lunch. You want to join?"

As the lift descended past their floor, Sindie got much closer, a coy smile forming on her face. "I know a secret, out of the way room. You want to have dessert first?"

Arhus looked down into her eyes. "That sounds like a bad habit to start."

"Hey," she replied with a small shrug of her shoulders, "you can't blame a girl for liking her dessert, can you?"

"Didn't you get enough dessert last night to last twenty-four hours at least?"

Sindie turned her head and looked away before looking back. "It's your fault for me liking it so much."

A few seconds passed before Arhus responded. "I take full responsibility. But I still need food for my blood sugar."

"Fine," Sindie said, turning away, but rolling her shoulders as she did so. "If you want to torture yourself until later, I won't stop you."

The lift doors opened and Sindie straightened. Arhus let her walk out first, trying to keep his eyes elevated as she did. He succeeded, at least most of the time.

Around two in the afternoon, Arhus got a summons from Montoya's office. Unable to think of a way to avoid going, he steeled himself the best he could as he made his way there. To his surprise, they met in a different conference room that was laid out with a central table and chairs. The attendees were also greater in number than the previous 'secret' meetings. Taking a seat as far back as he could get, Arhus leaned back and tried to remain inconspicuous. Montoya stood at the far side of the room from the door with his hands clasped behind his back. He began once most of the seats were occupied.

"Thank you all for coming," Montoya began with a greater-than-normal amount of civility. "I am sure by now you have all seen and discussed what was in the news today. The discussion panel has brought up several issues that are drawing significant attention. The one we are here to discuss today is what information on our visitors will be released to the public.

"Now, I know that not all of you have seen the reports and it is intentional that you are here. You are here to represent the public, who also have not seen the reports. Together we will decide, I mean recommend, what should be released and what shouldn't."

"How are we supposed to decide that if we haven't seen the reports?" Being so far back in the crowd, Arhus could not see where the question came from.

"Information will be provided in the meeting and we will discuss if it gets released." Montoya made the comment as if it was obvious.

"But if we don't see the whole report, how do we know if there isn't something that shouldn't be released?"

Arhus marvelled at the moxie of the questioner. *Then again, maybe people aren't as worried about losing their jobs now.* Another thought hit Arhus. *If Montoya is here, does that mean the meeting assigning access space to the ship is over? Or was Montoya not invited?*

"I am going to share all of the information the Council has approved to be shared with you. That doesn't mean that all that information needs to be shared with the public." Montoya turned toward the other side of the room.

"Share it all," Arhus announced, figuring he had nothing to fear from Montoya. Standing for emphasis, he looked straight at Montoya. "The World Council was founded on the principle of open communication after the Nuclear War. Since then, it has withheld more and more information from the public with every year. Now is not the time to be withholding information! The arrival of the visitors is too significant, too world-changing to be seen as secretive. Release all the information. If you don't and the public finds out, they won't care about whatever argument you give them."

"A very noble sentiment," Montoya said with a practised laugh, "but a naive one."

"And if the aliens' visit doesn't end up being so noble? Who do you think the public is going to take it out on?"

The comment caused a stir in the room. People leaned toward each other while others stared at Arhus. Montoya's expression was not pleasant. Arhus thought Montoya was doing a good job of restraining himself, since he looked like he wished to physically throw Arhus out of the room himself. Montoya's pause gave room for others to speak.

"Aren't you the guy who went into the alien spaceship? I saw that on the news feeds." The question was asked from across the room, but Arhus kept his gaze on Montoya.

"Yes, I am."

"Then you could tell us everything that is in the report," the voice continued.

Is that why I am here? Arhus wondered. *So Montoya can get the information to these people without giving it out himself? If so, he is putting on a good act of being upset. Or is he baiting me, daring me to say something so he can have me fired? Or maybe Montoya hasn't received the information himself yet and is hoping I say something?*

"I have filed my reports through the proper channels," Arhus responded.

Montoya looked relieved. "That is the proper way to distribute information. Mr. Gint is here to ensure accuracy, and to provide needed linguistic support, of course."

"But my opinion still stands," Arhus said. He chose his words carefully. "There is nothing in that report that couldn't be released to the public. Why any of it would be suppressed is beyond my understanding."

Montoya's comfort level appeared to rise again. *Typical,* Arhus thought, *hear the words you want to hear.*

"There are considerations you do not know," Montoya continued, turning from Arhus and looking toward the whole group. "The information from Mr. Gint has been processed by the appropriate persons and has been provided to this group. I suggest we get started. The applicable information for discussion has just been sent to your interfaces."

As everyone lifted their wrists and addressed their interfaces, Arhus sat down. He did not pull up his interface at first because he figured he knew what had been shared, but then thought about it and put it on his display. To his surprise, very little had been left out. The information that was missing concerned his own physical condition and the offer of the Subordinate to heal him. While people would understand excluding personal information, the ability to heal medical conditions would be of extreme interest to many. *Maybe that is why it was excluded, to prevent a mob-like response demanding that knowledge.*

Throughout the meeting, Arhus listened. His contributions were confined to nods of agreement. It was all the contribution he wanted to make. He saw several and could feel other eyes on him during the meeting. He couldn't decide if they were waiting for him to make another scene or were just curious. Either way, he did not like the attention and planned to exit the room as fast as he could when the meeting had finished.

The meeting took the full hour and a half allocated by Montoya. There were some who wished to continue the discussions, but a couple of minutes before the scheduled time, Montoya presented a summary and ended the meeting. Arhus was surprised that of all the information, they had agreed to withhold only a few minor details, several of which had not been discussed due to time. The instant after Montoya closed the meeting, Arhus rose and made a determined effort to leave the room. He almost succeeded.

A woman in her mid-forties stood in his path to the door. "Mr. Gint," she said, "a question, if you please."

Arhus nodded in reply and stopped walking. She took a breath and straightened to a determined stance.

"I was wondering if you could give me an idea of how much in your report wasn't presented today. No details, of course, just an idea." The woman's eyebrows went up once with the last statement.

"It was missing a few insignificant details," Arhus replied.

"Oh, come on," the woman said, turning her head to show the other side. "You don't have to give me the 'official' answer."

"It is the real answer," Arhus replied. "Now, if you will excuse me."

Without giving any further attention to the lady, Arhus walked around her and out the door. He was sure that several others tried to get his attention, but he ignored them as he made his way out of Montoya's office area and into the hallway. He hadn't taken six steps before Ms. Smith was standing next to him. He had not seen her in the meeting, but then, he knew of no reason she would not have been there.

"Going somewhere?" she asked.

"Back to my office," he answered, walking around her. She fell in step with him.

"Upset?" she asked with a lilt in her voice.

"Tired of people making everything harder than it needs to be," he responded.

"They have to have something to do," Ms. Smith said with a small laugh.

"Have you ever thought," Arhus asked, "how much would get done in the world if people stopped doing the unnecessary?"

"If we fix all the world's problems, what would they need us for?"

Arhus reached the lift. "Is there something you wanted?"

"Entertainment?" Smith gave him a coy smile.

"Are you that bored?" Arhus stepped onto the lift and asked for his floor. Smith followed.

"What else has been going on for the last week?" She raised an eyebrow. "I heard you have forsaken Montoya's inner circle. Why?"

"I hate the political manoeuvring. And I hate feeling used."

Smith snickered. "Not as dumb as you look, huh?"

Arhus looked the woman in the eye. "So is he using you, too?"

"We are all using each other. It's the game."

Arhus looked away. "When did serving the people become a game?"

"It has always been a game."

As the lift stopped, Arhus looked back at Smith. "Not for me," he said and then walked off the lift. Smith didn't follow.

Arhus checked his interface, amazed it hadn't sounded while in the meeting. There were six unassigned requests that had arrived during the meeting. The thought that somehow Montoya had arranged to have messages withheld from his interface during the meeting concerned him. The possibility that it wasn't an automatic feature of the meeting worried him. He made a note to himself to ask Johann about it.

Sitting down at a table, Arhus took care of the requests. When he was finished, he noted that many people looked like they were preparing to leave for the day. *It doesn't matter, particularly with all that is going on.* He retired to his office so no one would feel self-conscious about leaving.

In the next half-hour, Arhus found himself lost in thought a lot. *So much is still unknown.* He checked for any word about the allocation of space around the ship and found that the Council claimed an announcement would be made at six, two hours away. He imagined the anticipation many were feeling and the uproar that would follow.

After the noise subsided outside the office, Sindie walked in. "You waiting for the announcement in your office?" she asked.

"I can say I don't care what happens," Arhus said, recognizing the weariness in his own voice.

"I just thought you might want to get safe and snug at home before the chaos starts, since you live so close to it." She raised an eyebrow with the statement.

Tapping his finger several times, he replied, "You have a point. Not enough time to go out and eat."

"We can pick up something on the way. I'm flexible, you know that." A smile appeared on her face.

Arhus tried not to respond to the smile. He tapped his interface to shut it down and pushed away from the desk. "It will depend on whose line is the shortest, I suppose. You don't think people will be mobbing the roads before the announcement?"

"Like they will afterwards?" Sindie asked with a little surprise.

"You seem to be counting on people showing some restraint." Arhus moved around the desk to join her at the door.

"I wouldn't call it restraint," she replied as she turned. "More like indecision where to go."

"Another good point. We better be locked in at least half an hour before six." Arhus opened the door for her.

"Fine by me," Sindie said, a twinkle showing in her eye.

"By the way," Arhus said, ignoring the twinkle, "I guess I don't need to know where the meeting was."

"And I suppose you don't care that it is still going?"

Arhus stopped walking. "That means Montoya wasn't in the meeting."

"So?"

"Could mean that a power play happened. Montoya was assigned to some minor task to get him out of the way or as a punishment. Either way, it's a step down for him." He started walking again.

"Does that upset you?" Sindie asked.

"No." It was Arhus's turn to smile. "Just the opposite."

Chapter Fifteen
Chaos and Other Misdemeanours

The coffee table was a collage as if someone was expecting to be quarantined. Arhus was sitting on the couch with the curtains open to show the alien ship in the distance. Sindie soon joined him, taking the time to change into pyjamas before eating. Two plates and two sets of silverware, the real stuff, waited for her on the table, along with two tall glasses filled with beer. The food was of various ethnic types, per Sindie's choices, but looked like someone had been lost in indecision or kept forgetting what they had already bought. Having waited for her, Arhus handed her a plate and silverware when she sat down, his still empty.

"Why, thank you. You're such a gentleman," Sindie replied as she took the items.

"Only the best for my guest," Arhus said with a haughty voice.

"Guest?" Sindie said, her voice rising in tone and volume as she did.

"Well, you haven't moved in yet," Arhus replied, keeping his voice even. "Besides, it rhymed."

"Who says?"

"Half a bag of clothes and a toothbrush is moving in?" Arhus's brow furrowed.

"I'm not materialistic," Sindie said with a shake of her shoulders and her plate headed toward the food.

"Kind of taking it to an extreme, aren't you?" Arhus, in slow disbelief, moved his plate toward the food.

"I needed new clothes anyway," she said matter-of-factly. "Too many of mine were hand-me-downs."

"Darn wear-proof fabrics," Arhus mocked.

"Besides, there may not be a reason to keep saving all that money anyway," Sindie said as she piled food onto her plate, something from each container.

"That's a depressing thought." Arhus piled food between Sindie's reaping. "I would hate to see an economic collapse when our guests leave."

"You going to turn on the news?"

"And ruin my supper? No way."

Six o'clock came and went while Arhus and Sindie enjoyed being in the presence of a person they liked. With the windows and patio doors shut, the noise from the street did not penetrate the room. The view of the ship was far enough away that they could not see any activity there. The experience convinced Arhus of one thing. He had heard long before that the average man thought about sex every three seconds. Whether that was a frequency of occurrence or total time of the day was not clear. He did decide, though, that the time interval was too high for some females.

The observation was never acted on. The first hint of irregular activity was several dozen drones flying toward the alien ship. One or two would have been natural, but the large number ensured one's attention.

Arhus and Sindie stared out the patio door and watched the drones pass. Then, a thin line of smoke could be seen near the ship. The drones, floodlights on, circled the area. A look between them was all that was needed to prompt Arhus to turn on the news. A scene displayed with people running from the ship area and overhead drones firing at a group near the ship. A few in the group fired at the drones, trying to cover the runners, and a drone exploded at the end of a missile trail.

"What the hell?!" Arhus voiced. "Computer, play starting before the incident."

The display changed to a calmer scene. People were hurrying to get around the ship. Some still carried signs, chairs, and drinks, or pulled food containers.

"There!" Arhus said, pointing. The group he pointed at was different than the others. They carried no chairs or food and were all dressed in long, over-sized coats. They also kept to the middle of the crowd, allowing themselves to be pushed along.

"They look way too suspicious for security to allow them through," Sindie said. Arhus changed the view to the entrance, where hundreds of individuals pushed their way past the guards. The throng of people made any attempt to stop someone other than on the periphery suicidal.

"They may have planned on checking after people took up their positions," Arhus commented. "Computer, follow that group."

As commanded, the view followed the group in long coats. The throng spread out around the ship, but the group in focus stopped in front of the entry to the ship. Around thirty in number, they tried to stand without impeding those passing around them. As if on signal, they faced inward toward each other for a short while. When they turned back toward the ship, weapons appeared in their hands. They pointed them toward the ship.

The first shots were at the guardians at the ship's entrance. Taken by surprise, one guardian was hit by several shots, both solid projectile and beam weapons. The guardian staggered, first backwards and then to the ground, kneeling. The shots continued, one slug taking the guardian in the head. The guardian was knocked onto its back and lay sprawling on the ground.

The second guardian fared better. The first shots went wide, with one glancing blow the exception. The poor shots gave the guardian time to extend wings from behind his back and wrap them around his body. The wings, though translucent, appeared to deflect or absorb any further arms fire. Drawing a flaming sword, the guardian advanced on the shooters as half their number rushed the ship.

The few drones that had already been on patrol near the ship opened fire on the group with paralyzing yellow bursts. Several of the attackers were hit and one fell. Arhus assumed their long coats hid some kind of protection. Several attackers not running toward the ship opened fire on the drones, causing one to burst into flame. The other drones concentrated on the group returning fire.

If the attackers had any hope of defence against the flaming sword, they were convinced otherwise when the first of their number was cut in half by the guardian's sword sweep. The sword looked longer than Arhus remembered from the incident in Indonesia, leaving him to wonder if the length was variable. Four of the attackers attacked the guardian, trying to bring it down by weight of numbers, while the others tried to bypass it for entry into the ship. One was cut down by the guardian. Of the four who attacked it, two were killed before reaching the being and the other two did not have the strength to move it, much less tackle it to the ground. Both men were killed in short order.

To Arhus's amazement, the guardian did not return to the ship to deal with the other attackers, but continued to walk toward the group now firing at drones. Several fired at the being as it advanced, but did not slow its progress. The reason it did not return to the ship was soon clear. Two more guardians walked down the ramp, wings deployed and swords drawn. A credit to their bravery or stupidity, the men never paused, charging the guardians with weapons firing. It proved to be futile. With both guardians able to block entry into the ship, the attackers were cut down as fast as they came within reach of the flaming swords, which dismembered people and weapons alike. As the last of their number was cut down, an explosion filled the ship entryway. Fire and smoke obscured the view for a few moments. When it subsided, the ship and guardians stood as they had before, the human bodies scattered by the blast.

As the fighting raged, the crowds panicked and screamed. Most people ran from the scene in whatever direction seemed available, but several knelt in prayer while a few stood in their place in defiant refusal to give up their acquired positions. At least, they tried to stand in place. Some of these got knocked over or swept away with the crowds. Arhus winced while imagining that those who lost their footing were trampled. Several of those praying were also run over. The flow of the crowd prevented security from making headway toward the attacking group. The need to affect a quick exit of the non-involved proved more urgent. Even when people left the confined area near the ship, they were still not out of danger. Several news crews disappeared in the rush, their fate not clear. The news drones turned and left the area, their cameras still pointed at the activity. The automatic focus and zoom functions made sure that the views provided did not lose any integrity.

The scene caught up with the one that had greeted them initially. As the security drones approached the standing group, three miniature missiles emerged from the centre of the group, each exploding one drone. The momentum of the drones carried them beyond the action, two landing between the attackers and the evacuees and one bouncing off the ship without leaving any mark from the impact. The security drones circled the standing group and suppressed them with lethal force, concentrating on those firing missiles first. One more drone was lost before the group was all killed, the firing so confused Arhus could not tell from what. The guardian that had been advancing on the group stopped and took up position a few metres away, staying there even after all slumped on the ground. The immediate area had cleared of non-combatants, leaving the lone guardian and a pile of bodies. The sword still flamed, held at the ready. The drones took up sentry positions.

With a background of muted screams, the guardians on the ship ramp descended to take up station at the bottom. Behind them came two humanoid beings carrying long staffs. As these new beings walked, they touched human remains or equipment with the staff. The touched items disintegrated into dust, which then disappeared from view. As one continued near the ship, the other walked to the pile of bodies under guard, dispatching those in-between as it went.

"Talk about an efficient clean-up crew," Sindie said. "They're not even going to let us take the bodies to be identified?"

"Why did they even try this?" Arhus asked. "Didn't they know they had no hope of succeeding?"

"Guess not," Sindie replied. "I wonder who they were."

"After all the technologies the aliens have demonstrated, how did they think they would succeed?" Arhus cocked his head and stared for a moment. "A better question, how did the aliens not know this was coming?"

"What do you mean?"

"They're telepathic! How did they not know these people were outside their ship with weapons?" Arhus stared with his mouth open. "Unless they wanted them to attack. Do you think they could have even put the idea in their heads?"

"What in the world are you talking about? You think the aliens got some crazies to attack them? Why?"

"I don't know, just wondering. Why would they allow people to attack their ship?"

"Because they hadn't done it yet?"

"But they had to know it was coming. Why allow it?"

"A demonstration?"

"That's possible," Arhus said, sitting back. The news continued to show the aliens cleaning up the scene. "Maybe that's not what we have to worry about. Maybe we have to worry about our reaction."

"You mean the Council?" Sindie asked after a pause. "Do you think they would strike back?"

"At the aliens?" Arhus laughed. "I doubt it. Someone else? Just maybe, and in a way that will take innocent people with it. I don't know who planned this and what resources they have, but their next step will be bigger."

"Pfff." Sindie laughed. "You've watched too many action movies."

"Have I?"

"Do you think there is some secret organization out there planning on taking down the aliens? Why would they? It's not like the aliens have forced us to do anything." Sindie's mood had changed. She turned to face Arhus instead of leaning against him and her hands were getting into the discussion.

"Because people are stupid?" Arhus offered.

"Well, that's always hard to dismiss, but how do a few guys with guns hope to take down an alien ship?"

"Maybe they are trying to spark a fire. If the aliens react hard enough, they might think the World Council would be forced to defend Earth." Arhus talked in an even tone and hoped the emotion of the discussion stayed at a low level.

"Fat chance! There's no way the Council is going to attack that ship in its backyard. The Council members don't have the guts!"

"Maybe everyone doesn't think that way." Arhus paused, tapping his finger in the air. "Or I guess it could be one of the countries or factions."

"Attack the ship this close to Jerusalem? That'd be nuts!"

"Yes, it would be. First, they would have to have independent forces, and then they would have to be suicidal, because they know the Council would retaliate even if they weren't successful, not to mention the aliens."

Sindie gave him a very concerned look. "You don't think Indonesia would do it, do you?"

"Projectile Jerusalem? No way! Besides, they have enough of their own troubles right now with all the unrest going on."

"Revenge, then, hoping the aliens take it out on Jerusalem?"

Arhus shook his head. "If they think that, they don't know our visitors. I'm sure they already know who is responsible for the attack. It will be interesting to see if they tell us."

"This is so unbelievable," Sindie said, sitting back into the cushions of the couch.

The news report showed the two beings with staffs finishing the clean-up process and then heading back into the ship. The body of the assumed dead guardian was carried into the ship by the other original guardian, who followed the two beings into the ship. Once inside, the scene as far as the ship was concerned looked just as it had before the attack. General mayhem continued among the crowd. Some had stayed to watch the aliens at work. Security was in the process of clearing everyone from around the ship. Arhus was sure anyone who was allowed to return would be thoroughly checked beforehand.

"Yes," Arhus agreed, "the whole situation is surreal. The aliens act like it's just another Tuesday." After they both stared at the scene for a while, Arhus asked, "Did you see if any bystanders were hurt during the attack?"

"I didn't notice any," Sindie answered, "but I will admit I wasn't paying attention."

"Computer, is anyone reported dead or missing from around the ship other than the attackers?"

"Not at this time," the voice replied.

"What about any who were entering the ship?"

"Entries were halted while access was being granted to the allotted groups."

"At least there's that," Arhus said with a sigh.

"Is your secret committee going to ask you to talk to the aliens tomorrow?" Sindie asked.

"Don't know, don't care. Computer, end news display. Play some soothing music."

As light jazz caressed the room, Sindie went back to laying her head on Arhus's shoulder, her body strung out across the rest of the couch. She sighed. "Well, that was a mood killer."

"I know what you mean," Arhus replied, staring into the distance. The smoke had disappeared and darkness was settling outside. Stars started to appear where the sky was darkest, just above the mountain tops.

They sat in silence for a time. When Sindie yawned, Arhus tried to remove himself, which brought Sindie up with a jerk.

"Where you going?" she demanded.

"If we're going to fall asleep, it might as well be in bed."

"I was comfortable," Sindie protested.

"That made one of us. Come on, tomorrow will come too soon, I'm sure."

Chapter Sixteen
Calls and Answers

Arhus's interface blared at six in the morning. Awake but not much, Arhus managed to open his eyes. It wasn't the first time in the night they had been awakened. Around two in the morning, an announcement had been broadcast that all work had been suspended for the next day and everyone was supposed to stay home, and they had made sure everyone heard it. With the opportunity to sleep in, Arhus had looked forward to a lazy day. The second alarm promised to cancel that expectation.

Rolling over, Arhus looked at the interface. It took a while for his eyes to focus on the wording displayed.

"Who is it?" a half-asleep female voice said next to him.

"Montoya," he said as he flopped onto his back.

"You going to answer it?" The interface beeped again, softer this time.

"No, he can go hang himself for all I care." Awake, Arhus rolled over to face Sindie, who was face-down into the pillow. "Besides, we're not supposed to be out on the street today."

Sindie's face slowly rotated toward Arhus. A smile formed with as much effort as she seemed to be able to manage. "Whatever will we do?"

"Oh, I'm sure we'll think of something." Arhus leaned toward the smiling face.

ARHUS GINT!

The voice was so loud that Arhus sat erect on the bed as if it had been electrified. It took him a second to realize that he had not heard the voice with his ears. Blinking several times in rapid succession, he rubbed his head with his hands.

"You don't have to shout so much."

We apologize. Please, when you are ready, join us at our ship.

"Who you talking to?" Sindie asked.

"The Subordinate."

It was Sindie's turn to sit upright with a jerk. "He's talking to you?"

"Yes. Wants me to meet him at the ship." Arhus moved the covers and turned to the side of the bed.

"Does everyone have something against us spending time together?"

Arhus chuckled. "Besides the assumptions that makes, I doubt they even think about it."

"If our friends out there are telepathic, won't they know?" Sindie raised one eyebrow.

Arhus turned back toward her. "And it would be interesting to hear their opinion on the subject, if they've even thought about it."

"The only thing I am interested in," Sindie responded, flopping back on the bed, "is them leaving us alone."

"Not going to happen." Arhus stood up and walked toward the bathroom.

"What do they want, anyway?" Sindie called.

"My guess would be the same thing Montoya wanted." He left the door open after entering the bathroom.

"Selfish bastards." Sindie stared at the ceiling for a few seconds before noting that the bathroom door had not been closed. Throwing the covers off, she sprinted after him.

The World Council blue shirt shimmered when sunlight hit at the correct angle. The official insignia on the top left shoulder (it was deemed too arrogant to wear them in full frontal view) was not necessary for someone to recognize the outfit, but was part of the formal-dress outfit, as was the darker blue, full length pants with a crease in the front of each leg. Arhus was surprised the clothes fit so well after not wearing them for several years. Today felt like a good time to wear it—half of the security personnel in the streets let him pass without questioning.

The gates in front of the alien ship were closed and a whole squad, or several squads as far as Arhus knew, stood shoulder-to-shoulder in front of them. Picking out the commander in charge by his uniform, Arhus walked over and waited for the man's attention. Arhus had not met him before. *Someone new in charge isn't a surprise.*

As the man turned Arhus's direction, he looked up and down. "The Council want something?" the man asked.

"I'm sure they do," Arhus replied, keeping his voice calm and his volume low.

"Who sent you this time?" the man asked.

Arhus pointed at the ship, causing the man to give him a confused look.

"What does that mean?"

"Our visitors asked me to come," Arhus said.

The man took a breath. "Listen! I don't know if you are a nut job or…"

The man stopped talking as his head jerked back and his eyes went wide. Arhus waited until the man breathed again.

"Quite overwhelming, isn't it?" Arhus asked.

"Yeah," the man managed to say. "That was…" He pointed over his shoulder.

"Yes, it was."

The man looked back to Arhus, still not recovered. "Should I inform someone?"

"Whoever you wish. May I pass?"

The man turned and then waved at the guards at the gate. "Let this one pass!" he shouted.

The security guards at the gate looked almost as surprised as their commander at the order, but complied, making just enough room between themselves for Arhus to get through. Once through, they closed and locked the gate behind him.

Comforting. Like being thrown to the lions.

Arhus walked to the ship ramp. The guardians did not move or even look at him, nor did they bar his way. He stopped at the bottom of the ramp.

"Permission to come aboard, captain," he said out loud.

"You already had permission," the Subordinate's voice said from inside the light at the top of the ramp. His body came into sight as he descended.

"Old tradition," Arhus replied.

"Please," the Subordinate said, holding out his arm toward the centre of the ship when he reached the bottom of the ramp, "join us."

"Thank you." Arhus gave an abbreviated bow before stepping onto the ramp.

"Still so formal," the Subordinate said with what might have been a chuckle. "Did you inform the Council that you were coming?"

"No, I did not." As they cleared the outgoing light, the ship appeared just as it had on Arhus's previous visit.

"Why not?"

No need to lie. "I tire of their politics."

"Politics," the Subordinate mused. "That is something we do not share."

"You're better off without it." Arhus tried to keep the snide tone from his voice.

"It would be quite impossible," the Subordinate said as if the fact was obvious.

"Why?"

The Subordinate looked at him as they walked. "We are the EO-AY."

"I pretty sure I don't understand what that all means."

"We are one." The Subordinate said it as if it was an everyday fact.

"You mean one consciousness?"

"We are so much more. It would be difficult to explain to someone of your existence."

The hallway was the same, as was the common area. There were a few more people than Arhus's last visit and the plants looked more matured than would have been normal.

"Please, let us sit," the Subordinate offered, indicating a table and chairs to one side of the room, a short walk away. As they sat down, a messenger walked up to the table, holding two glasses. The one he set in front of Arhus appeared to hold apricot juice.

Of course they would know what I like to drink. He picked up the glass and sipped the most delicious apricot juice he had ever had, chilled to the perfect temperature.

"You have questions," the Subordinate said, not touching his drink.

"You knew there was going to be an attack before it happened," Arhus said.

"Yes."

"How far ahead?"

The Subordinate shrugged. "Does it matter? No one else was hurt."

"But you allowed the attack to happen. You didn't even warn your guardians."

"It was the best way to prevent others from being injured. Or worse." The Subordinate looked so calm as he talked.

"So you care if others had been hurt?" Arhus was not sure if he would get the real answer.

"It would have complicated the situation." It was said with no emotion.

"With the World Council?"

"In many ways."

Arhus pushed aside questions about what the answers meant and continued, leaving the analysis for later. "So why not leave the bodies of the attackers for us to identify? We could have stopped future attacks, maybe."

"The matter was concluded to our satisfaction." Again, no emotion.

"Will you at least provide the Council with a list of the attackers so their relatives can be informed?"

The Subordinate appeared to think for a moment, then said, "We will discuss that."

"Are there more out there planning another attack?"

"You need not worry about that. We will take care of any others that come."

I bet you will, Arhus couldn't help thinking. "Do you blame the

World Council for the attack?"

"Of course not."

"What about your guardian? Is... he... okay?"

"It is very nice of you to ask." The Subordinate smiled. "He is being attended to."

"He appeared pretty hurt." Arhus knew there was no tricking the Subordinate into giving out information, but had decided beforehand that he should try to find out what he can.

"He is not beyond... healing. We are quite advanced at repairing damage."

And you are so good at not giving out information, Arhus thought. After he did, he almost expected a thank-you from the Subordinate, but received none.

"As I am sure you know, humans are going to worry about any retaliation for the attack. It would make them much less nervous if you would make a statement that there will be none."

"Can you not relay this message for us?"

"It would mean much more coming from you."

"We see." The Subordinate appeared to ponder the idea for a short while. "We will send a representative to make a statement."

"Thank you." Arhus could not think of anything else to say in response.

"You are not here for your leaders and yet you ask the questions they would ask." It was the first non-bland statement the Subordinate had made.

"Just preparing for when they ask me," Arhus replied. "I'm sure they have been informed that I am here."

"Will you be in trouble?"

"No, I doubt it." Arhus chuckled. "At least your invitation will give me an excuse for ignoring their summons."

"We are glad we could be of assistance." The smile that went with the statement made Arhus wonder if the Subordinate had made a joke.

"How is the... gathering... going?"

"It was proceeding well, at least before the attack yesterday. Will your authorities now hold up those who wish to join us?"

Arhus took a deep breath. "I do not expect them to, after they feel that the situation is being handled and another attack will not happen, that is."

"And how will they do that?"

Arhus just stared at the Subordinate for a moment. Deciding he was being polite, Arhus said, "They will search everyone who is given access to the ship. Of course, those wishing to join you will be also be searched, but from what I have seen, they will be less of a challenge to search."

"Would it help if we stationed our guardians to address those who are joining us?"

Arhus waited for some hint of other suggested meaning, but found none. "I can ask. If Security agrees, how would you like them to inform you?" *That was a stupid question.*

"Have them inform the guardians outside. We will not be offended if our offer is declined."

Arhus took more than a sip of his drink. The Subordinate followed suit. Arhus felt some of his tension ease.

"Have you thought any more about what you will leave here when you return home?" Arhus asked.

"We have discussed it," the Subordinate said as he put his glass down.

"Have you come to a decision?"

"None can be told at this time."

Arhus paused, trying to decide what to ask next, if anything. *Do they just need more time to decide? Or are they avoiding an answer?* He decided on a different tack.

"Do you have any questions you would like us to answer?" Arhus asked.

Very small facial responses, not more than small twitches, showed either surprise or amusement, Arhus could not decide. The statement did bring a slow smile to the Subordinate's face. Arhus tried to keep no reaction and wait.

"Would you like us to fix your health condition while you are here?" the Subordinate asked.

Arhus just stared at the Subordinate, his mind a blank. It started working again enough for him to respond. "You would do that?"

"Of course," the Subordinate said easily. "We would not offer unless we had intention."

"Why would you do that? Aren't you afraid everyone will expect you to heal them?"

"We wish only to demonstrate our good will, and we only heal those that are chosen to be healed."

I don't know what that means, but I don't know if I care, Arhus thought. *Not hypoglycemic? That would be great! Not having to worry about eating on schedule! I'm not sure how that would feel. But, hell, I sure want to try!*

"What would it take?" Arhus asked, trying to remain calm.

"A few moments in one of our chambers is all. We can show you if you like."

Arhus shrugged. "Sure."

They stood and the Subordinate led Arhus to the same hall with the sleeping chambers as on his last visit. *It makes sense,* Arhus thought. *The chamber would have analytic and medical capability handy in case something went wrong.*

The Subordinate indicated a chamber with his hand. The chamber opened, extending the bed outwards. "It will take a few moments. The chamber will scan your body and then heal it. You need to but lay still."

Arhus stared at the chamber.

"Do not worry," the Subordinate continued. "We will let you out once the chamber is finished. You may be awake the whole time if you will. It will not hurt."

"Ah, okay. Do I need to remove my clothes?"

"That will not be necessary." Maybe a small chuckle came from the Subordinate. His hand swept the bed. "At your pleasure."

Tentatively, Arhus sat on the bed and swung his feet toward the wall. As he lay down, a pillow appeared at his head as if inflated from the bed. "Can you leave the lights on?"

"If that makes you more comfortable," the Subordinate answered.

"Yes, please."

The bed moved back into the chamber. Being inside the lighted chamber made Arhus think of being inside a lighted coffin, but he pushed the thought from his mind. After hearing the seal close, a blue beam came from the ceiling to the centre of his body. Arhus felt nothing as the beam appeared to travel to random places on his body, avoiding his eyes. Arhus was sure the locations were not random, but since he did not have a medical degree, he could only guess.

The blue light disappeared and a thin cylinder extended from the chamber wall to his throat. He felt a slight pressure and some liquid entering his body. His throat felt warm for a while, then the feeling spread to other parts of his body, decreasing in temperature as it did. If the fluid made it to his lower legs, he couldn't tell. After a few moments, another cylinder extended, this time to the centre of his body. He felt a small pressure, but no other effects. The light in the chamber changed from a yellow to a white colour. Arhus lay there and waited. The blue beam came back and again scanned his body. When it finished, the lighting went back to yellow and the bed started to move outward.

The Subordinate was still standing outside the chamber. When the bed stopped moving, Arhus swung his legs to the side and stood up. He didn't feel any different and there were no marks on his body or clothes. *Nice trick,* he thought.

"We can provide you with information for your medical experts to demonstrate your condition, if you wish," the Subordinate said.

"I don't think that will be necessary. I don't know if they would believe you anyway." *And I don't want to be stuck in a lab the rest of my life.* Arhus stood, not knowing what to do next. "I feel like I owe you something."

"You owe us nothing. This is our gift to you, to show you we mean only good for mankind."

"Then why not make such treatments available to everyone?" As soon as he said it, Arhus started to think of answers to his question.

"That is not why we are here and cannot be done with order, as we are sure you know."

"Yes, I know. Sorry I asked."

"There is nothing to forgive, it was a very human question. It shows your heart. Shall we go?"

Arhus followed without comment. As they passed the common area, he couldn't help but look at the food table. *Am I free of this tie to sugar? Can I now eat whatever I want whenever I want?* It sounded too simple for something that had ruled a large part of his life.

As they walked down the ramp, the Subordinate again spoke. "Thank you for coming. I hope your people find some reassurance in our words."

"You will tell them?" Arhus asked.

"Yes, we will send a representative."

Breathing what he was surprised to find was a sigh of relief, Arhus said, "And thank you for what you did. Truly, I appreciate it."

"Of course. If we wish to speak to you again, we will call." The Subordinate made a slight bow.

"Just hold down the volume," Arhus said with a smile, performing a somewhat deeper bow.

"Of course," the Subordinate said with a smile of his own.

The sun was in full display and blazing as Arhus walked to the guard station. He couldn't help but feel that time moved at a different rate inside the ship, but dismissed it as due to the strange surroundings. The station appeared to be getting back to normal, with a line of people waiting to approach the ship. They were being checked with enthusiasm. *Has security been withholding people until I return?* He did not want to ask.

"Everything fine?" the security officer asked as Arhus passed the gates.

"Yes, fine. You can allow people to enter when you are ready." Arhus was sure he had no authority to say that, but also knew it was what the officer wanted to hear. *If I get in trouble, who cares.*

"Thank you." The man turned to the other security personnel at the gate. "Sergeant, begin the procession."

"They have offered to help you screen people, if you wish," Arhus told the captain.

He turned back to Arhus with a shocked expression on his face. Shock gave way to worry. In a stumbling voice, the man managed to say, "I don't think that will be necessary."

The first person waiting, a woman, jumped with joy as she was directed to proceed. Once she had taken a dozen steps, the next person was released. Arhus watched just long enough to see them enter the ship. A look of joy filled the people's faces as they walked toward the ship.

I hope it's worth it, Arhus thought before turning to walk back to his apartment. *I should pick up breakfast on the way home. Nothing too filling.*

The interface didn't demand attention until breakfast was almost finished, something Arhus considered a minor miracle. *Maybe communication is slow with everyone gone,* he mused. He felt like ignoring it, but the emergency tone was something no one was allowed to ignore in any circumstance. The second surprise was whose face appeared, Arlan Morresette.

"Good morning," Arhus managed to say through his shock. Sindie made no effort to hide or stop eating.

"Mr. Gint," Arlan said without pause, "am I correct in that you have been on the alien ship this morning?"

"Yes, sir," Arhus said in staccato.

"Why haven't you filed a report?" It sounded more like an accusation than a question.

"Everyone was ordered to stay home."

"You can create a report from home, can't you?" Again, more accusation.

"We are not allowed to file reports from home," Arhus responded, regaining some confidence in the conversation.

"You quote regulations to me at a time like *this!*"

"I have not received written permission to ignore them, sir." *Chew on that, asshole.*

Arlan seemed flustered for a second, but recovered. "What did the aliens tell you? Are they holding us responsible for the attack?"

"No, sir, they are not." Arhus kept his voice even.

"Why did they destroy the bodies? How are we supposed to know who is responsible for all this?" Arlan's mood was not dampening at all.

"They know who attacked them."

The statement caused Arlan to pause, face and all, in the middle of forming another sentence. His head went back. "Are they going to tell us?"

"I asked them to share that information, but they haven't decided yet, though it's hard to tell. I also got them to agree to make a public statement that they do not hold the rest of us responsible." *And you are welcome very much.*

" *When?*"

"They don't seem to hurry to do anything, so I don't know. They are very careful how they talk, as if working out statements in detail."

"Hell!" Arlan seemed to relax a bit. "Everyone here is panicked. They might give us a little more consideration."

"You say that like you expect them to care."

The implication hit Arlan like a slap and did nothing to improve his mood. He scowled, his face twisted in raw emotion, then turned his eyes back to Arhus. "If you have any more contact, call my office at once. And you will be receiving that *written* permission shortly."

The interface went blank and then back to the default screen. Arhus turned it off.

"He didn't even say thank you," Sindie said in mock surprise.

"Bureaucrat," Arhus said as he put the interface on the table. "If I had been told by the aliens they were going to retaliate, would I be sitting in my living room eating breakfast? What an idiot."

"Well," Sindie said in a drawn-out manner as she leaned close, "I appreciate your efforts and intend to show my complete appreciation."

Arhus looked over his shoulder. "I thought you did that already."

"Maybe I am *really* appreciative." She gave him a sly smile.

Arhus laughed. "You might want to check your record, I think it's stuck."

"Nope, just trying to maximize my day." She gave her eyebrows a wiggle.

"Plenty of time for that. Right now, I'm hungry. I actually did something today." Arhus turned back to breakfast.

"I did, too. Don't you remember?"

"I wasn't counting that."

"Why not?" Sindie gave him a pout.

"I wasn't done," he said as he put another piece of bagel in his mouth.

"Oh! Goody!"

*   *   *

The visitors made their announcement around one in the afternoon. Every broadcast aired it. *Afraid to lose viewership for five minutes.* After the statement by one of the messengers, the news spent the rest of the afternoon talking about the two-minute statement. Experts were called upon to explain something that had sounded clear to Arhus. World leaders comforted those listening that they had nothing to fear and that all future incidents would be prevented while avoiding the 'how could this have happened' statement as much as possible. Any explanations revolved around not wanting to limit people's access to the visitors. Arhus could stand it for only so long before diving into his archive for a movie that he hadn't watched in a long time. He settled on "Time Bandits." Sindie had never seen it before and laughed through most of the movie. The costumes were cheesy and the effects were poor, but that was half of the charm of watching. Plus, she thought Sean Connery was cute. *She's just trying to make me jealous.*

Fascinated by the old movie, Sindie asked for another and Arhus jumped to "The Fifth Element"; the original, not the remakes (first or second). At least he had some ammunition if Sindie said anything about cute leading men. Sindie kept saying the movie seemed familiar until Arhus listed the films that were knock-offs. One, "Your World Should Be Destroyed" Sindie had a hard time believing was a knock-off until Arhus explained it. The list led to a discussion of the differences and their political meanings.

By the evening hours, the curfew was lifted, which seemed ironic for curfews. Sindie was ready to get out of the apartment, insisting on going out to eat. It was hard to argue with the request. The bigger topic ended up being where to go. Arhus was finding out that Sindie's tastes were far spicier than he was used to, and he had put up with Josef's taste in restaurants for years. The first couple on her preferred list were vetoed outright. They settled on one that let you add the extra spice, though Arhus could not imagine that it was required or survivable.

The street was crowded with people. Most were more cautious than carefree, but that changed as the night went along without explosions or security guards rushing about. News broadcasts displayed in restaurants showed people once again taking up positions around the ship. Arhus hurried past one bar because they had the volume up so high that you couldn't avoid listening. He wasn't alone. He noted many who looked like they just wanted to find a quiet, enjoyable spot.

"Do you think we should tell people who you are?" Sindie asked as a mischievous smile grew from her lips.

"Hell no," Arhus replied with enthusiasm.

"Don't want to be a celebrity?"

"Not in the least. Besides, you want strangers taking up all my time?"

"Ouch!" Sindie made a mock response, pulling her head back. "Hit a girl where it hurts."

"Just asking." Arhus raised his beer glass, tipped it to her, and took a drink. "Besides, I am sure the Council is suppressing the vids that show me coming and going as much as possible, so there goes my proof."

"And won't they just *love* you becoming a media darling and taking their spotlight." Sindie giggled.

"Not a fight I want to fight." Arhus put his glass back down.

"What about afterwards? You would think it would come out somehow."

"Depends on what our visitors do afterwards. Is one of them going to stay? Are they going to leave 'instructions' to be followed? Will we be on our own?" Arhus shrugged. "Who knows?"

"They do," Sindie said with a biting tone, "but they don't like to share."

"And I'm not sure I can blame them." Arhus leaned closer. "If they told us beforehand, how many people do you think there would be arguing about the decision day and night?"

"Too many, for sure. The news would be filled with it."

"Precisely." Arhus leaned back in his chair.

"What do you hope they do?" All traces of sarcasm had left Sindie's voice. She rubbed her beer glass between her hands as she talked.

"Me? I hope they just go and leave us alone. Not like we need someone starting a new church or something." Arhus played with his fork as he talked.

"Would you still work for the Council?"

"Don't think I'd want to." Arhus stared at his glass. "Not sure it would be wise, anyway. Too much politics around and people worried about what I might do."

"So, what would you do?" Arhus noted that Sindie's eyes had softened.

"I guess I could always teach. Some small town surrounded by farmland out in the middle of nowhere." Arhus looked off into the distance. "My mother had a garden. She'd spend hours tending the plants and turning the soil. When I asked her why, she said it helped her relax. Guess I can understand that now."

"You could write a book and then go on the talking circuit," Sindie said, her eyes looking playful again. "A lot of money in telling people what they want to hear."

"Why would I need the money?" Arhus asked, looking sideways at her.

"I might want to live a particular lifestyle," Sindie responded, not looking at him until she was done with the sentence.

"Pff, that's your problem," Arhus said, reaching for his drink.

"Thanks a lot!"

"You're welcome."

Chapter Seventeen
I Have a Secret

It wasn't long after Arhus got into his office the next morning that Johann showed up. He looked haggard and his clothes were wrinkled. Arhus had not seen him look that way since finals week in college, at least when he was sober. That morning, he was sober and excited.

"What's up?" Arhus asked as Johann closed the office door, making sure it closed.

Johann took a seat in a hurry and leaned forward. "Remember I talked about the aliens using sunlight to mask their signal?"

"Sure, it wasn't that long ago. Have you slept since then?"

"Some, I think." Johann waved his hands in the air. "That's not important. I found it! The aliens are using sunlight to mask their signals. They're not the same frequency, it's more like a complementary frequency, but if you weren't looking for it, you'd never find it." He took a deep breath.

"These guys are good, I'm telling you, they're really good. Even though I found the signal, I have no idea how they generate it. It's so... delicate... but it has so much power. We can't duplicate it."

"So you are saying we can listen, but we can't send?" Arhus asked.

"At least for the moment, yes. If we got the big boys in on this, they might be able to figure out something." Johann had a far-off look.

"And who knows how our visitors would react," Arhus added.

The comment brought Johann's eyes back to his. "True, very true. Oh, did I tell you there was more than the message delivered by their rep?"

That brought Arhus's head to full attention. "You mean communication with their servants?"

"Yeah, though I am not sure what it means." Johann shook his head, either to clear his head or in memory of the message.

"Lay it on me."

"It was short and not in human language of course, at least most of it. The part I could understand went something like 'Stand where you are.' Of course, it would help if we knew where they were..."

"How did you translate any of it?" Arhus asked.

"Comparing the message to the statement made by the rep, which, now that I think about it, you would be a lot better at. I used translation software. You know, that stuff that you complain about doesn't translate real well..."

"Never mind that," Arhus said while waving the statements off with his hands. "Send me the messages, will you?"

"Sure, it's audio files, but I'll send it to you. Wait, I brought it with me!"

Johann reached into his pocket and took out a data storage pod that he handed to Arhus. He appeared to have a weight removed from him when he did.

"Go home, try to get some sleep," Arhus told his friend.

"Yeah, I should do that. Not going to be much good if I can't function. Got caught here yesterday when everyone was told to stay home, so I worked through the day and night. Bad time not to have a pillow around."

Arhus stood up and moved around the desk. "Come on, I'll show you out."

"Thanks." Johann stood up, a slight wobble to his stance. "Hope this helps. You'll let me know, right?"

"Of course, after you get some sleep." Arhus's light touch was on Johann's elbow as he started moving, to make sure he didn't fall. By the time he reached the door, help wasn't needed.

"How's it going up here?" Johann asked as they walked through the office area.

"Fine. I think most people are waiting for the other stein to drop."

Johann laughed. "As long as we don't get charged for them like all those we broke in college, huh?"

"Yeah, let someone else pay the bill this time." Arhus waited for the lift to appear. "Take care and keep your head down, you hear me?"

"Yes, sir, boss," Johann said with a laugh. He stepped into the lift. "You, too. Ground."

"Always."

"Tell me another one I don't believe," Johann said as the lift descended.

When his friend was out of sight, Arhus turned and walked back to his office. Josef gave him a look as he passed. "I'm going to need some time alone," he told his friend in response. Josef nodded and turned back to his interface.

Three hours later, Sindie walked into the office.

"Hey Mr. Secret Mission, you going to stay locked up all day?"

"The door was not locked," Arhus replied with slight irritation.

"What's got you bunched up?"

Arhus took a breath and let it out. "Trying to decipher the undecipherable."

"You got something new!" Sindie hurried to stand next to Arhus.

"You might not want to know," Arhus cautioned.

"All the better!" Sindie stared at the display. "What is this? Where's the text?"

"There is no text." At a muted volume, Arhus played a short stretch of signal.

"Is that music of some kind?"

"It's a signal from the alien ship," Arhus started. Then his eyes went wide. "Crap! That's a good idea!"

"What's a good idea?" When Arhus stared at the interface display instead of answering, Sindie added, "Tell me, I want credit for it, whatever it is."

"I've been looking at the individual tones, but there is a lot more to music than just the tone. There is the speed of the tones, the rhythm, and the pairing of tones that create more than the sum of the parts."

"Sure, everyone likes a good beat. Language is similar."

"But not as extensive as music, or as ingrained. I can say the same word different ways and still convey the same meaning, but in music it would be considered a different song."

"So you think what they say also depends on how they say it? Geez, makes it sound like a musical language."

"Maybe that's why it takes so long for the aliens to communicate with us." Arhus made some final, harder taps on the interface and sat back. The display went into furious activity. "And it's going to take longer to translate."

"Wait a second," Sindie said, straightening from the display, "where did you get this?"

"Better for the person involved you don't know."

"Better yet, how did they get this? I hadn't heard that anyone had intercepted any signals from the alien ship."

"No one has except us." Arhus turned his head and gave her a smile.

"Hell, Ar, you have a copy of a signal from the alien ship and you haven't given it to anyone?" Sindie's mouth stayed open.

"I have a copy of *something*. It might be a signal from the alien ship and it might be the music they play in their private study. Until I have some kind of idea, I'm not telling anyone that we have intercepted commands from the ship." Arhus turned back to the display with a huff. "Besides, it's not like anyone on the Council deserves to know. The first thing they would want is a translation."

"But the aliens have to know you have it, right?" Some worry showed in her voice.

"Yes, and they haven't made any response, so I am assuming that while I keep it to myself, they don't mind. Of course, if they do know, they also know I can't understand it." Arhus waved his hand at the display.

"What happens when you do?"

"No idea." Arhus sat back in his chair.

The look of worry had taken over Sindie's entire face. "I'm not sure you should be doing this."

"Why not?"

"Because I'm concerned about your safety!" Sindie's volume had risen. She spoke softer with the next statement. "What if they don't want you spying on them? They seem to shoot first and ask questions later."

"I think the Subordinate would have asked to talk to me if they were worried about it," Arhus said.

"I'm not sure you want to count on your 'special relationship' with the aliens."

"That seems to be a reasonable assumption so far."

"Said the man falling from the plane. This is your life we're taking about!" Sindie's stance went still with her arms at her side. "Something I have an interest in!"

Arhus looked at Sindie's face. He noticed the slight quiver and the concern in her eyes. He reached up and touched her face with his palm. She nestled her face in his hand with a sigh before he turned back to the interface.

"Computer, if you find a result, don't display it, just inform me."

"As you wish," the computer responded.

"Does that make you feel better?" Arhus asked Sindie.

"A little, though it still worries me. What are you going to do with it if you get something?"

"Once I know, I suspect that it won't take long for our guests to know. I'll wait and see if they say anything. If not, I'll assume they don't care." Arhus shrugged.

"Don't you think it would be better to ask them?" Sindie said it in that half-question, half-suggestion tone mothers use with their kids.

"I'll think about it. I promise."

"Look," Sindie said, taking his hand away from her face and holding it in hers, "you're the one who can walk up to that ship and ask to speak with these guys, so I suggest you use that privilege. Don't assume anything!"

Arhus smiled. "Getting pretty protective, aren't you?"

"Ever known me not to be?"

"Just saying, it's rather refreshing in a relationship." Arhus's smile added a playful tone.

"There some reason to wait?" Sindie said without any playful tone.

Arhus stood up and wrapped his arms around Sindie. She responded with a tight hug of her own, her head buried in his chest. She gave no indication of wanting to let go.

"I haven't had anyone worry this much about me since my mother," Arhus said.

"They're stupid," came the soft response.

"My mother?"

"No, you know who."

"Oh, good. It would have made introducing you to her awkward." The response was a quick fist to his back. Arhus laughed. He stood there, letting the minutes pass by. After a while, Sindie spoke.

"Are you hungry? I didn't have breakfast."

"Why not?"

"Someone didn't make it for me."

Arhus laughed again. "So now my duties include making you breakfast?"

"You bet," was the response.

"Wow, now you are getting demanding."

"I'm worth it."

"I thought you wanted food."

"Now, yeah."

"Come on," he said, patting her back, "let's get you something to eat."

Chapter Eighteen
Fallout

"Holy crap!" Arhus said after answering his interface. Even though they had gone to lunch early, they still did not finish before the emergency request came through.

"What is it?" Sindie asked, placing her fork on her dish hard enough to make an unavoidable noise.

"A general session has just been called. Everybody is going! We'll need everyone from the office for support." Arhus raced his fingers across the interface, passing requests.

"Everyone?"

"Yeah, everyone. We better get back, this is going to be chaos until it starts."

"Right." Sindie picked up the brownie sitting on the small plate. As they hurried to the lift, Arhus gave her a look. "What? Not like I was going to leave it there. Hey, did you get enough to eat? You know, with your sugar and all? You need me to save this for you?"

"No need," Arhus said as they left. He entered an emergency code on his interface. "The aliens fixed me."

"Fixed you? What does that mean."

"They cured my hypoglycemia, they claim." They entered the lift, not waiting for it to come to a complete stop.

"Cured? How did they do that?"

"One of their chambers. Don't ask me how it works, I have no idea, but it seems to be real, at least so far." The lift used faster than normal acceleration as it climbed floors.

"Why'd they do that? Or better yet, what do they want in return?"

"They said it was to demonstrate their benevolence." The lift slowed as it came to the floor.

"Right. And we believe that?"

"For now." Arhus walked into the office area. "Okay, everyone, as you saw, we have an emergency session called thirty minutes from now. Get your stuff and head to your stations. Don't wait for anyone else. We might have enough time to make equipment checks, but I'm not counting on it. Don't ask me what it's about, I don't know and I doubt anyone but the people who called it do. Let's do ourselves proud today!"

People had stopped when Arhus talked. To their credit, most were already getting their equipment together. At the end of the speech, they transformed into a bustle of activity. A few preferred reference pads to their interfaces, permitting use of multiple sources at a time, and some had to take multiple language references. Arhus knew that the hard part would be synchronizing with the assigned persons or groups from the other end of a connection. He studied his interface for any assigned matches but found little of use. With a sigh, he hoped the information would come soon enough to establish the routes before the speeches started.

Sindie walked up to Arhus. "You have the lists yet?"

"No," he responded as he checked his interface again.

"No? Great, last minute assignments again. That means grumpy diplomats." Sindie rolled her eyes.

"We do the best we can. I'm leaving now. Maybe there will be more information at the conference room." Arhus turned to leave.

"Right! Be optimistic. See how far that gets you."

As Arhus walked to the lift, Josef fell into step with him. "Any idea what this is about?"

"Take a wild guess," Arhus said with a sarcastic laugh.

"They're going to debate it in general committee?" The lift was moving to their floor before they reached the entrance.

"Seems so."

Josef huffed in disbelief. "This ought to be interesting."

The doors opened and both men stepped onto the lift. As it descended, Arhus checked his interface again. "Being stingy with information."

"Aren't they always?"

"Now is not the time," Arhus said with a huff.

"Want me at the hub?"

"Yes, for now. No idea who we'll need where." Arhus's head came up with a small smile. "You want to translate for High Priest Gideon?"

"Do you think that's a good idea?" Josef said with his head cocked to one side and a frown. "After last time? Besides, she brings her own people."

"Just offering," Arhus said, looking at the lift door. "Just thought you might want to redeem yourself."

"Hey! I was right!" Josef poked Arhus with a finger. "Not my fault if she didn't like what that guy was saying."

"How long have you had this job?" Arhus's smile turned mischievous.

"Longer than you."

"One day."

"That's longer by anyone's count." Josef puffed up his shoulders as the lift doors opened.

"Just get to the hub," Arhus said with a resigned sigh and watched Josef walk off. Arhus went into the main room and searched for someone who looked like they were in charge. No ready target presented themselves, so he walked to a small area hidden behind and beneath the main podium called the staging area. As expected, people were installing electronic equipment and loading software from their interfaces.

"Is the person in charge around?" he asked the small group. One person looked up, pointed behind Arhus, and went back to his screen. Arhus turned and went to 'stage left' as it was called. It was little more than a waiting area for speakers, so it was an odd choice for someone who was supposed to make this meeting happen. The explanation came as Arhus neared and heard one side of a conversation. The woman was using an ear plug and sub-mandible mic for a measure of privacy.

Arhus was ready to wait for the conversation to stop before introducing himself, but who he found in the area preempted the introduction. He still waited while standing within eyesight until the woman tapped her ear.

"Ms. Smith."

"Arhus. Good to see you again." She read his expression in record time. "Surprised to see me?"

"Yes. I didn't know you handled these matters."

"Only on special occasions." She gave him a smile. "Official?"

"Yes. Translation services have been given no details."

"Who'd you bring?"

"Everyone."

"Good, we'll need them." Ms. Smith moved back into the main room.

"Who's coming?"

"Everyone." She said it with no emotion.

"Everyone? As in everyone everyone?" Arhus used enough emotion for both of them.

"Yes, all representatives from all countries and factions. Even the scientific ones." Ms. Smith made her way to the technicians.

"Are there assignments that I can pass along?"

"No, all being done on the fly. Hook up to the main server. Assignments will be handed out as needed."

Arhus stopped as if he had run into a wall. "You're kidding me."

The expression on Smith's face showed no hint of anything but command. "No, I'm not. You'll have to cope. If you feel like you can't, get someone else to do the job. Now go do your job."

Smith turned back to the technicians, leaving Arhus where he stood. The self-preservation spirit inside of him warned him to move before something bad happened and his legs obeyed. It was half a dozen steps before he tapped in for Josef.

"Yes, sir, boss?" Josef answered.

"We're flying blind," Arhus said into his mic.

"You're kidding!"

"Nope, and don't say word one if you want to keep your head. Surprised mine's still on. Make sure everyone has the main feed and is listening at all times. They might need to play catch-up."

"Good thing you have your best man at the wheel, then," Josef said with more mirth than Arhus felt.

"Don't let Sindie hear you say that," Arhus said, making a very small recovery.

"That's why they make private channels." Josef clicked off.

Arhus knew Josef's job had just become easier in the short run and a lot harder in the long. Transferring central control to Josef with his interface, he placed his own name in the assignable pool, but with last priority. *I'll help if needed, but I want to pay attention to what is happening as much as possible. Translators can get lost in the forest for all the trees rushing by if they keep being reassigned during the conversation, which is the source of most mistakes. Context preservation has to be maintained. I'll also have the luxury of gauging the political movements in the meeting.*

People started to arrive, the minions of the representatives who attended to everything from technical displays to the correct seat cushion. Arhus laughed at the thought of some of the requirements he had heard in the past. *Just normal human comfort desires or superstition? Maybe there's no difference.*

Without a lot to do besides note where people, including his, settled, Arhus tracked Ms. Smith's movements as much as possible. She seemed to be concerned with technical details to a greater extent than required. It made Arhus wonder what presentation was planned. It had to be connected to their visitors, but he could not think why so much technology would be required. *Are they going to link in the visitors? I can't imagine they would agree to that.*

A request came over his interface. It would have been routine, except for the fact that it came from overseas. Arhus stared at it for a moment before making an assignment, his mind still processing the implication.

Overseas? That means they are tying in other countries? No wonder there is so much activity down there. The spiderweb of connections made his head spin. *Are they going to let foreign leaders make comments? That could snowball like crazy! Did they insist on being linked in or do they even know to where they are linking?*

The implications made Arhus want to run and hide. He flagged Josef on his interface. "I just got a request for overseas connection.

The last time foreign leaders have been linked into a council meeting was before the World Council decided not to get involved in the Lower Sahara War."

"I know," Josef replied. "It turns out that even in 2258, people didn't care about that part of the world. I saw records of the meeting in college. A student from that part of the world had managed to find a copy. It wasn't considered the Council's brightest moment. He was using it as proof that the Council didn't care about them. The fact that the event had happened forty-four years before left people unconvinced. Anything more than five years is considered ancient history by most college students today."

"Makes we wonder, and nervous," Arhus said before ending the conversation.

The flow of arrivals became heavier, changing from the 'fashionably early' crowd to the 'don't want to be late' crowd. The mood was sombre, with less interaction than Arhus had observed before other meetings. Confidence was not in abundance, either. Both characteristics made Arhus nervous. *Tensions rarely go from high to low in meetings. Starting a meeting with tense people leads to bad endings.*

"Josef," he said into his interface, "are you scanning the crowd?"

"A little busy here," Josef replied in a distracted manner. "Did you know they were including other countries?" His voice tailed up with the question.

"I saw that. Just wanted to let you know it doesn't look cordial out here."

"Great!" Josef huffed. "At least I will be out of fist range."

"Be extra careful with any assignments."

"Like you need to tell me that? Much to do, must go." The connection was broken.

Checking his interface again for other information, Arhus continued to watch people enter in a no-nonsense manner, taking their places and setting up displays. The amount of equipment was unusual, making him wonder how many were creating a direct link with the home office. He couldn't help chuckling to himself, but did resist the urge to call Johann to see if he was pulling his hair out yet.

"Mr. Gint."

The comment caught Arhus off-guard, causing him to jump. When he turned, he found Ms. Smith behind him. The idea that he had been so distracted or that Ms. Smith was so sneaky did not make him feel any better.

"Can I help you?" Arhus managed to push out his lips.

"I have set aside a place for you near the front. I would like to show you where."

"What?" Arhus's eyes went wide. "Why?"

"In case you are needed."

"Needed for what?" Arhus's confusion still reigned in his head but he was getting used to it.

"Because of the topics we will be discussing. Please follow me."

Smith turned and started walking toward the podium. Arhus followed. It took a dozen steps for his brain to kick into something besides shock. He lifted his interface to his mouth.

"Josef, I'm being kidnapped. You may be on your own."

"What?! Are you kidding? Don't tell me this is Sindie, because if it is…"

"No, official." Arhus looked around to see if anyone had heard.

"Crap! Well, we who are about to die salute you."

"I think that should be my line. Deal the best you can, I gotta go dark."

"Wait!"

Arhus cut the connection and put his interface on private. Whatever was going on, he didn't want it spilling over to anyone else. The seat he was led to was not in the front row, but anyone who knew him would have no problem picking him out of a shot that didn't focus on the speaker. As he reached the seat, Smith turned back to him.

"Stay here the whole time, unless I dismiss you, that is." Her look was total seriousness.

"Should I go to the restroom now so I don't have to get up?" Arhus asked, maintaining as serious an expression as he could. To his surprise, Smith reached into her pocket and then held out her fist. He placed his hand underneath and she dropped a white pill into it.

"Take the pill so you don't have to. I would suggest doing it now." With that, she turned back toward the technicians.

For some reason, I feel I should salute, Arhus thought as he popped the pill into his mouth and swallowed. The pill was slick and mint flavoured, much better than the last time he had taken one. While standard equipment for his work, he hated the pills. *I'll have to drink a gallon of water, just water, not beer or anything else, after the meeting and spend several hours near a restroom. At least it's been a long time since I've taken one. Rumour is that if you take them too close together or too many times, you get crystals in your kidneys. There's medicine that could deal with that, but it's something I would rather avoid.*

The worst part about sitting in his assigned location was that it was hard to watch people walk into the room. Diplomatic etiquette did not allow him to sit facing backwards. He pulled up the display embedded in the chair in front of him, an advantage of not being in the front row, and pulled up a picture of the room. It was too small to give details and zooming meant he missed much of the room in order to see details. After some adjusting, he found a compromise that was not satisfying but somewhat informative. It felt like he was spying on people, but he could use his job to justify the view if someone asked.

Most of the chairs had been filled when Arhus began to wonder if the one next to him would remain vacant. With the importance of the meeting, it was hard to imagine any seat would be left empty. The last of the seats were being taken when someone finally sat next to him. The man wore the dark green dress uniform of Council Security. Arhus's heart sank a little, wondering if he was considered a threat, until he recognized the face.

"Lieutenant Benjamin Amster, nice to meet you again," Arhus said, extending his hand.

The man's face was neutral until he saw Arhus's. A smile emerged as he shook the hand. "Mr. Gint, good to see you again, too. Didn't know you'd be sitting here."

"I'm surprised you remember me." The handshake was firm, but not aggressive, and lasted three pumps.

"You were on our watch-for list," Amster replied.

"Sounds ominous," Arhus said with a slight laugh in his voice.

"No, no." Amster chuckled. "The list of people likely to show up, not the other kind."

"Good, I never felt dangerous before and would hate to think I was now." Arhus turned back to the podium as Mi Kutua approached.

"A man who speaks the truth is always dangerous," Amster whispered.

Arhus did not let his surprise at the comment show. *Deep thoughts for a security officer,* he told himself. *Definitely more to this guy than his job.*

Silence filled the room as Mi stood at the podium. She looked over the crowd, head turning back and forth. It was the first time Arhus wished he could see the whole scene to find out if she was looking at anything in particular. It was one o'clock to the second when Mi started talking.

"Thank you all for coming. This meeting, in my opinion, has been put off as long as it could be and longer than it should have been. Everyone across the world has been talking about our off-world visitors in secret meetings and hushed whispers. It is time for that to change. Yes, we are all afraid. Afraid of technology that they have and we do not. Afraid of their true intentions, not helped by their lack of communication with us. And afraid due to their demonstrated strength in Indonesia and in our own backyard.

"But we can no longer afford to be afraid. Events no longer permit us the luxury of waiting and watching. We are here today to discuss the events of the last few days and the actions that should be taken because of them. This is still our planet and still our world, no matter what some alien says or claims. And might does not make his claims true!

"We have scheduled a series of testimonies from informed individuals to convey what has happened since our visitors arrived. After all the facts have been laid out, we will entertain recommendations for action, which will be voted on by the assembly. All assembly members present will vote on all measures. Some of the recommendations have been prepared and some will be taken from the floor. All issues and recommendations will be heard, though we will have to limit debate on each item if you want to get out of here before the weekend."

The comment brought general laughter from the crowd, the kind that signalled that they knew she was speaking the truth. It didn't do anything to lighten the mood.

"There are two issues we are here to discuss today. The first is the presence of our visitors and the second is those who are joining them. Based on information presented to you today, we cannot verify that their participation is voluntary."

The statement caused a stir of voices and a gasp from the crowd.

"We have an obligation to protect the people of Earth, which means that we must be sure that they are not being manipulated. Events have unfolded quickly, too quickly for us to be sure of everything that is happening. We do not have all the answers yet, and I personally feel that we are due answers."

Applause came from the crowd. An empty feeling started in Arhus's stomach. He had never been part of peace negotiations, but the meeting was beginning to have that feel.

"The Earth and the World Council has to stand united!" More applause. "Today we will decide what we stand for. Do we let aliens come and do anything they wish without so much as a whimper? Or do we let them know that we of Earth are not owned by any alien race? Do we let them know that humans are intelligent, self-aware people who are in control of their own destiny? Do we stand in fear or do we stand in resolve?"

The crowd was exuberant now, cheering and clapping. Lieutenant Amster was not one of them. He sat in an attention-like pose, as unresponsive as the crowd was responsive. Arhus leaned his direction.

"This worry you as much as me?" Arhus asked.

"More," Amster replied.

Kutua waved her hands to quiet the crowd. It took a good thirty seconds for the enthusiasm to die down. Kutua smiled at the crowd as they did.

"First, we will present the facts. Please hold questions until later or queue them into your interface. Some of our technicians may be able to answer questions while the presentations are being made. The rest will be tabulated so the most common can be answered.

"Let me introduce Ambassador Montoya. He has been gathering information about our visitors since their arrival and has been asked to present what he knows. Ambassador Montoya?"

With an arrogant walk, Montoya took the stage, dressed in full diplomatic garb, complete with sash. His beard had been restyled and he wore a huge, self-satisfied smile. As he started talking, Arhus tuned him out.

I know all this. Montoya's a good speaker, but he enjoys holding the audience in thrall too much. Let him enjoy his fifteen minutes of fame. He'll probably not get another. I wonder who will be next? I am sure they will be crucial to Mi getting what she wants.

Montoya received sufficient applause for his speech and spent a little too much time accepting it, in Arhus's opinion. He expected Kutua to walk back up to the podium, but she didn't. Instead, American Ambassador Greg Mallard took the podium.

"So much for restraint," Arhus mumbled.

"This ought to be interesting," Amster replied.

"My fellow delegates," Mallard started, "the history of many of our countries records times of oppression by others, whether from those outside of our country or from within. Each of these oppressors have been resisted and overcome by the efforts of brave men and women, common citizens who stood up to the forces that wished to overcome them.

"Today should not be a day when we dishonour those who have come before us. Today should be a day that we follow in their footsteps and do not allow our independence, our self-determination, be taken from us."

Wild applause erupted as Mallard stopped to take a breath. He let it die down before speaking again.

"Now, I know that some of you are worried that I am calling for war. Let me assure you, I am not. While we are all members of the World Council, we are still all sovereign states, and as sovereign states, exercise control of our own borders."

More applause, not as loud or wild, followed the statement. A small, single laugh came from Amster just loud enough for Arhus to hear.

"As such," Mallard continued, "it is my belief that each country should decide which of their citizens should be allowed to enter the alien ship and which should not." Louder applause. "Control of a country's border has been a right of a country since civilization has existed and I see no reason to give that up now. The United States of America only asks that the World Council acknowledge that right and not interfere in our exercise of it."

Mallard smiled as applause resounded throughout the room. He raised his hands as if to welcome the adoration. Seconds went by with Mallard giving no indication of wanting it to stop. *Most likely he doesn't. I wonder what new position Mallard will use his fame to acquire?* Finally, the response died down.

"I would like to move that the General Council call for a vote on a resolution stating that each country has the right to regulate its own citizens with respect to access to the alien ship." The statement caused a stir, with some calls to the affirmative. "But we are not doing that right now."

Laughter rippled through the crowd. Some applause in appreciation of the joke was included. Mallard chuckled along with the crowd.

"I promised to keep this short," Mallard finished, "and cede the floor back to Senior Commissioner Mi Kutua."

With that, Mallard turned, made a small bow, and exited the podium as Kutua retook the stand. Kutua gave him a nod as she passed. More applause followed Mallard from the stage, but he didn't turn and acknowledge it.

"Now we will hear from Kuwa Tammil, representative of the African Confederation." Mi turned and lifted her hand to the right to welcome Kuwa to the stage. He was dressed in full African garb from head to foot, a multicoloured display. While the formal dress was not unusual, Arhus noted no insignia or indication of the World Council on his person.

"Thank you, Senior Commissioner," Tammil started. He let the polite applause die before speaking. Arhus was sure people were holding their breath. "Mr. Mallard has made a very vigorous speech. Possibly a very dangerous one."

Arhus felt a subtle stir more than heard it. Looking to the side, he could also see some people nod their heads.

"We have all seen what our visitors can do. We also all know *for a fact* that there is nothing we can do to restrain them when they choose to act. Some of you may dismiss Indonesia as not representing mankind's true capabilities, but it cannot be denied that readings were taken during their actions and that our visitors have technology we cannot match. It is also *a fact* that they have demonstrated fierce determination to get what they came for. To challenge this in any form can bring us *peril.*"

Murmurs were starting to be heard in the crowd. Arhus wondered what their reaction would be to such words. *Booing is considered bad form, but that doesn't mean it wouldn't happen. People who don't attend regular general council meetings may not know or care about unofficial rules.* As Tammil spoke, Arhus tried to zoom in with his display on the crowd, searching for the discontent. The Americans were an obvious choice, along with some of the more stringent countries like in the Far East. The smaller countries' delegations that he could find appeared to agree. The neutral responses were what took him by surprise. European delegates looked unaffected, as did central Asian and Middle Eastern. *That might just mean they already have plans in place,* he reminded himself. *Would some king want to keep his son from going or insist he be taken along? I guess that depends on how many he has.*

"By risking force, a country risks violence on us all!" The comment brought some enthusiastic applause. "The African Confederation will not risk violence upon our people! The result would be greater loss of life and destruction of what we hold dear. Do not deceive yourselves into thinking that you can dictate to this alien what he will and will not do. They have come here knowing that we cannot prevent their plans. What we should be doing is cooperating with them so that they will give us technology to use against the next aliens that have similar ideas. If we cannot do that, then we know what we are facing and must come together to develop technology ourselves before the next visit."

The comments brought a sustained, if not wild response. *A cautious plan, but a reasonable one, though it may not be popular with a lot of people. It sounds a lot like rolling over and playing dead, which is how those who disagree would spin it, I'm sure. But then, people have always been too willing for others to die.*

"The African Confederation will not support any measure of

restraint against those willing to join with the aliens. It is unwise and goes against every standard of freedom claimed by the World Council!"

Now the applause got wild, accompanied by shouts of agreement.

"Trump card," Arhus muttered.

"The man has a point," Amster replied, not joining in the applause.

"Hey, we would hate for principles to get in our way of doing the right thing, wouldn't we?" Arhus responded. The comment brought a snort from Amster, suppressed as soon as it started. Arhus decided he liked the man more and more.

"Stand with us!" Tammil shouted. "Stand with us against those who invite violence upon our heads! Stand with us against the foolishness that has plagued mankind throughout his history! I beg you, stand with us!"

Tammil raised his arms, fists clenched, encouraging the applause that followed. Some booing started to be heard, but it was muted. After less than half a minute, Tammil lowered his arms, bowed to the crowd, and walked from the stage without acknowledging the Senior Commissioner.

That fact alone speaks volumes, though without additional information, I can't make a conclusion.

"And the race is on," Amster said.

"To what is the question," Arhus replied.

Mi looked self-satisfied. *Does she want this division?* Arhus thought. *Is she going to use it as an excuse to do nothing, deflecting blame with the divided will of the people? Or is she going to use it as an excuse for the Central Committee to assume authority to act?* Mi gave no indication with her expression about which side she preferred. She didn't even flinch at Tammil's snub, as if she was expecting it. *Either she has some scheme or she doesn't care,* Arhus decided.

Four more speakers followed, their speeches predictable, if one knew the country or organization associated with the speaker. Both sides of the issue were presented with equal time. Mi even allowed one speaker who couldn't seem to make up his mind, jumping from one side to the other.

"The perfect politician," Arhus commented.

"You expected less?" Amster replied.

"True, there are quite a few around here," Arhus conceded. Amster laughed once under his breath.

Mi Kutua took the podium when the speeches were complete. "I want to thank each speaker for presenting their views. I believe it is time to call for a motion. Do I have a motion from the floor?"

Chaos erupted. The volumes people used dwarfed those previously heard. Arhus tensed, knowing that every option was available to Kutua and that the one she would pick would provide insight to her leanings. She did not allow the shouting to go on for long.

"Ambassador Mallard, you have a proposal?" Mi said, pointing.

The response from the floor of the section was even louder. Angry shouts of protest reminded Arhus of old British Parliament sessions. People were standing and even pumping their arms at Kutua. In reply, she pressed a spot on the podium, causing a gavel-like sound to be sent through the audio system. It took several presses for everyone to calm down.

"Please, all motions will be entertained," Kutua said. "They will be taken one at a time. Mr. Mallard."

"I propose," Mallard stated in a clear voice, "that a motion be passed by the General Council that states that each country or governing party is to be tasked with setting their own policy with respect to the emigration of their citizens to the alien ship and that this policy will not be counteracted with respect to their citizens by any other country or governing body."

While heated words erupted again, Arhus considered the motion. *It sounds reasonable, deceptively simple in fact, since it would nullify any future measures passed by the World Council. Would Kutua hand all that power over to the states? It could be seen as the start of the dissolution of the power the World Council has over alien relations. Is that the game she is playing, trying to obtain an advantage for her own country over the others by special relationships with extraterrestrial powers? That's a bold play and one that could be seen as world-dominating by others. Has she made some deal with America, splitting up spheres of influence like the Molotov-Ribbentrop agreement?* The thought was scary.

"We have a motion on the floor. Do we have a second?" Kutua asked.

"Second!" The statement came from the section with Western Pacific Conglomerate representatives. The tension inside of Arhus rose. Such an obvious move could not be ignored by the other delegates.

Is Mi trying to get the motion killed? Arhus wondered.

"We have a second. Please put the motion on the display." A copy of the wording appeared on the general display and in each of the personal displays. "We will now take a vote."

Arhus held his breath, feeling that the fate of the world was at hand. Even with all he knew about the different contingencies, he could not guess how the vote would come out or how it would be enacted. *For all of Mallard's nation thumping, he did not give any indication how America would respond to the motion. Do they think they can negotiate with the aliens, getting something in return? Do they want to make sure that those chosen are not 'the best' of the nation and not be told that they couldn't try to talk their people out of going? Or do they think they can beat the aliens?*

Arhus was stunned out of his concentration by the sudden appearance of the Subordinate next to the podium. A communal gasp went through the crowd, followed by a hush. Mi Kutua turned, eyes wide and mouth open. She looked lost. The Subordinate wasn't smiling. He looked over the crowd, ignored Kutua and turned to face them.

Chapter Nineteen
Take A Deep Breath

We have seen what is in your hearts, his voice said in Arhus's head. *Some of you are rebellious and head-strong. Such attitudes do not serve you well. We have only come to you with kindness and patience, admonishing those who have wished to forestall our wishes. We will not be patient forever.*

The Subordinate's expression turned hard. *We have come for what is ours and we will gather them to us. All those who wish to contend with us will be punished, as we have demonstrated. We implore you, do not be like these rebellious ones who think they can foil our plans. It will end in your grief and sorrow.*

Looking out over the crowd, the Subordinate did not get any happier as he talked. Arhus felt the Subordinate was looking into the minds of the delegates, reading their thoughts as he spoke. To read so many at one time was a daunting, frightening thought. *If they can know the thoughts of so many at once, how could any scheme be successful? But then, maybe it is all a bluff. But are we willing to risk our lives on it?*

We see that you are not all convinced, the Subordinate continued. A fearful murmur went through the crowd, while some maintained defiant expressions. Mi Kutua started to back away from the podium toward the technician pit. People stirred in their seats, the thought of running from the room hard not to read. *A demonstration may be in order.*

The Subordinate raised his right hand. Not having panicked up to this point, Arhus now felt it flow through his body. Lieutenant Amster rose from his seat. Arhus's head swivelled to take in his surroundings, his breath becoming short. Visions of destruction filled his mind, along with a panicked crowd and the resulting harm to those involved.

Don't do this! Arhus thought as hard as he could toward the Subordinate, not knowing if he would hear.

The Subordinate's hand stopped. He did not turn toward Arhus, but appeared frozen in motion. *Why not?* filled Arhus's head.

The sense of panic did not leave Arhus, but it changed. Suddenly, he felt that his next words would either prevent or allow an Armageddon-sized war to take place. *Hundreds or thousands of lives could be in the balance based on my next words. What can I say? What can I tell the Subordinate that they don't already know? Am I the best representative of humanity to argue our case? Is there a case? I have no influence with the Americans or other factions that want to stand up to the aliens.*

Time seemed to stand still, waiting for Arhus's response. *Can the aliens even do that?* No one moved, no one seemed to breathe. He could feel the presence of the aliens in his head.

How did I put myself in this situation? Arhus wondered. *At least no one else will know. Will they? Here goes nothing.*

Because it won't get you what you want, Arhus thought to the Subordinate.

This time the Subordinate turned toward and looked at Arhus. *What do you mean?*

Trying not to think how much attention the Subordinate's stare would draw, Arhus thought, *If you move against people who have not attacked you, it will cause them to resist you more. People love nothing more than a martyr and if you kill them now, that is what they will become. I am sure you have other ways of influencing people. If you are the first to initiate violence, everything that happens will be your fault.*

So we wait for them to attack?

I don't know that they will. An attack on their part could cause people to favour you instead. Plus, they haven't said that they will stop people from going. They might just be baiting you.

Baiting?

Trying to get you to act first so they aren't blamed for the result.

But they are thinking violence.

But they aren't doing it. If they know or think you can read their minds, they will use that to make you believe that they are planning something, even if they aren't.

The Subordinate turned away. As far as Arhus could tell, the Subordinate just stared at the crowd. *Is he communicating with the others? There is no way to tell. Or is there?*

Setting his interface on private and lifting it to his mouth, Arhus keyed in Johann. It didn't take long for Johann to answer.

"Are they talking?" Arhus asked.

"Who? Oh, yeah, they are, like old busybodies. What's going on?"

"Trying to prevent Armageddon. Tell you later." Arhus broke the connection. When he looked up, Amster was looking at him.

"Was that alien talking to you?" Amster asked in a voice far from hushed.

"Ah, yeah," Arhus replied.

"About what?" Amster's voice was insistent.

"Just trying to keep the world in one piece." Arhus managed to swallow.

"What is he about to do?"

"Nothing, I hope." Arhus didn't think he sounded convincing, but that didn't keep him from hoping.

Now other people were looking at him, though the Subordinate was not looking at anyone in particular, more toward the ceiling. Not knowing how many people suspected he had been talking to the Subordinate, it was hard to know how many expected something from him. When Arhus didn't do or say anything, more out of fear than resolve, they started to look back toward the Subordinate. Arhus tried to breathe in a normal manner, though he could feel his heart beating like a hyperactive drummer.

Again the Subordinate looked at the crowd. He smiled and crossed his arms on his chest.

We have decided to do nothing for now, the Subordinate's voice said in Arhus's head. *If our own are prevented from joining us, consequences shall ensue.*

With that statement made, the Subordinate disappeared in a flash of light. *Was he really there or not? It could have been a mental projection like with the messengers. All this 'we' stuff is not very reliable.*

Arhus reactivated his interface. "What now?"

"Nothing," Johann stated. "Everything's quiet. What happened?"

"He left, without killing anyone." Arhus sighed.

"That's something, at least. What did you tell him?"

"We'll talk about it later. Stay cool."

Of immediate notice was that the level of muted conversations had gone up with the Subordinate's departure. Mi Kutua was making her tentative way back to the podium. She kept looking around as if expecting someone to jump out at her. Taking the podium with both hands, Mi pressed the gavel button.

"There is a motion on the floor to allow each country to dictate the terms of their own people's emigration to the alien ship. Please vote."

Watching on his display, the numbers tally was slow at first, but then picked up speed. The positive votes came in first, but the negative caught up, though the total was still low. As time went on, the positive votes increased in number until obtaining an almost two-to-one margin. No one abstained. The total turned green as the vote total reached one-hundred percent.

"With all votes tallied," Mi announced, "the measure has passed. I am calling for a fifteen minute recess. Please return at the appointed time."

Shaking, Mi Kutua walked away from the podium. People stirred, both verbally and physically. Some left the room while most others activated their personal interfaces. Arhus put his head back on the head-rest of the seat and looked up.

Hoping that it was all over, Arhus's peripheral vision intruded into his calming process. From both sides, he started to notice how many people were looking at him. He tried to dismiss the looks, but they continued.

How could they have known? The conversation was telepathic,

Arhus thought. *True, he did look at me, and Amster was questioning me.* His nervousness started to grow.

Arhus closed his eyes, hoping to discourage attention, but he still heard footsteps that seemed to be coming closer. He prevented himself from groaning. When he opened his eyes and looked away from the ceiling, twenty people were standing close by, staring at him. A few whispered to each other. Standing up, Arhus nodded to the crowd.

"You are Arhus Gint, are you not?" a man with a Middle Eastern accent asked. "You are the one who has entered the alien ship."

"Yes," Arhus replied, nodding, "that I am."

"Why did you not speak today?" the man asked.

"I wasn't asked. Besides, I am only an interpreter."

"I don't care what your job is," a woman took up, "we want to know what you know!"

"Ambassador Montoya went over the information." Arhus kept his voice even, as he did when interpreting.

"You don't think we believe he told us everything?" the woman replied.

"That is not important!" the Middle Eastern man said, taking back the conversation. "You were talking with the alien, were you not?"

For a second, Arhus weighed the options and political consequences, more out of reflex than anything. *Hell with that,* he thought to himself. *Someone else can play that game.*

"Yes," Arhus said, "I was."

"What did you say to him? What was he going to do?"

Taking a deep breath, Arhus began. "He was about to demonstrate their power. How, I cannot say, but I am sure it would not have been healthy for at least some individuals in this room. I asked him not to, telling him that people would not react in the manner he wanted. He then said they would wait."

The statements caused the people surrounding Arhus to pause in thought, but not for long.

"So what are they going to do?" someone asked.

"They are going to see if those invited are prevented from joining the ship. If so, I cannot say what their response will be."

"Would they send out those angels of theirs and kill more people?"

a voice asked.

"Why not?" another answered. "They've already done it before."

"What are we supposed to do?"

"What can we do? You saw what happened in Indonesia. We can't stop them."

"You mean Indonesia couldn't stop them," someone said with derision.

"And you will do better?"

"There is something you may not understand," Arhus put in, waiting for people to stop talking before continuing. "There is evidence that the aliens can read our minds whenever they want to."

Arhus could feel the shiver that went through those around him. The conclusion that this particular information had been withheld was clear on their faces. Some reacted with worry, others with grim, analytical looks of what the statement meant.

"Why you?" someone from behind asked.

"I'm sorry?" Arhus replied, turning to look for the questioner.

"Why did he pick you to talk to?" Arhus couldn't place where the delegate was from by his dress or speech. *A conglomerate, most likely.*

"Because I happened to be there when they came out? I don't know the answer except that the Subordinate, the one who appeared, likes people without political ambitions."

"You mean to tell us," the man laughed, "that given all this, you now have no political ambitions?"

"No, I do not," Arhus said in a firm voice. "In fact, the faster I can get away from all this, the better."

"Right," the man replied with a small huff. "We'll see."

"Mr. Gint!" The firm voice came from behind the group. Those between Arhus and the voice parted with reluctance for Mi Kutua. She looked as far from happy as Arhus thought possible. "You are not a representative of the World Council and will not talk to anyone about these matters!"

"You are right. I am not a representative of the World Council."

The statement hung in the air. Kutua did not change expressions, but some of those around Arhus started to smile.

"You still work for the World Council and as such are ordered to return to your office and resume your duties."

"Excuse me, representatives," Arhus said with a small bow, "it appears I am needed elsewhere. Good day."

As Arhus left the group to walk up the aisle to the exit, he was joined by Mi and several of her people, making a fence of human flesh around him. *I might like a copy of this video footage.*

"What did you think you were doing?" Mi insisted.

"Talking, you know, like normal people."

"You have not been cleared to talk to anyone about our visitors!" Mi said in a sharp, low voice.

"Everyone is talking about the visitors," Arhus noted. "Are you going to prevent them from doing so also?"

"I could have you fired right here on this spot!"

"And lose your connection to our visitors? I don't think you'll do that. I doubt you can afford to do that." Arhus could see his easy manner grinding on Mi.

"Then I will have you arrested for dissemination of council secrets."

"Oh, I am sure our visitors would just love you for that." Arhus gave her a smile. "Care to find out?"

As they exited the room and entered the large foyer, people cleared a path for the group. It did not prevent them from staring as the group passed. Arhus could see cloistered conversations starting.

"You think you are in a position of power, Mr. Gint. Don't be so foolish." Mi waved a hand at their escort and they turned toward the private lifts.

"I know what position I am in and I think my actions earlier show how much power I have." Arhus's voice lost all softness and his eyes became hard. "I just stopped a possible war in your backyard and you know it. I don't know what game you were playing up there and I don't care. I care about the people in this town who would have to pay the price for all your politician's games!" The lift opened and the group entered. Arhus waited for it to start rising before speaking again. "Let me be very clear. I don't care about power plays or who comes out on top in all this, because I believe that by the time the aliens leave, there will be no top. Everything will change once they are gone, haven't you figured that out yet? You expect people to go back to their normal lives knowing that there are races out there who consider us their property to be farmed?"

"They will need our leadership more than ever," Mi said with confidence.

"And who will they blame for not knowing and protecting them from the aliens?"

Arhus watched Mi's head turn toward him. He could tell she wanted to reply, but the answer was running through her head as she did so.

"It doesn't matter if there was no way for us to know," Arhus continued. "It won't matter. Enough people will find 'evidence' of past visits in history and then start asking how you could not have known, and if you did, why you were covering it up. And then the conspiracy theories will fly and fly hard. Religious leaders will spout how they have now been vindicated after generations of ridicule and people will flock to them. Whole new churches will be created because of the aliens' visit. Philosophy will be turned on its head and the history of the world will be rewritten. And you think you will survive all that?"

Mi turned back to face the lift door, straightened herself, and took a breath. "We are survivors, we will survive anything."

"Ha!" Arhus couldn't prevent himself from saying. "Keep telling yourself that."

The lift had stopped moving, but the doors had not opened. Arhus had not seen any of the group address the controls. *One of the group must have a remote. With rank comes privileges.*

"Am I fired?" Arhus asked.

"It will be taken under consideration, but for now, no. Good day, Mr. Gint. Oh, and by the way, don't try telling anyone you are not a politician.

Arhus's brow furrowed. "What does that mean?"

"That little speech you gave was not one from a simple translator. I am beginning to wonder if you are making your own play here." Mi's head was lowered, not looking at Arhus as she made the comment.

"I have no idea what you are talking about." Arhus turned back toward the lift door.

"We'll see."

The door opened and Arhus walked off, not even checking if he was on the correct floor. When he walked out of the small hallway, he found himself in the back of his office area. Turning, he looked back from where he had come, but could not see the lift door.

"I always wondered what that hallway was for," he said to himself before turning back into the room. It was empty. Checking the time, he wondered, *How many people will bother to come back to the office after the meeting? Not that it matters at the moment. They are still processing, like everyone else. Tomorrow is soon enough to get back to work.*

Arhus went to his office and called up the interface display. No messages waited for him. His next step was to turn on the news reports. A sigh came out as the picture went to Reverend Owens.

"I have no idea what the government is planning," Owens said in a boisterous voice, "but if the government is planning on preventing people from getting on that ship, then they are interfering with their religious rights, rights guaranteed by the conventions of the World Council! They will find themselves in contention with our guests and their own people!"

Arhus sat back in the chair. "How the hell do they know already? This couldn't have been Mi's plan all along."

"It is time the Council acknowledges the facts in front of them. They can no longer keep pretending that our visitors are not the God of the Bible and deserve to be treated as such. If nothing else, they are representatives from somewhere not here! And how are they treated? Where are the official receptions? Where are our dignitaries to greet them? They are treated almost as an enemy. Anyone who treats God as an enemy will suffer a terrible fate!" Owens raised a finger to the sky.

"Pompous windbag," Arhus said to the display.

"Who's a pompous windbag?" Sindie's voice asked from the door, her head leaning into the room.

"Our American friend, Reverend Owens," Arhus replied as he waved her into the room.

"What do you expect, he's a preacher." Sindie walked into the room with more caution than Arhus would have thought needed.

"Are you okay?"

"Yeah," Arhus said, his brow furrowing. "Why wouldn't I be?"

"I saw you being led out by Kutua." Sindie walked around the table. "You still have a job?"

"For now," Arhus said with a shrug. "Not sure I want it anymore, so not worried about it."

Sindie sat on the table in front of him. "Did you talk to the alien?"

"Yes," Arhus said on an exhale.

"About what?" Sindie leaned closer.

"About them not executing their righteous anger on the delegates."

Sindie's mouth took a round shape and her eyes went wide. They stayed that way for a few seconds. "They wouldn't do that, would they?"

"I got the feeling they would."

Sindie still looked horrified. "My God, that would have been…"

"Scary? Yes. Bloody? Yes. The start of a war? Most likely."

"How did you convince them not to?"

"I think the Americans were baiting them, trying to get them to make the first move."

"How? By the vote?"

"No." Arhus shook his head. "By thinking violent thoughts."

"Using the aliens' telepathy against them." Sindie nodded as she spoke.

"You got it."

"Their delegates were taking a huge risk of being dead."

"True, but they would have also been martyrs and gone down in history, if that is any consolation."

"For being dead? Not in my book."

"You're not a politician." Arhus poked her knee while he said it.

"Too much to enjoy still," she replied, smiling.

"Where's Josef?"

Sindie rolled her eyes and then gave Arhus one of those 'you really know how to kill a mood' looks. "He's still running things. It's a mess up there."

"Thought it might be. I owe him big."

"For doing his job?"

Arhus cocked his head. "You have met my friend Josef, haven't you?"

"Hey," Sindie replied, poking him in the chest, "you're his boss."

"Which he agrees with when it suits him, or haven't you noticed?"

"Threaten to fire him," Sindie said with a quirky smile.

"And have him quit instead? Besides, what would I do without him?"

"Oh, maybe rely more on your best employee," Sindie said as she tapped her chin.

"You want to run the booth next time?" Arhus raised one eyebrow.

"Ah, on second thought, no."

Arhus threw up his arms. "So much for ambition in the ranks."

"Hey! You're the one talking about quitting." Sindie crossed her arms.

"Maybe I've met my ambitions," Arhus said with a wag of his head.

"Shoot low often?" Sindie cocked her chin.

"It keeps me from being disappointed."

Sindie let out a single laugh and then looked up, shaking her head. "Why do I even try?"

"Because you're a female and can't help it," came from the doorway. Josef walked into the room. "What are we talking about?"

"You," Arhus replied.

"Of course!" Josef said with a wave of his arms. "What else is there? By the way, oh swami, you owe me big time for today."

Arhus looked at Sindie. "Didn't I just say that?"

"I believe you did," Sindie said with a shake of her head. "And I said..."

"I was correct, didn't you? So where do you want to eat to celebrate afterwards?" he asked Josef.

"Wait a minute..." Sindie started.

"The Grand!" Josef shot back.

"Hold on a minute..." Sindie tried to interrupt.

"Done. I'll call them." Arhus looked at Sindie. "You coming?"

"That's not... The Grand! Of course I'm coming. I have to change first, though." Sindie hopped off the table.

"You want to bring someone?" Arhus asked, looking back to Josef.

"Sure. Just one?" Josef replied.

"Just one. No parties. You can do that later."

"Well, I guess it will do," Josef said as if strained.

"You want *me* to pick?" Arhus asked.

"No, heck no. I'll do my own picking, thank you very much. You concentrate on the restaurant."

"Fine. Seven?"

"Try six, it will be easier." Josef waved his hand at Arhus, already lost in thought.

"Six! How am I going to be ready by then?" Sindie protested.

"Start right away?" Arhus offered.

"You don't have to tell me twice." Sindie made a quick beeline for the door.

"Ah," Josef said as he watched Sindie race by, "can I have the rest of the day off to get ready, too?"

"No, you're back on in five minutes." Arhus shrugged.

"What about you?" Josef said with a smirk.

"I was told to leave. I'll walk you to the door," Arhus said, standing up and turning off the interface.

"She has a key to your apartment, right?" Josef asked as they watched Sindie enter the lift from across the room.

"What do you think?"

"Knowing her, she made it herself."

Chapter Twenty
Aftershocks

When Arhus walked out the door from his apartment building in the morning, the street was filled with news crews pointed his direction. After the shock passed, he put his head down and started walking his normal route. When he made it to the wall of news crews, it did not part. The lenses pointed his direction and the questions he had been ignoring still came. An attempt at a different location gave the same results. Arhus turned to go back into the building, but found he was now surrounded by news crews who gave no indication of moving out of his way. The questions came at a steady pace.

"This is kidnapping, you know," Arhus said in a loud voice.

"The world has a right to know what is happening!" one of the mouth-pieces said.

"Who says? Where is that in the law?" Arhus shouted back.

"The right for people to know has been known for centuries," the speaker threw back, his back straight and his pose righteous.

"No, it has been repeated by news reporters endless times when they want to convince people that they should tell them something. The right *not* to say something has been established by law, that is a certainty." Arhus was speaking louder than required, but the adrenaline in his body contributed to his volume. "The law has also stated that restraining someone against their will is kidnapping.

Where's a cop when you need one?"

"You don't think with all that is happening, the people don't deserve to know all that they can?" The speaker looked stunned.

"It is my definite opinion that the less people know, the happier they are. Now get out of my way."

Arhus pushed at the news eye in front of him to find there was a second layer of news crews, making the creation of a path impossible. "How many of you fuckers are here?"

"You must make a statement for the people!" a different speaker stated. "The whole world is on the verge of panic! Someone has to do something, say something!"

"Blame your delegates for that!" Arhus shouted back. "They are the ones who created the situation!"

"But didn't the aliens create the situation by coming to Earth?" another insisted.

Arhus chuckled. "So what is this now, blame the victim? Do you think humans have been hospitable to our visitors since they arrived?"

"But they don't have the right to take people!" another said.

"They're not forcing anyone to get on that ship. In fact, there are plenty who want to go, but our visitors are not letting them."

"But how do we know they aren't mentally forcing them?"

"How do you know that the World Council isn't?"

The comment caused a pause and some chuckles in the circle. "The World Council doesn't have that ability, no one does."

"How do you know? How would you know that if they do and are making sure no one finds out? How do you know that they aren't communicating to the aliens by telepathy? How do you know that the World Council didn't invite them here using it?"

The circle stirred with looks and murmurs. Some touched earpieces and talked to interfaces. While some became confused, others maintained their smug expressions.

Are these people that easy to confuse?

"Everyone knows that the World Council has no telepathic abilities," a man said.

"And a month ago, everyone was sure that aliens had never visited Earth, at least anyone with any credibility," Arhus replied. "In the absence of evidence, you can't prove a negative. Now good day and get out of my way."

To Arhus's relief, security forces arrived. Their first task was making a path for Arhus to exit the circle. The effort was welcomed, but he was sure there was more to it than helping a citizen. As he passed the security officers, a man in a suit walked up and took his arm.

"What the hell do you think you are doing?" the man said in a hushed voice.

"Making media mouth-pieces look bad?" Arhus replied.

"You have not been authorized..." the man started.

"Hey! It wasn't my idea so don't go blaming me!"

In short order, Arhus and the man were surrounded by security personnel as they walked, all with serious expressions on their faces.

"Do you think we could stop so I could get some breakfast?" Arhus asked.

"No," was the reply.

"How about coffee? I'll buy."

"No."

"Breakfast I understand, but how is a guy supposed to function without coffee?" Arhus asked with a huff.

"Cope."

Arhus looked at the man for a few seconds while they walked and then looked back to where he was walking. "I bet you're the life of the party."

"I am, actually."

"Sure, whatever you say. By the way, are we going somewhere in particular?"

"The Chairman of the Special Council, Arlan Morresette, would like to talk to you."

"Took him long enough," Arhus said with exaggerated surprise.

The man glanced at Arhus. "You know, that attitude would be better to be stored before we get there."

"What's he going to do, fire me?"

"He could do much worse."

A group formed in front of them. From what Arhus could see, it was made up of citizens. Security immediately formed a wedge and plowed into the group, pushing people away when required. Obviously not used to resisting, the group parted for the procession. Some tried to ask questions as he passed, but he ignored them.

"Like what?" Arhus asked.

"Like imprisonment," the man replied.

"Do you think the aliens or the public would stand for that?" Arhus considered for a moment. "In fact, let him. It could raise my status among the crowd. I might be more popular than ever."

"If they knew."

"And no one is going to put two and two together after you are recorded escorting me from my home. Right. What do you think this is, the twentieth century?"

The man's face took on a note of anger. "We have other options."

"You guys slay me," Arhus said with a laugh. "You never learn that your best option is to do nothing."

"You would say that," the man said from the corner of his mouth.

"No, think about it. How many people can you think of in history who were imprisoned, beaten, killed, exiled, or otherwise abused for what they said or believed? Now, how many can you think of that were ignored?"

"How are we supposed to know about them if they were ignored?" the man asked, looking out of the corner of his eye.

"That's my point!"

The man's expression didn't change much, but Arhus was sure he was thinking. *That's good,* Arhus thought. *I don't want to find out what's in the 'something else' category.*

Arhus didn't speak during the remainder of the trip. They took the private lift to the top floor, one Arhus noted wasn't an option in other lifts. *So much for the banishment of privilege,* he thought. *I hope they have coffee.*

The lift opened to a hallway. Arhus was led to a door. The man opened the door and then gestured for Arhus to enter. Once he was through, the man closed it without entering. In front of Arhus was a younger man sitting behind a desk with an active display. To one side was a couple of plants and some well-cushioned chairs. On the other side was an espresso machine that was popular with high-end restaurants. The cups at the table looked like china.

"Mr. Morresette will be a few minutes," the man behind the table said without looking up. "Please feel free to have some coffee."

"Of course," Arhus said to himself. All the cups appeared to be on the small size. "This is going to take several trips."

Arhus chose a cup, set it on the receptacle, and told the machine his selection, erring on the more, not less side when it came to things like sweetness. The resulting cup was creamy and very sweet. Downing the cup in one swig, he replaced it and asked for a second. The second one he took to a chair with him.

Once seated with the cup on the small table next to the chair, Arhus checked his interface. It was clear, which made him suspicious. He sent a message to Josef, telling him that he had been detained in a meeting and did not know when he would be in the office. The notice that the message had been delivered took longer than normal.

Great, reading my messages now?

Arhus picked up the cup, leaned back in the chair, and decided to enjoy a cup of coffee that he guessed cost more than he could afford to pay on a regular basis. *I can't taste a difference, but I'll enjoy it as if I can.*

Before he reached the bottom of the cup, the man behind the desk spoke again. "Mr. Morresette will see you now."

Since there was only one door on the other side of the room, Arhus headed toward it. The door opened as he approached, swinging open all the way as his foot reached the sill. Once through, the door shut itself.

The room Arhus entered was luxurious in every way. Plush carpet covered in places by oriental rugs, solid wood chairs upholstered in antique fashion with tacks, a wooden desk that looked like mahogany at least six feet across, crystal lighting, and real or simulated marble walls greeted him. It was hard not to gasp. Two walls of the room were glass, with a view of Jerusalem with green countryside in the background. From this angle, the city looked different. Arhus was able to see intricate detailed designs on the tops of buildings that were not visible from the ground. He also noted that you could not see any people from here.

"Please take a seat," Morresette said, standing behind the desk and indicating the chairs in front of it. Composing himself, Arhus walked in front of one and they sat down. "Thank you for coming."

Arhus felt like saying something about not having a choice, but his common sense told him to stay silent.

"You've drawn quite a lot of attention of late," Morresette said.

"Having the Subordinate like to talk with you will do that, I suppose," he replied.

Morresette frowned, but then gave a dismissive huff. "I have heard that you have a view of your own significance."

"Doesn't everyone?"

The comment drew a look from Morresette. "Of course they do. I asked you here to discuss the information you have been supplying to delegates and the media. There are some who are concerned about this information."

Morresette paused, but for once, Arhus made no comment, just looked at the man across the desk. Morresette continued.

"Many are of the opinion that we have to control the type and amount of information that is disseminated. It would appear that you do not agree." Morresette's right eyebrow lifted and he again paused. When Arhus said nothing, he added, "Would you like to clarify?"

"I am a translator. Information is given to me and I pass it on to someone else. That is the basic function of my job. It is not up to me to decide what should or shouldn't be passed along." Arhus kept this neutral posture as he spoke.

"That is correct, but you have not been authorized to pass this information to other parties, I may point out."

"At the time of the event, I was not given specific directions not to pass it along."

This time Morresette gave a genuine smile. "Yes, I have heard that you are a person who can use procedures to your advantage. Not that it will help you advance your career." Morresette turned back to his display.

"I am not trying to advance my career," Arhus stated. The statement caused Morresette to stop and turn back to him. The man tilted his head and pursed his lips.

"So you are telling me that you have no political or career aspirations?" Morresette looked surprised.

"Yes, that is what I am telling you," Arhus replied, still in a neutral voice.

"Some would say that makes you a dangerous man, Mr. Gint."

"Or an honest one."

Morresette turned back to his display. Fifteen seconds went by without conversation before he continued.

"Quite a few suggestions have come to my office about what to do with you. Some are rather... extreme."

"Like your man that escorted me here hinting that you could make me disappear?"

Morresette chuckled. "I'm afraid that Kelvin has watched too many spy movies. People don't do that anymore. We're civilized. Others have suggested firing you, but that would appear to be setting you free into the world without any supervision, which sounds even worse to me. Others have suggested publicly censoring you, discrediting you, in other words."

"Kind of late for that, isn't it?"

Another chuckle from Morresette. "Yes, so it would seem. Still others have suggested transferring you to a post on the other side of the Earth."

"You like speaking in non-specifics, don't you?" More emotion showed in the statement than in all of Arhus's previous conversation. Morresette shrugged.

"Bureaucratic habit, I suppose." Morresette regained his posture. "Because I am the head of the Special Committee, I have taken it upon myself to decide what to do about you. At least that way, it will be a final solution instead of all this constant side-show distracting us from our work. Unless you had something you wanted to state?"

Morresette looked at Arhus from the top of his eyes above his glasses. Arhus stared back for a few seconds.

"I am giddy with anticipation at your decision," Arhus replied.

Sighing, Morresette looked away. "I tire of your attitude, Mr. Gint. I find it irritating. Please stop."

"I tire, too, Mr. Morresette. People trying to use knowledge about the aliens to their political advantage. People acting like they have the best interest of their citizens at heart when they are actually trying to obtain an advantage from the aliens. People acting like they don't have firm opinions when they do." Arhus stopped talking long enough to breathe in again. "I am very curious what your decision is."

"I am sure many people are disappointed in many things." Morresette closed his eyes, took a breath, and then opened his eyes again. "I have decided to do nothing about you. I have no instructions, limitations, or threats. You are free to do as you will. You can continue at your job, which it appears you are quite good at, for as long as you want. Unless your performance changes, of course."

Arhus sat back in the chair without comment. No thoughts wandered through his brain. No other shoe dropped. Morresette worked his interface display as if Arhus was not there. After a while, Arhus raised an eyebrow.

"Is that all?"

"Yes, you may go now," Morresette said without looking.

Standing, Arhus made his way to the door. Halfway there, he wondered, *Did Morresette listen to the conversation through town?* but decided not to ask and ruin everything. When he exited the office and walked through the reception area, the man at the table did not look up or say anything as he left. *Better that way.*

The first worry he had was how he was going to call the lift, since he did not see any buttons or mics on the wall, but the door opened as he approached. First checking to make sure the lift car was there, he entered. *I've watched too many old movies,* he told himself. The door shut behind him and the lift started to descend without requesting a floor.

"I don't know if this is creepy or just superior technology," he said to himself. "Not like it would be hard. They would have to make a lot of assumptions and be willing to tolerate a lot of false starts. Of course, coming from the top floor gives you two obvious options."

Without a view, Arhus remained facing the door. It caused a wistful feeling, since the view would have made the trip more special. "I guess you can't have everything," he told himself. "Prevents assassinations, too, I guess."

When the lift stopped and the door opened, he thought he recognized his floor. After exiting, he realized that he had never exited the lift on a different floor and thus could not tell if they all looked the same or not. Walking a short distance confirmed his assumption. Several inquisitive looks were sent his way, but they just waved and smiled as he walked to his office. He did note that Josef and Sindie both made paths in the same direction, Josef more direct about it.

Arhus did not even make it to his desk before Josef walked in, spreading his hands in question. Smiling, Arhus waited for Sindie before saying anything.

"You have to put up with me for a while longer, at least," Arhus said to both friends.

"So? Nothing?" Josef asked as Sindie sighed in relief.

"Nope. Morresette is going to do nothing." Arhus walked around his desk but didn't sit down.

"Not even a stern lecture?" Josef asked, unbelieving.

"Nope."

"That's kind of disappointing," Josef commented, a resigned look on his face.

"What?"

"Maybe it would make you smarter," Josef said, leaning toward his friend. "Wake you up to the realities you are dealing with."

"Oh, shut up," Sindie said.

Josef turned to her, shocked.

"You want someone else to tell you what to do the rest of your life?"

"I like living," Josef replied.

"They don't do that anymore," Arhus commented.

"Right. That's what they tell you right before they do it some more." Josef's voice grew a little more excited.

"Paranoid," Sindie said all but under her breath.

"Living," Josef countered.

"Enough." Arhus put a little force behind the word. "I think Morresette is just giving me enough rope to hang myself with, or so he thinks. It's that or he doesn't want to ruin his chances with the aliens. Either way, it doesn't matter. I think he is going to tell everyone to get off my back."

"Which also means they'll stop trying to use you to get favours from the aliens?" Sindie asked.

"We can hope. I expect that violating it would break the truce, so to speak, and open the floodgates. As long as they leave me alone, I don't care." Arhus took a deep breath, let it out, and rubbed the top of his head.

"Are you sure the aliens didn't manipulate Morresette into making this decision?" Josef asked.

"No, and I don't care. If they did, then thank you very much to them."

"Maybe the guy isn't as stupid as he acts," Sindie commented.

"It's a nice thought," Josef said with a smile, "but I'm not holding my breath."

"So," Arhus said, trying to conclude the conversation, "the long and short is that it's back to work as normal." He raised his eyebrows at them.

"As if anything is normal nowadays," Josef mumbled. He stood there while Arhus stared at him. "Oh, that's my cue. Right."

As Josef walked out of the office, Arhus turned to look at Sindie. "Something else?"

"We need to talk," she said in a serious manner.

"About what?"

"The future." When Arhus gave her a questioning look, she added with a roll of her eyes, "Not that. Heavens no. Too soon, anyway. I mean what we are going to do in the future."

"How far in the future?"

"You getting picky now?"

"Just trying to be clear," Arhus said with a shrug.

"As far as we can: tomorrow, next week, next year. The farther, the better."

"You want to do that now?"

"Yes."

Arhus thought he saw some worry in her eyes. "Is something in particular bothering you?"

"You mean besides the whole world going nuts? Heck, no." She tilted her head to the side.

"It's not a bad idea, but I don't know if we can plan yet."

"The way things are going, if you said you wanted to run off to Tibet and live off yaks, I might not argue." She appeared to deflate a little.

Arhus looked in her eyes for a few seconds, seeing what he figured would be the same in other people's eyes. "I appreciate that, I really do. I don't think I would choose yaks, but I know what you mean. Plus, I don't know what our friends in the ship might think about me leaving."

"I thought their telepathy reached around the whole world?"

"One of them has assumed a human-like form that I am assuming comes with limitations."

"Could you just ask them?"

The simplicity of the question made Arhus want to kiss her right then. "Yes, I could, though I don't know if they would give me a straight answer or what a 'no' might mean."

"Still, might be worth a try." There was a little pleading in Sindie's voice.

"I will try if the situation is right. Course, I don't know when they will talk to me again."

"At the most inconvenient time, I am sure." Sindie switched to her work face. "You need anything?"

"No, I think…" Arhus's interface demanded his attention like an angry child. He hadn't even checked to see if it was active. He activated the personal display. Johann's face came up. "What's up?"

"Alien radio is going wild!" Johann was literally hopping up and down on his seat.

"Do you know what they are saying?"

"No, but it has to be big!"

The interface at Arhus's desk started flashing. Sindie's interface also flashed yellow and the sound of activity could be heard from the office area. They both headed that direction.

"Let me know right away if you decipher anything, okay?"

"Sure, but I don't think we'll have to."

Arhus cut the connection as he entered the general office area. All the interfaces were flashing, but people were gathering to watch the central display. A view of the alien ship sat central in the screen. A smaller view showed the Subordinate standing on top of the ship beside the open top port.

"What's going on?" Arhus asked.

"Not much yet," Josef answered, "but America is about to vote on an emigration bill."

"That didn't take long," Arhus commented.

"Almost like they had it ready and waiting?" Josef asked.

"You don't think the idiots would try and keep people from leaving, do you?" Sindie asked.

"In a word," Josef replied, "yes."

"And from the ship's response, I take it they already know how the vote will go." Arhus stared at the Subordinate on the screen for any sign of what he might be thinking, but the alien was as unreadable as ever.

"Maybe it's just a threat," Josef said.

"I don't think 'just' is a word to use with our visitors," Arhus answered.

Another small view in the corner of the display showed the American legislature and a tally count. Everyone's eyes turned to that area. The numbers started to appear, the 'yea' vote outpacing the 'nay' count. Soon it was clear that the measure was going to pass.

"What are they voting on?" Arhus asked.

"To give the government the power to deny a citizen the right to leave the country without cause. The arguments were based on the fact that they could not know if the aliens were using undue influence on people."

"Shit. And how are they going to decide if undue influence was used?" Arhus asked.

"They weren't very specific about that."

"They can't be worried about people from that flake's church, are they?" Sindie asked.

"No, but I heard that Shawn Yun was visited by one of the angels." Josef said the comment without emotion, but looked to be expecting a response.

"Shit!" Sindie said. "Shawn Yun? No wonder they're pushing this!"

"What?" Arhus asked with fake surprise. "You think that they don't want to lose the top quantum theorist and the guy who is driving all the advances in their *defensive* system development?"

"Yeah, I would bet money on that," Sindie replied.

"Anyone know if he even wants to join our visitors?" Arhus asked.

"Since he was visited, he's been in protective custody, if you believe the reports," Josef said.

"Protection from what, himself?" Arhus asked.

"Of course." Josef nodded his head.

"The guy's a huge space nut," Sindie said, "and has voiced several times that he would love to visit other planets if it was possible."

"Definitely a flight risk," Josef said.

The numbers stopped scrolling. Fifteen 'nay' votes had been cast. The numbers and the title of the bill turned green. Clapping could be heard from the floor of Congress. Everyone held their breath.

On the alien ship view, beings started flying out of the ship at speeds too high to allow recognition. A secondary view zoomed in on one. They were the four-faced creatures and they were all flying west. The first of the beings appeared to fly slow enough for those following to catch up. The exodus continued for a few minutes until a formation took shape. The group, as a whole, increased speed. The display showed a number next to the group: two hundred. Then they disappeared from view.

"What the..." more than one person shouted.

"Were they real?" Josef asked.

"If they are, it's quite a show of force. Plus they have stealth technology we can't track."

"Or they are just making us think we can't see them," Sindie said.

"Works either way," Arhus said.

"Put up the American feed," Sindie shouted at the central display.

The view changed to a map of the American coast. Circles were overlaid, indicating the sensor fields that covered the country. Red pinpoints looked like the location of defensive sites. Yellow points moved across the map.

"Why are we looking at this?" Arhus asked.

"It's what the Americans are broadcasting," Sindie responded, working her interface.

"But why this? This is their defensive grid, isn't it?"

"Filtered, I'm sure, but yes." Sindie did some fast fingering on her interface. "It appears all the other feeds are being shut down."

"News, private, everything?"

"Yes, everything. They're isolating the country."

"So they get to tell their own version of the story?" Josef asked.

"Most likely. Maybe they just don't want everyone else to know how bad they screw up." Arhus noted a new feed. It wasn't located on the main display but to the side, which wasn't possible. He pointed. "What the..."

Someone near the new display walked up and passed their hand through it. The view did not change. The picture became sharper until it was clear that they were looking from the perspective of someone flying through the air at great velocity. Single word questions were voiced by more than one person.

"You don't think..." Sindie said, looking at Arhus.

"Yes, I do," he said with a sharp exhale. "Our visitors are providing their own feed from one of the creatures. I guess that tells us they're real."

"But it's so... clear. I mean, shouldn't things be going by faster?"

"Who says it's a real view and not a telepathic one?"

"Who made them media savvy?" Josef asked.

"You don't think they've been sitting in their ship playing cards, do you?" Arhus replied.

"How long is it going to take them to get there?" Sindie asked.

"At the speed they used last time, not long."

Attention was commanded by the new display. It was a peaceful scene. Clouds floated by, the occasional plane could be seen in the far distance, and shadows moved over the water below. Arhus thought the whole view felt strange, given where the view came from and the capabilities of the creatures. At intervals, he would look back at the American display, but no indications of the creatures appeared.

Can they defeat the sensors or do they just keep people from seeing the creatures in their heads? Arhus wondered. *The Americans have automatic systems. Can the visitors override them also?*

As Arhus watched the American grid, two hundred green dots appeared scattered across the eastern seaboard. Yellow dots converged as red dots started to blink. The green dots were travelling so fast, some of the yellow dots failed to catch them. The view from the creature showed a trail of white smoke coming toward it and missing as if it had no lock on the target. The view swung to the right and a very brief view of a plane went past. One of the yellow dots on the American screen disappeared, followed by several more. The green dots passed Washington, D.C. and kept going, converging toward the middle of the country.

"What's there?" Arhus asked, pointing.

"Old missile silos converted to underground bases. Whole network of them. Supposed to be the safest place on the planet," Josef answered.

"How do you know all this?" Arhus asked, not able to hold back a chuckle.

"I pay more attention than people give me credit for," Josef answered. After a short pause, he added, "And I dated an American girl from the military once. Did cross-country skiing. Very athletic."

Time didn't matter as they watched. More yellow dots disappeared. Red dots stopped blinking. The green dots converged in North Dakota. The view from the creature showed green fields of grain, trees, and rivers as they passed. The view seemed to slow as they approached a group of concrete structures painted green and brown. The paint scheme might have been effective camouflage if the creature hadn't been looking at the buildings the whole time.

As the view got closer, defensive batteries sprang from the ground and opened fire. The view changed to one where the top of the grass could be seen. From the swaying back and forth, Arhus assumed the creature was performing an evasive manoeuvre. The end of a fiery sword could be seen just before it passed through a battery. Without sound, Arhus could not verify that the other batteries had been destroyed, but he assumed they had been. The view stopped in front of one of the doors on the concrete bunker. The display from the Americans vanished.

The smaller view from the creature appeared on the central display. Arhus watched a hand extend the flaming sword into the door and carve a hole. When the door section fell, two soldiers appeared, firing their guns. They didn't fire them for long. The view then walked into the building and a hall that spiralled downward. At one point, two robots appeared, spouting flame at the view. The flame appeared to have no effect except to be channelled around the view. Arhus assumed it was caused by the wings, invisible to the view. The flaming sword cut through the robots with the same ease as it had cut through the men. When it did, the robots exploded. After the smoke cleared, the view returned to one of progress down the spiralling hallway.

The creature reached the bottom of the spiral, where the floor of the hallway merged into the floor of an open area surrounded by walls with other hallways leading away. Men stood at intervals in the area, but did nothing but stand. The view turned to the left to proceed down a hallway. Two men stood in the way, weapons at rest, but not moving. When the view came to the men, it stopped and a hand waved at the men. The men did not move. The men were grabbed one at a time and thrown behind the view. The view then proceeded down the hall.

After several turns, two guards could be seen standing in front of a door. The events from the hall were repeated, but this time with a difference. After the second man was thrown from the door, he stood up and started firing a pistol at the view. Tiny sparks where the high-density needles hit the creature's wings appeared. A second creature made a swift swipe of his sword, bisecting the man. The cut was made so fast that the top half hit the ground first. From the view, it could be seen that three creatures had walked down the hallway.

The view turned back to the door, which was cut open. The door was pushed open to reveal a very comfortable-looking room. Inside the room stood Shawn Yun, his eyes wide in anticipation. The view walked up to the man.

Do you wish to join us?

"Yes! Yes, I would very much like that!" Yun nodded vigorously when he spoke.

A creature came into view, his back to the viewer. He appeared to open his robe. After looking, Yun stepped toward the creature, disappearing from view. The creature closed his robe and then turned back to the view. From what Arhus could see, he could not tell any difference between that creature and any other he had seen.

"Did it eat him?" Josef asked.

"It must be a special carrier unit," Arhus replied. "I don't see a sword hilt hanging from its side."

"Talk about being taken by angels," Sindie said, awe in her voice.

"That's right," Arhus responded. "The Bible does say something about that, doesn't it?"

"Yeah," Josef said, "they carry you to Heaven."

"The theologians are going to shit themselves," Sindie added.

"Like they haven't already?" Arhus asked.

The view showed hallways again, looking down one into the open area with the spiral walkway. Several creatures were fighting men, or more accurately massacring them, but in the distance, Arhus could see several men positioning a large weapon. When the weapon fired, an orange beam hit the wings of one creature. His wings started to glow with an orange light. As the view disappeared behind a wall, another creature charged the weapon, sword raised.

"Isn't that..." Josef said. As he did, the screen shook and an orange wave of energy passed in front of the view from left to right down the cross hallway. Its progression could be seen as a ripple in what Arhus thought was the wings in front of the creature.

"Christ!" Arhus said.

"They just destroyed a neutron beam weapon," Josef said, shock in his voice. "They breached the core!"

"I can't believe the Americans would use the weapon in their own facility," Arhus said.

The view once again moved into the hallway leading to the open area. The two creatures were gone. The men were gone. The weapon was gone. The floor, roof, and walls around where the weapon had been were gone. The area was a strange, glowing black colour. The view moved quickly through the hallway, the room, and up the spiral. An orange glow was maintained in the view far up the spiral walkway.

"Everything is just... gone," Sindie said.

"Everyone on that floor and who knows how many other floors are dead," Arhus added.

"That glow doesn't look healthy either," Josef said.

"Let's hope for Yun's sake the creature's wings can protect or absorb the radiation," Arhus commented.

The view changed so fast that Arhus assumed the creature must be flying. It came to the door and proceeded out the building. They were greeted by the sight of an ongoing battle. Creatures were destroying weapons or killing men, some just by flying close past them. There was a brief view that looked up to see a creature leaving at high speed. Several others rose from the ground to join it.

"That must be the one with Yun," Arhus said. "Is that a satellite killer?"

"It is," Josef said as an orange glow appeared in the top left corner of the view. "And they are firing it."

"But if they hit the creature with Yun in it, they will kill him!" Sindie said.

"I think that's the idea," Josef replied.

The view changed to centre on the vehicle that had fired. The view zoomed close to the vehicle. The flaming sword plunged into the side, carving large pieces from the vehicle. In a few seconds, the last piece of the side armour fell away to reveal the machinery inside. A large black cylinder, angled off-vertical, was in full view. The sword drew back.

"He isn't going to ..." Sindie said.

The view changed to an altitude shot high enough that individual men or machines could not be seen. An orange, glowing sphere bloomed on the ground. It grew larger and more translucent as it did. Arhus could not guess the size of the sphere when it faded away. A small black dot was seen before it disappeared in the distance.

"Damn," Josef uttered, more out of reflex than purpose.

"When they make a statement, they really make a statement," Sindie said.

"How many did they lose?" Josef asked.

"At least three, but no way to tell how many more. Look." Arhus pointed at the screen. A view of America similar to the first one had appeared, but no green lights showed. "They must have gone back into stealth mode."

"It would make sense," Josef agreed.

"How could the Americans have done this?" Sindie asked. Her voice sounded far off.

"Done what?" Arhus said.

"Gotten so many of their people killed."

"The power containers on the neutron lasers are supposed to be ballistic proof and laser proof," Josef answered.

"But not alien proof, it seems," Arhus added.

"Idiots," Sindie said with disdain. "They should have never created those weapons."

"And the aliens are not neutron chamber proof either," Josef said. "Not totally, that is."

"Why do they use such dangerous weapons?"

"Before today, they were considered safe. Plus they are very effective." Josef turned from the display. "I think that's about it for today."

"The way the day's been going, I won't count on it," Arhus said.

The central screen changed on its own. The American Congress hall appeared. All seats were filled, but Arhus's eyes were drawn to the front of the room, where the Subordinate and two messengers stood.

"Like I said…"

Chapter Twenty-One
Warnings

The room gasped as one person. From their faces, the congressmen were equally surprised. Everything seemed to stand still for a moment. Then the Subordinate moved his head to look around the room. He was standing on the floor in front of the podium. The messengers stood to either side, almost to the aisles for the back doors. Neither messenger moved, standing at attention, and neither carried a weapon.

He's not there, Arhus thought to himself. *He's projecting their presence. Just like at the General Council meeting.*

Sindie grabbed his arm with her shaking hand. The other hand soon followed.

Everyone waited. The Subordinate finished examining the room and faced the middle of the assembly again.

We *have been patient,* came into Arhus's head. *Before now, we have shown mercy. But you are a rebellious and stubborn people. You withhold what is* ours *from us. We* have seen your hearts and *know you do these things. Your hearts cannot be hidden from us.*

We *will no longer show mercy. Those who rebel against us will be punished. Those who do not rebel but accept us and obey us will be rewarded. Those who hide and tremble in fear will have nothing from us.*

If you try to prevent ours *from joining us, we will punish you. If you kill ours, we will destroy you. Do not be mistaken.* We *will do these things. The time for testing is over. The time for mercy is over.* We *did not intend to destroy you. Why would we?* We *created you! But if you continue being foolish, we will do so.*

You have your instructions. Follow them.

The voice stopped, but still, no one moved. The Subordinate remained standing before them. After a few seconds, a man near the front of the assembly rose from his chair. He was balding, overweight, and less than average height. His face was red and his eyes blazed. His demeanour gave Arhus a sinking feeling.

"Why should we listen to you?" the man said, finger pointing, as he got close. "You are not God! You have no authority over us. Why should we let you tell us what to do? You are a thief and a murderer!"

The Subordinate reached out and appeared to touch the man on the head with one finger. As he did, the man stopped talking mid-word. His mouth remained open and his body stiffened, but then it began to slightly quiver all over. The quiver lasted about five seconds. No sound came from the man. When the quivering stopped, the man fell to the floor as if a rag doll.

So shall be everyone who defies us! shouted in Arhus's head. The Subordinate and the two angels disappeared.

Arhus tore his eyes from the display to the room. Some people swore, others acted like they had trouble getting their breath. Most looked at each other as if seeking assurance that what they had seen was real. Arhus felt his heart sink, but tried to concentrate on the people in the room and their condition.

"Did he just kill that guy?" Sindie asked, her voice barely heard with her head buried in Arhus's chest.

"I would say… yes," Josef replied in the same manner.

"They didn't just kill him," Arhus said, keeping his voice low also, "they telepathically killed him."

"What do you mean?" Sindie's voice sounded blank, the confusion not well hidden.

"The Subordinate and those angels weren't in the room. It's the same trick they used in the General Council yesterday. They projected the image of the Subordinate and the angels in the room."

"But he touched that guy," Sindie protested.

"It looked like he touched him. The more disturbing aspect is that they targeted him, from Jerusalem."

"How can you know that?"

"Because the Subordinate has taken a human-like body. So unless you think they can teleport, they're weren't actually there."

"Christ!" Josef said louder than Arhus would have liked. "If they can do that to him, they can do that to anyone!"

"I think that's the point." Arhus noted that people were forming small groups of two to five and appeared to be talking or comforting each other. He breathed a little easier. "They just demonstrated in two different ways that no one is beyond their reach."

"He should have demonstrated that before the vote, shouldn't he?" Josef asked. "It's kind of wasted on the congress now."

"The demonstration wasn't for them," Arhus replied.

"The President!" Sindie turned, her eyes lighting up. "He still has to sign the bill!"

"Yes, he does," Arhus agreed. "That demonstration was directed at him to suggest he not sign it."

"You think they'll kill him if he does?" Josef asked.

"Would you risk finding out?" Arhus asked back.

"Shit, I won't have been this stupid to begin with. I wonder how long we will have to wait for the President to decide?"

"Not long would be my guess."

Arhus looked at Sindie. Her face and eyes were drooped in sadness. He extended an arm and she walked into it. He gave her a firm hug, feeling her breathing steady. When he looked up, Josef had much the same expression on his face. Arhus extended his other arm and Josef also accepted the hug. There was nothing but comfort in the efforts. Arhus understood the need. *The world has been changed. We are no longer the dominant species, no longer in control. Hundreds of years of technology made us feel that we could do anything, and in one week, we were proven wrong. Who knows what else is out there to beat down our assumptions?*

Two more people walked up and Arhus nodded. They joined the communal comfort. Other groups formed.

In the past we would have been mad, Arhus thought. *Why aren't we angry? Why aren't we resolving ourselves to resist? Have we been without war for so long we have turned soft and pliable? Was that the aliens' plan all along? To turn us into sheep?*

The hug ended. People looked less sad.

"What now?" Sindie asked.

"Now we wait and do our jobs until something else happens," Arhus answered.

"Is that all there is, just go about and do our jobs?" she asked.

"If someone has another idea, I'm ready to hear it," Arhus said louder so that others in the room could hear.

"But what's to be left after the aliens leave?" Eymen asked.

"If I knew that, I'd be buying stock." People laughed at Arhus's joke, the kind that relieved nervous tension. "Look, I'm not going to stop anyone from doing what they think they need to do. If you want days off, take them. If you want to go visit your relatives in Guyana, no one is going to think bad of you. If you want to start a cult that worships the aliens, I'm sure you'll have plenty of company."

People appeared to relax. Arhus looked around. *How little I know about most of these people. I know the basics, but only a handful I've spent time with outside of work on a regular basis. I don't know much about the rest. What are their families like? Do they even have them, and if so, do they even like them? With Jerusalem's history, many people come here to start over, to get away from their past. Plus, it is so easy to isolate yourself today. Not in physical proximity, but in the ways that count. No one is bothered by strangers anymore. Is that why the aliens showed up now? Because we are so disconnected?*

The milling around and talking continued. It was the most socializing Arhus had seen by the group in years.

"Maybe that's been our problem," Arhus said to himself.

"What's been our problem?" Josef asked.

"We haven't had a real crisis or enemy in more than two generations," Arhus answered.

"What are you talking about?" Josef said.

"No real communities. Not in the historic sense."

"But you can go VR and find a community of anything you want," Sindie put in.

"Yes, but they are not right next to you, touchable."

"You can add that feature if you want," Sindie pointed out.

"Sure, but you still know it's not real. And anytime you get tired of them, you can leave. You don't have to deal with people, solve problems, live next to them day after day. There's been no reason to band together, face a common foe, whether it's been an army, disease, famine, heck, even typhoons have been tamed."

"Isn't that good?" Josef asked.

"Is it?" Arhus asked back. "When life stops being a struggle, what happens to us? Do we become soft, complacent, easy to conquer? Do we just accept what's happening?"

"I don't think the Americans just accepted what was happening and look what it got them," Josef said.

"Maybe they would have been smarter about it."

"Besides," Sindie said, "it's not like science and technology has stood still."

"But what about us, as a people? How often do we come together and celebrate our community, our common bonds?"

"Why would we?" Josef asked. "If the world is one community, why would there be a need? We outgrew nationalism and statism."

"But does that make us easier targets?"

Josef and Sindie just looked at him for a minute. Josef opened his mouth several times as if to speak, but then closed it again. After a while, he said, "I don't know."

The discussion was interrupted by the central display. A view of the American president sitting at his desk filled the display. He appeared worn and worried, fatigue showing in his eyes. He looked straight at the viewer, his shoulders squared and head held up.

"I would like to address the world so there are no lingering questions," the President started. "I have made my decision even though the bill has not yet reached my desk. I am making this statement in order to quell any speculations or actions that may result from those speculations. Concerning Congressional Bill 451, I will veto this bill. If Congress overrides my veto, I will not enforce the bill. I consider this legislation as grievous as the Alien and Sedition Acts and will have no part in it. We cannot maintain our citizens' freedom by restricting it. We cannot deal with the world and, it appears now, the universe by closing ourselves off from it.

America has always been about freedom, and that includes the freedom to leave. We will, of course, regret any who leave, but I will not have our forces stand in their way. Thank you for your time."

"Wow," Josef said as the view disappeared, converting to the default. "Talk about a pre-emptive strike."

"More like a plea to the aliens," Sindie said through twisted lips.

"Can't say I'm surprised," Arhus said.

"Surprised?" Josef responded. "No. He just got his ass kicked by some... whatever they are... and has a mess to clean up in the middle of the country. Guess he didn't want another."

"So the bad boys of the block call it quits," Sindie said. "That leaves the Western Pacific Conglomerate to cause trouble, if anyone."

"I'm pretty sure they would rather be in bed with the aliens than fight them," Arhus said.

"That's for sure!" Josef said with a laugh. "They must be drooling for that alien technology."

"Heaven help us if they get exclusive access," Sindie said, returning to snide mode.

"True, but I don't think the aliens are that stupid," Arhus said.

"Do they care?" Sindie's face showed indignation.

"I think so. They claim us as their own. They might want to come back later." Arhus knew the argument had no basis but hope.

"You're assuming that the human-like emotions you see in them are real," Sindie returned.

"Yes, I am."

"I hope you're right," Sindie said, looking away.

"You think they might come back again?" Josef asked.

"Why not? Since we are 'ready' in their own words for, whatever, why won't they?"

"Fool me once...?" Josef replied. "Then again, it's not like they have much to worry about here."

"At least if they have some kind of 'claim' on the Earth, that might prevent others from doing the same."

"Unless they sell the rights." Josef pointed at the ceiling.

"They don't strike me as capitalists," Arhus replied.

"You make our planet sound like a sports team," Sindie said.

"More like a farm team," Josef replied.

"All of which is getting us nowhere since we don't know." A bit of edge showed in Arhus's voice, causing the other two to look at him with some surprise. After letting the air settle for a while, he added, "So, what now?"

"Drink!" Josef responded.

"That doesn't sound very professional," Arhus said.

"Hey, who ever accused me of being professional?" Josef asked.

"Hmm, I'll have to get back to you on that one." Arhus got a far-off look in his eyes.

"And what are you thinking?" Sindie asked.

"I'm wondering if our visitors are going to want to talk," Arhus said.

"Don't they normally do that first thing in the morning?" Sindie asked.

"Yes, but it never hurts to be prepared."

"At least we could eat lunch," Sindie said.

It was Arhus's turn to be surprised. Without the normal signals warning of hypoglycemic conditions, he hadn't even thought about lunch. It was a nice feeling, as if he had been freed from something. Plus he wouldn't have to worry about what he ate, either.

"Of course," he replied, "no reason not to."

"Unless the workers are so preoccupied with everything going on that they didn't fix any food," Josef said.

"I suppose there is that," Arhus agreed, "but we won't know until we go down there."

"That's just what we need, the whole world coming to a standstill," Sindie groaned.

"If nothing else," Arhus said as he started toward the lift, "there's food at my place, if we are forced to go that far in our search."

"You might decide not to come back," Josef said as he followed.

"Her or me?" Arhus asked.

"Yes," was Josef's reply.

Chapter Twenty-Two
Don't Ask Me!

The three managed to find a restaurant that was serving, though the selection was limited. With lunch done and being out of the office building, Josef and Sindie both stated that they weren't going back today. Since even his interface was quiet, Arhus didn't disagree with them. Sindie said she needed to check in with her family while Arhus was sure Josef was going to find a drinking party somewhere. *Won't be hard for him to find one. Even in the restaurant, people looked depressed and worried.*

The office area was almost empty when Arhus returned. He made it back to his chair behind the desk before hearing the summons.

Mr. Gint, came the voice that was now very recognizable as the Subordinate's, *we would like to talk to you.* The voice was learning control, because it used a normal volume.

"Be there as soon as I can," Arhus said aloud as he stood up.

As he walked to the ship, he noticed the amount of foot traffic had diminished. It didn't surprise him, but seemed out of place. As he walked, he figured out why—the normal traffic of people going to the ship was not there. There were still people making their way in the same direction, but not news crews or onlookers.

Did the scary aliens chase them away? he wondered. *What, not so warm and fuzzy now?*

The ones who were 'called' still walked the streets. He could recognize them from the dreamy look in their eyes. A few were escorted by one or two others. The companions tended to look more worried than anything, though it was hard to tell whether it was about their friends leaving or being rejected at the point of a sword. A few pleaded for the called to go back home with them.

If they made it this far, I doubt they're going to change their minds now, Arhus thought with a small huff. *If they even can, that is.*

As Arhus approached the gate to the ship area, the security office waved him inside on sight. *The perks of being well known, I guess,* Arhus thought. The line of people was as steady as ever and even a little heavier than before, if he judged right. *People have had time to get here, I guess. Or else they are processing them faster.*

Arhus stepped into the line, not noticing someone coming out of the processing building at the same time. The person, a woman with tanned skin, gave him a look.

"Don't you have to be processed?" she asked.

"I'm just visiting," Arhus replied with a smile.

"But… Wait! You're him, aren't you?" The woman's eyes got wide and she almost stopped walking.

"My whole life," Arhus replied.

"What's it like, I mean, talking to one of *them*? What are they like?"

"The one who has assumed human-like form is much like a normal person, though one just learning social skills and speaking idioms."

"What about the other ones?"

"I've never spoken to them, at least any more than anyone else in the world, that is."

"Are you going with us?" The ship was getting close.

"I haven't been invited."

"But… why not?"

"Don't ask me, ask them." They neared the ramp. "I hope it goes well for you."

"Oh, I'm sure it will!" The woman waved as she stepped onto the ramp. Arhus waved back. A messenger walked down the ramp toward Arhus.

"Please follow me," the messenger said before turning and starting back up the ramp.

"I wonder what he would do if I didn't?" Arhus asked himself playfully as he followed. When the messenger didn't turn around, he let it drop. Led through the part of the ship he had been through before, they took a turn until they came to a small room. Inside were two chairs with a small table between them. It could have been a personal meeting room or one used for romantic dinners. The angel gestured but did not enter. Arhus went in and sat on one of the chairs.

He didn't have to wait long. When the door opened, Arhus stood up out of habit. The Subordinate smiled as he entered.

"Please, you can remain seated," the Subordinate said, gesturing toward the chair. Arhus nodded and sat back down. The Subordinate took the other chair. "Thank you for coming."

"Of course," Arhus replied. "Wasn't doing much else anyway."

Arhus waited, but the Subordinate didn't say anything. After a short while, the door opened again and an angel brought in two glasses and set them on the table. They were filled with apricot juice, which made Arhus wonder where they got it.

Maybe they make it themselves, he thought. *Out of... what?*

"You made quite an impression the last two days," Arhus said.

"That was the intent," the Subordinate answered. The conversation continued in the slow method that the visitors seemed to do everything, except fight. "What is your impression of the Americans?"

"I'm pretty sure you've made your point." Arhus stared for a moment. "Don't you already know that?"

"Your insights have been useful in the past," the Subordinate said in such a way that sounded as if he meant it. "Do you anticipate any others causing concern?"

"Of the same type? No, I don't, but then, there are some out there that can be unpredictable at times." Arhus picked up the glass and took a drink. *Perfect.*

"We are aware and they are being watched." The Subordinate did not touch his drink. "Are there other concerns?"

Arhus's brow furrowed. "I'm not sure what you mean."

"Do other groups give you concern?"

"Well," Arhus said, trying to think, "not in the sense of being dangerous, but then, I don't receive those briefings."

"What about ones that are not physically dangerous?"

Arhus almost laughed. "You mean like the Reverend Owens out there? He's just looking for an angle."

"Angle?"

Arhus took a breath while he thought. "He is trying to find a way to make the situation work to his favour. I assume he was not called?"

"No, he was not."

Arhus thought he almost saw a laugh at the suggestion.

"Then he has no control of the situation and won't until after you leave, if you don't leave someone behind to represent you, that is."

"So he is looking for power," the Subordinate said with a small nod of his head.

"Yes."

"And how would he do that?"

"By claiming to know the truth, or by responding to what people want and making himself their leader. His religion will be called into question after you leave. I'm sure he is looking to try and ride the next wave, so to speak, and maintain some kind of position in the new world."

"How can he know the truth if we don't tell him?"

The question demonstrated to Arhus how much the visitors didn't understand about humans. *How can they be God if they don't understand? Or does God need to?*

"He doesn't need the absolute truth, just something that people believe as the truth." As he said it, Arhus could hear the rottenness of the statement.

The Subordinate nodded. "We understand. We feel that the truth would eventually be discovered, as you have seen happen to many non-truths from your past."

"We can hope so, but what happens in the meantime might not be... desirable."

"We do not think in the near term."

The statement piqued Arhus's interest. "Just what do you call 'short term'?"

The Subordinate seemed to consider the question. "One hundred years."

"You know, that is longer than most human life-cycles."

"On your planet, yes. There are several considerations that you have not or could not change that could prolong that lifespan."

A shot like lightning went through Arhus, causing him to want to ask questions he knew he was not trained to understand. *How could they extend our lifespan? By protection from ultraviolet rays? By curing the limited division of cells? Is it possible?*

"Do you plan to tell us about them?" Arhus asked.

"It would not benefit you. Your technology is not able to perform them." The Subordinate was talking about human lives and he was talking about them in a neutral voice.

"You could give us the technology."

"Do you think that people are ready to live longer?" the Subordinate asked. "Do you think they deserve to?"

It was Arhus's turn to think. "Some, yes. Those like Mr. Yun could do more good with a longer lifespan."

"And the others?"

Arhus forced himself not to react to the statement and give a measured answer. "I'm not sure a longer life would be of much benefit to society as a whole, and there are some that I don't want to see live longer. Of course, everyone would want a longer life and if we could not distribute the benefit to everyone, there would be a lot of tension."

The Subordinate smiled. "We see you have answered your own question."

Arhus took another sip of juice. The Subordinate seemed content to let the conversation lag for a few moments. After setting the glass down, Arhus asked, "Have you given any thought to my question of leaving something behind when you leave, in exchange for those that leave, so to speak."

"It is a complex issue. We are still considering."

So much for quick decisions, Arhus thought. "Is there anything else?"

"Are you concerned about our intentions? Do you doubt that we are letting people decide on their own?"

A simple question, but it caused Arhus's head to go back. He felt nervousness growing inside him and maybe a little sweat. "Have you been monitoring my thoughts?"

"No, we have not."

"Why not?" After asking, Arhus wanted to kick himself.

"We could, but we prefer not to intrude in any more minds than is necessary. We prefer a willing response."

"So you understand how easy it is for us to wonder if you are manipulating people into wanting to join you?"

"Of course we do, it is natural for you to think so, given what we can do. But we assure you that each person has made their own choice."

"And we have your word on that." The way Arhus said it, a human might have been offended.

"Of course. Why would we not speak the truth?"

"I can think of no reason why," Arhus replied.

"We are not human, as you know." The Subordinate gave him a wry smile. Arhus could feel a small amount of heat in his cheeks and doubled efforts to control himself.

"I believe you, but I'm not sure everyone else does or would."

"We are aware of their feelings. We can hope their feelings change with time."

They stared at each other while Arhus thought about the Subordinate's apparent show of emotion. He had to ask. "Are you somehow becoming human or just getting better at acting human?"

"All behaviour is learned," the Subordinate responded through the small smile. "A study of humans can show which behaviours make them comfortable and which are considered strange. Then one has but to practice these behaviours. Does this make one human? The question could be debated."

"But are you physically becoming human?"

"We choose to appear in a form that you would see as human, though it is not human as you understand it. The differences are less physical, though your scientists may be able to identify some of them, given a chance."

"I think I understand," Arhus said. "Is there anything else you would like to ask?"

"No. We were most concerned that we still had your confidence.

And that you would still talk to us when requested."

"Of course. Anytime. Well, almost anytime. I do need sleep, you know."

The Subordinate responded with a chuckle. As he stood, he said, "You will be escorted out."

"Thank you," Arhus replied as he stood. A messenger was waiting outside the room when the door opened. The Subordinate walked out and away as if all thought of Arhus was forgotten. Arhus followed the messenger from the room.

The line coming into the ship looked heavier than when he had entered. Overawed, the people took no notice of Arhus exiting the ship. Arhus made a mental note to ask security how many people had entered the ship, to settle his curiosity. At the base of the ramp, the messenger stepped aside and made a small head bow as Arhus passed. Again Arhus had a feeling of unreality as he exited the ship, though he still did not know why.

Everything I see inside can't be an illusion. That would destroy the Subordinate's credibility, wouldn't it?

Lost in thought, Arhus did not notice how close he was to the gate or the man who walked up to him until he was within a couple feet of his face. The shock of noticing the man caused him to draw back.

"You're him, aren't you?" the man said in a quick, excited voice. "You have to get me on the ship!"

"Sir, I can't..."

"Talk to the aliens! Tell them I want to go with them!"

"Sir, I have no influence..."

"Me too! Me too!" a woman came up and insisted.

Before Arhus could even think, he was surrounded by people grabbing and pleading with him. The multiple hands pulled him back and forth and his head connected with at least two of theirs. The words from so many sources became incomprehensible and unanswerable. There was no escape route from the petitioners. Arhus's head began to spin.

Then the *zit* of stunners could be heard through the crowd. In a moment, the security guards were forcing their way to him, petitioners falling to the ground before them and in their wake. With the same speed he had been surrounded by his petitioners, Arhus was surrounded by security guards and ushered to the gate. He did not resist, carried along. His thoughts took refuge inside his brain, recognizing where he was once he was inside the security station under care of a paramedic.

"Do you hurt anywhere?" the woman asked.

"My head hurts," Arhus replied.

"You took a couple of blows to the head, but they don't look serious. Here, swallow this. It will take care of any swelling."

The woman handed him a pill, small and easy to swallow. After taking a few breaths, Arhus could feel it working.

"Are you here with anyone?" the woman asked.

"No."

"Then we better have a guard escort you home, just in case. Will anyone be there to make sure you don't have any other symptoms?"

"Yes," Arhus replied. *Sindie may or may not be there, but I don't want a stranger sitting in my apartment all afternoon.*

The paramedic looked at his eyes one more time and pronounced Arhus good to leave. A security guard fell in step as he made his way to the door. Stepping outside revealed a crowd, but this time of news crews, all looking his direction.

"Nothing like someone getting mugged to draw the newsies," Arhus said.

"You want us to clear them out?" the guard asked.

"I would like to make a statement." Arhus took a step toward the crews.

"You sure that's wise?"

"If it gets people off my back, yes."

Arhus walked at a measured pace to the news crews, to their surprise. All the eyes turned his direction. Nervousness grew as he realized that he had never been in front of so many lenses at one time. When he got just out of arm's reach and the questions started, Arhus held up his hands and waited for quiet.

"I will only be making a statement, not taking questions." The disappointment showed in their eyes and their moans. "I want to clear up what caused the scuffle that I experienced a few minutes ago.

"I have no idea who is on our visitors' list. I was not consulted on who would or should be on the list. Our visitors have not discussed their intent on this matter with me or asked my opinion. I have no influence on who is accepted onto the ship, nor have I asked for any. I do not want to be involved.

"No one should ask me to get them on the ship or an audience with the visitors. I can't help you. That is my final word on the subject. Good day."

Arhus turned from the group and, with the guard in tow, walked away. At first, his goal was just to get away from everyone. It was several blocks before he noted where he was and corrected his course. *Strange that the guard made no issue about my route, but then, maybe he doesn't know where I live.*

It was halfway to his apartment that Arhus's head started to hurt again. Maybe it was the sunlight, maybe the noise of the town. All he knew was that by the time he reached his door, he was glad to be inside with peace and quiet. The guard did not enter, just watched him go inside and shut the door. Arhus did not care what happened to the guard after that.

The first stop was the kitchen for two beers, because he didn't want to have to get up for the second one. The next and final stop was the couch. Shoes came off and feet went on the coffee table. All displays stayed off. His interface was turned off and tossed on the table. One beer went on the table and one went in his hand, top removed. After a drink, his head went back.

After a while, his head felt better again. The lack of noise and people must have helped, but he gave most of the credit to the two beers. He was debating a third against the unavoidable physical effects when the door opened. Two small feet rushed in, slamming the door as they did.

"Ar! You here?" Sindie's voice was loud compared to the quiet he had been in.

"Couch," he replied at a lower volume.

Sindie rushed into the room and jumped onto the couch, managing not to land on Arhus. "You okay? I saw the vids. I came right over."

"I'm fine," Arhus said in the same voice he had used with the paramedic.

"Sure you are. Let me look at your eyes." Sindie put gentle hands on either side of his head and turned it toward her. Then she used her thumbs to open his eyes all the way and stared hard for a few seconds. "Your eyes look alright."

"Since the paramedic sent me home, I'm pretty sure I'm fine," Arhus said.

"Physically, sure. How about mentally?"

"I'm not crazy, if that's what you mean," Arhus said with a chuckle.

"No, dummy. You were mugged. That can… leave effects."

"I'm fine." Arhus rolled his eyes. "Not the first time I've been yelled at, you know."

"But the first time you've been mugged, no doubt."

Arhus tilted his head to look at her. "You ever been to a mosh pit?"

It was Sindie's turn to look at Arhus sideways. "No way, you didn't. Don't tell me, it was Josef's idea."

"Yes, and yes, we went, and no, I never went again. Once was enough." Arhus looked back at the ceiling.

"Was it as violent as they say?" Sindie's voice had gone from concerned to curious.

"I doubt it. But then, it's not the twentieth century either."

"Geesh, I can't believe they still exist."

"They don't except on very special occasions and with a lot of regulation. I'm sure the regulation has something to do with lack of violence. Can we talk about something else now, like nothing?"

"Your head hurt?"

"Just tired of everything."

"Sure. You hungry?"

"I got liquid bread." Arhus held up his bottle and then looked at it. "Guess I need another."

"Coming right up."

Chapter Twenty-Three
Get With It

Making it into the office felt like a relief to Arhus. It had been several days since the incident at the ship, but he still kept an eye out while walking around. He did note the increased number of people walking toward the ship, but forced himself to ignore them. None seemed interested in him.

"Well, look who showed up," Josef's voice greeted him when he entered the office area. "I was beginning to wonder."

"A guy takes a couple of days off and everyone panics," Arhus moaned, but smiled.

"Maybe we are just tired of doing your job for you," Josef countered.

"Then who is doing your job?" Arhus asked.

"I'm doing that, too!"

"About time you pulled your weight." Arhus laughed at Josef's fake shock. "Hey, I have a real question. My office?"

Both men walked into Arhus's office. He waited until the door was shut before asking, "Do we know how many people have entered the ship?"

Josef looked up from the corner of his eyes. "Well, the rate was about one person every thirty seconds, or about four thousand a day. The rate increased after the American incident, almost doubling."

"Which means they should have just about everyone they want,"

Arhus said.

"It has to be close. I suppose we could ask the security office and see if they will give us a number. We would need a good reason. Is something going on that I don't know about?"

"Not that I know. I just thought they should be getting full pretty soon. Doesn't the media have an idea?"

"Yeah, lots of them. I can get you a dozen different numbers if you want them. Security is probably who knows the real number."

"No, I want the real number. I'll try asking security and see if they will tell us."

"What excuse you going to use?"

"Hey," Arhus said, spreading his arms, "I'm the chosen one, remember?"

"And when they ask why you don't ask our visitors for a total?"

"I am confirming their count."

Josef rolled his eyes. "Good luck with that. Don't mention my name, by the way."

"But it was your idea. I thought you'd want credit."

"No, thank you. Am I clear?"

"Go to work," Arhus said with a wave of his hand.

Josef exited the room. Arhus made his way to his chair and sat behind his desk, transferring his interface signal to the desk display. No messages awaited him; he had cleared them out the day before from his apartment. He manipulated the display to call security. A pleasant-looking young lady in uniform appeared.

"How may I help you, Mr. Gint?" the lady asked.

"I was wondering if I could find out how many people have entered the alien ship?" he asked.

The lady's eyes twitched. "I will have to refer you to someone else for that information."

"Please do, I'll wait."

The screen went to a pastoral screen with soft music. Arhus tried to place the location, but couldn't find enough clues. *Maybe that is on purpose. I could ask the computer, but that sounds like cheating. Plus, if it was a fake or altered scene, it would ruin the effect.* Arhus had moved the scene to the side and started attending to other business before his call was answered.

"Good morning, Mr. Gint," an older man in a fancier uniform said from the display.

"Good morning, Mr..."

"Officer Chinua."

"Officer Chinua. I was trying to find out what the official count of people going onto the alien ship was."

"Can I ask why you want this information?" The man did a good job of not acting suspicious when he asked.

"You know who I am, right?"

"Of course I do." He gave Arhus one of those 'Do I look stupid?' looks.

"Since I might be called by our visitors at any time, I just thought it would be a good idea to keep abreast of the situation. You know, so I'm not surprised."

The man stared at Arhus. Arhus tried to retain a neutral expression back.

"I will tell you," the man said, "that we have counted over twenty-four thousand people entering the ship. Not counting yourself, of course."

"Thank you. You have been most helpful."

The man looked down, but then looked up again. "Would you consider a request?"

The question took Arhus by surprise. "Maybe. I can try, at least."

"We're losing a lot of good people to the aliens. It would be nice if we got something in return. You know, so we don't feel used." The man's eyes softened as he spoke.

Has he lost someone?

"I have already mentioned that to our visitors, but have not received a reply yet."

"Mentioning it one more time can't hurt."

"I will if given the chance."

"Thanks."

The display disappeared, leaving Arhus wondering. *How many people are going to feel they've lost something when the ship leaves? There's no way they will ever see those people again. Will they hold memorial services? What kind of legal mess will it create? Do we declare them legally dead? Or do we wait seven years? I suppose they could return in their lifespans, but hundreds of years may have passed here. That would be a legal mess.*

Without orders to the contrary, the display switched to the news. Arhus was not listening, but the activity on the display caught his attention. The scene was the gate at the alien ship with the news mouthpiece talking to a security person. The person was Lieutenant Amster and the interviewer seemed quite excited. Arhus turned up the volume and listened.

"So are you saying," the interviewer said, "that we have almost reached the limit of the ship and that those in Jerusalem are the last that will be boarding?"

"I am not saying that," Amster replied. "We are here to record who goes on the ship and to keep the peace."

"But we are approaching twenty-five thousand, correct?"

"We are approaching that number, but I am not saying that twenty-five thousand is the number of people who were invited to board the ship. We do not know how many were invited."

"But the number of people coming to Jerusalem has all but stopped."

"That may be true, but that has no bearing on how many were invited, or if more will be."

"The estimates that have been circulated for the ship's capacity are all around twenty-five thousand…"

"…based on human technology. We have no idea if the visitors' technology is more or less space efficient."

Arhus thought that Amster was doing a good job, but he could see signs that the lieutenant wanted the interview to be over. When his interviewer failed to ask another question in the same breath, Amster put an end to the interview.

"I have things to do, so you will have to excuse me." With an abbreviated bow, Amster turned and left the mouthpiece behind.

The view changed to one of Reverend Owens. Arhus felt his stomach turn. The reverend looked fresh and excited, impeccably dressed. He had a big grin on his face.

"The end is almost here," the reverend said. "Then we will find out what kind of people we are."

"What to you mean by that?" a voice said.

"Do we accept the truth before our own eyes? Will we acknowledge God and His rights? Will He leave us new instructions to follow?"

"You mean a new set of scriptures?"

"They obviously know much more than we do about the universe. Why wouldn't they tell us? Do you think God will just leave us here with no more idea of what is out there than before He arrived? Before they came, we had not even found life anywhere in the heavens. I think we can now say that there is. What is it like? Who are they? Are they friendly? Can we expect them to come here? Are we to spread God's truth to them also?"

"So what are you proposing we do?"

"Here it comes," Arhus said to himself.

"We need to make sure that there is a representative who stays here so we can know what to expect, how we are to progress. If God just leaves, we are in darkness just as much as before He came. I think we deserve more than that. He needs to give us direction."

"And who do you expect to be this representative? Someone from the alien ship?"

"Well," Owens said as he hitched himself up, "that is for God to decide."

"Would you volunteer for such a job?"

"If asked, I would feel it was my duty to God and the human race to take such an undertaking."

"And there it is," Arhus said. "What do you want to bet he says he was asked, even if he wasn't?"

In disgust, Arhus turned off the display. He wondered how much longer it would take to get the last of the people on the ship. With the news crews there, it couldn't be long. While he thought, his interface buzzed with a demand. He triggered the device. Montoya's face came up.

"Mr. Gint. I know that I am not the person you want to speak to at the moment, but I had to call you. I assume you have seen that the people the visitors invited are almost all on board."

"Yes, I did," Arhus said in a bland voice.

"What the news did not say is that we expect the last of these people to be on board by noon, if not earlier. We expect the visitors to leave shortly afterwards, the next morning, if their pattern is consistent. This leaves us very little time to make a final request of them."

"I am not asking them for anything for you." Arhus's voice took an edge.

"This is for the human race! Don't you understand that?"

"What I understand is that our visitors don't have any sense of human give-and-take." Arhus was all but shouting. "If they are going to leave us anything, it will be on *their* terms. Us pleading for something won't make a difference! Good day!"

Arhus had heard that verbal communication used to have hand-held receivers that one could slam down to disconnect. At that moment he wished he had one. *Maybe I could get the interface programmed for a slamming sound,* he thought.

The door opened and Sindie stuck her head in. "You okay?"

Arhus sighed and deflated. "Yeah, just dealing with the world."

Sindie snuck into the office with minimal door movement, made sure it was closed, and walked over to his side, sitting on the edge of the desk. "You were shouting pretty loud."

"Montoya."

"Oh, that explains it." It was her turn to roll her eyes.

"You know," Arhus said with his eyes closed, "as soon as these aliens leave, we are getting out of here."

"The farm in the Netherlands?" Sindie asked.

"Yes. Somewhere out of the way."

"I'm pretty sure we can swing that. I have money saved up. Besides, there are fewer people out there now, I hear." She smiled.

"If it's not enough, I guess I could always go on a speaking tour." Arhus shook his head while he said it.

"I thought you wanted to stay out of the limelight."

"While the iron is hot, you know."

"Sounds like a good way to get burned, if you ask me."

As she was saying the words, Josef stuck his head into the office.

"Come on in," Arhus said, waving, "join the party."

"Ah, you have a visitor," Josef said nervously.

"So?" Arhus asked.

"An important visitor," Josef answered.

Sindie jumped up and made a fast pace out of the office. Arhus stood up and tried to shake off his mood. It had to be someone important to make Josef nervous.

Arhus stood in time for Arlan Morresette to walk into the office. The man was in one of his formal three-piece business suits. When he entered the room, he nodded to someone outside of the door and closed it. Arhus was too shocked to say anything.

"Mr. Gint," Arlan said, "please excuse the interruption."

"Of course," Arhus said, "anytime. Please, take a seat if you want."

"I won't have time," Arlan said as he waved off the offer. "I just wanted to make a quick stop. As you have undoubtedly heard, the people who were invited on the alien ship are almost all aboard."

"It seems to be the topic on people's minds."

"I am sure that's true. As you are also aware, there has been no reciprocity on the aliens' part."

"That seems to be everyone's concern." Arhus started to get nervous.

"We want to try and make sure we take every effort so that doesn't happen." Arlan made the statement the same way most people said they needed you to stop and pick up milk on the way home.

"I'm not sure I can help you with that."

"You are the only one who can help us with that," Arlan said firmly.

"What do you expect me to be able to do?" Arhus couldn't help feeling like an axe was suspended above his head.

"Go to the ship and be prepared to ask them what they are going to leave us in compensation for the people they are taking." Arlan asked the question with all seriousness.

"They don't think that way," Arhus said. "They say that they own us. If they truly believe it is anyone's guess, but it would appear that they do."

"Then they should want to help us advance, to become better. We're not fruit trees they can just pick what they want from us and then leave!"

"To them, we might be."

Arhus waited for Morresette to hit him for the comment. Instead, Morresette just took a deep breath. He looked at Arhus with eyes that conveyed no kindness.

"Will you go to the ship, Mr. Gint?" Arlan asked.

"Yes, I will, but I make no promises as far as the results."

"That is all I ask."

With that, Arlan Morresette turned and left the room without further comment or attention to Arhus. Standing there, Arhus was both relieved and disappointed. *I am used to being dismissed, but not over something so important. I wonder if Morresette expects me to succeed?*

The second surprise Arhus received was that no one came into the office when Morresette left. After settling himself, he decided to exit the office for the general office area. Morresette was gone. He found people staring at him. Saying something seemed to be expected.

"No big deal," Arhus said, raising his hands. "Just the top brass fussing over what they can't control. Nothing to worry about."

"They've never visited *here* before," Eymen said.

"And we have never had aliens on our doorstep before, either," Arhus replied. "The next day or two might be crazy. People are expecting the ship to leave soon, so events might get frantic. Don't panic and do the best you can to deal with requests. If you can't, you can't. Don't stress over it."

Arhus brought his hands down together in front of him and gave everyone a big smile. He couldn't tell if it helped, but people turned back to their work. Except Eymen, who walked up to him.

"You know," Eymen started in a low voice, "I was invited to go with the aliens."

"Yes, it's hard to forget. Have you decided to stay?"

"I'm still not sure." Eymen looked around and then at the floor. "One minute I want to go and the next I want to stay. I'm not sure what to do."

"What do you want to do?" Arhus asked in a soft voice.

"That's what I'm trying to figure out. It's kind of a non-changeable decision either way. I guess if I knew more about where I was going, I might be able to decide better."

"You want to ask them?"

Eymen's head jerked up, eyes wide. "I can do that?"

"I don't see why not. If you want, I will go there with you to ask."

"Wow, I'd appreciate that." Eymen looked at his hands and looked back up. "Do I need to take anything?"

"No. If you decide to go, I'm pretty sure you can't take anything with you. Do you want to go now?"

"Is that okay?" Eymen looked around again. "What will the others think?"

"That I decided to take you with me somewhere. Don't worry, I was ordered to go to the ship anyway. You better leave your interface here."

"Yes." Eymen looked away.

"Then let's go. I just need to tell Josef that I'm going out. Meet me at the lift."

"Sure. Be right there."

Arhus walked to where Josef and Sindie were watching. "I got an assignment from Morresette. Be back in a while, I hope. I'm taking Eymen with me."

"Eymen?" Sindie asked. "You never take me to the ship."

"I don't share well," Arhus responded, making both of them laugh a little.

"As often as you're gone, makes me think I run this place," Josef said.

"You might want to get used to it," Arhus responded.

"Do I want to know what that means?" Josef asked as Arhus walked away.

"Probably not," Arhus said over his shoulder as he kept walking.

Josef looked at Sindie, who smiled. "Oh," was all he said.

Eymen seemed nervous the whole trip. Arhus tried to talk about anything else, but it didn't seem to help, so he changed tactics.

"How's the family in Turkey?"

"Fine, but they worry about me being in Jerusalem."

"Did you tell them?"

"Of course I told them." Eymen looked at the ground as he spoke.

"What did they say?"

"Some said don't go and others said to go. Of course my mother doesn't want me to go. She still thinks I need to provide her grandchildren. She has seven, but still thinks she needs more. I think it's more about me being settled down, conventional."

"Do you want to settle down?"

"I never wanted to settle, but I have been wondering what I wasn't settling for."

"Age will do that to you." Arhus looked up toward the sky. "I think when you are young, it is about not being your parents, but then you find that everyone is their parents, or at least close enough not to matter. A few go and do something different from their upbringing, but they act normal for wherever they end up. If not, then people just think them strange."

"Where I am from, if you remain single, you are strange. Any pairing is looked on as better than none."

"They think you selfish or greedy?"

"Yes, selfish. Which always surprised me, when most everyone grew up in large families."

"People expect the same to continue from now on."

"I suppose so. I am not sure why."

"Human nature? Makes them feel secure?"

"That has changed, hasn't it?"

Eymen looked up with the last comment. He had a smirk of a smile on his face. Arhus had to laugh.

"I suppose so," Arhus replied. "So does that affect your decision?"

Eymen thought before answering. "Most likely."

They came to the entrance to the ship. With but a few people standing outside, the line leading to the security building was almost non-existent. He guessed that soon everyone that was here would be inside the fence or the ship. A guard approached them.

"Can we help you?"

"Arhus Gint. Just standing here at the moment."

"Do you want me to tell the captain you're here?"

"Captain?" Arhus's head spun around to look at the man.

"Yeah, we've been upgraded." The man gave Arhus a knowing smile.

"No," Arhus said, "that won't be necessary. I'm not sure we are even welcome, if you know what I mean."

"If you're the guy from the news, I'm pretty sure you are always welcome. Suit yourself, we won't interfere." The man walked back to his station.

As he did, Arhus looked toward the ship. A messenger walked down from inside, then headed their way. As it drew close, Arhus could feel Eymen's tension without touching him. The messenger stopped in front of them.

"You are both invited to the ship," it said before turning and starting back.

Arhus looked at Eymen, who gave a small nod, and started the same direction. Eymen's steps, irregular at first, became more steady as they walked. The messenger proceeded into the ship. Eymen stopped at the sentries and eyed them with some fear in his eyes.

"You were invited, so you have nothing to worry about," Arhus said.

"I know, but they still scare me," Eymen responded. After a few seconds, he continued into the ship.

Coming to the top of the ramp, they found the Subordinate waiting for them. He was smiling, though it still did not hold the conviction that a human's might. The Subordinate gave them a slight bow as they stopped at the top of the ramp.

"Welcome, we are glad you are here," the Subordinate said. Looking at Eymen, he added, "Have you decided to join us?"

"Why... where are you taking the people who join you?" Eymen asked.

"We are taking them to another planet that we have prepared to populate."

Arhus turned to find Eymen awe-struck, mouth open. He debated for a second whether to say something or not, but then worried Eymen might not reply if his state wasn't broken by something.

"You don't have to go," Arhus said. The Subordinate showed no response to the comment.

"I know, but I think I'm going to." Eymen turned to Arhus. "Will you say goodbye to everyone for me, and tell my parents?"

"Of course I will. Take care of yourself."

The hug was quick and unexpected. Arhus patted Eymen's back several times. As they parted, he could see that Eymen's face had softened. Eymen turned back toward the Subordinate, who gestured into the ship. Walking slowly at first, Eymen walked faster as he went until he did so eagerly. Arhus smiled to himself.

"I assume that not everyone you invited has accepted your offer," Arhus said, still watching Eymen go down the hall. "Will you invite anyone to replace them?"

"We always knew that everyone might not accept. Our plans made accommodations," the Subordinate said. Then he added, "No, there will be no other invitations."

"I'll make sure people know that," Arhus said, turning to face the alien.

"We will, though, extend an invitation to you and one other person you may wish to bring with you, a life-mate, if you wish."

"Me?"

"Yes. Do you find the invitation surprising?"

"Well, yes. I did not receive a visit from one of the messengers and it's kind of last minute. Why now?"

"We... have grown fond of you. It is true that we did not send a messenger to invite you. Through our interactions, we have found other aspects to make you desirable as a person to join us. If your companion has any deficiencies, they can also be fixed."

"Why didn't you just do that for anyone who would want to join?"

"Why should we when we can choose those who are... better?"

Arhus stood in shock at the coldness of the statement in spite of all its implications. *Is that how they see us? Are human emotions that alien to them? Do they have none of their own? Are we so small to them?*

As Arhus thought, the Subordinate stood with what appeared to be infinite patience, waiting for an answer. The more Arhus thought, the less he could find reason to give a 'yes' to the question. All the wonder and awe had been drained away.

"No, thank you, I think I will stay," Arhus said.

"It is your choice." The Subordinate smiled for a moment. "We hope that answers some of your earlier questions."

"Oh," Arhus chuckled, "it's not that easy. Have you made a decision about leaving someone or something here when you leave? A representative, maybe?"

The Subordinate's smile vanished for a moment, but then returned. He tilted his head to one side. "Would you consider being our representative?"

Arhus was about to say, "Me?" again but caught himself. The question seemed even bigger than the previous one. "How would that work? I mean, I don't know that much about you. How could I be your representative?"

"The necessary information would be provided to you. We would also leave several of our servants under your authority so that you would be able to exercise power so that others would not take advantage of you."

"And my mission?" Arhus could hardly believe he was even asking.

"To help guide the development of those on this planet. To make them even more valuable to us."

The last statement put a bad taste in Arhus's mouth. "Is that all we are to you, a commodity? Do you buy and sell us to other races?"

"No, of course not." No humour showed in the Subordinate's eyes as he spoke. "You are too valuable and rare to sell to another."

The statement did nothing to take the taste out of Arhus's mouth. If anything, the taste got stronger. He tried to control his thoughts but couldn't help wondering, *How long will it be before we can break whatever bonds the aliens hold over us? Not in my lifespan, but I can still hope for the future.*

And shove those smug looks back down their throats, Arhus thought.

Arhus stared back. "No, thank you, I think I'll pass."

"As you wish. We will respect your decision."

A sudden panicked thought went through his head. "Will there be anyone else as your representative?"

"It is unnecessary. You are developing well now. We feel confident in your continued future development." The Subordinate's smile may have been called a smirk if Arhus thought him capable of one.

"But you have made all these changes to your body... being," Arhus said.

"They are easy to change back," the Subordinate said without emotion.

"And anything else?"

The Subordinate shook his head.

"Well," Arhus said as his eyes wandered a little, "There will be a lot of people disappointed, but, as you say, it's your decision." *And I'm not telling anyone any details so they don't think I blew it.*

The Subordinate made a small head bow.

"Anything else I need to know?" Arhus asked.

"No, there is not. Please know that talking with you has been of real interest to us and we hope that the rest of your life is successful."

"Thank you." Arhus felt nerves starting. "You know, when you leave, the world will get chaotic."

"It will be temporary."

"Temporary to you is a lifetime to us." Arhus could feel an edge starting on his voice. When the Subordinate shrugged, it made him want to yell and scream at the alien about what he was doing to the world without caring. But then another part of him said that it wouldn't do any good.

"Then I guess I will be going." Arhus made a small bow and turned.

He half-expected the Subordinate to say something else and debated whether to even acknowledge if he did, but no other words were forthcoming. As his feet left the ramp, the last of the invited were walking onto it. As the last woman did, the guardians turned and followed her. Arhus stood and watched. He could hear the gasps and shouts of the people surrounding the ship as it did. Hurrying to the guard station, Arhus watched security talking to each other. They appeared to be getting organized for something. He could hear shouts of, "They're going to leave!" from the crowd.

Arhus ran for the gate. He was met by a tsunami of people headed the other direction. He tried to brace himself and run sideways, but there was no resisting the wave. His shoulder slammed into the ground. Curling himself up into a ball, he tried to tuck his head into his body. Feet stepped on him, legs and knees tried to kick him around like a soccer ball, but he was too heavy to be driven very far. People screamed in panic of being left behind and for others to get out of their way. He felt someone fall over him, providing a stop to his progress. It did not prevent more kicks and feet finding his body. The wave still managed to drive him and his companion on the ground along.

A person dropped next to him. Risking a look, Arhus saw a stunned, unconscious look in their eyes. The *zit* of stunners grew over the sound of the crowd. More people dropped around him. The crowd must have gotten the idea, because feet and knees no longer drove him along the ground. Hands grabbed and lifted him from the ground. Extending his legs brought pain, but he fought through it to stand on his own.

"We have to get you out of here!" a security guard was shouting, the sound barely audible.

Arhus turned toward the ship. The crowd had reached the ramp and had been met by two creatures, their swords swinging into the oncoming crowd. New cries reached his ears of people in pain or dying. The creatures' work was effective, but did nothing to deter the desperate. Some ran around to the side of the ramp and were climbing up. Two more creatures appeared from inside the ship, their work as effective as those at the bottom of the ramp.

"You have to do something!" Arhus shouted at the guard.

"What? Besides, our protocols say to stay away from the ship." Arhus could see the fear in the man's eyes of being close to the creatures.

"Send in the drones then!" Arhus shouted back.

"Their programming won't allow them and there's no time to change it."

"You can't just let all those people die!"

"There's nothing I can do." The guard turned to the others around him. "Get this man out of here!"

Looking back at the ship, the cries of the desperate and dying rang in Arhus's ears. He watched the guardian's swords come up and swing down, knowing that each swing meant the death of one or more people. Sweating and shaking, he searched for an answer, something to forestall the massacre.

"DO SOMETHING!" he shouted at the ship. "YOU CAN STOP THIS. STOP IT NOW!"

Why should we?

"Because people are dying!"

They knew the consequences of their actions.

"But they aren't thinking straight! They're desperate and don't know what they are doing!"

"Who's he talking to?" the guard to Arhus's right asked.

"How should I know?" the one on the left replied.

What do you want us to do? The question was dispassionate.

"Make them stop! Have them get away from the ship!"

You would have us overcome their free will?

"YES!"

After all that we have done to make sure that those who joined us were free to choose and act on their own wills?

"Yes! These people are not thinking straight! You must help them. Don't you care?"

We care about our own.

Silence followed as people continued to willingly run to their deaths. Arhus held his breath, waiting, hoping.

You help them.

"I don't have the power to stop them."

We give it to you.

Liquid light filled Arhus's head, causing it to expand well beyond his skull. His knees grew weaker and he allowed the guards to carry him along while his mind adjusted. When his eyes opened, he not only saw everything around him, he felt it all in his mind, every person outside of the ship. While he could see all of the crowd, it was as if he was also with each of them individually at the same time. He felt several as they were cut down, felt the sword cutting through their bodies, felt their lives ending, almost as if a part of him had died. *I can't wait!*

Pushing the guards away from him both physically and mentally, Arhus stood on his own and held his hand out in front of him.

"STOP!"

All movement stopped, even the swinging of swords. The loss of sound felt deafening.

"MOVE AWAY FROM THE SHIP."

Touching the minds of those on the outside of the crowd, Arhus directed them away from the ship first, followed quickly by the next layer.

"GET MEDICAL TO THE SHIP TO HELP THE INJURED," Arhus directed to security. They moved with no question.

Arhus could feel some who resisted his control. A man near the front, determination filling his mind, struggled to move forward.

"Don't," Arhus told him.

"I must!"

"It will mean your death!"

"I must try!"

"Why?"

"Because my life isn't worth living if I fail!"

Despite Arhus's efforts, the man broke from his control and took two steps toward the ramp. As he did, a guardian's sword swept through his body. Arhus let go of the man's mind before he could feel the man die.

Searching the crowd for another, Arhus's mind came to rest on a familiar feeling.

"BIEL! What are you doing?"

"I have to get on that ship. Please help me."

Arhus could feel his control start to slip. "Don't! Come back! You'll die!"

"What do I have to live for? I've ruined everything I've touched." Arhus could feel her tears on her cheek.

"No, you haven't! Please, don't do this!" Searching his mind, Arhus looked for a solution that did not require reasoning with her. To do more would violate her free will even more. *What choice do I have? Let her die?* He couldn't do it.

"Sleep!" he sent to Biel's mind. He felt her lose consciousness and fall to the ground. *It's the best I can do.*

Is this what you wished us to do? came into Arhus's head.

"Yes." He was starting to feel exhausted.

How very... human... of you.

"You mean humane, don't you?"

No, human.

Feeling the rest of the crowd leaving the ship, he could also feel their drive to board the ship wane, replaced by sanity and regret. His connection to each of them started to dissolve and his head started to shrink. And throb. Falling to the ground, tears of his own ran from his eyes to the ground. His breath came in short, quick gasps. Men once again grabbed his arms and lifted him. The ground passed under his feet. The slight pull on his shoes felt like the earth trying to drag him back to the ship.

Do you wish to reconsider our offer?

"No," Arhus said out loud. "No one should have that power."

But you used it.

"Call me a hypocrite if you want."

Maybe you start to understand. Goodbye, Mr. Gint.

At that moment, it felt as if something left Arhus's mind, something that had been there that he had not known existed. So many emotions raced through him, he could not tell what they all were.

As he was carried to the guard station, Arhus saw the ramp to the ship close. Even without the aliens' help, he thought he could feel the disappointment running through the bystanders. When the ramp had disappeared into the outer skin of the ship, the ship rose from the ground, the landing gear retracting as it left the ground. As slowly as it had descended, the ship rose back into the sky, continuing to do so as Arhus was carried into the infirmary.

The bed in the infirmary was either very comfortable or Arhus felt really bad. They had given him a shot for the pain of his bruises and his head. Happily, no bones had been broken, though his ribs hurt like heck. His eyes refused to focus and his head drifted back and forth as if he was in a dream.

"I demand you let me in!" came a voice from outside the room.

"That voice sounds familiar," Arhus said while his eyes wandered.

Arlan Morresette pushed his way into the room and walked directly to Arhus. "What's wrong with him?"

"He's been through a lot. We gave him something to settle him while he heals." It was a woman's voice, one Arhus didn't recognize.

"Well, wake him up, now!"

"I wouldn't recommend…"

"I don't care what you recommend! The fate of the world hangs in the balance! Wake him up now!"

Arhus felt pressure on his arm. His eyes started to clear and not swim so much, but he hurt more. Blinking helped clear his eyesight, but did nothing for the pain in his ribs and legs. And his arms. And his head. All of him, in fact.

"Mr. Gint, report!"

"Getting stampeded hurts," Arhus managed to say, noticing how dry his throat was suddenly.

"Stop all this foolishness. The aliens are leaving. What have they left us?" Arlan's face wasn't more than a few centimetres from Arhus's.

"Nothing," Arhus croaked out.

"Nothing?"

"Yes, nothing."

"That is unacceptable! Why? Didn't you ask them?" At least Arlan's face moved away from Arhus's as he waved his arms in the air.

"They said we were doing fine on our own."

"You failed, Mr. Gint! You utterly failed!"

"So sue me." Arhus looked away from the man.

"You think this is fun?"

"Well, not at the moment, but I am sure later…"

"Mr. Gint, you are a disgrace to the human race and the World Council. Your association with us is terminated. Do not bother to come back to the office. Give me his interface."

Arlan grabbed the interface from a woman's hand. "Good day, Mr. Gint."

As Arlan walked out, Sindie rushed in, pushing past the man while giving no deference.

"And that applies to her, too!" Arlan shouted before leaving.

"Ar! You okay?"

"If this nice lady would give me another dose of those drugs, I would be great," Arhus said with a smile.

"Sorry, not for an hour at least," the paramedic said with a frown and real sympathy in her voice.

"Then the marriage is off," Arhus said with a wave.

"What marriage? Ar, what are you talking about?" Sindie took his head in her hands.

"He might be a little out of it for a while, ma'am. Don't worry too much about what he says." The woman packed up things in the room.

"So what else is new? I need to get you home right away. Don't worry, I'll take care of you."

"He shouldn't walk, if he even can," the paramedic said over her shoulder.

"Then get me a chair and I'll push him!" Sindie sent back.

"Sure, sure, no problem. Everyone's so grumpy."

Getting into the chair was accompanied by a lot of 'ouch' from Arhus. The paramedic gave Sindie a pill with strict instructions to wait at least an hour before giving it to Arhus. On the way out, Sindie asked, "What did Arlan mean, goes for me too?"

"I managed to get us fired."

"About time."

Outside, they were met by a whole troop of security. The captain was waiting just outside the infirmary. Green uniforms were everywhere while white-uniformed personnel led disoriented people away from where the alien ship had been.

"Is he going to be okay?" the captain asked Sindie.

"I think he'll be fine. A little beat up, it seems."

The captain knelt down to be eye-to-eye with Arhus. "Thank you for what you did."

"Just don't tell anyone, if you don't mind." Arhus took a sip from the straw near his mouth.

"Don't worry, I'll tell them we think it was the aliens."

"It was."

"No, it was you. Take care of yourself." The man gave a salute.

"You too, Captain."

"I assume you are going to tell me what that was all about," Sindie said as she pushed the chair.

"Do I have a choice?" Arhus asked.

"No."

"Then you assume right."

Epilogue

Arhus pulled the weeds from between the broccoli plants, laying them on the cut grass piled around the plants after shaking off the dirt. He never could understand how the weed seeds got through the thick mat to the dirt below, but some always did. All the weeds pulled, he stood to move to the rows of herbs next. As he stood, Sindie walked up. She looked indecisive.

"You have some visitors," she said.

"And who would they be?" he asked.

"Some guys in suits. I think one is the new head of the Common Workers Union. At least, he looks like the guy on the news." Sindie's eyes looked on in anticipation at Arhus's answer.

"Why do they keep coming to me?" Arhus said with a shake of his head. "I'm a vegetable and herb farmer now, small scale. What do they think I can tell them?"

"Don't you remember? You were the chosen one, at least for a week or so." Sindie's smile was almost a tease. "Besides, who else are they going to go to?"

"Anyone but me," Arhus said, kneeling down next to the herbs to look for weeds.

"Well, after your speaking tour, you *are* the person to go to. They kicked out the politicians, remember? Some even made laws forbidding elected officials to receive pay or not hold other full-time jobs. You're the only name left from before." Sindie walked up and knelt next to him. "Besides, I think you're pretty smart. I wouldn't want them going to someone else for advice."

"How about you answer their questions?" Arhus said without looking.

"Don't drag me into this," Sindie said, raising her hands. " *Your* kids keep me busy enough as it is!"

" *My* kids?"

"The way they have been acting lately, they're *your* kids for sure." Sindie stood back up. "So, do I tell them you're coming?"

Arhus sighed. "I guess I'll get it over with. But I'm not cleaning up to meet them. If they can't deal with a little dirt, that's their problem."

"You look better with a little dirt on you, dear," Sindie said as she kissed his head and walked away. "Don't take long. A little wait adds to your mystique, but too much just makes them antsy. Plus it gives *your* kids too much time to cause trouble."

Arhus stood up and removed his gloves. "At least they're on my side."

Joseph could see there was a small crowd of people near the gate making the noise. He estimated fifteen to twenty people, but they were packed tightly together, making them hard to count. They did not seem to have a chant or common statement, placing their shouts in competition which each other.

"Very inefficient," Joseph said with a frown as he walked.

As he drew close, he noted that the shouting crowd had the same demeanor and dress as the protesters he had seen yesterday, only a lot more of them. Half a dozen guards stood inside the fence, rifles held in both hands across their chests, staring down the protesters who were bold enough to rattle the fence. One of the guards turned his direction when he was within five feet.

"Sir," the guard said, taking a step in Joseph's direction, "you shouldn't be here."

"What the heck is going on?" Joseph craned his neck to look around the guard.

"They suddenly got excited. I think it was the shooting. Now, if you'd be good enough to move away from this area…"

"One heretic down! The rest of you next!" came a shout from behind the guard.

"That's your solution, just shoot everyone?" Joseph shouted back, stepping around the guard.

"Sir, don't speak to them…" The guard tried to move in front of Joseph.

"That's what happens to blasphemers!" the man shouted back.

"And somehow a simple farmer was offending God? How pitiful is your god, anyway?" Joseph shouted back, his face starting to turn red.

"Sir, I must insist!" The guard grabbed Joseph by one arm.

"He spoke to God and lied! He deserved to die. He was a heretic!"

"He was my father!" Joseph tried to shrug off the guard as he shouted as loud as possible and shook his fist at the man.

"Shit," came softly from the guard next to Joseph. The man swung his rifle around his shoulder and grabbed Joseph with both hands. "Mr. Gint, it is not a good idea for you to be here. I will be removing you from here now!"

"It's the heretic's son," one of the crowd said, slightly softer than a shout.

As Joseph's view was taken up by the face of the now determined guard, he heard one or maybe two loud bangs. The guard was driven into Joseph, knocking him to the ground and landing on top of him. Joseph's head hit the road hard enough to bring stars into view. The impact of the guard's body made his head come back up, at least as far as it could with a soldier carrying twenty pounds of body armor and equipment.

Sirens wailed. As his vision cleared, Joseph heard more bangs and the sound of pulsation rifles, fewer of the latter than the former. The guard on top of him groaned.

"Shotguns," Joseph told himself. "Get your head in the game, Gint, it sounds like we're losing."

Reaching down along the the body on top of him, Joseph felt around until his hand found a pistol grip. The first tug resulted in no movement of the weapon. Cursing himself, Joseph found the latch and released the weapon. Groaning, the guard on top of him moved, landing an elbow into Joseph's face.

"Not helping," Joseph said to the man as he pushed him off in the direction of the weapons fire. Rolling to his side, Joseph pointed the weapon over the man's body toward the crowd and pulled the trigger.

About the Author

Dale E. McClenning was born in Illinois and lived most of his life in Indiana. He went to Ohio State for Mechanical Engineering and was an engineer for 33 years mostly doing industrial turbine engines (generator sets). He has a wife of 33 years, two boys (32 and 28), one daughter-in-law and one soon to be, and one grand-daughter. He has been reading science fiction since grade school and writing since junior high. He has read a lot of history and theology as well as science fiction.

CPSIA information can be obtained
at www.ICGtesting.com
Printed in the USA
LVHW030534030419
612795LV00001B/22/P